Ella Shawn

Âmes Brisées

Âmes Brisées

A Broken Souls Novel

ELLA SHAWN

ISBN: 978-0692-06611-9 (Paperback)

Book design by Vickey Browne.

Printed in the United States of America.

First printing edition 2018.

ellasenchantedlife.com

DEDICATION

For the one Soul created to bind with my own and constantly reminds me that Souls are not designed to break, and neither am I. I love you. For the three Souls who chose me as their guide and watcher, I love you. For every Soul that has been broken by love, pain, and self-doubt; you are stronger than you realize.

Ella Shawn

ACKNOWLEDGMENTS

I could not have completed this project without the encouragement of my family and friends. It is not a simple task to ask the people who depend on you to release you to your writing cave and forgo cooking and cleaning and sometimes, eating to indulge in the one other thing besides them that brings you joy. I am humbled to have shared this experience with a few people who gave me so much feedback; my beta readers, Tina. and Jaimie. Your feedback was invaluable and without your honesty and attention to details, this book would not be as wonderful as it is. To my editor, who busted my chops with her no-nonsense approach to editing and the mantra I have now come to write by: *To thine own self be true.* Thank you for your tough love and your amazing knowledge of all things literary. V. Browne of Brownstone WES Consulting Group. To my brother, A. Walters, thanks for helping me with my attempt to design my first book cover, you make it look easy when I know it's not. Lastly, to my first fans… I hope you enjoy my first foray into my new life as a professional writer. I write the stories I want to read and hope they somehow reach an audience who loves what I love.

Ella Shawn

ENLIGHTENMENT

"What hurts you, blesses you. Darkness is your candle."

— Rumi

PROLOGUE

There is not a man anywhere in the world who will admit to believing in love at first sight. That is not to say some men don't believe but trust me when I say one would be hard-pressed to find a man who will say it out loud. We are not expected to fall for bullshit like love, fairy tales and happily-ever-afters. No, we are expected to be the big, strong knight in shining armor there to save the day, rescue then fuck the damsel in distress and ride off into the sunset to search for our next conquest. Men will admit; however, they use the bullshit fantasies of desperate women to get what they want from them…and sometimes, the women may get a little of what they are taught to believe is love.

Love. An emotion people are willing to kill for, die for and lose their minds for. Why? Who in the hell needs love when you can fuck without the complications of needy, clingy women? I'll stick to what I know, and trust me, what I know has absolutely nothing to do with love…it is all about pleasure. My pleasure; and to some degree her pleasure. Really, her pleasure is as important as my own. When I slide 'Jughead' into a woman, I want to own and possess her in every way. If I can't own her pleasure, then what the hell do I have a dick for? This was what I believed, what I practiced and how I conducted my relationships...at least it was—until her.

Honestly, I never thought love would find me, but it did and when it hit...I was not prepared for it at all. The lovers I had before her were not lovers. They were easy lays, well most of them were easy lays, but the first lust—the first woman to have me was old enough to know better and naughty enough to not care. She taught me how to use my, what did she call them…. natural talents to ensure whatever I desired, I could get. She gave her knowledge to me as she took everything that may have been good and innocent from me. That was a part of the deal. She thought emotions were best expressed through power and sex, as a master of my universe, emotions were not a necessity. Emotions were not for the powerful people who inspired awe and wonder in the eyes of those they looked down upon.

I thought she was the beginning and end of all things true and real. Man, was I wrong! It wasn't until I ran into her, that something thawed inside of me and I knew I would never recover from the slow, melting, burn that crawled down my throat and landed in my heart...a burn which usually landed in my crotch...Nope, this woman would be the methodical and perfect death of all of me. Maybe she could save me. Heal me. Love me? Maybe, she could make me strong enough to love myself.

~1~

Every day is the same. I wake up, make my bed, take a quick shower, brush my teeth, brush my hair, get dressed and go downstairs to have breakfast and wait. Wait for my life to start. I'm sixteen years old and nothing has changed in my morning routine since I started taking care of my own hygiene. I lumber down the stairs of the modest, two-story house where I live with my mom and her husband, I can't help but wish for something...anything to remind me I'm still alive. Right now, I'm feeling as if I never took my first breath. It feels like I've been holding it in until something worth breathing for comes my way. I have yet to find it, and I'm one hundred percent sure I won't find it in the bowl of Fruit Loops I'm having for breakfast.

"Same shit, different day." Those are the words that hit me in the chest accompanied by my stepdad's fist as I land on the last step before touching the stained yellow and brown linoleum. "What the fuck are you doing taking showers at night and in the morning? You got any money to pay the fucking water bill? ...No, you don't! You little shit. I know you don't because I didn't give it to you and your sorry ass mama never got two cents to rub together." He sucks his two front teeth, smacks his thin, pale lips and smirks at me as he continues his disrespectful tirade about my mom. "…but with the way she sucks me off...I'll always make sure she gets what she need." *Stop talking about my mom like she's a whore, she's not. I can't wait until she realizes she could do so much better than your trashy, white ass. How can you control my mom's money when you don't even have a damned job?*

I look up at him wishing I wasn't such a punk-ass and then I let my head fall back down into the locks of my shoulders. *Like I'm praying to a god or some shit.* I am defeated before my day even starts. "There ain't no law against being clean, but maybe it should be a law against walking around smelling like piss and shit all day." I mumble my unsolicited response in a voice that I hope will go over the intelligence level of this in-bred son-of-a-bitch my mama picked up at the local trailer park. She was so excited to show her ass-backwards family her new, white husband. His skin color was the yardstick against which all things were measured...even me. Especially me.

I never met the man who helped to create me; I have only heard stories about him. So many stories, they became the stuff of myths and legends in my mind. I have pieced my biological father together from the stories and faded photos I found in a box in the back of mama's closet. In my mind, he stood about 6'8" and was lean and muscular, but not bulky...kind of like a distance runner. I imagine he has large and powerful hands he uses to express what his mouth can't say. I am assuming my bio-daddy was dark; I say was because I don't know if he is alive or dead. I make this assumption about his color based on the fact my mama is so light, she could damn near pass for white with her silky chocolate hair that hangs down her back in waves that roll on like the ocean. And big green eyes.

There is no way my father could have been anything other than blue-chip black. I mean really, I'm the color of a perfectly baked German chocolate cake...my eyes are an interesting shade of brown...kind of like melted chocolate with pieces of golden wrapper mixed in for no reason at all. They are not flat or lifeless, but deep and soulful. I didn't inherit any of my mother's features...well maybe my keener than normal nose, but that seems to be all my mama graced me with of the features belonging to her. That and my bio-daddy's name: Jonathan Ranard Ellis, Jr. She gave me that.

***

It was pretty obvious to everyone...well everyone except me, neither of my biological parents gave two shits about me or anything having to do with me; which left the perfect opening for the woman known in the neighborhood as *Auntie* to swoop in and have her wicked way with me. She was known for her warm smiles and sweet, magnolia hellos throughout the community, but for the teenage boys who lived in the neighborhood; she seemed to have an entirely different approach to showing southern hospitality.

It was a well-known, but unsubstantiated fact among my friends and me that if Auntie took an interest in one of us...we had basically hit pay-dirt. Auntie like her boys young and fresh. *At least that's what the porch-sitters say about her and I hope for once, they were right in their furphy.* I prayed every night to whoever was listening that she would take a special interest in me. *That anybody would take a special interest in me, really.* My long-lost-maybe-dead daddy must have heard my prayers and sent a special gift my way. I was not in summer school, but I learned more that summer before my senior year than in all my years of going to school.

~2~

I managed to get through my eleventh-grade year with little or no physical damage from my stepdad, but I would have rather worn the bruises my mother sported than the ones Earl left on my mind, my heart and especially my soul. He made me watch him beat my mother and then he made me watch him have sex with her...not sex that made sense...the sex he made me watch was angry and punitive. I looked into my mother's bloodied face and saw enough tears of embarrassment to drown us both. *Many times, I wished they would...drown us so we didn't have to exist in hell anymore.*

"Mama, why can't we just leave him? You're the one with the job...we can leave, or you can call the police on him, can't you?" I asked her this question so many times and every time, my mama would just shake her head and let fat, oil-slick tears roll down her swollen, blue cheeks. I hated her in those moments. I hated her because she didn't fight back, she didn't try to protect me or herself. I hated her in those moments because she knew when Earl was going to lose his shit, and she did nothing to stop it from happening. I felt hopelessly out of control in that house...Auntie was the perfect distraction for me. Being with her gave me the time and structure I needed to not only survive but rise above my messed-up situation.

***

"Hey John." Auntie's voice was the stuff of wet dreams. It didn't really matter what she was saying, her voice traveled from my ears straight to my dick and all I could think about was how the lips that had spoken to me would feel wrapped around my rigid shaft.

"Hey Auntie. How're you doing?" I tried to keep my voice even, but I was in an awkward phase where my voice was changing and some of my words came out as growls instead of the smooth, velvet baritone I was developing.

"You lookin' for something to do today?" The bullet of awareness shot through me and almost knocked me on my ass. *Pay dirt, here I come!* I was so hard by the time I made it up the seven steps to her front porch, I could hardly move. At sixteen, I was already tall and had filled out as a result of playing varsity football and baseball for the last three years. Auntie stood up and prowled towards me, she looked like a lioness hunting a large mouse. *God, please let me the mouse she wants to catch between her sexy lips...either pair of them will be fine with me.*

"You look like you could use a cold drink. Why don't you come on in my house...my air conditioner keeps things nice and cool. I hope you don't mind the dark, I have this thing with being in the dark…" She let her voice trail off and slid her eyes over my face and smiled as she licked her lips. "...There is something so mysterious about dark, cool places. Her eyes raked over my body, dressed in basketball shorts and a Grant Hill jersey, I knew I looked older than my sixteen years and I also knew in my basketball shorts, my erection was easy to spot. I was too turned on to be embarrassed...in fact, I wanted her to see how big I was, I wanted her to get wet thinking about what I might feel like moving inside her. *Of my friends, I think I was the only one who had not had sex with anyone...Shit, if my first piece of ass was going to be Auntie...it was worth it.*

"Yea, Um, I'm a little thirsty. It's *hard* staying cool in the summer heat." I noticed how her breath caught when I emphasized the word *hard*. Her eyes dropped to the large bulge in my basketball shorts and a broad smile graced my face. I hoped I had her attention. The dimple in my left cheek ensured she would at least let me touch her breast today. I had only pulled on the nipples of girls waiting for the bus, but I honestly didn't know how to really touch a woman's breasts in a way that would turn her on...turn me on.

She hadn't lied. The inside of her house was dark and cool. So damn cool, I watched her large nipples turn into beaded points under her sheer camisole. *Shit, she's not wearing a bra...* "You mind if I turn on some music while I fix you some sweet tea?" I was busy looking around her living room, it didn't look like a kinky twenty-something year old lady lived here. *I think she's twenty-something... no more than thirty.* It looked like my grandmother lived in this house I hope would bring me to my knees and not in prayer, either.

"No." I answered after the CD had already started playing. "What are we listening to?" Her disembodied voice floated into the living room and took up residence in my already painfully hard dick. "I've really been feeling this singer, Des'ree, she's British, but her music sounds like she may be from the islands. This is one of my favorite songs by her. It's called, *Feel So High.*" The smooth chords of an acoustic guitar started a sultry, mature voice floats into singing.

This was the sexiest music I had ever heard. It was mature and made me think about fucking. I decided at that moment I needed to expand my music library. Auntie seemed to read my mind, because she snatched the thoughts that were floating around in my head and spoke them with that wet-dream voice of hers. "I know this is not what you young boys listen to, but I think it is important for *you* to expand your horizons when comes to music, books, movies and *experiences*." She walked over to me and placed a tumbler of what I thought was just sweet iced tea in my right hand, but the moment the brown liquid hit my tongue, I knew she had spiked my drink. She stepped a few feet away from me and was watching me like a hawk as I tried to swallow the brown fire burning a quiet river of bedrock in its wake.

"This is really good." That's all I could get out before I

started coughing like a baby taking its first suck of milk from the bottle. She rewarded my inexperience with a smile that didn't reach her eyes, but in my sexually aroused state, I thought she was looking at me with admiration and awe...I had never been more wrong in my life.

Auntie was in my face within seconds of my first sputtered cough. Her long, slim fingers snatched the tumbler from me and in the next moment, she grabbed my dick and balls in her right hand and my face with her left. I vaguely remember wondering where she had put my drink. Her right hand tightened around my man parts and her perfect nails dug into my face as her mouth sealed over mine. I had kissed a girl before...just one, but I had kept my mouth closed the entire time. This was no spin-the-bottle kiss. Auntie pried my lips apart with her warm, wet tongue. She licked at the seam of my mouth and when I gave in and opened, her tongue slid next to mine and we became a frenzy of tongues, lips and teeth. The entire time she kissed me, she massaged my dick and balls...almost to the point of pain, but mostly it was the single most pleasurable thing to happen to me in...*ever*.

"You have a sweet mouth, Jonathan. Your tongue is strong; I'll have to teach you all of the amazing pleasures your tongue can bring..." I opened my eyes and looked into the face of a predator. In that moment, hunting became my favorite sport.

"You still got my dick and balls in your hands, Auntie." I heard the stupid words fall from my mouth and immediately regretted saying them because just then, Auntie squeezed my shit with equal pressure on my balls and my dick and I came long and hard all over my self. I was so embarrassed, I could have died right there, but then she did something that changed my life...forever.

While I was still coming, she yanked my pants down and

wrapped those beautiful lips around my still spurting dick and sucked me dry. All the while, she dug her nails into my ass cheeks and began to hit them violently...the pain mixed with the feeling of coming made me come even more. When it was all over, my dick and balls were heavy and more than a little sore from where she had squeezed, sucked and bit them...my ass was in as bad a state as my manhood. Odd thing was...I didn't care. Whatever Auntie had done, I wanted her to do more of it...much more of it.

"Jonathan…" Auntie called my name in such a way it made me wonder if I would ever allow anyone to call me *John* again. "I do hope you enjoyed your time with me today. I would love to have you back over...I'm sure I have some work around the house you can tend to. You should just plan on spending your summer with me...helping me clean up my bush and shrubbery. Don't worry; I'll pay you for all the *work* you put in." If my stepdad had given me the keys to a new, candy-apple red 1990 Ford Mustang 5.0, I could not have been happier. *Holy shit, Auntie had chosen me for her summer fun. Learning to fuck from an older woman might as well be a gift from the gods...*

Every day for the next ten weeks, I crossed the road and made a left heading towards the entry to our subdivision, stopping at the stop sign to check for traffic before making a right onto the next street...one, two, three houses down, stood the pretty yellow house with the white wrap around porch. The pleasure I derived while inside her house, inside of Auntie...there are no words to describe it. *I never thought I would experience anything greater than Auntie's strange and dark love.*

With each caress of pleasure Auntie gave me, she cut it with the sting of bites, pinches, floggings, spankings, and hot wax. She trained me to give myself to her in a way that was purely for her pleasure, if I somehow derived any pleasure from something she was doing to me, I would pay dearly for it...usually with tears and sweat. The crazy thing is, I *loved* it. Every bruise, every harsh word, every bite, slap, pinch...her pleasure from my pain gave me pleasure.

And because I didn't have the fear of pain anymore, I was stronger and less easily scared by my stepdad. Auntie gave me what I needed to not only please her and her singular need for me, but she also equipped me with what I needed to stand up to my stepdad. Of all the lessons Auntie taught me, teaching me another person's pain could become my pleasure was the lesson that would save my life.

I fucked Auntie like I had been born to do only that. She even told me once, that my dick had been especially made to fit her pussy. She loved me in every hole her body had, and I loved the way she punished me for making her come. I tried every day to make her come at least three times, because I knew when she came, she would punish me and leave me bruised, sometimes bleeding and every lick and bite left me hard as stone and ready to fuck her again.

~3~

There was a particularly hot day, and I had been out in Auntie's yard pulling weeds from her rose bushes. I was sweating and panting like a slave. Just when I thought I couldn't take anymore, Auntie came to her back door wearing a smile and nothing else. She looked like snow that wouldn't melt. Perfect breasts sit high on her chest, her pecan colored nipples already hard...inviting me to take them between my teeth and bite them...hard. I lapped up her sexiness in small sips, I did not want to gulp her down...no; what I wanted was to experience every aspect of her unique flavor...let it linger on my tongue and slide down my throat and saturate my senses. That could not happen.

She crooked her long, manicured finger and called me to her without uttering a word. Judging from the look in her eyes, I knew that I was in for a rough afternoon, but after dealing with my mom and her shit-faced husband for two days, I was in need of whatever Auntie had for me. I hated the weekends...I couldn't see Auntie on the weekends...only Monday through Friday.

As I stood and walked toward the back porch; my head down...I wasn't allowed to look at Auntie without permission. I stood on the bottom step and waited for her to tell me what she wanted me to do next. "Jonathan, baby." Her voice snaked its way into my mind and took me to the place deep inside of me where it was cool and dark and sexy. I loved that place, that place was where I found my pleasure. "You are filthy, Jonathan. Take your clothes off and leave them on the first step...you need a bath, baby." Auntie had never given me a bath before. *Fuck, this is going to be sexy as hell. Having Auntie wash my body with her own hands...Oh God, I hope I don't come in the bathtub.*

I stood before Auntie, naked and limp. I had to learn to

control my erections. Auntie did not want my body to respond to hers until she gave me permission to do so...that lesson was hard learned, but so worth it. Anything that made Auntie happy was worth the pain I had to endure to make it happen. "I like you dirty Jonathan, but I need you clean for what I have planned for you today. Turn around and bend over...touch your toes and don't move until I tell you to do so. Do you understand?" I wasn't allowed to speak to her without permission, so I simply nodded my head and did as I was told. Standing there, naked and exposed to her, made me feel like a child. A child who was loved and cherished. A child that mattered to someone. I loved that Auntie set boundaries for me and made sure that I stayed within those boundaries. I stayed within the boundaries because I knew what the consequences were when I got out of line. Her rules and punishments were clear and consistent. When I stepped out of bounds, I knew exactly what my punishment would be, and that the punishment would always fit the offence.

What is she going to do to me? I thought that I would be going into her house and into a bath that she had run just for me...I thought that she would use her hands and mouth to clean every inch of my body...I guess she has other plans.

"Don't move and don't let me move you."

Auntie's voice was a sand polished stone surrounded by shallow water. Her tone was unlike anything I had ever heard from her. *Shit, something was different.* I felt the hairs on the back of my neck stand up and I knew that today would change our relationship forever. It would either end today or something new would begin. I didn't have time to consider which one I would rather have happened before Auntie started in on me.

"Do you remember seeing those white cops turn the water hoses on those Black people who were fighting for the right to vote, to go where the hell they wanted to go...to be treated like the fucking human beings they were? Do you remember learning about that shit in school?"

I couldn't answer, she had not given me permission to speak to or with her, yet. All that I could do was stay as she had instructed me to.

"I want you to know what that feels like. Not just physically, Jonathan. I want you to know how it feels to have your power stripped away from you and know the only way to regain it is in death or through violence."

My heart was beating so hard, I thought I was having a heart attack. *Auntie thought that she was my summer school teacher and in many ways, she was. She taught me so much more in my time with her than simply how to fuck.*

Before I had time to consider how I would learn today's lesson or even what today's lesson really was, I felt the stinging bite of ice cold water pelt my ass cheeks.

"Don't you move one inch...you will stay and take it." Auntie growled through clenched teeth. I had no choice...I planted my feet wide on the patio and locked my knees enough to keep me standing, but not enough that I might pass out. The water felt like bullets hitting my skin. My mind worked overtime as it tried to make sense out of what was happening to me.

"How does it feel to have no control over what happens to you? If I gave you permission, what would you do to make me stop?" A tear leaked out of my left eye as I tried to take whatever Auntie thought I needed to take from her, but this was too much.

Auntie had moved in front of me and the water left large, angry footprints across my skin. The only thing I could think about was how brave and courageous those *freedom riders* were during that time. How strong those Africans were when they were brought over here and worked like animals. Something in me clicked...the pain and humiliation poured from my body as the sweat, water and blood dripped onto the patio and I was left with three robust emotions: anger, pride and lust.

"Jonathan…" My name was a soft purr that dripped from her beautiful lips. "...I give you permission to try. And. Make. Me. Stop." That was all I needed to hear. I stood up swiftly and grabbed the hose from her...water went everywhere. I quickly coiled the hose around her slick body and used the water pouring from the spout to fuck her thoroughly.

"Oh my God!"

The sounds that spilled from Auntie's throat were like nothing I had ever heard from her. She sounded like a lioness mating for the first time.

"Jon-ath-an... Like that...m-ore of th--at."

When she was begging for me to finish her off, I pulled the hose away from her sex and uncoiled it from around her body. She stood there, soak and wet for more than one reason. She was breathing hard and trying even harder to entice her clit into giving her the orgasm that I would not let her have.

"Don't touch yourself, Auntie." I did not recognize my own voice. Gone was the in- between stones-in-a-can voice. My voiced spilled from my lips and flowed like rich, black oil. I watched it spread across the patio and crawl up Auntie's leg...she squirmed as my words set fire to her blood and chilled her soul.

I saw her shudder and then it happened. Auntie lowered her eyes and her body became compliant…I knew that look, it was the look of a submissive. She had given me what only she could give me...the opportunity to take my power back...I would never be able to repay her for that gift.

I took auntie into her house, ran a warm bath in her bath

tub and placed her carefully into the warm, lavender scented water. She wouldn't look at me. Her beautiful eyes stayed downcast, it was hard to see her looking so contrite, but there was a peace that poured from her that told me this is where she wanted to be. I knelt beside the bathtub and soaped my hands with the fragrant beauty bar; I noticed how her breathing had picked up and how hard her luscious nipples had become. I could smell her arousal...she was so hot for me...my touch...my, *command?*

"Auntie, you can look at me." My voice was strong and sure. I watched with fascination as Auntie's head swept up and turned to the right so that she could stare into my face. "What is going on Auntie? Why are you behaving like this?" Although I was enjoying the sudden change of events, it made me nervous. I knew that I would never be able to be to Auntie what she was to me. She stared blankly into my eyes as if she was waiting for something. Then it hit me in the face like a wet rag...she was waiting on me to give her permission to speak directly to me. *What was going on in her fucking head?*

"You can speak to me, Auntie." I had to remind myself that I was in charge and there was a certain tone I needed to use to assert my dominance over the woman who had demanded my submission just thirty minutes ago. She took a deep breath and blew it out slowly through her sexy lips...those lips that made me want to come every time I saw them.

"J-Jonathan. I have searched all my life for you. One so young and beautiful and passionate and strong. Strong enough to demand my submission." *Her words echoed my own thoughts. I always wondered how she was able to do that and wondered if I stayed in this role, would I develop that uncanny ability, too.* "Do you know how difficult it is to always be in control of everything and everyone around you? Do you have any idea how badly I have wanted to submit to a man? This is usually the part in my summer relationships where I tell the young boys goodbye. Jonathan, if I ever have to say goodbye to you, I do believe that I will die...on the spot. I will die without you."

Once she was done talking, she lowered her eyes and turned her head towards the front and waited for whatever I had to give her. I wanted to run screaming and yelling from the house and never return. I had never felt so needed, so desired and it scared the shit out of me. Auntie had shared herself with me in a way that she had never shared herself with anyone else...maybe ever. The responsibility that came with being with her in this new way made me question myself and if I could really do what she wanted me to...if I could really be who *she* thought I was. *What the fuck do I know about controlling her...hell I can barely control myself. I need her...but, now she seemed to need me more.*

"Auntie, tell me your first name." My days of asking her anything were effectively over. I had only to tell her what I wanted, and she would make it happen. The power she gave me was astounding and then...another wet rag in the face. Auntie trusted me not to abuse this power, just as I had trusted her when I willingly turned my power over to her. And I knew that I could never abuse her trust in me the way Earl abused my mom's trust in him. "You can speak to me, look at me when you tell me your name." My voice was low and soft, I did not want her to feel threatened. Auntie was hand-feeding me my manhood, my future...myself. She was giving me what I had been looking for my entire life...a reason to take a fucking breath.

"My name is Della. Do you want my last name, too?" Her voice was so soft, so sincere. Like a child. She was simply amazing.

"Yes. Tell me your full name...first, middle and last."

"Della Regina Venial."

"That is a nice name, but nothing about you says that you should be called Della."

"What do you want to call me?"

"You look like a Violet. In fact, don't share your new name with anyone. The secrets you have belong to me and I will not share them. Do you understand?"

"Yes. I understand."

I soaped the towel and began to wash her. I let the now lukewarm water run down her back as I moved the towel over her neck and down around her shoulders. Once I got around to her breast, I saw a silent tear spill from her right eye. She broke my heart. I finished bathing her and helped her out of the bathtub. Pulling one of the extra fluffy towels, the ones she would not even let me look at, from her linen closet and wrapped her in the smell of spring meadows and softness.

"Lift your arms, Violet." She did so immediately. I wrapped the towel around her and tucked it in on itself. I noticed that her arms were still raised above her head. "You can lower your arms, Violet." She did so immediately.

I led her to her bedroom and began to dry her body. I was extra gentle, extra careful with her. She was like a newborn baby. She needed to know that I would never hurt her beyond what she needed...I had to show her my true self before I helped her discover her own truth. I removed the towel completely from her body and told her to sit on her bed. She did not hesitate to do what I told her.

"You keep your lotion on your dresser." I did not phrase it as a question. She nodded her answer.

"Walk over to the dresser and get it for me, Violet.

Bring it back to me and sit on the bed where you are sitting now."

Upon her return, she sat on the edge of the bed and kept her eyes and her head lowered.

"Give me the lotion. Look at me while I take care of you."

I took the jar from her delicate hands and turned the cap. The scent of lavender and vanilla filled the room and my nostrils. I loved the way Auntie smelled...clean and sexy and fresh.

"I'm going to lotion your entire body and then I'm going to fuck you real slow, real deep and for a long time. You will not come until I tell you to. Do you understand me, Violet?"

"Yes. May I ask you a question?" Her voice was so soft and low, I had trouble hearing her.

"What do you need, Violet?"

"What do I call you, Sir?" *Sir. Is she talking to me? Shit, I didn't think about what she should call me.*

"John. Call me, John."

"Yes, John. Thank you."

I lotioned her with the attention a new father lavishes on his newborn baby girl. I picked her up in my arms and held her to my chest. I placed her in the middle of her bed and watched her. I had never been allowed to stare at her. To appreciate how beautiful she was. Auntie was 38 years old, but to look at her you would think she was in her late twenties at most. She had married early to an old Korean man who had one foot in the grave and one foot in hell. He had more money than balls and many people say that she married him for that reason and that reason only. He died eight years after they were married.

"Lay back Violet and close your eyes. Don't open them

until I tell you to."

"Yes John." Her voice was liquid sex and my dick...limp until the moment she spoke my name, jumped to action. I got so hard, so fast...I felt a little dizzy with all the blood rushing from my head to my dick...

"Open your legs. Wider. Wider...yes like that. You have such a beautiful pussy, Violet. It's lavender and pink and soft and warm. *The fucking flower of life is what's between her legs.* Are you wet for me, Violet?"

"Yes, John. Only for you."

"Give me your right hand." I took her hand and move it towards her sex. I was so turned on, I hoped that I could last through this little game I was playing with her.

"Touch your clit, Violet and then tell me how it makes you feel when you rub it hard and then soft."

Her index finger moved to her clit and began to move in small, expert circles. Her hips immediately began to lift and ride the ecstasy her long finger was providing. Her mouth was opened, slightly. Her nipples hard and tight. There was a rosy pink color creeping up her neck and staining her cheeks. I had never been allowed to watch her as arousal, hot and heavy slid through her body. It was the most erotic thing I had ever seen.

"Tell me how you feel when you finger your clit softly." My own breathing was labored and I realized that I had wrapped my right hand around my ever-thickening cock and I was stroking it slowly.

"It feels…" I cut her off. "Tell me how you feel, Violet. You; not your sweet, little pussy."

"I feel...hot and chilled at the same time. Like there are little bugs crawling all over me and kissing my skin from the inside out." She was still massaging her clit and her juices were flowing like a river from her slightly parted slit. I wanted to shove my dick into her and fuck her until we were one body, one heart...one soul, but I refrained. I had to see this through to the end.

"Harder. Rub your clit hard, but don't you dare come."

Her index finger was joined by both her middle and her ring finger. She placed her index finger and her ring finger on either side of her swollen vulva and used her middle finger to vigorously rub at the epicenter of her arousal. Her hips began to buck into her hands and her mouth was open in a silent scream of passion. She was so damned beautiful; it hurt to look at her...hurt to not be inside her. I saw her pussy start to tremble and I knew that she was close...so close that she would not be able to stop the orgasm that was threatening to shatter her whole body.

"Violet!" My voice harsher than I intended, but getting the desired response from her. Immediately, her hand stilled, and she worked fervently to calm herself down and stave off the impending explosion waiting to happen in her body.

"Tell me how you feel when you finger your clit hard and rough like you just did."

"I--I... feel, uh...um. I feel..." Her voice was so shaky it was obvious that she was having a hard time stringing her thoughts together. She had taken me to this desolate place where pleasure and frustration made love and gave birth to total dependency on the one who holds your power in their hands. I loved and hated that place, but seeing Auntie so tied to it, made me realize why she loved to take me there and leave me...wanting and needing, also knowing that I did not have the right to ask for anything.

"I feel like bubbles being blown by a small child who

only blows them to chase and pop them. I feel like a kite. The wind picks me up and takes me up so high, and when I want to go higher...a cruel child yanks my string and pulls me back down to the land of small people." Damn, she broke my heart, again. But...I could not let her know how deeply she affected me. She did not need my softness, she surrendered herself to the stronger, more confident me...I owed it to her to give her that.

"Good...I want you to feel that way. You need to know that I own and control your pleasure, Violet. I will blow you and then pop you before you have a chance to reflect the colors of the rainbow in your prism. I will take you higher than you thought you could ever go and then yank you back down...down on your knees looking up to me...waiting for the chance to make me come." *I was talking a lot of shit for someone who had just been given the reigns to the horse and buggy. Damn, but it felt good to finally have power over someone and more importantly, power over myself.*

Her eyes fluttered and her breathing became a harsh pant. I watched her chest rise and fall as if the air she needed to live was being withheld from her. I had no idea I had this much power inside of me. For a sixteen-year-old boy who had been ruled by everybody in his life, this felt like I had taken a hit of crack and it went straight to my balls and made them bigger, stronger and more virile.

"Pull your knees up and keep your legs open, Violet. I am going to fuck you...I will let you know when you can come. If you come before I tell you to, if you open your eyes before I tell you to, if you touch any part of me before I tell you to...You will be punished. For every act of disobedience, I will bite you ten times on your clit...bite you hard."

I climbed onto the bed and allowed my eyes to close momentarily as her scent floated up to my nose and plummeted to my balls, making my dick even harder...damn, it *hurt*. I am glad Auntie had taught me how to control myself, or this would be over before it even got started. I let my hot flesh lie between the lips of her sex and felt the greedy sucking of her pussy along the length of my dick. She was so wet, so warm...I wanted to be inside her immediately...but I had to draw this out. Had to make her wait, need, want, beg for me to fuck her.

"Tell me what my dick feels like against your wet pussy, Violet."

"It feels like...the sun is shining just on that one spot...it's so warm and heavy and... Oh, God!" Her response to the role of my hips as the head of my penis brushed against the opening of her sex, made me want to hear more of those helpless cries spill from her beautiful lips.

"Like that, did you?" My voice sounded like Satan had taken up residence in my throat and was working hard to lure Auntie into the depths of hell. She was more than willing to join me in hell, too. She lifted her hips in answer to my question. I realized she had kept her eyes closed and her hands off me...she wanted this. Wanted *me* like this.

"Open your legs wider, Violet. As wide as you can get them."

I fell heavily into her swollen, wet flower. I didn't stop surging forward until I bottomed out at the end of her. It always shocked me that Auntie was so tight. I thought with all the sex she had that she would be loose and wide, but she wasn't. Her pussy felt like she had never had sex before in her life. I never had the right to ask her how she managed to stay so tight, but now I could, and I knew that she wouldn't lie to me. I stayed deep inside her, not moving, just staying...rigid and unyielding. I felt her cervix...it was hard and soft all at once. I move a little to the left and pushed a little further, I wanted all of me buried deep inside of her...she let a moan escape her lips...filled with pain and reverence. She was lost to me.

"Violet, the first time I fucked you, your pussy was as tight as one that had never been fucked, but what about the neighborhood boys...how are you so tight? You may speak to me." I moved a little to see her face and heard her keening softly in the back of her throat.

"Before you, I hadn't had sex in 16 years, John. I have had plenty of boys in my home, they pulled weeds, painted my rooms, cleaned out my shed...just wanted to give them something to do and put a little money in their pockets. You are the only person I've been with like this. I was so tight because before you, I had only had sex once and then after that…not until you. Didn't you notice?"

My dick got harder, longer thicker and I knew that I was getting ready to come...I felt my balls draw up and get tighter...*Fuck, I can't come like this. Focus Jonathan...focus on control.* I forced my body to submit to my will. Amazingly enough, the lesson that Auntie had taught me worked. Another wet rag to the face. Auntie had known all along I was who she was looking for. She wasn't teaching me how to behave the way she wanted *me* to, she was training me to teach her how to behave the way I wanted *her* to. Auntie knew...she knew what was hidden from my dumb ass.

A smile flitted across my lips, and then I bent down, grabbed Aunties left nipple between my teeth and slowly bit down on it. She moaned, her sex clenched around my dick. She felt so good. *Wait, I'm only the second person she's ever been with...I was a virgin when I fucked her the first time...She belongs to me almost as completely as I belong to her. I'm so fucking glad I never told my friends about what Auntie and I did in her house.*

"No. I. Did. Not." Each word was punctuated with a

small thrust of my hips that made her gasp four times. “I told you I was a virgin and I had no idea what I was doing. Why did you give yourself to me? Why did you choose me?” I had to know. I had to know before I fucked her brains out and left her senseless and sore.

“I saw in you what I see in myself. I saw your power, coiled and restrained by assholes who think they are better than you. I saw your nurturing heart that was becoming harden because it seems the only thing a gentle heart would get you is beaten and mistreated. I saw your honesty and willingness to give as much as you received. John, in a word...I saw *you*. And I wanted whatever you had to give me.”

I was not expecting that. She took my breath away and I felt my hips moving against her. I had to give her this gift. I must give her all of me. She never let me give myself to her the way I wanted to, but now she would take what I gave her and relish in the feelings. Auntie would never forget this night and neither would I.

~4~

I looked at Auntie and realized that her eyes were still closed. I knew that at some point, I wanted her to look at me...to know that I am the only one that will ever put that soft look on her face, but right now...I wanted her to concentrate on how I could make her feel.

"Violet." I let her name linger on my lips and I swear that I felt her wet nether lips brush against my mouth. God...I wanted to taste her sweet, salty flavor.

"I am getting ready to fuck you, real slow. Don't move your hips...this is my show. I am in control of you, not the other way around. Do you understand?"

She nodded her head and continued to hold on to the pillow. She was so sexy, so beautiful...I knew I would never get over *loving* or *fucking* or *being* with her...I don't know which one my honest emotion was.

Deliberately, I pulled out of her warm wetness and waited just long enough to make Auntie want to move her hips up to pull me back inside of her warm walls, but she did not move. She lay there, like a dead body...she was so good at being obedient. At this point in my miserable life, I needed to have someone who would listen to me and do what I told them to do. I felt powerful and confident...like I could do and be anything I wanted to be and right now...I wanted to be so deep inside Auntie she could suck my dick without opening her mouth.

"Fuck!" I grunted as I slammed into Auntie's amazingly tight sex. "You feel so fucking good, Violet. Shit. I don't want to come, yet...but God. You are so perfectly wet and warm and tight and soft and—shit." I felt myself getting ready to find my own release...not now. I will not allow myself to come, yet.

I moved back out just as slowly as I had moved out of

her the first time and slammed back into her with such force, her eyes flew open for just long enough for me to notice.

"Did you just open your eyes, Violet?"

"Y-Yes, John. I did."

"What did I tell you would happen if you did any of the things that I told you not to do?"

"You said that you would bite my clit ten times...bite it hard."

"Then let me pull my dick out of you and give you your punishment. This is not for you, so don't come. You have disobeyed me by opening your eyes and for that I will punish you. Do you understand?"

"Yes."

"Yes what?"

"Yes, John. I understand."

"If it gets to be too much for you, say Della, and I will stop. If you don't say Della, I will continue, assuming you are alright. Okay?"

"Yes, John. I understand."

I pulled out of her and heard the sexiest sound I had ever heard. It was an inverted sucking noise. Her pussy was so wet, so greedy...it tried to suck me back in. I loved it.

My head dipped between Auntie's parted thighs and I started my diabolical pursuit of feasting on her beautiful clit.

I blew my cool breath over her hot flesh, trying to gentle her and make this easier for her. Her aroma filled my senses and made me almost crazy with the need to have my mouth on her.

"Open your eyes, Violet. I want you to see me

punishing you and then maybe next time you will follow directions. Okay?"

"Yes, John."

"Ask me, Violet."

"Ask you what, John?"

"Ask me, Violet. I will not tell you again to do so.

She realized that I wanted her to ask me to bite her clit hard...hard enough to bring intense pleasure and inflict just enough pain to keep her on edge. Ask me, damn it.

"John. Please punish me by biting my clit ten times."

"Good girl."

I parted her soaking wet lips with my thumbs and gazed inside her and thought to myself that she was designed just for me. The first nibble was soft, reverential even. I licked the entire length of her clit, then without warning or provocation, I bit down into her soft, sweet nub. Oh, she was amazing. The muffled sounds of helplessness and need made me want to fuck her...stop this bullshit and bury my painfully hard dick inside her over and over again. I didn't. I couldn't. She was expecting me to punish her and part of me knew that she was still testing me to see if I had the courage of my conviction to really dominate her the way she wanted me to...I had to go the distance, had to prove to her she could trust me to take care of her as I had trusted her to take care of me.

She was silent and soaking wet. Every bite left her more swollen, slicker, more eager for me to be inside of her. Bite number ten proved to be her undoing. She was shaking with the need to come, but I had not given her permission to do so and I knew that she was reaching her breaking point and that is exactly what I wanted to happen. I knew I had to break Auntie all the way down to build her into what I needed her to be...what she needed to be for me. Tears fell helplessly from her eyes and slid towards the bed. She wanted me to let her come...she needed me to let her come, but I could not. I had to see this thing through.

"Don't you want to come for me, Violet?" I teased her because she had done the same thing to me. She taught me how to train her to please me by training me to please her.

"I'm so hard right now; if I put my cock in you...I'll hurt you, Violet. You won't be able to take all of me. You don't want me to hurt you, do you?"

"Tell me what you want." I knew that if I gave her the choice and she made one for herself that did not take into consideration what I wanted and needed, that I had a lot more work to do with her.

"I want...w-what you w-want for me...how you want m-me."

That is exactly what I wanted and needed to hear. She was mine...to do with as I pleased.

"Come, now." I bit out through my clenched teeth...I was so close to coming myself, I had to fight myself to stop the explosion threatening to rip my body in half. I have never needed to come so badly in my life, but I had to watch Auntie's first orgasm after turning her power over to me. I had to see it roll through her body and see it ravish her delicate features; turning her into something altogether belonging to me. I waited until her eyes turned soft and began to lose focus before I slammed into her warmth. I began stroking in and out. Rocking my pelvic bone against her clit; rubbing the head of my dick over that sweet spot just inside her slippery walls. I watched as her orgasm etched a painful expression of pleasure and submission and then I heard her. Rather, I didn't hear her. She was so still, so quiet. I almost stopped what I was doing, fearing I had hurt her, but I was too far gone to stop...But, I still listened to the cacophony of silence as I started coming inside of her. I had never come that hard. It seemed the more I came, the longer her orgasm lasted.

It was long minutes before the convulsions racking our bodies stopped. I lie inside her and felt the wetness of her tears as they leaked from her closed eyes. I held her and kissed her tears away, and she kissed mine away, too.

I was finally breathing on my own.

.

~5~

I left Auntie wrapped in her favorite blanket and a smile that I had never seen on her face. I was amazed I was the one who had put it there. She came down from her orgasm and looked at me with such gratitude and wonder; I knew I would kill to have her look at me that way every time we saw each other. I walked home that night knowing my power and feeling invincible. I knew if I wanted Auntie to continue to trust me to take care of her needs, I would have to learn to trust myself to take care of my own as well. *Now to figure out the million-dollar question of what it was I really needed.*

The door closed soundlessly behind me as I made away across the front room. I was so caught up in my own thoughts and feelings; I didn't even see it coming until it was too late. *What the fuck*...my mind struggled to understand what had just happened. I reached up and touched my head and felt the sticky, unmistakable feeling of blood coating my fingers.

"Where the hell you been? You little shit." I looked into the eyes of the devil and for some reason; he began to look comical to me. So much so that I could do nothing to stifle the laugh that tore from my throat and landed in his face with the satisfying pop of a right hook. His eyes turned cold and I felt the frost of his stare try to penetrate my soul...but I was on fire and I knew that the fire burning in me was fueled by my need to remain strong for Auntie...Being strong for her meant I had to first be strong for myself.

"Where the fuck you been, *boy*?" I glared at Earl, whose face was a masterpiece of confusion and fear. "Where is my mother?" I looked at his hand, loosely wrapped around my baseball bat that had my fresh blood on the tip and then I noticed it…Splatters of dried blood all along the length of the bat. His hands clenched around the bat and his stance changed slightly.

He looked taller and more threatening than I had ever seen him look before. *I like this look. This is one that I will have to adopt when I am with Auntie. Powerful and imposing, yet nimble enough to make quick move seem effortless. Get it together, John. Focus...where is your mom...*

"Your mom is where I left her silly ass. I see why you are such a stupid fuck!" Earl shouted the words through too thin lips that had sucked on one too many beer bottles. "Your stupid mom had one thing to do today. Nothing especially hard, just cook me something and then feed me and then suck me off." His smile looked demonic. "That stupid cunt of a mom you got couldn't seem to do even the most basic things. She's so fucking stupid, I'm tired of her and you. It's time to move away from all this family-man shit."

"What did you do to my mom, Earl?" My voice was so low and soft, I hardly recognized it and that's when I saw a shadow of fear pass like fog through his eyes and then it was gone. "So help you God, if she is hurt…"

I couldn't finish the sentence because Earl raised the bat and swung at my already bleeding head. Something in me snapped. It was the same feeling that came over me when Auntie was spraying me down with the hose in her backyard...the feeling of anger and fear...lust even. I grabbed the bat as it came towards my head and I snatched it from his hands; adopting the stance that he had just showed me, I passively gazed at him...seeing only the hurt, fear and pain in my mom's eyes. The way he had broken her down over the years.

"Where is my mom?" I whispered as the bat came down across his left shoulder. I heard the first bone crack and then the shrill sound of pain. I lifted the bat again and watched as his right hand came up, ready to deflect the next blow from the bat. He flinched as I brought the bat down again. "I am going to ask you one more time, Earl. Where the fuck is my mom?" I stood over him and felt my body tightening with leashed power and I knew that tonight, one of us would die and it would not be me. He held both his uninjured and his injured arms up in supplication and I simply stared at him with no emotion on my face.

"I left that whore of a mom in the bedroom. I hit her until her silly brains spil…" he never had a chance to finish his thought. I brought the bat up and then down in one quick movement against his skull. I heard the most satisfying crack I had ever heard. *Better than when I hit a homerun on the baseball field.* Blood ran from the center of his head down his fleshy, white faced. He looked up at me, eyes unfocused and breathing shallow. He tried to open his mouth to say something, but then a look of consternation and pain danced a slow waltz across his face.

"Shit." I watched as he struggled to stay upright and watched as he struggled to focus on my face, watched as his thoughts scrambled in his head and watched as his life seeped out through the massive split in his skull. I watched with detachment, because I knew he had already killed my mom and that there was nothing left to do except the call the police.

***

"Yes sir. When I walked into the house, I heard my mother screaming and I yelled for her. As I walked towards the hallway to go to her, Earl blindsided me with the bat and cracked my head open." I took a deep breath and allowed my eyes to linger a little longer than necessary on the large blood stain that had soaked through the carpet. Blood left by the monster of white trash that had single-handedly taken everything from me. I wanted to smile, but felt that would be out of line...suspicious even. So, I looked up at the cop with what I hoped was a look of pain and contrition. *Must have worked, because I vaguely heard the older cop tell me to take my time.*

"Once I realized what had happened, a sick feeling came over me. I was instantly worried for and about my mom and her safety. When I no longer heard her crying or yelling, I Knew that Earl had killed her...he finally *killed* my mom." I took a deep, shuttering breath and closed my eyes before continuing. "I wrenched the bat away from his hands and hit him as hard I could. I—don't know how many times I—I hit him, I just know that I wanted him to suffer the same way he had made my mom, whose only crime was trusting and loving him."

I let the words tumble from my mouth with not-so-quiet conviction, because it was the truth. When I was done telling the police what had happened, he looked at me with such pity and in that moment, I hated him, too. *Don't pity me, you fool. I just killed a man who had been slowly killing my mother for the last 12 years, I am not pitiful...I am powerful.*

Because the police found evidence of the 12 years of abuse to both my mother and myself at the hands of Earl, they did not bring me up on charges...they let me walk away without so much as a fingerprint. I was a sixteen-year-old orphan. There wasn't a foster home in the state that would take a sixteen-year-old boy, who had watched the murder of his mother and then murdered the man who killed her, into their home. I was assigned a caseworker, guardian ad litem, and a psychologist by the judge in family court. The state was not sure what to do with me, because no one wanted to take me in. Not my aunties, not my uncles...no one wanted a murderer in their house. Then the funniest thing happened. He showed up at the second hearing...looking like an older, more polished version me. I gaped at the man that had only been a part of a myth that I created to validate my lineage to myself.

"Excuse me sir, these court proceedings are closed to anyone not directly involved with this case. Now, who are you and what interest do you have in this matter?" The snow-capped top of the judge's head was in direct contrast to the smooth, brown skin of her face and hands. She was a stern looking woman; one who looked like she wouldn't take any shit from anyone. She looked like the kind of woman who would protect her child at all cost, would have given her last to ensure that the life she was responsible for was safe. Judge Daniels looked like the woman my mother should have been for both me and herself.

"Uh...yes ma'am. I'm...uh. This boy is my son. I am the boy's father." He looked nervously at the judge and then slid his eyes over to me with a look that was darkened by guilt, grief, greed? I don't know which was present, but none of them seemed as if they would work out well for me.

"John, dear." *The way she said that made me think about how Auntie would call me 'dear' just before she punished me for whatever transgression I had committed. The thought of her made my dick twitch and I had to fight for control over my body and my mind. Down Ellis, now is not the time.* "Do you know this man to be your father or…?" She let the alternative linger in the air. It hovered like a dense humidity...waiting for just the right moment to turn all the grass and flowers shiny with dew.

"Judge Daniels, I don't know who that man is. I've never seen, met, nor heard tell of my father...so I can't say if he is or is not who he claims to be." I tried to look contrite and confused all at the same time...I was becoming quite the actor.

"Then sir, that settles is. Please remove yourself from these proceeding or the bailiff will be more than happy to assist you should you so desire." She turned her harden brown eyes away from the man who probably was my father and looked softly at me. *What the hell is it about me that makes older women look at me like they wish they were younger or that I was older?* No time to think about that now...had to get the judge to grant me emancipation from the state and classify me as an adult, capable of making my own decisions and more importantly, handling my own money. Money coming from two insurance policies totaling a little of 200,000 dollars.

"John. I understand that you would like to be considered for emancipation from becoming a ward of the state." It wasn't a question, just a stating of a fact.

"Yes ma'am. I have been taking care of myself for most of my life and although I know I am only sixteen years old, I am confident I will be able to not only look after myself, but ensure I have a bright future. I have plans to attend USC in Columbia and study accounting. Once I graduate with my MBA in international business, I will secure a job with one of the top firms and work my way up." It was important to me that she understands that I wasn't some wayward, dickhead who intended to go through the insurance money buying cars and jewelry and clothes and stupid shit like that.

"Well. I can see you have put some thought into your plans. I like seeing that in a young man such as yourself. I believe you are more than capable of not only making your own decisions but also taking care of your financial well-being, as well." Her eyes lingered on my broad shoulders and slowly moved up to my mouth. I gave her the smile that showed off my dimple and showcased my naturally white, straight teeth. *Holy fuck. I just made the judge blush.*

"John. I will have to insist that you continue under the guidance of the state provided caseworker and the state-appointed guardian ad litem. You must also continue to attend school and maintain your current 3.9 GPA or *get it up*, if you can." *Holy fuck! Did she just say that to me with that look on her face?* She continued in a voice that had become a little husky and a lot sexy. "You will need to check in with your caseworker once a week and with your guardian ad litem three times a week.

I also feel it is necessary for you to continue seeing your psychologist until such a time as he deems you ready to move on. Do you understand the conditions of your emancipation?"

"Yes ma'am. I do." I did not want to say more or seem too cocky. I really wanted Judge Daniels to know how much I appreciated her ruling...*I never know when I may need a judge to help me out. With my luck...it will be sooner rather than later.*

I walked out of the courtroom with a plan, a home, a car and most importantly...freedom. I was finally free from the expectations, disappointments and brutality of what was my nightmare. With this new freedom and with my new role as Auntie's Dom... I realized I truly was the master of my universe.

"I'll check in with both of you at the appointed times next week." I threw over my shoulder, as I walked into the open arms of Auntie. I could not wait to get her back to her place and share my emancipation with her...freeing her from herself and taking all the worry, fear and insecurities away from her. That would always be my gift to her...I loved being responsible for someone who really needed me. Who really wanted *me*. Who really understood just how fucked up I was and still found pleasure in submitting to me.

"Good morning, Violet. You look like my favorite wet dream." As I slid into the car, I noticed the man who claimed to be my long-lost father staring daggers into my chest. I had a feeling that that was going to be the last time I would see the bastard.

~6~

Time seemed to stand still once I got out of Auntie's car. She had been deathly quiet on the drive back home. There was something on her mind, but she didn't know how to say it. God, I hope she doesn't think I'm completely insane and will become violent with her. I only want to make her feel as good as she makes me feel. *That's what you get for killing a man, dumbass. People are afraid of you; with good reason.* I walked around to Auntie's door to open it and let her out; the key still in the ignition, the CD player still playing '*Sun of '79'* by Des'ree and her, still buckled up in her seat belt.

"Get out of the car, Violet. I have plans for you and we need to talk." I used my new Dom voice and somehow, I even managed to emulate the power stance Earl adopted right before I bashed the fucker's head in. The effect was immediate. Her breath hitched, her eyes dilated, and her lips parted. She was damn near panting before I even reached across her chest, letting my fore arm brush against her erect nipples as I unbuckled her seat belt and coaxed her out of the passenger side. "I've missed you, Violet. Have you been missing me, too?" With her eyes averted, she nodded her head and I watched as one lone tear slid down her cheek. It looked like a diamond against her beautiful chestnut skin.

"We will talk about this in the house." I had no idea what to say to her, or what the hell the matter was. I had never seen her like this before...hell, I had never seen any woman like this before. As we entered her house, all of what was holding her up seemed to seep out of her and pool at her feet on the floor. I saw her collapsing and managed to get to her just in time to keep her from hitting her head on the corner of the table. *Fuck! What the hell was wrong with her? I was scared shitless and beyond confused about what she needed me to do for her.*

"Talk to me, Violet!" There was a sharper edge to my voice than I intended, but at that point...I was reminded that I was only sixteen years old and had no parents, and a 38-year-old mistress who was totally dependent on me for her sense of self.

What the fuck was I thinking...I need somebody older than me to do this...Wait! Why am I doubting myself? I'm sixteen years old, with a 38-year-old mistress and no parents to tell me what the hell to do or when to do it. I am the master of my fucking universe and the master of her fucking universe, too Game on Ellis. Game on.

"I—I don't know what to say." Her voice was so soft, I could barely hear her. In that moment, all the responsibilities I had as her Dom clicked into place. I had to make her feel safe, cared for, and most importantly; I had to let her know that she could trust me to be strong enough to deal with whatever came up in either my life or hers. I swept her up in my arms and carried her to the couch where I sit down and held her on my lap. Kissing her hair, her temple, her eyes, her cheeks, her nose and finally her chin. She was shaking like a leaf and then I felt her tears on my chest through the thin Henley I was wearing.

"Talk to me, Violet. Tell me what's wrong so I can fix it." My voice was softer, more concerned than I realized. I didn't like seeing her like this...weak and incapable of taking care of herself without the assistance of a male figure. She looked too much like my weak mother...I didn't want her like this.

"I thought I had lost you. I thought that chicken-shit Earl had took you away from me." The fire in her eyes helped me to release the breath I had been holding. There was the Auntie I knew. Her voice stronger now, but still filled with unshed tears, she voiced what her face had already told me. "I thought he had killed you. There was so much blood. When I saw them take that body out in the bag, I just knew that it was you in there...dead." She begin to shake her head back and forth as tears kissed her cheeks and continued to soak my shirt. "God, John. I ran home to get my pistol...I was going to shoot that motherfucker right between his eyes." Reluctantly, a smile pulled the corners of her mouth up into a sexy, innocent smile. I wanted her, hard and fast, but I knew she needed time to get over what she thought had happened to me. To lighten the mood, I asked her if I should be worried about have a pistol-shooting girl. Her reply was a simple, "Yes. You probably should be." Her voice was so much like the one she used only days ago before I took that hose from her, before she gave herself to me, before I became her Dom. *She cannot take back this power she gave me. I am the Dom; she belongs to me, damn it. Then get your pansy ass up and act like the Dom you have become.*

I placed her on the couch and stood up and over her. I straightened to my full height and took my power stance and lowered my voice to a low rumble. "You. Bedroom. Now. Your pussy should be naked and wet. Leave the pearls on and your bra. Everything else folded neatly beside the bed. When I come in there, you should be on the bed with your legs spread wide and your knees pulled up to your ears."

Her gaze dropped and all she said was, "Yes, John. How ever you want me." *Damn that had been a close call. I almost lost control of Auntie. Man up shit-for-brains!*

***

I walked into her room, roughly ten minutes later and saw her laying on the bed--just as I had instructed her to be. She was so beautiful and so mine. I didn't say anything to her as I walked towards the bathroom. I left the door open and took a shower. I stayed in the hot water much longer than I normally would have. I wanted her to wait; I needed her to know that she was no longer in control of this relationship, of me...not even of herself when we were together. I had to demonstrate that through sex and then we would be able to talk about other things. Right now, Auntie was being punished for her crass remarks and forgetting herself and her place in this relationship. I was punishing her for making me doubt myself and my newly acquired position of power. I left her assed-out for a little while longer.

"Violet." I snapped her name out like the wet towel I had just hanged up on the towel rack in her bathroom. She did not answer and I knew it was because I had not given her permission to do so. "Speak Violet." I spoke in my most authoritative voice and in my mind, I saw her wilt and submit further.

"Yes John?"

Was there a question in her voice and if so, why?

"Are you still lying in the position I told you to stay in?

"Yes John. Does that please you?"

"Yes, it does, Violet. I'm contented."

"John, may I ask you a question?"

Is she having a hard time breathing while having to hold her shapely thighs spread and raised? Maybe I should end this punishment but damn it...she has her safe word.

"Yes."

"Have I done something to displease you?"

"Yes."

"John, may I ask you another question?"

"Yes."

"Are you punishing me, now?"

What the fuck? Does she want me to punish her...does she expect a more physical form of punishment? I don't know if I could ever hit a woman...not after seeing what my weak mother went through.

"Do you think that you deserve to be punished, Violet?"

"Yes."

"What have you done that would make me punish you?"

"I—I spoke out of turn with you and forgot my place in our relationship."

How the hell did she pluck that shit out of my head? Maybe Auntie is the witch everyone says she is.

"What punishment do you think you should receive?"

I hope she couldn't tell that I was asking for help in deciding what her punishment should be...I hope that she didn't know that I already thought I was punishing her.

"Well. I have behaved off-color and my actions did not reflect well on you as my Dom, so I think the only thing to do is...spank me. Hard."

"Spank you hard." My voice a little higher than I wanted it to be and I pictured her smirking at me from behind the wall separating us. "With what? What should I use to spank you?" I didn't care if she figured out I had no fucking idea what I was doing, she was willing to teach me through her submission and I was more than willing to learn all I could from her.

"Your hand would be the most appropriate tool, to start the punishment. John."

Deep breath. Holy fucking hell, she wants me to spank that beautiful ass with my hand. Shit, I'm hard. There is something extremely sexy about having this conversation with a wall between us.

"Stay as I have instructed you and I will be out shortly. Violet. Think about how my hand is going to feel against your soft ass, against your wet pussy. Think about how my dick is going to pound into your tight cunt...and how you're going to want to come, but you won't...not until I tell you to."

I had to stay a minute and jack my shit, because if I had gone in there like this...it would be over before it ever got started. Ten minutes later, I emerged from the bathroom with a limp dick and a menacing look on my face. I saw her straining to keep her legs up in the prone position, I was pleased that she had obeyed me and stayed as I told her to.

"You have pleased me, Violet. But as you know, your transgressions overshadow what you have done to please me and for your transgressions, you will be punished. We'll go with fifteen licks. Remember, you can always use your safe word. I will stop whatever I am doing the moment I hear it. Tell me your safe word." I waited for her to answer and she whispered, "Della."

On an exhale, I reward her. "Good girl."

"Good. Close your eyes and raise your arms above your

head. I am going to bind your hands with my belt. Let me know if it is too tight." My heart was in my throat and I could barely breathe. I did not want to hurt her, didn't want to lose control...mostly, I didn't want to lose her trust in me to know how far I could take her.

The bed shifted as I pulled Auntie from the middle of the bed to the edge closest to me. I quickly bound her hands with my leather belt. Tight enough to be uncomfortable, but not so tight as to hurt or bruise her. Her legs were still in the position I had designed to be her punishment. God, in that moment, I fucking owned her...*Please don't let me go too far...please help me make her enjoy this. Please, God, don't let me lose her faith in me.*

"You have agreed to be punished by me and have accepted what that punishment would be. You understand that you can use your safe word and I will stop, immediately." I gave the words that she had given to me so many times, back to her.

"Answer me, Violet."

"Yes John. I understand why you are punishing me and I accept the punishment and I will use my safe word if I need to."

I caressed her left, then right butt cheek. Her breathing almost came to a halt. She really wanted my hands on her. I looked at her pussy and saw how wet she was. I hadn't even touched her yet. She wanted...no, she needed this punishment. I had to give this to her, it is the least I could do. I lifted my hand from her butt and ran my index finger down the length of her beautiful, plush sex and I thought she was going to come right then, but she didn't. *Thwack!* I brought my hand down against her right ass cheek and felt the stinging in my palm. She didn't make a sound. I rubbed my hands softly over her warm cheek before I repeated the action against her left cheek. The third hit landed in that spot where her ass and her pussy met. *Thwack!* She moaned low and deep in her throat and damn if my dick didn't get hard. That was the pattern. Right cheek, left cheek and then the meeting place. She seemed to get more turned on with every searing lick I gave her. Her arousal was like a homing device for my arousal. I wanted her so badly.

"Three more licks, Violet, and then I'm going to fuck you. I'll tell you when to come." My breathing was harsh, and I slowly began to understand how fine the line really was between pleasure and pain. I understood why I enjoyed it so much when Auntie punished me...I needed her to; needed her to show that she cared enough to give me boundaries. That she cared enough about me to punish me when I stepped outside those boundaries. It made sense that I enjoyed punishing her as much as she was enjoying the punishment. Boundaries...that's what the fuck I needed and now that she had given me some...it was easy to reciprocate. The last lick reverberated off her pussy and that's when I saw a small, secret smile grace her full and perfect lips.

"Good girl. You're wet for me, Violet." That's all the warning I gave her before I slammed into her with so much force, she cried out, loudly. I didn't stop pounding inside of her. Her legs had been in that strenuous position for almost an hour. I pulled out of her and flipped her over on her belly, spread her legs and slid back into her decadent folds.

"You feel so incredible, Violet. I love how tight you are, how wet you are, how you smell." I knew my words were ratcheting up her need to come, so I kept it up. "I'm so hard and so deep inside you, I feel your stomach muscles tightening. Do you like the way my dick feels inside you, do you want more, Violet?" Her moans and stifled cries made my balls tighten up and my cock even harder. I wanted to come so badly, but I had to wait. Had to show more control. "Talk to me, Violet. Tell me what you like." *Shit, I needed some reassurance that I was doing this thing right. I needed to know what she liked so I could remember it for later.*

"I—like it when you're so deep…" I rolled my hips and hit the left wall of her sex. She stopped mid-sentence, I smiled. "...that you hit the end of me."

"Like this?" I pushed hard into her and felt the tip of her cervix. She moaned and spread her legs wider, giving me more room to fuck her deep. "Yes, John. Like that."

"What else do you like, Violet?"

"I love that you fuck me like you can't get enough." Her body began to tighten around me, and I knew she was working hard to stave off her climax. "Do you want to come, Violet?" I knew she was close. I continued to taunt her, pushing her to her limits. I wanted to drive her crazy with the need to come, wanted her to surrender her pleasure completely to me. "I feel your sweet, little pussy clamping down on me. You get so hot, so greedy when you're about to come. Makes me want to fuck you for the rest of my life."

"Please John. Please...I can't--" Her words were lost in a heart-wrenching moan that caused her muscles to clamp down on me so tightly, I almost came my damn self.

"Please. John. I. Can't...You're...Oh God, John." I knew she was about at her limit. I rolled my hips to screw a little deeper inside her and when I hit the spot I knew she loved for me to hit; I whispered between clenched teeth, trying desperately to stop my own volcanic eruption, "For fuck's sake, come Violet." The words were barely out of my mouth when I felt her grow hotter and tighter and wetter and then I was coming. Coming harder than I had ever come in my life. I felt her body tense as she milked my dick again with her orgasm. Her orgasms feeding my wild thrust like oxygen feeds a fire. We were both too hot to put the flames out. I don't know if she had one long orgasm that prolonged my own or if the constant jerking of my dick made her orgasm repeatedly, but it didn't matter. What mattered was that I had punished her, fucked her and controlled her pleasure and my own.

When I rolled off her, I got off the bed and went into the bathroom to find some baby oil to rub her ass, which was the same shade as the roses I had just weeded a few weeks ago. When I returned, she was on her stomach, looking like the cat who caught the mouse. Pride welled up in my chest, because I knew that it was me who put that satisfied look on her face.

"How was that?" I asked as I freed her wrist from the constraints of my belt and gently rubbed them, making sure she wasn't bruised...

"So damn perfect...so good."

"Good. It was good for me, too."

I rubbed her ass with baby oil and listened as she winced in pain but didn't seem too bothered by the discomfort.

"Does it hurt, much?"

"Yes, but I deserved it, and this is what I needed." Her voice was so low on that last part of what she said, I almost didn't catch it. *She needed my hands on her, she needed me to set the boundary for her and then hold her feet to the fire if she stepped away from that boundary. I couldn't help feeling like I had passed some sort of test.*

"Yes. You did. I enjoyed punishing you, Violet. Does that make me a *monster*?" I needed my teacher to tell me that I was normal and not some spawn of Satan. I needed her to give me permission again...permission to breath.

"John. I want you to enjoy punishing me...May I speak frankly, Sir?" I realized she was getting ready to teach me what I needed to know about punishments, sexual dominance, and afterwards. Even as I massaged the oil into her thigh and leg muscles. "Yes, be as frank as you need to be, just don't grow a penis." My attempt at humor brought a throaty laugh from her more-than-kissable mouth.

"I won't grow a penis if you promise not to grow breast." I smiled at the easy way our conversation was flowing. It was nice to be able to relax with her, to not have to be the Dom or the sub... just having to be me; a sixteen-year-old orphan with $200,000 in the bank and a woman more than 20 years older than me who wanted nothing more than for me to happy.

"You were going to be frank with me…" I said with a teasing smile in my voice. But I am sure she could hear the anxiety that was there, as well.

"Yes. When a person assumes the role as a Dom for someone else, there is a level of power that comes with the position. But as you are learning, with *that* much power over someone, comes a lot of responsibility. I realize I have placed quite a bit in your lap, but I trust you and I know you are learning and you will still need my guidance.

You are doing such a great job, John. I don't ever remember feeling this safe, this cared for. Please know, I will never undermine your role as my Dom, but I am here to guide you and make your transition from sub to Dom as smooth as possible."

I took a deep breath and relaxed for the first time in what seemed like a long time. I wanted to stay up and talk with her all night, but I was tired, and I just wanted to feel her body next to my own.

"What about a bath?"

"That sounds nice."

"Good. I'm staying with you tonight?"

"Thank you for the privilege of waking up to you in the morning, John." And just like that, I was back in the driver's seat of this relationship. One day, I will find the courage to go back to the house I lived in with my mother and her sadistic husband, Earl. Both of whom were dead. One at the other's hand and one at my hand. Sometimes I am not sure which of the two I killed. Maybe, I killed them both...maybe...*Who the fuck has time for maybe...you only have time for right now. And right now, you have a bath date with the oh-so-lovely Violet. Get your ass in gear, boy.*

~7~

The rest of the summer was a blur at best. I rarely went to the house that had been my home for the last twelve years; most of my time was spent with Auntie and the rest of the time, I made myself scarce around the neighborhood. It really wasn't that hard to do, seeing as though all the people who gave me their, 'I'm so sorry your mama got you living like that.' bullshit before the incident, disappeared as soon as I killed the son of a bitch who had murdered my mom and tried his best to murder me, too. All the guys I used to hang with, play ball with, go after girls with...those dumbasses were nowhere to be found. *Can you blame your neighbors and your friends for stepping away from your crazy ass? The only reason Auntie hasn't left you is because she is just as fucked up as you are.* I was tired of this nagging voice in my head. I knew that it was just my conscience talking to me, but shit. Hearing it all the fucking time made me feel like maybe I *was* crazy.

Today was the day I was meeting the realtor at the house I used to live in with my mother and her husband. I moved my things into Auntie's house three days after the courts emancipated me. People would talk, but hell...they were already talking. What the fuck do I care what those porch talkers say about me? They don't know me or what I've been through, so in the great words of every angry Black man, fuck'em.

The sun was especially oppressive on the Tuesday morning the realtor was supposed to come over. I lived in a decent neighborhood of mostly Blacks, but a few white families had moved into the area recently. Most of the people in the neighborhood worked blue-collar jobs and tried to make a better life for their families than their people had made for them. I hoped that the commercial cleaning crew I hired had done a good enough job cleaning the filth of that night away. I had to have new floors, new paint...shit, just about every damn thing in the house was new. I even had the outside of the house redone with newer vinyl siding and shutters.

There was no mortgage on the house, my mom was smart enough to get a payable upon death insurance policy that paid the house off in the event she died before she had paid the mortgage in full. She also had an insurance policy on Earl in the amount of one million dollars that nobody knew about. She made me the beneficiary of the policy if she passed before Earl did...She seemed to be planning a better life for me after she died. Almost like she knew she would not survive Earl and he would not survive me. Maybe she did know; either way, I had more than enough money to do whatever the fuck I wanted to do and what I wanted to do was sell that house and move me and Auntie to a new city. I was planning to attend The University of South Carolina in Columbia...so I thought moving to Columbia, finishing the last year of high school would be a good start. I had enough credits to ensure what I would graduate at the age of seventeen. *Shit! My birthday was coming up...So much fucked-up shit has been happening, I completely forgot God cursed me to be born to a weak woman who couldn't choose a good man to save her soul. August 20, 1991. Three days away.*

"Hello. Jonathan Ellis?" A pretty little, blond woman greeted me as she walked up the steps to the front porch where I was swinging mindlessly in the swing I had installed to help sell the house. She was much smaller than Auntie and she looked frail. *I would probably break her boney ass in two if I fucked her like I fuck Auntie. Wait, where did that thought come f*rom?

"Yes. I'm Jonathan Ellis. Thanks for coming out, Cynthia, right?" I flashed my megawatt smile that showcased the dimple in my left cheek and rose to my full height of 6'5". I watched her eyes travel up my body and pause a little longer than was necessary when she reached the zipper of my shorts, then my chest and she licked her thin lips when her eyes rested on mine. *Yea, I could fuck her right now if I wanted to, but I have never been into white girls. Not enough cushion for the pushing. But, what the fuck do I know? I've never been with a white woman, but I knew that this skinny one would not be my first.*

"It's nice to meet you. You are, er, younger than you sounded over the phone. Are you old enough to sell this house?" She flashed her smile, I guess it was supposed to make me feel more comfortable, but her already too thin lips completely disappeared and all I saw were teeth and gums. Made me think of Fire Marshall Bill from my favorite show, In Living Color. I had to work hard not to cringe. I returned her smile with my own and hunched my shoulders.

"I assure you, Cynthia. I am plenty old enough to sell this house." I adopted my new Dom stance and allowed my voice to drop down half an octave. "Both of my parents, unfortunately, passed away and the courts saw fit to emancipate me so that I could handle my affairs as an adult instead of having child protective services involved. So yes, I am old enough to sell and buy anything I want to." I reached around her slight frame and placed my hand on the small of her back to lead her into the house. I heard her breath catch the moment I touched her. *This is too easy. I'll bet she's already wet. Not interested.*

"Well, Jonathan. This house is lovely. It looks like your parents did a great job keeping the home in tip-top shape." Her large, gray eyes scanned the family room that led into the eat-in kitchen; appraising the floors, paint, and furniture as she moved towards the kitchen proper. "Oh my. This is a contemporary kitchen for the age of the house. Was the property recently remodeled?"

"Yes. I had some work done to the house to bring it up to date. Before my mother took ownership of the property, it belonged to my grandpa. When he passed, he left it to my mom. She and her husband didn't really do anything to make the house more modern...more *livable*, but I was fully aware that if I want the house to sell, certain things needed to be done." I was standing behind her. She ran her small, pale hands over the stainless-steel appliances and the granite counter tops. I moved in closer, I wanted her to feel my heat behind her. For me; at this point, everything is about power. Whoever has the power has the upper hand. Auntie taught me that and so far, it has proven to be the most valuable lesson she's gifted me with.

"I honestly don't think we will have any trouble listing this home and selling it. All we need to do is agree on an asking price and we can do that by looking at any comparable homes in the neighborhood and seeing what they are either selling for or have sold for." She finally turned her heart-shaped face away from the upgrades in the kitchen to look up at me. Her eyes told me that she knew what had happened in this house and was waiting for me to confirm. She didn't say anything just took a step back and continued to look up at me.

"Is there something else you need know, Cynthia?" People always find it unnerving when they are addressed by their given name. *Creates a power shift.* I watched as her breathing increased and her delicate hands smoothed her already perfect hair.

"Uh...er. I heard that a double murder...well. We have to tell prospective buyers if someone died in a property and as nice as this…" I held up my right hand to stop her from talking. Her eyes stretched open and I saw what looked like fear and panic sift through her gray gaze. I stepped towards her and looked down into the stormy pools before I said a word. When she couldn't look away, I spoke in a soft, monotone voice.

"I think we both know that two people died in this house. I also think we both know my mother died at the hands of my stepfather and my step father died at *my* hands. I get that you must let people know that a double murder occurred in this house, but please, Cynthia. Let's not bullshit each other." My face was impassive and conveyed my disinterest in anything she might say. I watch as her alabaster skin went from creamy to pink and then to full-blown red. *That's right, bitch. If you are scared, you should be. Don't try and dick me around. I may be young, but I'm not your average sixteen-year-old.*

Her throat worked on a swallow and she looked like she was on the verge of passing out. I stepped away from her and decided that I would put her out of her misery. "Listen, Cynthia. I don't think you are the right realtor to sell my home. Thank you for coming out. I hope it was not too much trouble or took much time out of your busy day." My relaxed and friendly tone had returned to my voice and I could tell she was more than confused at my quick change in mood. *Keep them guessing. As long as they can't stick you in one category, you will always have power over them.*

"I am sorry, Mr. Ellis. I really would love to work with you, but I fear you may be right. I don't think I am the right person to list and sell your home." The quiver in her voice betrayed the brave, professional front she tried to slide into this strange conversation. I smiled at her and placed my large hand on the small of her back to usher her out of the kitchen, out of my house and out of my life.

"Thanks so much for coming out. I do appreciate the small bit of information you were able to share with me. I think I may list it as a FSBO. The process will be a lot easier." By the time I was done talking, she was standing on the last step of the large front porch, looking confused and bewildered; almost like she didn't know how she had ended up on the step or how she had been dismissed by a sixteen-year-old-too-smart-for-his-own-good boy that she had just addressed as 'Mr. Ellis'. I smiled at her once again and turned to walk up the steps and into my unsellable house. *Shit! What the fuck am supposed to do with this damn house. I knew never to get rid of real estate, but I couldn't be responsible for a house here and get started with my new life in Columbia. I guess I will rent this bitch out. Problem solved.*

I dug my cell phone out of my back pocket and called Auntie's number. She answered on the first ring. "Yes John." Her voice was breathy as if she had just finished working out or fucking.

"Violet." I used my lowest register and smiled when I heard her quick intake of air. Completely enjoying the power I had over her. "What have you been doing, Violet?" Not giving her a chance to answer, I continued with my questioning. "You sound winded, as if you've been exercising or..." I left it open, allowing her to fill in the blank. "Being that I have been at my house for the last two hours, I would hope that you decided to go for a jog." I left it in the air and frowned when I heard the fearful plea in her voice when she asked for permission to speak to me. "Yes. Speak."

"John. I was out back working in my garden. It has been quite neglected sense our arrangement changed. I forgot to bring the cordless phone out with me and had to run into the house to catch your call. I didn't want you to call me and not be able to reach me."

I smiled and I'm sure she heard it in my voice. "Good. I am a jealous guy and you belong to me. I never learned to share, and you mean too much to me for that to even be a consideration. I'm on my way over. I should be there in about an hour. There will be a package delivered to your door. I want you to put it on and be ready in the front room in one hour. If you are not ready, I will punish you, Violet. Do you understand?"

"Yes, John. I understand." She sounded distracted and then I heard her doorbell ring and excused her from the phone so that she could collect the dress, shoes and jewelry I had sent to her for a special evening out. I had to tell her we were moving to Columbia and she really didn't have a choice if she wanted to continue our 'relationship'. I needed her more than I would ever tell her, but again, she needed me, too. *There will come a time when you will outgrow her, what will you do with and for her then? You will find someone more suited to you, and then what happens to Auntie? Will you assume responsibility for her while you forge ahead with your life? Will you turn her out into the streets when you no longer have need for her...when you have found someone else to replace her?*

As these thoughts dinged around in my head, I realized that I hadn't even thought that far in advance. I have been so focused on the right now...getting through every day; one day at a time. I would never leave Auntie out there on her own, but I also knew one day, I would find a woman I wanted to marry and have a family with. What the fuck would I do with Auntie? *End this bullshit relationship and take your horny ass to Columbia and start living your life. This is not rocket science, dumb ass.* Easy for you to say...you're just a voice inside my head that's driving me fucking crazy. Shit. Now I am talking back to myself.

~8~

I used the key that Auntie had given me at the beginning of the summer to let myself into the house that we shared. She was waiting, just like I told her to be, in the front room. She looked like something out of a high fashion magazine. Auntie was a beautiful woman and there was an innocence about her that pulled at my heart. I was sure I was not falling in love with her, but I couldn't deny I cared more for her then I had ever cared for any other person.

I stood in the door and let my eyes roam slowly over Auntie's perfect curves. She had her hair pinned up in the back, while around her beautiful face; loose curls framed amazingly sharp eyes. She was gorgeous. "Stand up, Violet." She stood and smoothed the emerald green dress that fell just above her knees. The coloring of the dress somehow made her lilac colored eyes appear more feline and dangerous. The spaghetti straps showed off her amazing shoulders, collarbone and arms while the sweetheart neckline drew attention to her full breast. There was just enough beading on the top of the dress to negate the need for excessive jewelry. Auntie's small waist and the sexy curve of her hips and thighs were emphasized by the cinched waist and slightly flared skirt.

"You look...words are failing me, Violet." The look in my eyes said I was thinking about fucking her...hard, deep and for a long time. I watched as she squeezed her thighs together in an effort to stop the throbbing at the apex of her thighs.

"Walk over to me. Slowly." My voice was a whispered command that had the same effect on Auntie as if I had barked out an order. She walked towards me with her eyes lowered and chin held high. Everything about Auntie was a moving contradiction. She was sexy and innocent, powerful and submissive, everything and nothing. The mystery of her made me want to protect not just her, but all the complexity that made her who and what she was.

"Violet. You look so beautiful, so damn sexy. I want you now, but I really want to take you out to dinner and maybe a drive to my favorite spot by the beach. Later. I'll have you later. You'll be my dessert:" I always tried to make sure that Auntie knew she had options, even when I forced my will on her, even when I required her submission to me. I could not stand to break her as I had watched that fucker, Earl, break my mom.

"John, you can have me anytime you want to. Dinner and a drive not required, but I do appreciate you doing this for me. You make me feel cherished, cared for." She broke my heart everyday...makes me wonder what kind of life she had. Her eyes remained lowered as she spoke to me. I loved her contrition when it came to me. I wanted to pull that dress up in the back, rip her white lace thong off and shove myself into her wet warmth, but I couldn't. I needed to stay in control if I was going to convince Auntie to pick up her life and move to Columbia with me.

"We have reservations at Traditions and then I want to take you to the Lighthouse at Huntington Beach. We have things that need to be decided tonight and then I want to bring you back to my house and fuck you raw." She looked at me with fear and trepidation in her beautiful eyes, I couldn't imagine why, but I didn't want to take the time to ponder it, either.

I held my hand out to her and led her out of her front door into the passenger side of my brand new 1991 Ford Mustang Cobra, 5.0. The candy-apple red color only added to the flashiness of my car, purchased courtesy of the one-million-dollar life insurance policy my mom had on Earl. *Thanks a lot, mom. You didn't do shit for me when you were alive, but I guess when you won't do shit to make your own situation better...nobody else's situation matters either.*

"You look beautiful, Violet. Do you like what I am wearing? This is only my second time wearing a suit?" I still needed Auntie's approval as much as I needed to dominate her. She was, after all, my teacher and student. "Yes, John. You can really hang a suit, you look older, and more sophisticated...more dominant. This is already the best night of my life." She crushed me every time she showed such appreciation for what I considered small acts of kindness. *What the hell kind of life did Auntie have that would leave her so utterly broken?*

"Well, if this is already the best night of your life, I can't wait for you to experience the rest of what I have planned with and for you." Looking into my eyes as I moved the manual transmission into reverse, she smiled the shyest, sweetest and most child-like smile I had ever seen. *I will not hurt this woman, ever. I will always be here for her...regardless of what choices I make...she will always be taken care of.* The finality with which that thought buried itself in my mind made me uneasy. Then, one look at the smile on Auntie's face wiped that uneasiness away.

"Have you ever been to Traditions?" I was having trouble making conversation with her...I was nervous for some reason. Then it hit me...another wet rag in the face. The entire time Auntie and I have had this *arrangement,* we have only ever been in her house. As much time as we spent together, most of our relationship is about sex, domination, submission and control. I realized that I didn't know much about the woman I had been fucking for the last two and a half months. *What are people going to think when they see this sexy, thirty-something-year-old woman with a sixteen-year-old boy? Now you think about that dumbass? You are stupid...Earl was right about you all along.*

"Violet, er...it just came to mind that we know the nature of our relationship, but nobody else does. People can't find out that we are having sex...they won't understand, and I don't want you to be locked away for child abuse. I love what we have, and I will do anything to protect it, but I'm not quite sure what to do...how to present us in public." I let the words tumble from my mouth, hoping I still maintained my dominance in the obvious moment of weakness. As usual, Auntie guided me through the situation without making me feel inferior.

"John, may I speak openly?"

"Yes."

"What we have does not need defining, but I understand others need to label relationships and those who engage in them. Don't worry, I'll be whatever you need me to be for the public, but please don't ask me to pretend to be nothing to you."

"Auntie...uh, er...Violet." I stuttered over my words, feeling off my game and confused. Was she in charge or was it me? I felt her wide eyes looking at me, but not in my face and then I heard her soft voice...her submissive voice asks, "John. Who do you want me to be, tonight?" Just that quickly, she gave me back my power...*Christ*! I guess old habits die hard.

"Tonight." My voice more authoritative than before. "You will be my older cousin coming to help me straighten things out with my mother's death and such." I pulled into the parking lot and gave the valet my keys as Auntie and I got out of the car. I had taken my matching tie off and unbuttoned my dress shirt at the collar. I had a more casual look that made Auntie shine even more. Men were eye fucking her the minute we walked into the restaurant. *These fuckers keep looking at what belongs to me like they want to die tonight. I've killed already...take your damned eyes off. She is mine!*

As we walked through the restaurant, I had to remind myself that tonight, she was my older cousin...not the older woman I was fucking. We sat at our table and Auntie's eyes zeroed in on mine. "John? Please don't be concerned with any of their looks. We know what this is, even if they don't." Her voice; soothing and sexy, did little to calm the irrational jealousy that was burning a path from my head to my fists, which were balled up in my lap. "I know—it's just that…" I lowered my voice to a pregnant whisper, "You are mine and I don't fucking like it when strangers look at what belongs to me like they have a right to do so." I realized I wasn't thinking straight, but I didn't care at that moment. I wanted to get up and walk over to Auntie, pull her from her chair, bend her over the table and fuck her hard...so every shit-eating man in the restaurant would know she was mine.

"I love it when you look at me like that, John." Auntie's voice was a low murmur in my ears and what she whispered to me sent an electric bolt straight to my dick. I hardened immediately. "You are the only man that has ever had my heart, that will ever have me and right now, if you want to take me out to your car and fuck my brains out...I don't need this...but I do need you to remember who you are to me and who I am to you. You own me, John." *How does she do that? She knows all my insecurities, because they are the same ones that she deals with, but where she can reassure me...I don't know if I am returning the favor. I must do that for her...for me.*

In that moment, I realized that I really had nothing to worry about, because Auntie would be coming home with me and she would be lying next to me and she was mine...completely. I relaxed and decided to enjoy this evening out with my *cousin,* Violet. *I smiled at that thought…no way were the thoughts running through my head appropriate for my cousin.*

"Do you know what you want to eat?"

"What will you be having, John?" Without even trying, she turned the control back over to me and somehow managed to contain herself for the on lookers. *Amazing...fucking amazing is what Auntie is.* "I'm going to go with the porterhouse steak and potatoes with asparagus."

"May I order something different...I am not really keen on eating steak tonight." The waiter walked up to the table with a basket of sliced brioche and warm honey butter. "May I take your drink orders?" His eyes were glued to Auntie's beautiful face and slowly swept down to her cleavage...I wanted to shove that pen in his neck, but I kept my cool. Besides, I wanted to see what Auntie would do...would she stay in sub mode, or would she step up and take over?

Without looking at the waiter, never giving him the attention he obviously wanted her to give, she lowered her eyes slightly and spoke only to me. *God, I love who she is and who she makes me...I am a lucky bastard.* "John. What do you suggest I drink? Oh remember, I don't drink alcohol." Her face and voice dripped with contrition but her countenance exuding confidence.

"I think sweet tea with extra lemon would be a good choice...when in the south, drink as the southerners do and all that." I smiled at her and turned my frozen chocolate gaze to the waiter and nodded my head. His smile faltered, and he scooted away without another look at the woman sitting across from me. She looked so pleased with what just happened and again, I felt as if I had just passed another test. *Damn, Auntie is a hell of a teacher.*

"John, may I ask you something?"

"Yes, anything."

"What really happened the night of the incident? You don't have to tell me, but I really want to know." I took a deep breath to center myself and slow the horses that ran in my chest. I considered her beautiful eyes and decided that she deserved no less than the entire truth. Even if she decides that my truth is too dark to accept...she deserved to know more about the man-child she was in a relationship with.

"Well Violet, the night of the *incident* was just the ending to something that began twelve years earlier." I stopped speaking as the waiter approached us with the drinks. I noticed this time that he only glanced in Auntie's direction long enough to place her drink down in front of her. "If you are ready to order, I will be more than happy to take that for you now, sir." I felt that familiar hum of power just under the surface of my skin. I liked that feeling almost as much as I liked coming. "Yes. We are ready to order. I'll have the porterhouse steak, medium rare, smashed potatoes with asparagus and hollandaise sauce. For the lady, grilled day scallops, parmesan risotto and braised spinach." Auntie had not told me what she wanted, but I felt confident that I had ordered something that she would love. I gave the oversized menus back to the waiter and nodded curtly for him to go. Auntie looked at me and a faint smile graced her full lips. She was pleased and damn if that didn't please me. *Another test passed. Shit, I should remember to bring her an apple.*

The food arrived, and we listened to the ebb and flow of conversations around us. I was grateful for the chance to be quiet because I knew that soon enough, I would have to continue the conversation that was started earlier, as well as talk to her about moving to Columbia.

"Are you enjoying your meal, Violet?"

"Yes. How did you know what I wanted?"

"I spend a good portion of my day inside you, watching you, wanting you...I pay attention." My answer must have shocked her, because she looked up at me through impossibly long lashes and showed me what I loved to see...her appreciation and her need for me.

"That you do...I don't know what I'm going to do with myself when it is time for you to return to school. I may have to come in and volunteer in the library or something." Her tone told me that she was only half kidding…

"Well, that's one of the things I need to talk with you about, but I don't want to have this conversation here. Did you want dessert?" I hoped like hell she didn't. I felt my resolve slipping...If I am going to do this...I need to hurry up and get it done. *This is what you get when you try and be grown...just because you fucking a grown woman, don't make you grown.* I am so tired of this voice...before it was just my voice, now it's taken on the voice of that motherfucker, Earl. Even in death, he keeps fucking with me.

"No, John. I only want to ease the panic that is walking slowly across your handsome face. I'm ready to go, if you are. Oh, and thank you for taking me on my first real date." I couldn't contain the confusion that replaced everything else on my face. "What the do you mean your first date?" I was glad that my voice was full of confusion and concern rather than anger. How could someone who looks like Auntie and fucks like her not have ever been on a date. I mean, admittedly, I have not been on many dates...unless you count sitting next to a girl at the basketball games and yelling at the same time a date. In that moment, I realized that I really didn't know her at all. The thought bothered me a little. Here I am assuming responsibility for this little-girl-woman and I haven't taken the time to know anything about her except for her body.

"John. There is a lot you don't know about me. Most of which I don't want to share, but I know that I need to be honest with you so that you can make an informed decision about continuing our...uh, *relationship.*

~9~

After the meal was paid for and we were seated in my car, I felt my nerves creep up and threatened to yank my heart right out of my chest. I knew what I wanted. I knew what I wanted to say, but something was holding me back. *That would be your chicken-shit heart...you should really stop playing house and stay in your fucking lane, little boy.* "Shut the hell up, *Earl.*" I mumbled under my breath and hoped to God that Auntie hadn't heard me talking to my dead stepfather. *Shit. I really am losing my mind. Get your shit together, John. She wants to be with you...stop second guessing yourself.*

The drive north on highway 17 was strained, at best. I had no idea what the hell I was going to say what I needed to say to make her want to move to Columbia with me, and I really wasn't sure that I had the right to ask her to do so.

"John. You've been quiet. Is everything alright?" Her voice broke through my muddled thoughts and brought my attention back to her. I glanced over to look at her and saw concern on her face. Time slowed down to nothing and I watched as she opened her mouth to say something to me...to warn me; but just as a sound like nothing I had ever heard, tore from her throat, the windshield exploded, and the car became air-born.

"Oh shit! Violet...Violet..." My voice was raw from calling her name, from screaming her name. The car was upside down and there was blood, glass and smoke everywhere. It didn't look like Auntie was anywhere near me or the car. "Violet!" I yelled her name and tried to reach my left arm over to see if she was there, a sharp pain burned through my senses making me cry out. *Shit. Is that gas...oh my God! This car is going to explode, and nobody will know or care what happened to me or Auntie. I have to get out of this car and find her.*

I managed to crawl out through the window and realized that I had probably broken my arm; there was also a lot of pain coming from my head, neck and back, but I could walk and that was good enough for me. I didn't even know where to begin looking for Auntie, not until I heard her soft cries coming from the other side of the road. I made my way across the highway and looked into the darkness, trying to follow the sound of her voice.

"John?" A whispered plea for help carried on the wind.

"Violet?" A whispered reply returned on the wind.

"Yes. Are you al…" A wet cough accompanied by a sickening gurgle in the back of her throat interrupted her inquiry. *I have got to get help. I can't leave her. God please let someone pass by...a cop, anyone.* As if my prayer had been heard and answered almost immediately, a police car with flashing lights drove up to the wreckage. I dropped to my knees and reached across the small ditch and touched what I hoped was Auntie's arm, but it felt like it was at an odd angle.

"Hey. Are you hurt?" The gruff voice of the cop broke through some of my haze and I was able to peel my tongue from the roof of my dry mouth and respond.

"I'm alright. The...my cousin is not...she needs to go to the hospital immediately. Please get an ambulance...I don't think she's going to make it." My voice broke on the last couple of words, but thankfully my tears and pain were effectively hidden under the cloak of a misty, dark sky.

"The ambulance is on the way. What's your name, son?"

"Jonathan R. Ellis, sir."

"Hey?" I knew what was coming next.

"Aren't you the kid who killed his stepdad over there in Plantersville?"

"Yes. How long will it be before the ambulance gets here? She is barely breathing." I tried and failed to keep the panic and mounting agitation out of my voice as the cop seemed to be stuck on stupid with the revelation that I had killed my stepdad. Just when I felt my temper flaring, I heard the siren of the ambulance barreling down the road towards us. "Thank God." I whispered to no one in particular. "Violet, just hold on baby. The ambulance is here, we are going to the hospital. Please baby, just hold on for me...for us." I heard a low keening sound escape from her open mouth...she was barely breathing; my heart stopped beating as the paramedics came with the gurney.

"Sir, if you can walk, please come with me. I need to check your injuries. Sir?" I didn't hear anything that guy was saying to me. Hell, I don't even know if it was a guy. I felt a tugging on my arm and the pain of that tug registered somewhere in my brain, but not enough to jolt me into my body.

"You have to hurry and get her. She's not breathing. Please, save her. Her name is Della...save her!" I felt what I thought were tears sliding down my cheeks, but I soon realized it wasn't tears, it was heavy, thick blood. I have no idea where the contusion was, and I really didn't care. My focus was on the gurney draped in blankets and an unresponsive Auntie making its way towards a waiting ambulance. I stood up, too quickly, in time to see Aunties face...or what was left of it. I didn't even recognize the person laying on the gurney as the woman I had left the house with earlier.

"Sir. Please get into the ambulance with Della...you both need medical attention." He extended his hand to me to help me into the back of the vehicle. Once settled onto a bench, my eyes slid towards the lifeless form lying flat on the table. The paramedics were working fiercely on resuscitating her, but they looked about as hopeful as I felt. *God, listen. I know that I am the last person who has a right to ask you for anything...but, I can't believe that you would give her to me and then just take her away from me. I need her. I need us. Please God...save her.*

By the time we arrived at the hospital, the medics rushed me towards the emergency room. I noticed that the fuss had died down around Auntie. A sickening chill ran down my spine and I didn't have to wait for them to tell me the news. My breath stopped flowing. My reason for breathing was leaving me. My beautiful teacher, lover and friend was not going to the sun of a new day. *What the fuck am I going to do without her...? I killed the only person I ever cared about. Maybe I am cursed...maybe I don't deserve to know love or tenderness.* "Stop this fucking gurney. I need to see her, I need to tell her…" The paramedics and nurses tried to hold me down, but sometimes crazy is a good thing. I bucked them off me and made my way to the gurney that Auntie was laying on. Not dead, but not alive. I leaned down, tears of sorrow and regret flowing freely from my eyes.

"Auntie."

"My sweet boy, John." A cough came up from her chest and let a small trickle of blood run from the side of her beautiful mouth.

"Don't talk, Auntie. I want you to know that I care for you...you're the only person I've ever cared for. I know that you have to leave…" I couldn't finish my sentence. Sobs robbed me of the ability to speak and I didn't care who saw me blubbering like a baby, because at that moment...I felt like a motherless child.

"John." Her voice is a siren's call. "...I love you...you…" More coughing, more blood. "...Thank you for giving me so many…" Gasp and cough and blood...so much blood pooling beside her head, running from her mouth. "...So many first...I'll never be gone...You have my..." Gasp. Gasp. Cough. "...Everything." Nothing. No cough, no gasp. Just nothing. Then I saw it. One tear sliding down her cheek and a smile gracing her disfigured face. She was beautiful. She was all I never knew I needed. She was gone.

"I'm so sorry, Auntie. I am so sorry." I felt the tears mixing with the blood running down my cheek and fell to the floor. Everything else was a blur and as I looked into the faces of white doctors and nurses and welcomed the blackness that was closing in on me. I welcomed the sweet oblivious warmth that unconsciousness provided. I hoped in that moment that I would die on the floor...facing tomorrow without her...I would rather be dead.

***

I had nothing left. A week later I returned to Auntie's house with a broken collarbone, shoulder and left arm. I had several cuts that required stitches and four broken ribs. I had a concussion and was told that I should not be alone for at least 72 hours. I was hoping that if I laid down and went to sleep...with the help of the pain pills they had sent me home with, I would not have to worry about waking up. As I made my way into the house, the cold, dark silence that had drawn me in at the beginning of the summer now felt oppressive and dead.

"Why?" I hit the wall with my right fist and welcomed the pain. Pain was better than what I was feeling. Pain made me feel something...I was numb. I continued to hit the wall until my knuckles were open and bleeding. I needed the pain...I needed to suffer. Tears, sobs and pain. *I miss you, Auntie. I want to feel your arms around my shoulders as I move inside you, Violet. I want to protect you from whatever broke you, Della. I need you.*

~10~

I found Auntie's personal papers under her bed in a locked box. I used the keys she'd given me to unlock the box should I ever need to. I found her last will and testament...it looked like it was newly printed. I found her life insurance papers, bank records, deeds and titles to various properties she owned…

"Auntie was loaded. Why was she living modestly? What was she saving it for?" I mumbled to myself as I absentmindedly went through her things. I read a letter that was addressed to me. *When did she write this letter…?*

My dear, sweet Jonathan,

If you are reading this letter, then my time with you has run out. I wanted to tell you so many times, but I couldn't bring myself to do it. I just wanted to spend the last months of my life giving and receiving everything that had been kept away from me.

When I saw you walking down the road looking like a grown man with the weight of the world on your shoulders, but still cocky and self-assured, I knew that I would have you... Only you. And more importantly...you would have me. I saw you, John. Saw exactly what you were. I was sure that you had no clue about the power and passion you possessed, but I saw it and I knew that I could bring it out of you.

You were amazing and funny and smart and humble and so broken. I wept for you every night you left my house. I wanted to heal you. Give you my strength; I knew that shortly, I would not need it anymore.

I want to say thank you. Thank you for loving me in a way that made me whole. Thank you for taking care of me, taking the trouble of making decisions away and leaving me with only the desire to please you. To make you happy. I gave you everything. My heart, my mind...even my broken soul.

John. I am dying of brain cancer. I refused any treatment...I wanted to stay in control of my life and my death. I have been fighting this battle for three years now, and finally...I am ready to concede...cancer wins. You made these last three months more than I ever could have wished for. Thank you. Please know that my death is not something to be sad about...be happy for me. I'm not suffering anymore. Be happy that you were able to give me pieces of myself that I had locked away years ago. Be happy that I was able to give you the gift of power...it is an invaluable asset. Be happy that our time together was not about sickness and pain...well, at least not the pain of cancer. (smile)

I know that you will be an amazing man, I want to help you become that. In the world we live in, money and property are power. I have more money than I would ever need to be happy, so I'm leaving my entire estate to the man that gave me something that money could not buy...his heart. Take what I gave you...money, power, sex, lust, hope, fear, pain, and my love and conquer the world.

My last request, John is that you never forget me. Hold me in your heart like you held me in your arms. Never fall out of love with me, even as you fall in love with someone else. Remember me always and I will always be with you. Listen for me in the wind and storms. Look for me in forgotten rainbows and clouds.

I love you. You are everything. You are my always...my forever. Be happy, John. You deserve it and so much more.

Forever Yours,

Violet

I stood in the middle of the bedroom where I had found so much pleasure laced with pain and kissed with something so precious, I couldn't begin to attach a word to it; and it was then that I felt the emptiness settling in my soul. Then, that I felt something break inside me; I didn't know what it was, I just knew it hurt like hell.

As far as I knew Auntie didn't have any family or friends to speak of and if she did, I had no idea how I would contact them to let them know what had happened. My eyes glossed over with unshed tears and I tried to contain my pain, but I had packed so much pain and hurt inside of me, I really didn't have anywhere to store this fresh pain. I knew that I had business to take care of and once I was done, I knew that I would never go back.

***

According to Aunties last will and testament, she did not want to be buried. As she had outlined in her will, she was cremated one day before I turned seventeen. I collected her ashes in an alabaster box, had the box sealed and took her back to her house. No one even cared that she was no longer alive. No one came to knock on her door to see what had happened. No one showed up with flowers, casseroles or condolences. When I got out of my rental car, I looked at the porch sitters and saw, for the first time just how vacuous they were. They seemed to be feeding on the misfortunes of those who existed around them. I walked up the driveway and walked slowly towards the porch.

"Hey!" One of the faceless porch sitters called to me. I had a mind to ignore her and continue on my way, but some part of me wanted to believe that the community that Auntie and I lived in wasn't so fucked up. I hoped that someone would ask about her, lament her passing, share in my grief...but when I looked into the face of the woman who had called me so crudely, I knew she was just searching for misery to feed her own selfish needs.

"Yes." My voice was as deadpan as I could make it. I didn't want any of my pain to become lunch for that mindless collection of malformed cells pretending to be human beings.

"Where that light skinned woman *what* lived in that house. Everybody already know she been letting you lay in her bed *wid* her, so where she at? Did you kill her *lack* you did your step daddy?" She smiled an almost toothless grin and I felt myself walking toward her as the heat of hurt and chill of anger and grief collided to create the perfect storm.

"What the fuck did you just ask me?" My voice was soft and barely above a whisper, but I knew she heard what I said. I could tell from the way her eyes turned into saucers in her too flabby face.

"Listen. I don't want no…" I cut her off without saying a word. I immediately adopted my Dom stance and glared and watched as the female porch sitter wilted under my obsidian stair…

"It surprises me that all of you fine, church-going folk feel that you have the right to sit high and pass judgment on those of us you think are below you. I wonder what *God* will say when you have to answer for being so mean and cruel to a woman because she was beautiful and your men folk tried repeatedly to fuck her." *Silence is what I heard and that was more gratifying than cursing that bitch out and behaving the way she expected me to.* "Have a nice afternoon."

Time spun around me like a vortex and one day became the next and I woke up in Aunties bed without Auntie. Tears stained my face and made my pillow wet as I cried throughout the night, missing my Violet. I showered, brushed my teeth and got dressed. By the time I made it downstairs, the doorbell was ringing some kind of gong sounding the ending of an era and beginning of darkness. I made it to the door in time to see a UPS truck pull away from the curb. I opened the door and looked around to see if anyone was up this morning, watching. I was relieved to see that no one was looking in my direction. I stooped down to pick of the package that had been left at the door. It was a large box, but not leaden. As I stood up, turned to walk into the house...the wind chimes on the porch made a beautiful tinkling sound that made my breath catch. Auntie had said that when wind chimes sing on a windless day, someone from the other side was saying hello. "Good morning, Violet. I miss you." I spoke as if she were standing in front of me and for some reason, I felt better. Not good, no, but definitely better.

I sat the box on the coffee table in the den and set down to open it. What I found inside made me gasp. A birthday card, two airline tickets to New York and two tickets to attend the NY

Giants' first game. I vaguely remembered telling Auntie that my favorite football team was the Giants and I would love to see them play in the MetLife Stadium someday. She remembered and gave me this gift for my seventeenth birthday, which I had forgotten about until the moment I saw the birthday card.

I opened the card and my eyes were immediately drawn to the beautifully pressed flower tucked neatly into the crease by the tantalizing aroma that lingered in the card. I gently removed the violet from the card and made myself read the handwritten piece of herself that she had left for me.

John,

I am so glad that I am here to celebrate this day with you. I know you think your birth was a mistake, but I really want you to know there are no mistakes, just opportunities to make situations better. I know this may seem like too much, but I wanted to take you to New York to see your favorite team play...I can't wait to show you the city.

I hope this small gift will make your birthday better. I love you in ways that probably aren't legal, but I would gladly go to hell and back to keep feeling the way you make me feel.

Enjoy this day...I will be back with you before the night falls. I have a pressing meeting today and will be out for the better part of the day. Don't start your party without me.

That card broke my heart all over again. I sat down on the couch in front of the table and let the anguish fall silently from my eyes. I could have sworn I felt Auntie's delicate hand caress my cheek and wipe my tears away, but that could not have happened. But, I smelled her sweet, citrusy scent floating through the room. My breath caught and I called her name...hoping against all odds that she was with me...that I had not killed her...that she was not going to die of brain cancer. But I knew. She was not with me, I had killed her and she would have died of brain cancer if I had not wrecked the car.

"Every fucking thing that can go wrong for me, will! Why even create me if the only thing that my life will consist of is pain, suffering and death. Why in the hell would you give me breath and then take it away from me? I'm sure you are somewhere laughing at the complete and utter clusterfuck of a life you gave me to live...well ha-ha, hilarious. NOT!!!!!"

I yelled at the four walls, hoping that whoever lived up there in the clouds could hear me and knew how really pissed I was for the shitty lot I had received.

"Why couldn't I have been born to normal parents who fucking cared about the child they created? Why did my mom marry that white-trash, Earl and then bow down to him like he was a goddamned messiah? Why did everything in my life have to turn to shit?" I screamed and ranted until my voice was gone and then I continued to squall until I could no longer hear any sound from my raw and ravished throat.

No one to answer my questions and I had no one to fight with. Just me, all alone in my 38-year-old dead lover's house.

This birthday was as jacked up as every birthday I ever had. Seventeen years-old. My net worth had gone from $0.00 to over 7 million dollars including the properties I now owned in Aspen, New York, and Martha's Vineyard. All my good fortune came as the results of three deaths. Two of which I couldn't care less about and one that left a big, gaping hole in my soul. I got up and started packing my things. It was time to go...time to find my happy...whatever the fuck that meant. My happy died in a car accident that I caused.

My happy left me more than 2 million dollars in cash and over 4 million in property. My happy was nothing more than ashes in a box sitting on her fireplace mantel. My happy was dead and as far as I could tell, so was I.

~11~

Three months ago, I was a seventeen-year-old Dom/child who had just killed my stepdad, buried my mother and cremated my thirty-eight-year-old submissive lover. I had lost everything that made me who and what I was up until that point. I was left with nothing that meant anything to me, but something that meant everything to most people.

At seventeen, I was worth over 7 million dollars and had the entire world before me...what the hell was I going to do with myself? How in the hell was I going to move on from the dead feeling inside me without losing my fucking mind? The only option I saw was to live for the moment, because in the end...that's all any of us have. A series of moments that we string together to make memories we hope will keep pulling us along until the next memorable moment.

***

I worked hard during my senior year at Hamilton Academy to prove to the rich, white kids whose parents actually gave a rat's ass about them, I was just as good as they were. They all thought I was there on scholarship and I would be an anchor for their sorry ass basketball and football teams. I worked hard in the classroom and even harder on the golf course. I loved golf. It required control and thanks to my role as Auntie's Dom, I knew how to exert control over all things. I was a natural athlete and chose to take up a sport that the 'haves' did not expect the perceived 'have-nots' capable of playing. My hatred of white people, thanks to Earl, led me down a dark and depraved sexual path during that senior year.

I had no desire to start a relationship, I just wanted to fuck anything that reminded me of all that Earl had taken from me. I remembered the way that cute, little white realtor looked at me and how I thought about fucking her...thanks to the 'Black Mandingo' myth, I had my pick of white chicks to fuck at Hamilton.

"Jonny…" I looked up from my copy of *Brave New World and* glared at the petite girl with dark brown hair and green-blue eyes. There was nothing remarkable about her features, but something about the way she looked at me caught my attention.

"Don't call me *Jonny" I* admonished in my most impassive voice. I went back to reading my novel and taking notes in my black and white marbled composition book. It was a warm spring day and I had decided to have my lunch outside under one of the trees on the front lawn.

"Um. I'm sorry. I just thought that maybe you went by that name. What should I call you?" She stepped closer to me...almost standing right over my head. I looked up and saw her shaved, pink pussy. *What. The. Actual. Fuck? This little girl didn't have on any underwear and stranger than that, I think she wanted me to see that she was naked under her dress. What the hell was going on?*

"You are blocking my sun; can you move your naked cunt out of my face and leave me the hell alone?" I did not want to see her or be that close to her. I knew when rich, white girls got caught with black boys, the first word to fall from their lips after the cum dribbles out, is rape. I was not trying to get caught up in that bullshit. I had plans and those plans did not include going to jail for fucking some white girl. *I didn't go to jail for murdering my stepdad in cold blood...there was no way in hell I would go for a piece of lackluster ass.*

"Why are you being such a douche bag? I'm just trying to get to know you, that's all." Her voice dripped with hurt feelings that were dipped in embarrassment. Her red cheeks and flustered look made me laugh. She did not back away from me as I asked; instead she opened her legs wider giving me full view to her barely-there sex. That was the thing about being with white girls, the pussy lips, just like the lips on their faces, were so thin…it was like sticking my dick into a wet hole and nothing else. "What do you want me to call you, then?" *Shit, she was not going to give this up. Well, if she wants to play...I guess I'll have to play.*

"You can call me Sir." I unfold my 6'5" frame and stood over her. I eased into my Dom persona and watched as she physically reacted to it. Her pupils dilated, her lips parted and her face flushed a really pretty shade of pink. I hadn't noticed the spray of freckles that danced across her nose. She wasn't all that plain after all. I needed to see how far I could take this...how far I could take her. "You call me Sir, and I will call you Viridian. What do you want from me, Viridian?" I dropped my voice to an even deeper baritone and purred her given name...her knees gave out. Reaching out my hand to catch her before she fell to the ground, I held her steady until I was sure she could stand on her own.

"Are you alright? Do you need to sit down?"

"No. Sir." Her voice was soft and feathery...I knew right then that I could take her wherever I wanted her to go. The question rattling around in my head was did I want to take her anywhere. I had been with plenty girls since coming to Columbia, but there was something about her. The innocence that she portrayed made me want to protect her, but I knew already there was nothing innocent about Viridian. I would take her and when I was done...I was done.

"Viridian. You never answered my question. What do you want from me? I won't ask you again." I stared down into her eyes and did not blink. My face impassive and controlled, I could almost smell her arousal mixing with the jasmine that was blooming all over campus.

"I just wanted to wel…"

"No lies, Viridian. Only the truth. So, tell me, do you want me to *fuck* you? Is that why you're out here showing me your pretty, peach pussy?"

"Um. I—I. Does that make me a slut?"

I smiled at her. Not my all-American boy smile, but the one that conveyed to the receiver of this gift, that I could deliver hard, deep, mind-blowing sex. She squeezed her thighs together and I watched a thin line of slickness meander down her leg, landing on her designer Jack sandals. I leaned down and put my lips right next to her left ear and asked if she wanted to skip the rest of the day and go to my apartment. I watched her small breast swell in her tight tee shirt and listened as she whispered, yes.

"Viridian." I purred her name again, letting my tongue caress each syllable. I licked my bottom lip and pulled it between my teeth. She was watching my mouth. I could tell that she was hoping that I would put my mouth on her...*No way in hell was I putting my mouth anywhere near this slut's pussy, but I would be fucking her today. Condoms on deck.* "Yes, you letting me fuck you today does make you a slut, but I don't mind if you don't mind. So. Are you coming or going?"

"Coming...I hope. Coming a lot, I hope."

I told her to follow me in her Volkswagen Cabriolet. We drove the 7.7 miles it took to get to my apartment in Pavilion Towers. Parking in the underground garage gave me the anonymity that I needed and a quick out if I need that, too. I could tell from the look in her eyes that she was impressed with my car and my home...I didn't care one way or the other if she was impressed, but seeing the disbelieving look in her eyes made what I had planned for her much easier to do.

"Do you and your parents live here? My best friend's brother lives here, but he goes to "USC. There are a bunch of college students in this building...are your parents building a house somewhere or is this all that you guys can afford?" I wanted to push her head into the elevator doors, but I just looked down at her in disgust and gave her an indulgent shake of my head. "No. I live here alone. It's close to everything I need to get to and I don't want to be responsible for another home. Renting is just easier for me right now." I knew she had more questions, but she got the hint that there would be no more answers coming from me. We rode up in silence.

"Come in, Viridian. Sit down on the couch and take your shoes off."

"Excuse me?"

"Viridian. I know you understand English. Do as you are told or get the fuck out of my apartment." I didn't bother to turn around and speak to her or to make sure she had done as I asked her...I knew she had.

"Sir?"

"Yes, Viridian." My voice was deadly soft and full of leashed power. I wanted her to fear me...afraid of what I might do to her. She swallowed, hard before she spoke.

"May I have some water, please? Sir?" Hearing her silky voice ask me for what she wanted made me think of Auntie and how perfect my name used to sound on her full lips. The thought of the almost nonexistent lips of the white girl touching me made my stomach flip, but I had already made up my mind...I would fuck this little girl and send home with a few bruises.

I walked from the kitchen with a tall glass of ice water

and three pieces of papers. One was an NDA, non-disclosure agreement, to ensure that any information I shared with this girl would not be shared with anyone outside of my apartment. The second was a permission form. This form ensured that I had permission and consent to engage in sexual activity with the signer of the document. The third and final was a sexual background survey. More than three partners and there was not deal.

"Please read over and complete these forms while you enjoy your glass of water. Do not ask me any questions about them...if you want me to fuck you today, you will need to sign them and be honest on the survey."

I'll be right back." I walked from the den and went into the second bedroom where I quickly showered and moisturized my skin using the new Kiehl's Facial Fuel moisturizer and changed into a pair of grey lounge pants and nothing else. I walked carelessly into the den and sat down in the chair adjacent to the couch where she was sitting with her shoes off. I knew the effect I had on her, and I loved the power rush I was getting from her reaction.

"Have you read and signed all of the papers?

"Yes, sir."

"Good. Any questions before I take you into my room?"

"Yes, sir."

"Well?" I lifted my right brow as I looked over her signed NDA.

"This seems a bit much just to have sex with you."

"That's not a question." I deadpan. "I was emancipated by the court systems and because of the court's decision; I am considered an adult. I am worth quite a bit of money and my lawyers want to make sure that I and my *assets* are protected."

"Do I get to ask you any of the questions you asked me on that how-many-people-have-you-fucked survey?"

"Watch your mouth, Viridian. How do you expect me to let you suck my dick pleasure me with such a dirty mouth?" Her mouth fell open and then she closed it just as quickly. I raised my left brow at her and smirked in her direction. I saw the frost melt away and knew it was time.

"There is a bedroom down the hall, the first door on the right. There is an attached bathroom, take a shower and dry and moisturize your skin with the items left in the basket on the sink. When you are done, stand at the door with your head and eyes lowered and your hands interlaced behind you, resting at the small of your back. I will be in shortly to fuck you." I watched as she stood and shuffled into the bedroom, she didn't scream...so she must be okay with all the toys that I have laying around my playroom. *I did more research into the lifestyle that Auntie had introduced me to after her death. I found myself immersed in a world that helped to make my world make sense. With my teacher and sub gone, I had to continue to learn how to become the Dom Auntie wanted me to be.*

~12~

I strolled into the room and did not spare one look in her direction. She did not attempt to look up, nor did she make a move to speak to me. *Such a willing submissive. I wonder if this is something that she has done in the past...Why? With whom? When? Not my concern, but I'm still curious.* "You look lovely, Viridian. Lift your eyes...only your eyes and look at me." Her eyes swept up to find me standing in front of her naked body. I watched as her breathing increased and the rise of her small breasts matched the rhythm of her breath.

"Do you have any questions about what will happen in this room and what you can talk about afterwards?" My voice was less menacing and more cajoling. I needed her to trust me and I didn't have a long time to build that trust. Her fear fed a need in me that I had not known was there until Auntie, but more than her fear, I needed her trust.

"Um…" Her voice was soft and shaky, but I heard the undercurrent of arousal in her utterance, too. "Will you hurt me? I—I don't have a *lot* of experience with sex, but there is just something about you that makes me want it." Her eyes lowered and that pretty pink blush that seemed to match the softness of her sex, stained her cheeks. At that moment, something in me opened up and I knew that I would have this girl for longer than just now. The Dom in me needed to protect her; needed to make sure she had what she needed and would be able to stand on her own when I was done with her. And, I would be done with her.

"Viridian? Do you believe I will hurt you and if you do, then why are you willingly standing in my room naked and wanting?" I asked her as I placed the index and middle finger of my right hand under her chin and lifted her round face so that our eyes met. The freckles across her nose were cute and made her look younger than her eighteen years.

"I don't think you will hurt me, physically...but, I don't know. I am afraid of you, but not enough to walk away from whatever you will do to me today."

"Well, aren't you a brave little one. I have no desire to hurt you...well not beyond what I believe will bring both you and me pleasure."

"I know you think that I am a slut because of the way I came to you on campus, but I'm not. I have never *chosen* a boy to have sex with and you are the first one that I am willingly choosing."

What the hell does that mean? I don't want to deal with a damaged girl, looking to me to heal her. Fuck, I can't heal her...I will only further destroy her. Shit...she's got to go.

"What do you mean, you have never chosen a boy to have sex with?

"I was the butt of a practical joke at a party I went to my freshman year at Hamilton. I don't go to parties anymore and I don't have friends anymore." Her head lowered, and I saw one tear slide down her pink cheek.

"What joke...what party? What the fuck happened to you, Viridian?"

"I got invited to my first party the fourth week of my freshman year. I was excited because I had never been invited anywhere by the kids I went to school with. When I got there, all the kids were drinking, dancing and hooking up. I got a soda and found a corner so that I could observe them...try and remember how they behaved so that I would know how to act at the next party I went to." She took a breath and kept her head lowered and her hands interlaced at the base of her belly; although now they were clenching and unclenching as she spoke. I was pleased that she had followed my directions.

"Go on." I spoke softly, encouraging her to continue telling me what happened to her. For some reason, I was becoming more and more angry. I had to work to control the tick in my jaw.

"I was a virgin when I entered the party and I wasn't when I woke up the next morning." Her voice broke as a languorous exhalation escaped her trembling lips. More emerald crystals fell from her deep, green eyes and then, nothing.

"What do you mean?" I needed her to tell me what had happened...to confirm my suspicion and give me a reason to kick some white boy's ass.

"Richard Carmichael asked me to dance. He was in the same grade as me, but his older brother was a senior and pretty much had his pick of any girl he wanted. We danced and his brother brought me another soda. I drank it, because I was hot. I felt funny...you know, like everything became fuzzy and I couldn't remember where I was or what I was supposed to be doing.

"They drugged you." Not a question, but a confirmation of what had happened to her.

"I guess so. I woke up in my bed with rope burns on my wrist and ankles and dried blood on and around my—my…" She could barely get the words out, but I needed her to tell me...to continue to fuel the slow rage that was wrapping itself around my mind.

"Blood where? Where was the dried blood, Viridian?"

"Blood on my private area and my anus...I had been raped and sodomized by at least five different people. My parents took me to the emergency room and had me...you know, checked out. The cops were called and a case was opened. The only names I could remember were Richard and Drake

Carmichael...that is where the arrest started, but they ended with six other boys. All from important families. I was labeled a slut, cock teasing bitch. According to the boys, I knew what I was doing. Even some of the faculty and staff members were whispering behind my back. I stopped hearing all the chatter after a while, even though none of it had died down; it still hasn't. I just choose not to hear it anymore."

"What happened to the boys?"

"Their parents got them off and had their records expunged. My parents wanted me to leave school and go to boarding school where I wouldn't have to see them every day, wouldn't have to endure the alienation that came with my new status as campus slut and tease. I told her no. If I left, then they win...I would not be ashamed of what happened to me." In that moment, I was so proud of the young woman standing before me. She continued as I really looked at her. "So, I stayed and now I'm graduating with 138 people that hate me and I'm okay with it, I guess."

"I want their names, even if they have already graduated and gone on to whatever shit life they have started." Images of my mom filled my head and the all-consuming guilt and pain that came with those images exploded as undiluted rage inside my broken soul. I did not protect her from Earl. I didn't know how to protect her and by the time I realized that I could protect her, it was too late. That trashy motherfucker had already killed her. I would never let another woman go through that shit if I could help it. Fuck Earl and every pompous piece of trash that thought they had a right to treat women however they wanted to.

I moved closer to her, my naked torso so close to her bare breast, I could see the tremor run through her body. "No lies, Viridian. Have you been honest with me about this? If so...I will make sure that those cock-suckers pay. I hope you know that none of that shit will matter to the right man who was made just for you. I am not that man, but I will make sure when that right man comes along, you will know what the fuck to do with him and how to protect and command respect yourself. Do you trust me?"

"Yes. I will never lie to you. It happened, but why do you care? You don't even know me?" Her voice was fine sand falling through an hourglass of her eternal pain.

"I don't know you, but *I know you.* You are a woman who has been victimized and is trying to find a way to become a survivor while still living with the guilt, shame and stains that come from someone taking from you what they can't give back. I don't know you...but *I know you.*"

One tear, two tears and then a slow and decorous trickle that broke my heart but shored up my resolve to make these fuckers pay for their sins. "Do you want me to fuck you? You can say no and I will walk you back to your car. No harm, no foul. I will still need the names of those boys who violated you...even if you do not want to fuck." I pulled her hands apart and lifted her face to meet my gaze. She was still crying silent tears, but there was also a look of longing in her eyes. She was still nothing spectacular to look at, but she was so broken and she needed me. *At this point in my life, I needed to be needed.* She needed to have me enter her...make her come. I shelved all other plans I had made for her today...she was not the slut I thought she was, and I would not treat her as such. I would still fuck her and fuck her good, but I wouldn't debase her...I couldn't.

"Yes. Sir. I would still like for you to fuck me. I won't talk about anything that happens between us." Her voice was stronger, but still vulnerable. I like that, it made my dick stir; just a little bit. "Good. I really want to fuck you today. Walk over to the bed and stand on the left side. Legs spread shoulder width apart and hands behind your back. Think about how good

I'm going to make you feel." I wasn't hard, yet because I wasn't really attracted to her, but I knew how to control my body and would get there when I needed to.

She walked over to the bed and stood as I told her to. She really was quite good at taking directions. I smiled as I sauntered up behind her and leaned into her petite frame. "Do you trust me to take care of you, Viridian?" She nodded her head once and remained still. I slid the 4" black, velvet ribbon under her wrist and wrapped it around until it looked like I was tying some sexy Christmas bow. Then I wrapped the loose ends of the ribbon around the middle, making separate loops around each of her wrist. I continued wrapping the ribbon around the middle until I was satisfied that she could not move her hands and was at my mercy. I checked to make sure that I could slide two fingers under the binding...I could and I was satisfied.

"How does that feel?"

"It feels...soft, sir."

"Is it too tight? Does it hurt?"

"No, Sir. It's not too tight and it does not hurt."

"Why are you breathing so hard? Are you afraid or excited?"

"I am both, Sir. Exited. Afraid."

"Good. I want you to feel both. Let your fear feed your excitement. Viridian, you must trust me and know I want you to experience pleasure, but only as I see fit to give it to you. You must give up your control and trust me. Choose a word that makes you feel safe."

"A word, Sir?"

"Yes. A word. I will not ask you again, choose. Now."

"Blanket."

"Good girl. If I am doing something to you sexually and you no longer feel safe, your fear overtakes your excitement, say the word you have chosen and I will stop whatever I am doing to you." I put my hands on her shoulders and gave her a light squeeze to get an answer from her."

"Yes, Sir. I will use the word, Blanket."

"If you tell me to stop, quit, don't do that...I will not stop. I will *only* stop if you use your safe word, Blanket. Do you understand how important it is that you use your word? Don't try to be something you think I need you to be, be honest with yourself and me...no lies, Viridian. Do you understand?" She nodded her head, keeping her eyes down.

"You may not speak to me again unless I give you permission. If you do anything that may displease me at all...I will spank your creamy white ass and watch it turn that pretty, blushing pink you wear on your face. Now, open your legs wider."

~13~

I looked at her body as I stood behind her. She wasn't tall, has absolutely no curves at all, and seems to be lacking any of the features that make a woman look like a woman. No hips, no ass, emaciated thighs that led down to chicken legs. There was no ass to smack, no breast to suck or pinch. *How the hell am I supposed to fuck this girl when she is the last thing I would consider attractive. Come on, Jughead...get hard!*

"Viridian. Bend forward at the waist and allow your chest and right cheek to lay flat on the bed." I almost laughed as I watched her bend forward and saw the flat shapeless butt cheeks fall open as she pushed her torso into the mattress. My breath caught in my mouth and I had to fight the overwhelming need to run from the room. I had never seen anything like the mangled rosebud that seemed to pucker; asking for a kiss...*What the fuck happened to her?* "Good girl. You look beautiful like this." I lied to myself more than to her...I needed to make myself believe that she was beautiful. It was hard, but I wasn't.

"Thank you, Sir."

"Did you just address me, Viridian? Because I distinctly remember telling you that you were not to speak to me unless I gave you permission." I paused trying to gage her reaction to the soft threat in my voice. "Do you remember what I told you I would do if you displeased me? I kept my voice cool and detached. I wanted her fear to overtake her excitement. I had to break her before I could fuck her properly. I watched her slight shoulders rise and fall with a breathy exhale. Her back arched instinctively...maybe fucking her won't be so bad after all.

"You said that you would spank me and make my cheeks turn pink."

"Stay in your current position. I am going to spank you

for ten licks and then you will not displease me again. Viridian, why am I doing this to you?"

"May I speak, Sir?"

"Yes."

"I am being spanked because I displeased you by talking to you without getting your permission."

"Do you think that you do deserve this spanking?"

"Yes, Sir. I do.

"You will count your licks...in Spanish. Do not scream in my presence. You will whisper each number and say, thank you, Sir for spanking me after each lick. Do you understand how this will work?"

"Yes, Sir."

Thwack! My right hand landed hard on what should have been a plump right butt cheek. I listened for her small voice.

"Uno. Thank you for spanking me, Sir."

Another hit to the left cheek.

"Dos. Thank you for spanking me, Sir."

The last smack landed at the juncture where her thighs and ass and pussy met.

"Diez. Thank you for spanking me, Sir." Her voice was a cracked plate. I knew in that moment that I had her. She was completely mine. I could do whatever I wanted to do to her and she would accept it, because I owned her. I had all sorts of evocative ideas going through my head about how I could get back at Earl, the realtor, and every other white fucker who ever made me feel like shit.

Then I remembered what Earl had done to my mother. I

remembered Auntie telling me that when a person chooses to give control over to another person, that person has an obligation to protect the giver. To respect and take care of the giver. Using the gift of the power exchange over someone to fulfill some sick need, is the same as taking control and power without permission...that's called rape. I heard her so clearly in my mind, I looked around the room searching for her beautiful face. I didn't see her, but I felt her. She was with me...guiding me into my new adventure. *God. I miss you, Violet. Please help me do right by Viridian. She is so broken…broken like me. Help me help her like you helped me.*

"Viridian. How was that?" My voice was deep and low, but not imposing. I did not want to take from her, I wanted her to feel empowered by her ability to relinquish control and still somehow find self-control through her submission to me.

"You may speak to me."

"I have never experienced anything like that in my life. I... I don't know how I feel about you hitting me...with what those boys did…" Her voice broke away and I heard a small sniffle. *Shit. Was I too hard on her...did I push her beyond her limit? I don't know how to fix this.*

"Your ass is such a beautiful color. My dick is so hard right now. I want to bury myself inside of you...so deep inside you. God, I *want* you now, Viridian." I wasn't lying. Something about having her submit to me, something about the way her soft voice turned into a pained whimper made me want to fuck her and show her what her body could do. I could give her back her sexuality...her body. Of that I had no doubt.

"That turned you on, Sir. Hitting me and hearing me count?"

"Yes. I can't tell you how much it means to me that you trust me to put my hands on you and not take you further than you were able to go. Knowing I can have you this way...knowing you relinquished control over to me...you chose to give yourself to me...I didn't take anything from you except the burden of making choices."

I stood behind her and dropped my pants. Stepping out of them, I took my penis in my right hand and began to stroke my length. I pressed the tip against her soaking sex. I wanted her to feel how much she turned me on. I needed her to feel sexy and powerful, even in her submission to me and my will.

"Is that your...um...is your…"

"Say it, Viridian" Ask me what you want to know."

"Is that your...uh...your *thing* touching me?" The way she said the word *thing* told me she had never used it in a sexual context. *How cute is that?*

"Do you like the way it feels against your cunt?"

"Yes, Sir."

"Do you want me to fuck my dick into your wet pussy? I promise if you don't like the way it feels, I'll stop. Just use your safe word and I will pull out. Okay?"

"You won't keep *doing it to* me if I say my word. You would stop and not hurt me?"

"Yes. One word and I stop. I want to give you pleasure...the pleasure those assholes stole from you during your freshman year. I'm not like them. Trust me?"

"Yes."

I reached into the drawer in the bedside table and retrieved a condom. As I slid it on, I let my erection touch her cheeks. She jumped a little. *And white people call us savages. Whatever those bastards did to her, fucked her up for real.*

I pushed her legs farther apart and began to feed my dick, which was too big for her, into her tight channel. She was so small and shallow. I didn't know how much of me she could take, but I wanted to give her all I could. All she could take.

"Oh my God. You're too big for me." Words fell from her lips and stroked my ego, making me want her all the more.

"Do you want me to stop? If you do, you know what you have to say."

"No. Please don't stop. Please, Sir. Just...take it sl…"

I stroked into her, balls deep. I could not let her think that she had any say in this matter. She was mine to do with as I please. She had her safe word and she had not used it. I felt a barrier; something was keeping me from reaching the last bit of her. I adjusted my stance, bent my knees a little and spread her legs farther apart so that I could get all of me inside.

"Holy. Fucking. Hell!" Each of the words were followed by the most animalistic grunts I'd ever heard. Her pussy wrapped around me like a vice grip and oh my...she was deliciously wet, deliciously tight.

"More." I didn't ask her, I told her that I was going to give her more. I waited for her to safe word, she didn't. I pulled out, slowly so that only the tip remained inside of her then, without warning...I slammed back into her. I looked down and saw that she was red and swollen. *She could not take me. I would not hurt her...I would not take her further than she could go.*

I fucked her with shallow thrust that didn't require much of my cock. All the while praising her for how good she felt, how good she was making me feel. I rubbed her ass, knowing that it was burning and would give her a different sensation as I pushed into her.

"Would you like to come, Viridian?"

"I don't know. Will it hurt?"

I reached around her and found her tiny clit. *Everything about this girl was small.* I placed the pad of my thumb on her nub and began to circle the small center of her. Her hips start moving, until that moment, she was as still as a statue.

"Yes, like that. Keep moving your ass like that. Shit. You feel so good. Your tight, little pussy is squeezing my dick so good." I kept praising her, wanting her to feel the power of pleasing a man with her body. Her response to my heated words was far more emotional than physical.

I pushed down on her clit and shoved my dick a little further inside her and it happened. Her body tensed, her breathing stopped, her pussy grew hotter and wetter, everything in her was pushed to the center of her core and began to radiate outwards. Her multicolored scream painted the walls and everything in my room a beautiful shade of blue-green. I refused to come. I wanted this for her. She had no idea what her body could do. I wanted to take her further, but I chose not to.

"How was that, Viridian?" I was rubbing her ass with aloe-vera gel after giving her a bath. She cried in the bathtub and I let her.

"Thank you, Sir. For…" Her voice trailed off and I knew what she was thanking me for, but I needed her to be able to say it.

"What are you thanking me for? The fucking or the bath." I let my amusement color my words. I chose to keep her blind-fold on for the remainder of our time together. She still could not see me.

"No, Sir. Not for the sex or the bath. Thank you for giving me...just thank you."

That was enough for me. I helped her get dressed and walked her to the door. I felt like I should let her know the nature of this arrangement.

"Viridian. You do understand we are not dating. We will not be hanging out at school or going out on dates on the weekend. If you want to play again, let me know...otherwise, don't expect anything else from me. I'm not prepared to give you anything more than this. Do you understand?"

"Yes. I understand."

"Good. I hope you want to play again. You are wonderful. I am grateful that you gave yourself to me today. Thank you. You are much stronger than you give yourself credit for. Will you play again?"

"Yes. Wait, you enjoyed me. You want to play again...with *me*?"

"Yes. I really would love to play again. You should know when I choose a play partner, it will only be myself and that play partner...until the game is over. Do you still want to play, Viridian?"

"Yes."

***

Viridian and I had standing play-dates for the rest of my senior year. It was fun giving her the gift of empowerment. When we parted after graduation, she owned her body, her sexuality and most importantly...she owned herself.

Welcome the University of South Carolina; Class of 1997.

FALLING

"Falling in love is very real, but I used to shake my head when people talked about soul mates, poor deluded individuals grasping at some supernatural ideal not intended for mortals but sounded pretty in a poetry book. Then, we met, and everything changed, the cynic has become the converted, the sceptic, an ardent zealot."
— E.A. Bucchianeri, Brushstrokes of a Gadfly

~14~

My time spent at Hamilton Academy taught me so much about myself as a student, a man and a Dom. I graduated with honors and was accepted into The University of South Carolina's Honors College with a full scholarship. I accepted the scholarship, even though I didn't need it. I thought that it was better to let everyone assume that I was some charity case who was completely on his own rather than allowing the gold-diggers to try and sink their teeth into me and my money.

It was hard to get Viridian to let go of our arrangement, but eventually she got the message. Our last time together we role played and I let her top me. She worked me over with a small, leather cat-o-nine tails. The ends were wrapped around small glass beads designed to bring the blood to the surface of the skin, but not to cause any pain. She looked excited and confident as she rained down biting licks over my chest and abdomen. Her eyes were lit with a strange fire I recognized as power...it was the same fire that lit my eyes when Auntie turned the reigns of our relationship over to me. She said it was the obligation of those of us who understood how to wield and shape our power over others to in turn teach them to do the same. That was Violet's gift to me and my gift to Viridian. In all the time we spent together, she never called me anything but, Sir and I never called her anything but, Viridian.

Shit. I didn't even know her real name. I guess that's good. A last name meant she belonged to someone...meant she had a father who loved her. With only a first name, she was nothing permanent. Just a passing of the moon. I wasn't looking for love. All my love was cremated over a year ago. I didn't have anything else to give.

It's amazing what thoughts cross my mind when it's idle. I realized that I had made my bed, put all my clothes away and had my small desk sorted out on my side of the dorm room that I was to share with some dude whose name I didn't even look at. At the end of my meandering thoughts, the door burst open and a large blurb of something fell onto the floor.

"Hey, man."

"Uh...Hey."

"My name is Richard. My friends call me Dick or Dickey for short. What about you? What's your name?"

"John."

"Well, John. Looks like we're gonna be roommates. I hope you ain't one of them neat, pansy boys. I'm all boy and that means pussy, sweat, and beer." He snorted and finally looked at the other side of the room. His eyes fell on my bed, my desk and my opened wardrobe.

"What did you say your name was...Dick, was it? Listen. I am one hundred percent sure that this living arrangement is not going to work out...why don't you go find some other "all-American-boy" roommate to whoop it up with." I never stood or took my eyes off his glassy, mud-brown gaze

"What the hell...you think you can just kick me out of my room. I see. You one of them rich Black boys who thinks he has papers on everyone?" His face was already red from whatever he had been drinking, but it somehow went into some horrible shade of lava that only succeeded in making him look even more like a clown than expressing the impotent rage I'm sure he was feeling at the moment. I was so entranced with his skin's ability to change colors, I didn't really hear what he asked me.

"What? You got hearing problems on top of being an

arrogant asshole, dude?"

"Listen, Dick. It's pretty obvious that you are drunk. Let's just go to the dorm manager and see what we can do about this." I took a condescending tone with him because I thought that maybe the only reason he had gotten into the honor's college is because of his last name and the number of zeros his dad was able to attach to his yearly contribution to the USC Alumni fund.

Dick was more than a little angry with the high-handed way I dealt with him, but something about the way I spoke to him must have appealed to his lower self because he went straight to the dorm manager and requested a room change. He was immediately obliged and that left me with a private room.

My freshman year started much as I thought it would. Getting to know my way around the campus, figuring out the best routes to class and which food was edible. For the first time in a long time, I felt normal. I felt like I was just another student making his way through college. Finding someone to spend my nights with wouldn't be a problem, but I didn't want to get involved with anyone. I decided after my time with Viridian, I would use my college experience to focus on me. On becoming the greatest John R. Ellis I could be.

I was doing a good job of fitting in and staying out of every college girl's bed. I have to admit I was not celibate, by any stretch of the imagination, but I managed to control the Dom in me enough to have mostly vanilla sexual experiences. They didn't satisfy my baser needs, but those meaningless fucks did help to take the edge off the animal that lived just under my skin.

I *was* doing a good job of staying true to my decision to not take another submissive, until one early afternoon in October. I had a one o'clock class across campus and I was coming from Cooper library; I took a shortcut through the Horseshoe and in my rush, I ran into the most beautiful woman I had ever seen. The world slowed down, my heart stopped beating in my chest and I heard the wings of the butterfly flapping. In a word, I fell dangerously in love with a flurry of molasses skin, strawberry brown hair and liquid caramel eyes. She was beauty.

"Uh...um. Excuse me. I'm so sorry."

"Really. I should be the one to apologize. I knocked your books and you to the ground."

"I was not watching where I was going, are you alright? Did I hurt you?"

"Stop." My Dom persona slid into place before I knew where it had come from. I watched the beautiful girl reacted in a way I had never seen someone react to me. Her beautiful lips parted and she stuck a small, pink tongue out to wet her full bottom lip. I watched her caramel eyes darken to a beautiful toffee color. Still sweet, but somehow darker and richer. More seductive, while somehow appearing more vulnerable. She absent-mindedly pushed her reddish-brown curls behind her left ear and took in ragged breaths. I watched her breast rise and fall with each intake of air. She was so damn beautiful; my dick was hard within seconds of contact. I violently wanted to dominate her, to show her that she belonged to me and that I could do anything to her I wanted, whenever I wanted. I wanted to be inside her...hard and fast. Just the thought of her beautiful auburn curls tickling my balls as I pushed deeper inside her. *Fuck. What the hell was happening to me? I have never felt this strongly before...not even for Auntie. I have to get away from her before I do something stupid; like attack her and take her right here in the middle of the fucking university.*

"I'm sorry. I didn't mean to yell at you, I just wanted to let you know that you're not to blame for this incident and should not feel responsible for what just happened." I stayed in my Dom role and gave her back the three books she had dropped and continued to hold her golden-whisky gaze a while longer than necessary.

"Thank you. I guess it's just always been easier to take the blame and walk away. It's just—you know... easier that way. Thanks for giving me back my books, but I think you can let my hand go now." Her words were a clear bell ringing in my heart. Her voice was innocence dipped in the promise of hot, dirty sex. I wanted her.

"I find that accepting blame when it does not belong to me only makes it easier for the person to whom the blame actually belongs...not the person who is usually the victim."

"I am nobody's victim. I am strong and very much aware of what is easier for me." Her eyes were accusations and flashed a fierceness and a vulnerability that was only overshadowed by the liquid daggers she was aiming at my heart. Both pain and defiance were at war in her eyes. It hurt me, physically to watch the duality within her. *What the hell is wrong with this girl...what happened to her?*

"I didn't mean to insinuate that you are victim of any kind, I believe you are strong and aware, but I just don't believe in taking the blame when I didn't do anything to deserve it. If this is how you choose to live, then more power to you...but believe me, living this way doesn't make you strong."

"Thank you doctor-know-it-all. I will take my blame and my books and myself and get to where I am going. Have a good day." She hardened her eyes and stood to her full height...*Jesus, she is tall and even more beautiful when she was pissed.*

"Thank you, little-miss-save-my-ass. You have a good day, as well." I tried to make my voice as cold as I could, but it was something about her that made me smile. She looked so damn adorable standing in the fall afternoon looking at me like she wanted to kick my ass while at the same time, having such a look of contrition on her lovely face. I had to get away from her. *Shit. Back to my dorm room. If I don't get rid of this hard-on, I will definitely not be able to make it to class. What the fuck did I do with that warming lotion?*

~15~

It's been two weeks since I ran into the beautiful girl in the Horseshoe on campus. Every time I think about her, my body has the same violent reaction...hard dick, painful balls and shortness of breath. I've been walking through the Horseshoe every day, hoping I would bump into her again, but maybe she was just a figment of my imagination because I never saw her there.

It was fall in Columbia, which meant absolutely nothing to the weather lords; I had on a pair of cargo shorts and a button-up polo shirt with my favorite flip-flops, the ones with the rainbow tag. With weather this great, I thought I would take a different route to my one o'clock class. I left my dorm room about ten minutes earlier than usual and took the scenic route through Pendleton and planned to make my way to Wardlaw. I guess I was just tired of looking for her and not seeing her...hell, not being able to catch a glimpse of her and it was starting to get to me. I felt like I was losing my fucking mind and I was tired of feeling like that. When reckless thoughts passed through my mind more often than not, was the time shit got crazy. It was time to move on. The best way to do that was accept she would not be mine and find a willing piece of ass to spend time with.

And just as I turned onto Pendleton, there she was. Walking with some tall, lanky ass white boy. He was looking into her eyes while his right arm rested on her shoulders. She looked slightly up at him, he was only a little taller than she was, and then she smiled at him. *What the fuck was she smiling at him for?* A felt the white-hot burn of jealousy and something akin to terror scorch a heated path through me and just like that, I decided I needed to save her from the biggest mistake of her life. *Not another Black woman submitting to some white son-of-bitch. Not on my goddamn watch.* Before I could stop myself, I was strolling over to the smiling, now laughing couple. I didn't know what I would say, hell, I didn't even know her name, but I had to do something to get her away from that fucking *white* boy. *This will not go down like shit did with my mom and that fucker, Earl. Not today, motherfucker!*

I let my books fall to the ground as I casually bumped into her. She wasn't looking where she was going and that gave me an in. A chance to talk to her again, maybe even get her name. "Oh my God, I'm sorry! I didn't see you there." Her humility humbled me, and I almost felt bad for the rouse...*almost*. While I still had a smug look on my face, she looked up and recognition danced across her beautiful features and settled in a hard, flat line on her kissable mouth. "You! I take my apology back. You don't deserve it...not one syllable of it." By this time, her features had morphed into something between a scowling smile and a pout. It was the sexiest, cutest thing I had seen in a long time...really in forever. So much raw power blanketed by a child-like innocence. I knew at that moment I would have her; in my bed, my life...shit, she may have already found her way into my heart. *What the ever-loving fuck*?

"Oh. Hi little-miss-save-my-ass. How's it been going?" I asked too nicely and too formally. I liked watching her emotions play out on her face. It was like looking at a long lost silent movie.

"Don't call me that, you ass." Her eyes immediately lowered and there it was again, contrition. *Interesting*.

"Um. Excuse me, how do *you* know Vivian?"

"I don't know her, Opie, but I would like to."

"Opie! Who the hell you calling Opie? Oh, I see." He laughs like I just told him the funniest fucking joke he's ever heard as he continues to yak away. "You got me mixed up with some scared, punk-ass—I'm not that white boy, word is bond." He kept his arm planted around Vivian's shoulder and turned his body protectively towards her so I could see his slightly red face. "Am I supposed to be impressed because you play basketball for USC? I'm not."

"I have no fucks to give about if you're impressed by basketball players, because I don't play basketball—number one. And number two, I don't want you to be impressed by me because of physical attributes, but if you want to ride my nutsack because I'm a double major in USC Honor's college on full academic scholarship maintaining a 4.8 GPA, feel free to do so. It's also the reason you need to fear me, Opie. I won't fuck up your face, but your future... that's up for grabs. *Word is bond.*" I had slid smoothly into my Dom persona and I knew the chill in the air was not the cause of Opie's shivering shoulders. I smiled to myself, happy in the knowledge that I owned this little prick and there was nothing he could do or say to regain control of himself.

"Vivie, I need to get going." His voice was bitch soft as he tucked his tale and turned away from what he had no right to lay claim to. "I'll see you later, maybe. Okay?" He peeled his arm away from her shoulder and walked around her body to get to the other side of the sidewalk. I just stood there, staring into the most expressive eyes I had ever seen. I got lost in them...I wanted to swim in them...make love while they watched me.

"Why did you do that? You really are an *ass*. I've been trying to get Kyle to talk to me for weeks now, and in one moment, you go and scared him away. What are you? Some kind of *sadist*?" She was almost yelling, and I saw the edges of crazy closing in on her, so I did what I thought was best in this situation; I grabbed both of her shoulders and gave a gentle shake that forced her to look at me. I pinned her with my most menacing Dom gaze and unleashed my tightly reigned in power.

Not enough to scare her, but enough to let her know I would not be challenged, especially not by her. The effect was immediate. Her shoulders relaxed, her pouty mouth opened slightly, her honey gaze went soft and relaxed with acceptance and then her breathing changed. I knew in that moment I could take her anywhere, do anything to her and she would be willing.

"Are you calmed down enough for me to let you go?"

"If you had not been following me around campus, I would have no reason to be so irate, God."

"Well in my effort to try and avoid running into you again, I thought I would take a different path to my class. I was not expecting to run into you."

"Why in hell would you need to avoid me? I don't even know you and you sure as hell don't know me."

"On bumping into you two weeks ago, I was...let's just say that I've had a hard time getting you out of my head."

"Well, it's not like you were all that easy to forget either...I haven't been able to stop thinking about you since colliding with you." Her face was unreadable, but her body language gave her away. Her words, her tone, her actions were at odds with each other and she was so fucking beautiful standing there trying to be defiant when all she wanted to do was give in to whatever this thing between us was.

"Then why the fuck have you been hiding from me? I've walked around that damn Horseshoe everyday trying to get a glimpse of you. Where were you?"

"I stayed away from the Horseshoe because you...you *scare* me. You scared me then, just like you're scaring me now."

"Scared you?" The thought of her being afraid of me

made my stomach hurt in a way that told me I was falling too fast, too hard and too deep. "I would never want to make you afraid of me. I just really want a chance to get to know you." I stepped closer to her and dropped my head so my mouth was just on the outside of her ear. I wanted her to hear me clearly. "I want you, Vivian." I felt the miniscule earthquake that moved through her body and it made me wonder what she would look like as she came apart on my fingers. "Listen, I want to show you…" I wasn't breathing. My heart, mind and the essence of who I was waited silently for her to fill in the space left by my unspoken words. I heard her sharp intake of breath and continued to wait.

"What will you do to me? I mean, I don't understand why you would want to…" Her voice trailed behind her thoughts, but it was too slow to catch up and the thought got away from her. She looked up at me and it felt like a kick in my balls. Her eyes leaked caramel tears and I couldn't stop myself from tasting them. I dipped my head and kissed the saline hope running down her cheek...she tasted like salt-water taffy.

"I will make you smile. I will give you the realest parts of me, parts that until just now, I didn't even know were still a part of me." This sounded like a load of bullshit even to my ears and yet, I meant every word of it.

"Vivian, there is just something about you...I can't reach high enough to touch it, but I know I want the chance to stretch and reach for it. A chance to figure you out. I can't promise you…"

She pressed her soft lips against my left cheek and applied just enough pressure to ensure her lip gloss would leave her mark on me. Effectively silencing me. She raised her regal head and looked me square in the eyes and said, "Okay. You had me at 'hard time getting you out of my head' I just wanted to see if you would work for it.

I don't know what made her do it, but hearing it caused all thoughts to slide down into my heart and transform themselves into a raw, primal emotion. I grabbed her around the waist and swung her around, the entire time we laughed and whooped it up in our excitement. "You will not regret this." I promised as we walked towards Wardlaw.

~16~

Four weeks later, Vivian and I were laying on my bed, while I read poems from a collection of Lord Byron. As I finished reading one of my favorite poems, "She Walks in Beauty", I felt her arms tighten around my waist. She was shivering as if she were cold, and then the unmistakable softness of a tear soaked through my shirt and landed over my heart. "What's with the tears? My reading couldn't have been that bad." I joked, hoping to lighten the mood. "No." She sniffed and swallowed back a whimper. "Your reading was beautiful. I love Lord Byron. That poem is one of my favorites, I'm just amazed it's one of your, too." I smiled and kissed the top of her head. *She is definitely too good for me, but I'm a selfish bastard and I'm not letting her go.*

We had spent every hour of everyday together when we were not in class or with friends. My college experience was narrowing down to just two things; Vivian Bruno and academic excellence. In the short time that I had known Viv, I learned she was an only child, her mother walked away from her, leaving her with her father—who died just prior to her starting USC. Like me, she was all alone in the world and unlike me, she was alright with her current situation. But even as she alleged that she was fine with being alone, something would pass over her face and darken her beautiful eyes to the color of whisky. I couldn't name it, but it felt like regret and shame.

"You know?" I let the question hang low in the space that strained between us. Rubbing the fingers of my right hand up and down her bared shoulder, I continued with my thought as if I had not taken a pause in my speech. She was just so soft and warm, I wanted to experience touching all of her. "You are a beguiling woman. I know we haven't known each other long, but I think whatever this is between us just might be forever." I felt her body tense up...the fear in her eyes as she looked up into mine, was the same fear I'd seen in my mother's eyes just before Earl would beat the shit out of her. It broke my heart.

"Hey, what's wrong?" Concern evident in my face and voice. She cast her eyes down...so much in contrast to the feisty woman who challenged me on pretty much everything I did or said. Deep breath after deep breath. She was trapped in some horrible memory and I couldn't reach her. Couldn't pull her from it. I continued to rub slow circles down her arm and whisper calming words in her ear. *Baby whatever it is, I'm here with you. Let me help you feel better. I'm right here...you are not by yourself anymore. I can take this from you...if you let me.*

Something I said seemed to pull her from wherever the hell she had gotten lost in. Her breathing was still fast and deep, but her eyes regained focused and she sat up in the bed and held me in her gaze. "John. I don't know what *this* is we have, but I don't want to; it's just that…" She was stumbling over her words and practicing shibhari knot-tying with her elegant fingers. She looked so unsure of herself. "I don't want to have sex with you. I have never had sex wi..." I cut her words off by placing my hands on her shoulders and giving her a little squeeze. I looked through her eyes and there it was...hurt, shame, guilt and fear. "Vivian. I only want you. I only want us to find our happy in each other. I will never ask you to give me something you're not ready to give.

I won't lie and pretend that I don't want you. I won't lie and tell you I don't dream, shit; that I don't fantasize about being inside you, finding a rhythm that belongs to just you and me. You are the most beautiful soul I have ever known. I only want to love you, nothing more and nothing less.

There is a difference in making love and fucking, Vivian. It's as different as writing a research paper and a poem. Poetry is living and moving… changing and growing all the time. When one person reads the poem, they get something different from the next person who reads it because poetry uses words to bind the writer's emotions to the soul of the reader. Research papers give everyone the same information because there is only one way to respond to facts: you either agree or disagree. When we fuck, we'll still be making love because the actions will bind our souls and there will be no room for anyone else to connect with us on that level. Do you understand why I'm in no rush to be inside you? Vivian, our love will create worlds. Fuck...this is not coming out right."

I continued to rub her shoulders and hold her gaze. A small frown defiles her perfectly arched brow as she tries to process all the shit that just spilled from my mouth into her lap. Her eyes lowered from my gaze and caught sight of the exposed ridges of my abs.

"Sex with you and me would be...just. I know you won't pressure me, but I've never done this before...I've never chosen a lover before." She looks up at me as her voice hitches up on the word chosen and quickly looks back down. I use my index and middle-finger to gently lift her chin up so she could look at me. When her eyes meet mine, my heart cracks.

"Hey."

"I'm not comfortable with the idea of sex...it's just...too—"

"Listen. If you and I never make love with each other, I won't go anywhere." I was shocked by the truth behind my declaration. I really meant it...sex was not what was driving me towards whatever this is between Viv and me. "I don't want you to think that I am only hang out with you because I want sex from you. I mean, I love looking at you and touching you and feeling you curled up next to me...but it's you I want, Vivian. Just you." I feel her relax and soften against me. Her body still shaking, though not as badly. Her tears watered the seed that she'd dropped in my heart about a month and a half ago...now they were taking root. I was starting to love her. My heart beat a tattoo in my chest as the realization settled in my blood. I couldn't call what I was feeling fear, it felt a hell of a lot like a panic attack.

The rest of the afternoon passed by with the staccato rhythm of the rain and the languidness of shared naps. Four weeks and I was in love with a girl who was as broken, if not more so as I was. I had made peace with my demons, I wasn't sure if I was ready to face her, but I didn't have a choice; I loved her. Looking down at her, sleeping in my bed, her right hand resting possessively over my heart, and her pouty lips slightly opened...jughead flexed as if to remind me he was still here and actively waiting for some attention. I was always semi-hard around her, but after her meltdown earlier, I knew I would have to use the control that Auntie taught me, so I took a few deep breaths and willed myself flaccid. I will not fuck this up. I closed my eyes with thoughts of what these feelings for Vivian meant for me.

It wasn't until I ran into her, that something thawed inside me and I knew I would never recover from the icy-volcanic lava that dripped down my throat and landed in my heart...when it usually landed in my crotch... Nope, this woman would be the methodical and painful death of me. But, maybe she could save me. Even heal me. Fuck! Could she love me? She could possibly make me strong enough to love myself.

~17~

The first semester of my freshman year was passing by in a dizzying blur of classes, work, meetings, and Vivian. Finals were just about done, it was cold and dreary in Columbia and most of the students on campus were planning to go home for Christmas break. I knew roughly where I would be for Christmas, but I wasn't sure where Vivian would be. From what she had shared with me, she didn't have any family to go home to.

The week before Christmas break found me trying to figure out what Vivian's plans were for the break. I had property all over the country, but I didn't want to go alone. Vivian was coming over and I was feeling as anxious about asking her to come to New York with me as I'd felt about asking Auntie to move to Columbia with me two summers ago. I planned dinner in my room. Mostly out of fear of driving and causing another accident that could potentially hurt someone I cared about.

The knock on the door made me jump. I had already opened the take-out boxes and was ready to start the evening and then a knot formed in the pit of my stomach and I thought that maybe I shouldn't assume that she didn't have plans. *Dinner was going to be awkward if I don't pull my shit together. I'm going to need my Dom for this...it's the only way I know how to get what I want from her without scaring the living daylights out of her.*

We had finished out meal and put the trash away. We were half sitting, half laying on my bed and she had her feet in my lap. *Here goes nothing.*

"So, Ms. Bruno. How has your first semester of college been?" I inquired as she enjoyed her foot massage. Her eyes half closed and her face relaxed, she looked like I had just made her orgasm. I really wanted to make her come, but I had to give her the time and space she needed. It was hard as hell to not touch her in all the ways I knew would make her feel good, but it would be much harder to be without her.

"It has been the best four months of my life, I feel like I finally belong to myself. You know? Like I have a choice in what happens in my life...I feel like what I want matters. Like...I don't know. It's been great and most of that is because of you." Her voice was so quiet on the last couple words, I had to strain to hear it, but once I heard it...I could help the smile that creased my face. *I made it great for her. I made her matter.*

"Well, Ms. Bruno. What will you be doing over winter break? Will you recharge your batteries alone or with family and friends?"

"I don't know. I don't have anywhere to go and I don't have a lot of extra money to go on vacation...so I guess I'll be on campus this break. What will you be doing Mr. Ellis?"

"I have been thinking about going to New York. A good friend of mine has a place in the city that she won't need it and I have the key and go ahead to use it. I would love to take this really great girl to the city that never sleeps for the break, but I'm nervous about asking her to come with me."

"Who's this amazing *girlfriend* who has a place in New York?

"Why, Ms. Bruno. Did you dip your sweet tongue in green paint before you chose your words?"

"Well, Mr. Ellis. I am an only child. I never learned to *share*." There was something about the way she said, share, that made me flinch, but it was gone before I could ask her about it.

"I am an only child, too. So, I guess I can understand your selfishness."

"Whatever. Who is this *friend?"*

"Her name was Violet. She was a cherished friend and unfortunately, she passed away two summers ago from brain cancer. She didn't have any family, so she left everything she owned to me. She was my first sexual experience, Vivian." I studied her face for a reaction and managed to keep my face impassive as understanding settled over hers.

"Oh."

"Oh?"

"Yes. Oh. How old was she, John?"

"Thirty-eight."

"She was your first?"

"Yes."

"Did you love her?"

"Yes. I do."

"Is she my competition?"

"No. My love for you is unique and different than any love I have ever known."

"She gave you sex. I have given you only my time and a few kisses.

"She gave me my sexuality, you will give me the other half of myself."

"Why did she choose you as her lover?"

"She saw in me what I couldn't see in myself. She saw *me*...I didn't even know who the fuck I was, but she knew, and she gave me that person."

"Who do you see in me?"

"I see a powerful, but unsure woman; who's too afraid of her past to enjoy her right now. I see a heart bigger than life with a need to please and keep the peace, but I also see a heart that's been broken and a soul that needs mending."

"I'm scared of who and what you see in me. I'm afraid you will see all of it and walk away from me. Away from us...before we even become an *us*."

"You don't ever have to be afraid that I will walk away from you. You are my other half, I will never leave you, Vivian. I—I love you."

"You *love* me? But. I haven't had sex with you...I won't even let you touch me. How can you love me?"

"Sex doesn't define love. You are special to me. You make me smile. I have a lot of shit on my mind and you… you make me forget about it all. When I think of you, when we are together...you make me believe there's a reason I'm still here." I watch as her eyes peek up at me and then immediately fall back to her lap. *Is she embarrassed by my words or does she think I'm lying out of my ass?*

"Will you take me to New York with you for winter break?"

"Yes."

"Will you make love to me over the break?"

"If that's what you want. Don't feel as if you have to give yourself to me in that way to compete with Violet or because you feel obligated to do so. I don't mind waiting for you."

"I want to, John. I'm ready to choose my *first* lover. Will you hurt me?

"Hurt you? No, I hope not. I don't want to hurt you."

What a strange question to ask. "Has someone you loved hurt you before?"

"I've never loved anyone before."

"Why do you think I'll hurt you?"

"Sex is painful."

"It can be, but pain and pleasure don't have to be mutually exclusive; they can be mutually beneficial if both people consent to engage in safe, sane sexual play."

"What do you mean?"

"I mean that through carefully measured pain, one can find an enormous amount of pleasure."

"Is that what you like? Pain, I mean."

"I enjoy giving pain during sex. Yes."

"Why?"

"It is what I know. Violet enjoyed a certain kind of sex, I was young and foolish enough to give that to her. Pain and pleasure were interchangeable with us. Learning to get through the pain knowing what pleasures waited on the other side; made the sex even more amazing. At least for us... it is not for everyone and if it is not for you, I don't need it."

"Will you show me?"

"Show you?"

"Show me how pain and pleasure can coexist and be enjoyable.

"I would love to share that with you, but not now. You are not ready, and I am not ready to go back to the place inside myself because it's a dark place and I don't want to confuse you, Viv."

"I'm not incapable of making a choice for my own sexual self. I think I know what I want and don't want."

"You may think you know, but you don't. Pain isn't all ways in the form of physical. You seem to be a little skittish about sex and how it should happen… I could hurt you and there would be no turning back from that. I don't want to lose you, us, or what we are building together."

"You think we'll be *forever*?"

"Even if I didn't want it, Vivian...we are forever. There is nobody else for either us. We. Are. It."

"You seem so sure."

"Yes."

"Then kiss me."

"Kiss you?"

"Kiss me."

"You don't have anything to prove."

"I know and that's why I want you to kiss me. For the first time in my life...I don't have to do anything except be me. I want you to kiss me, John."

"Where?"

"Here." She pointed to the juncture between her thighs. I stand there, totally befuddled for about an eternity. When she's aroused, she smells like fresh rain-water and honeysuckle, I've been wanting to taste her for a long time. I've wanted my mouth on her since I bumped into her four or five months ago. Hell yea. I'll give her this kiss.

"Are you sure?"

"Please."

"Stand up." She does

"Unbutton and unzip your pants."

"Okay."

"Pull them down and step out of them."

"Okay."

"Fold you pants and place them on the chair in the corner."

"Okay."

"Take your shirt off...I want to look at you."

"Okay."

"Fold your shirt and place it on top of your pants on the chair in the corner." Her white, cotton bra is covered in hot pink stars with a little pink satin ribbon in the middle. *Shouldn't be sexy, but for some reason, Jughead appreciates the innocence of it.*

"Okay."

"Lay down on the bed, place your arms above your head and spread your legs a part."

"Okay,"

"Beautiful. So amazingly beautiful, Vivian."

"Thank you."

I crawled up on the bed. I make sure to keep my clothes on, I'll give this to her and take nothing for myself. I run my fingers up the inside of her long legs and stopped at her knees. I pushed them up and out to make room for my shoulders. Her pink cotton panties with little white flowers strewn all over them are wet and up this close, she smells more like spicy cinnamon, and oranges and something else I can't quite name. I run my nose up the length of her pussy and inhale deeply through the soaked material of her innocent little panties. She tenses her thighs and her surprise escapes from her lovely mouth, but she swallows the sound down her throat.

"Is this, all right?"

"Yes. F-fine."

"Good. Tell me to stop and I will."

"Okay."

"Lift your hips up, I'm going to take your panties off."

"Okay."

"God, Vivian. Georgia O'Keefe couldn't paint you and get it right. There is a perfection about you and nothing can capture it… you're exquisite".

"Are you *really* talking about my… me, down there?"

"Yes. I really am talking about your beautiful pussy? Have you never seen yourself?"

"No."

I got up from my bed and grabbed the hand mirror from my wall, I use it to cut my hair.

"Here. Get up. Grab the mirror, you have to see what has my mouth watering."

"No. I don't want to. I don't need to see me down *there*. Please, I'll take your word for it."

"Vivian, take this mirror...look at how beautiful you are." She timidly takes the mirror and sits up on the bed. Drawing her knees up, she put the mirror between her thighs and gasps when her glistening, sex comes into view. The outside of her bare lips is a deep shade of purple, they looked so soft and full. She almost reaches out to touch herself, but embarrassment makes her pull back. With her legs spread, she can see the wetness of her arousal clinging to the inner lips of her pussy.

"I *do* look like a flower!" The wonder in her cause my lips turn up in an appreciative smile.

"Lay down. I'm going to taste you."

"Okay."

"If you don't like something, tell me to stop and I will. Okay?" It's important to me that Vivian knows she has all the power in this situation. Something about her told me she needed to have control in order to really let go. I could give that to her. She didn't have to know I was topping her.

"Okay."

She lays back and spreads her legs for me. As I push her legs wider and lowered my head to her, I'm almost high from her scent. I run my index finger down the length of her and she hums, low in her throat like one of the church mothers on Sunday morning when Pastor says something they really agree with.

"Good?" I ask as I run my finger up and down her center, not touching her clit and only grazing her opening.

"Yes."

"Good. I'm going to slip my finger inside you. Just one finger, alright?"

"Alright." She was scared and turned on and soaking wet.

"Do you feel that?" I push the tip of my index finger into her and began to slide the rest of my finger deeper, sliding against her wet walls. She was as tight as I thought she would be, but then I guess being tight isn't a prerequisite for being a virgin. Her breath is yanked out of her lungs and her muscles clamp down on searching finger. I groan deep in my throat, I'm so hard it hurt.

"Damn, Vivian. You're so responsive. Jesus Christ! I've never been this hard in my life."

"Really?" She questions as she whimpers and starts to move her hips to ride the finger that's pumping in and out of her. I add a second and third…I want to slip my entire hand inside her, but I know that would be too much for her.

"Yes. I want you so badly, but this isn't about me. It's about you. Have you ever had an orgasm?"

"N-No. I-I-Oh John. What are you? Do. Ing?"

I'd start rubbing my thumb in concentrated circles around her clit, she was riding my hand like I one day hope she would ride my dick.

"You like it?"

"Oh. God. Yes."

"I'm going to put my mouth on you. Keep your hands above your head...don't bring them down for any reason. Okay?"

"Okay."

I lower my head and lick her clit, then I suck her hard nub into my mouth. She was trembling in my hands. I pull my fingers out of her and lick her essence from my index, middle and ring fingers and smile as I swallow her down. The look of *oh-my-God-did-he-just-do-that* is one of the sexiest things I've ever seen. I lick the entire length of her dripping pussy. She tastes as good as she smells. She's so soft and wet and warm. My tongue spears into her wet cleft, while my thumb starts to massage her clit again. Her hips were bucking and she makes unintelligible noises as I pleasure her. *Ohmygooooo...John.*

Ican't. Take. Th—this. John. So good, Sogood. You. My, John. Oh God, John...So. Too good. Too good.

Hearing her helpless, nonsensical words make me crazy with the need to feel her orgasm on my tongue. I go wild, eating at her like I had never had this type of meal before. I'm all teeth, tongue, and lips. Sucking, licking, biting and thrusting. I was working so hard for her orgasm I barely noticed the fact that she's undone my pants and pulled my dick free. She kept stroking me...up and down. Up and down. Hard squeezes on the down stroke, and a counter-clock-wise twist on the upward ones.

She was going to make me come. On the last suction on her clit, she stiffened and squeezed her legs against my head, holding in that position for what seemed like forever, then her body starting to relax. I didn't realize that she had been screaming and bucking until she went still and the room was quiet, save for out heavy breathing. We were in an almost 69-position, except my dick was closer to her breast than her mouth and that's when I felt the stickiness on her belly and realized that I had come all over her, marking her as mine.

"Are you alright?"

"Yes."

"Are you sure?"

"Yes. Are you...are you alright?"

"I am more than alright, you are a-fucking-mazing. Are you sure you're alright?"

"You seem to enjoy my hands touching you too, John." Her shy smile melts me. She could ask me for anything and she could have it all...no questions. "Thank you." She smiles with her eyes. "I didn't know that I could do that."

"Wrong way around. You, my beautiful girl, are the

amazing one."

"Really, thank you, John."

"For what?"

"For showing me what my body can do."

"You are more than welcomed. So, are you coming to New York with me for winter break?"

"Is Cocky the biggest cock you've ever seen?"

~18~

I had never been to New York, but that didn't stop me from acting as if this was my second home. I had only seen pictures of the brownstoneI inherited from Auntie. The pictures did not do the space justice. We took a car from LaGuardia to the renovated brownstone that I now owned in Harlem. We pulled up to the curb on 119th street. I could not believe my eyes. The place was beautiful and I owned it. More than my reaction, Vivian's reaction made it feel like Christmas. In all honesty, sharing this moment with her was the first time I ever really felt like there was a reason to be happy during this time of year. Her eyes were the stuff Christmas specials were made of. She was exquisite.

"Oh my God. This is your place?

"I guess it is. I've never been here before. It was just too painful. I was going to sell it, but the estate planner talked me out of it...said that owning property in New York pretty much guaranteed my economic security. So, I didn't sell it. I did hire a couple of caregivers to stay in the home and maintain it for me. They are an older couple who stay in the basement apartment, but keep the property cleaned and lived in. Ready to go up? I'm freezing my balls off out here." She laughed and grabbed my hand as the driver carried our bags to the door. I still hadn't told her about the fact that I was a multimillionaire, I needed to know she loved me for me...not because I had access to money.

"I guess if your balls are freezing off than my girls must not be ecstatic out here either." She joked as she cupped her hands over her breast and smiled up at me. In that moment, I saw my forever and I knew it was her.

"Then let's get my balls and your girls inside."

"After you Mr. Ellis."

As we were walking in, we met the older couple who had been hired to maintain the property. They were on their way out. It was good to meet them face-to-face. They were both artist, who never found the level of success they hoped they would in their chosen arts but refused to live without their it and the freedom to be their authentic selves. I could totally admire that about the bohemian couple in the late forties. Mary was a singer/writer who worked several bars and lounges to get herself out there and her husband, Mike was a visual artist who chose to work in crayons. For them, landing this job, which provided them with free housing and a salary, was a dream come true. They could focus on their art and not worry about be out of doors. I guess it was a win-win for all involved.

"This place is beautiful, I have never seen anything so elegant before." Her eyes were scanning all the glossy woodwork that seem to start on the floors and work its way up to the crown molding on the ceiling.

"I have." I said as I looked down into her face. She blushed and smiled her shy smile. *She really is exquisite.*

"Which room will I sleep in while we are here?"

"I was hoping you would share the master with me. We don't have to avoid sleeping in the same bed just because we may not be having sex."

"Wait. What do you mean, may not be having sex? I thought you said if that was what I wanted, then you would make love to me." Her eyes looked panicked and she searched my face for a clue or a hint...something to hold on to.

"Baby. Calm down. I'm in no rush. I want us to enjoy this time together. I've never been to New York and you've never been here either, so...let's just enjoy the city and whatever happens, happens. Okay?"

"John, you can't possibly mean you don't expect anything from me after spending all that money on first class tickets, a driver for the three weeks we are here and God knows what else you have planned and paid for...I don't have money to contribute...All I have is my..." I was taken aback by the shit that was spilling from her lips. It was pissing me off and I really had to step back and get it together.

She continued, "And I really want to share it with you. I want to say thank you the only way I know how." Her words were barely a whisper, but in those soft confessions, I heard a truth that my mind just could not touch, but somewhere inside me, I knew that horrible, dark things had happened to Vivian and the damage was deeper than even she realized.

"I want nothing from you except your smiles and giggles and laughter. There is no pressure on you to make love with me. And anyway, how would we make love if you're in another room?" I joked, hoping to lighten the mood...it didn't.

"I know. I-I wasn't sure if you wanted to have sex and still have me in a same room. Isn't that how it works? Sex in one space and sleep in another? I know we have slept together many times, but that did not involve sex...once we start having sex with each other, you will surely want your own space to sleep in, right?" Her questions made me think maybe she was trying to be funny, but guileless eyes told me she was dead serious.

"Where did you ever get that idea? If we make love in New York, if we don't make love in New York...I want to have the pleasure of sleeping with you and waking up with you in the morning. If we make love, then I definitely want you sleeping in my bed and waking up in my arms." My voice was colored in the deep turquoise tones of confusion and disorder. I couldn't help the tone...I *was* confused and a little put off with her low expectations of me.

"Oh. I just. It's just that...Oh, never mind. Your room it is." She was so flustered, it reminded me of something I wanted to ask her about, but then she turned around and pinned me with her caramel eyes and spoke in her sweet, honey coated voice, "John. You will make love to me while we're here, won't you?"

"I really want to, Vivian. But, I don't have to. You don't have to. But yea, I really, *really* hope to make love to you."

"So, it's settled then."

"What's settled?"

"I choose you as my first lover, John. I can't wait to share myself with you." She turned her perfect all-American-girl smile on me and I felt myself returning her goofy grin. *Being in love obviously turns me into a goofball.*

"You've never had a lover before, Vivian?"

"A *lover*, no. I've never had a lover, but people have had sex with me before."

"So, you're not a virgin?" Something felt weird about the way she chose her words…they were so deliberate. I wanted to see if my misgivings were warranted or if I was reading too much into her tone.

"No, I guess not." Her brow rucked up as she thought about what I had asked.

"What do you mean, you guess not?"

"Oh, I mean my hymen was broken early in my childhood...I don't remember how it happened...I just know that it did." Vivian's face was so open and honest, but the mist of uncertainty sifted through her eyes like winter breath and my chest tightened.

"Oh. We'll take it slow. Remember, I don't need anything from you that you're not ready to give. Just you and me is enough." She nodded her head and I noticed a the corners of her mouth were turned down and her brows were drawn together. "Are you hungry?"

***

The kitchen was fully stocked and the house looked as if a family really did live here. Mary and Mike were going to be away for three weeks, visiting relatives in Puerto Rico. So, on that first night in the city that never sleeps, Vivian and I cooked dinner, looked at TV and cuddled on the tufted Cabriolet couch in front of the fireplace.

"Viv. It's getting late and I'm barely keeping my eyes open. I'm ready to turn in, but if you want to stay up, you can."

"No. I'm ready for bed. There's an ensuite in the master bedroom, right? I could use a hot shower."

"Of course. I was thinking the same thing." *Should I ask her if we could shower together*?" I used my best aristocratic voice, but I sounded more like a pervert talking to a little girl, trying my best to get her to do something she had no business doing. *Oh well, can't be good at everything.*

"Uh. You want us to shower together? Tonight?"

"We don't have to. I just thought since we both needed a hot shower, we could take one together. But I'll wait until you're done, if that's what you want." *What the hell? Vivian had me second guessing pretty much every thought that went through my head. This is not who I am. This is not who Auntie left her fortune to. Play time is over...it's time Vivian met my Dom persona.*

"John." Before she could say anything else, I stood and held my hand out to her. She grasped onto it like I was the only thing keeping her from drowning in a sea of anticipation and chaos.

"Vivian." My voice was only slightly deeper and my gaze was frozen coffee. I stood at my full height and angled my body towards hers, my shadow looming over her shadow. Everything about me said control, power, and sex. I could not allow Vivian to think I was weak. *She asked me to show her, well...here goes nothing.* I hope she doesn't run for the hills, but this second guessing and questioning has got to end. I said nothing else after calling her name. I let my Dom stance do all the talking. I knew what I was looking for and if she gave it to me tonight, her life nor mine would ever be the same.

And then it happened. She gave me what I needed to see. Mouth slightly opened; making room for the increase in her breathing, breast full and nipples forming tight buds under her shirt, pulse beating like crazy in her neck and of course; the heady scent of her arousal hitting me full force and making it hard for me to focus. I had her right where I wanted her, now what the hell was I going to do with her. She was not some damaged, doe-eyed white girl with a black Mandingo fantasy. No, Vivian Bruno was my forever.

"Vivian." I snapped out her name like a whip, giving her a lashing across her torso to connect with the full, round curves of her breast. Her shoulders slumped and the look she slid my way made me feel like a dog, but once I started down this slippery slope, there was no coming back from it.

"We will shower together because that will make me happy. I'm going to start making love with you tonight, but not complete it, because you need to learn to tell me what you want. While your limited experience is endearing, something tells me that you know exactly what you want from a man and I can't wait until you feel comfortable enough to tell me how, when, and what you want me to do to you." *This could go either way.*

She looks confused but turned on. Shit! Her look...Does Vivian wants to play? Yes, she does. Good. That is damn good.

~19~

With her hand securely in my hand, we walked up the stairs to the second floor where the master bedroom was. I opened the door and turned on the bedside lamp. Vivian was shaking like a leaf, I did nothing to calm her down. There was too much at risk to fuck this thing up by falling back. I had thought maybe Vivian would need me to take a back seat so that she could feel comfortable, well...truth is, I can't give up my control to her. I'm a Dominant, and if we are going to make this thing forever, she will have to accept this part of me.

"Vivian, I'm going to run our shower. You need to get undressed and sit on the edge of the bed with both feet flat on the floor and your hands on your thighs...palms down. Do you understand?"

"Okay, John." Her voice was a bloated, dead fish. Something was off.

"Good. When I'm ready for you, I will come to get you. Okay?"

"Yes, John." Still bloated. Still dead. Her eyes were as dead as her voice...something was definitely off.

Hearing her contrition, her submission gave me such a head trip, I thought I would pass out from the high I was riding. She is so perfectly suited for this...so ready to please. Teaching her to please me and more importantly, getting her to trust that I will take care of her in every way, will be the greatest accomplishment of my life. I walked over to the en suite and started the shower. I wanted the room to be thick with steam and heavy with lust; my lust for her and her lust for me. I stood in front of the mirror and removed my shoes and socks. I walked back into the bedroom where I found Vivian sitting on the edge of the bed, naked with her palms lying flat on her thighs and her feet flat on the floor. She looked so beautiful. I moved to stand in front of her and didn't spare a glance her way. I ran my hand down the length of her hair. I stroked her hair as if she were my favorite pet. I heard her breathing hitch and felt her relax under my touch. I was already getting hard.

"Vivian, unbutton my shirt starting at the bottom and working your way up to the collar." I wanted her submission more than I knew I did, but I couldn't shake the feeling that what I wanted would destroy the woman I wanted it from.

"Okay, John." Her voice, a quiet, strained piano chord that bordered on cacophony. I looked down at her for what seemed like the first time in hours. She looked so contrite, so eager to please, but there was something else in that look. Fear? Anger? Defeat? *Self-preservation*? I didn't want to see any of that in her eyes. And then again, those eyes didn't really look like they belonged in Vivian's beautiful face. I wanted to see joy and awareness or joy and awe.

"Vivian, look, at me." I kept my voice even and tried to speak in a more relaxed tone. "What are you thinking right now? And don't lie to me." Harsher tone, softer meaning. "I need to know what's going on in that brilliant mind of yours."

"I'm scared, John. This feels exactly like…" Her voice trailed off and her eyes went soft and wide at the same time. *What happened to you Vivian?* "I don't want to be controlled, I want to have a say in what happens to me, to my body." A tear slid down her cheek and an almost imperceptible whimper left her throat. "I don't want to be used and discarded like the trash *he*...I'm not toilet paper, John."

"Vivian, what the hell are you talking about? When have I ever treated you like trash…in Columbia; in my dorm room…you asked me to show you. Show you how pain and pleasure are just opposite sides of the same coin, this is the beginning of the showing."

"This thing you want from me." She continued as if I had not clarified what was happening. "It will hurt me and you said you would *never* hurt me." I set down on the bed beside her and took her right hand in my left and began to rub my thumb across the back of her knuckles in an effort to soothe her. I didn't say anything, just sat quietly beside her, waiting and listening. She didn't understand what she was feeling was the power exchange I created by having her undressed and sitting, while I was still completely dressed except for my socks and shoes and standing over her. She took a deep breath and held it in until she was forced to blow it out and her words rode the wave of air and spilled out on the carpet under of her bare feet.

"John, I'm sorry something I have said or done has made you turn into this; whatever this is, but if this is what you meant by what you and Violet shared, then I am not interested in any of it." I watched as more silent tears slid down her beautiful face. I felt like the worst kind of dick for showing her without explaining what she was seeing. I knew she was not ready and yet, I persisted. *Fuck! I'm out of my depth here. I need to do this right...I want her to trust me, to give me her submission...she doesn't trust me enough, yet.*

"Vivian." My voice soft and steady.

"Yes." Her voice soft and teary.

"I need to. There are some things you need to know about me." I slide my eyes over to her, hoping for a glimpse of something on her face, I get nothing.

"Okay." I feel her hand tense under the constant ministrations of my thumb.

"Vivian, I—" My voice dropped to a whisper. I wanted to tell her about my mom, Earle...the killings, my life, my money. Nothing came out. My mouth suddenly became the Sahara Desert.

"Yes, John." She looked up at me, hopeful and scared. It was the sexiest look for a sub to offer her Master. *What kind of sick bastard finds the look of hopeful fear sexy? A really fucked up one...and that would be me. One fucked up, sick, bastard coming right up.*

"I." Clearing my throat, I tried again. "I have never been in love before. You make me...no, not you, shit. I love you, Vivian. I want you in my life…forever. I'm not going to propose to you on this break, but...let me show you." I got up from the bed and went to the top drawer that I had unpacked my underwear in and pulled out a little blue box nestled in simple blue and white Tiffany and Co. bag. I walked back over to her and placed the bag with the box in it into her hands and stood back. She looked at me and the confusion on her face made me smile. At least she wasn't crying anymore.

"Look in the bag, there is a gift receipt...look at the date."

"John?" The noise of the paper bending in her foraging fingers and giving up secrets that it had protected for months made me feel weaker and stronger, somehow."

"Look at the date, baby. Tell me what you see." My voice soft and cajoling.

"John. This is dated September 21, 1992. God! That's the day I bumped into you at the Horseshoe. You bought this the first day we met...what is this?

"Open the box." Holding my breath and hoping to God I didn't pass out.

"Okay."

Waiting with my stomach in my throat and my balls where my stomach used to be; hoping against all odds that this doesn't scare her more than I had already managed to.

"Oh, my fucking God! No fucking way! John? What the fuck...you got this--Shit, John." By the time she stopped her string of profanity and steadied her eyes on me, I was doubled over on the bed laughing all pretense of my Dom persona stripped away by the confused utterings of the woman I loved. It was just so fucking hilarious to see her so flustered...she couldn't even form a coherent sentence.

"You jackass. Oh my god, this is the most beautiful thing I have ever seen." Tears of joy this time. Smiling face and deeply dimpled cheeks.

"I only want you, Vivian. I need to tell you something. For real." My voice was quiet with the austerity of what I was about to say. "Come and sit with me." Belatedly, I remembered that I was running the shower and got up to turn it off when I felt her hand on my arm; pulling me up towards the shower.

"Talk to me after we shower." *Okay, where is this assertive vixen coming from? Should I stop her or see where she takes this?*

Her fingers start at the bottom of my shirt and makes short work of the buttons before we clear the bathroom threshold, I'm only wearing my Levi's and underwear...barely. The bathroom is steamy and hot. Vivian is tugging at my button fly and pulling everything down and out.

"Vivian! Wait a minute. I need to tell you something. The shower can wai--" Vivian was running her fingers down my sternum and across the six-pack along my abdomen. Her nails sending tiny shock waves through my body with each pass of her fingers.

"John. You're beautiful. Every part of you is beautiful. Ebony skin stretched taut over lean, toned muscles. Your chest, broad with so much definition and abs so perfect, I want to lick every inch of you." I didn't know Vivian had this side in her, but damn I really liked it. Her hands were rubbing over my chest, around my shoulders to my back and back down to my hip and thighs. It was driving me crazy. I couldn't do anything to hide my erection, it was all I could do not to attack her in the bathroom and fuck her into the New Year. Before I knew what was happening, I had grabbed my throbbing dick in my right hand and had my left hand curved around Vivian's left hip. I watched as her gaze fell to my hand...moving languidly over my length. I stroked myself, my eyes never leaving hers.

"Shit!" I bit out through clenched teeth. "Vivian, I... you are so sexy and you won't stop touching me…" My hand is moving faster along my erection and my hips fucking my cock into my fist, fingers squeezing the broad head. My eyes rolling back in my head with pleasure. Her long, nimble fingers finding my nipples, hardened to points on my chest...she pinches them, hard. I growl from low in my throat and I hear a whimper from her. My left hand is flexing at Vivian's right hip, I can't control the movements. I want to move my hands around to her ass and squeeze, move it around to the front and sink my fingers into the hot, wetness of her pussy. I want to, but I don't. I just keep my hand flexing on her hip and let her watch me stroke my heavy cock. There is already pre-cum leaking from the slit and then she does the hottest thing I've ever seen. She passed her right thumb over the head of my dick and brought it up to my mouth.

"See how you taste, John. I can't wait to have you in my mouth."

"Fuck!" I managed to get out around her thumb as my lips closed over the tip. The salty essence of myself coated my tongue and made me wonder why Auntie never let me taste myself.

"John, are you close?"

"Yes." I was stroking my dick with brutal force. Almost crazy with the need to come...I felt my balls tightening up and knew that a few more strokes would send me to the moon and doing this in front of Vivian was so much more carnal than me just jacking *Jughead* by myself. Her eyes dropped to my hand and then she dropped to her knees and pushed my hand aside with such confidence, it almost made me come.

"Let me help you." Her voice was a kitten's purr that made all my pleasure points sizzle with need. She wrapped her full lips around the head of my dick and placed her left hand on my right hip, just as I had placed mine on hers. Slowly, she began to take my length into her mouth.

"Holy fuck, Vivian. Your mouth. Shit, baby! Suck me hard, make me come."

I felt her throat relax and she took me deeper into her mouth. When my balls were up against her chin and my dick part-ways down her throat, she started constricting her throat muscles and then relaxing them. I had never in my life felt anything like that before. Over and over again, she took me deep into her throat and then pulled me out to the tip only to do it again. When she felt my cock get bigger and my control falter, she went all in. By this time, I had grabbed her head in both of my hands and was pounding my dick down her throat and saying all kinds of nasty, filthy things to her about how I wanted to fuck her pussy the way I was fucking her mouth. I was so close...she knew it and so did I.

"Shit, shit, shit, shit.... oh God! Vivian, I'm—I'm go. Ing. To. Come. Sohard...Shit." And that was it. She wrapped her right hand around my balls and gave them a squeeze and pulled down on them the same time she bit, softly down on the base of my dick and that was it. I flooded her throat with my cum and she drank me down like a woman dying of thirst. She made these sexy little noises as she sucked me into another erection. I was done. Didn't want to be, but I was. Spent and so in love, I could only see and feel Vivian.

Standing under the shower head, clean and sated, Vivian told me that she would be willing to try to be what I wanted and I told her that I would be everything she needed. She didn't need to know I would take care of her for the rest of her life, she only needed the reassurance I would be there for her now.

"I love you, Viv."

"I love you, too, John."

Sleep was pulling at both of us. We went to bed, naked, happy and in love.

I know that something will come up and destroy this amazing feeling... I'll be prepared for it, because that's just how my life goes. Happy-happy, joy-joy and then a big fat fuck you, John!

~20~

Christmas in New York was amazing. I'm not sure if it was amazing because of the city or because of the woman I was with. Either way, I fell more in love with the city and the woman the longer we were there. We went to see all the touristy attractions, went shopping; where Vivian tried to refuse my generosity. Ultimately, she stopped complaining about the money I was spending on her and started enjoying herself. I knew that I would have to tell her about my financial status, but that was conversation for another day. Today was December 31,1992, we were going to bring in 1993 in Time Square...there was no other place to be.

The temperature was hovering at about 55 degrees and it was a perfect day for walking in the city. I finally got reservations at Peter Luger Steak House. I was so excited to take Vivian to this New York institution. I knew that she would freak out about the prices, but it would be worth the headache to have this experience with her. And, it would be a great chance to tell her some of my secrets and maybe learn some of hers.

We had slept together every night since we got to New York, no sex, no intimate touching; just holding each other and stealing kisses. I was determined to let Vivian set the pace on this. I knew that she would be worth the wait. Vivian had dreams, well more like night terrors. She would wake up, just cry silent tears and whimper as if she was experiencing soul-shattering pain. We hadn't spoken about the ring since I showed it to her, but I knew that it was constantly on her mind and that is precisely where I wanted it to be.

"Vivian, are you almost ready? Our reservations are for 6:30. I have never had Peter Luger, but the reviews make it sound like a must do experience. I hope we're not disappointed, but I doubt we will be." My mind was going a mile a minute. I was nervous and excited and scared as hell about this early date. I needed to tell Vivian some important things, but I was not sure how she was going to react when I told her about some of my darker moments.

"Um...yea. Give me just three more minutes. I want to look like I belong in a place like Peter Luger with a man like John Ellis."

"Look like you belong? Baby, never question whether you fit into a certain place or belong with a certain crowd. You were made to stand out, don't try to fit in... ever."

"John." Her voice was dripping in appreciation. "You have to say that, you're in love with me. But the truth is, I don't fit in with certain *people* and I don't fit into certain *places*. You are strong and confident, and I'm just…" I cut her off mid-sentence, I did not want to hear her tear herself down.

"And you are *just* amazing and beautiful and sexy and smart and witty...You are *just* everything I never knew I wanted and that's why I love you." I could tell she wanted to believe all I said about her, I could see the struggle in her golden topaz eyes, but there was something keeping her from doing so. I wondered if it had anything to do with those terrible dreams she had during the night. I intended to find out over dinner.

Peter Luger was everything the reviews said it would be. I tried to hide the check when the waiter placed it discretely on the table, but Vivian move quicker than I thought she would. "Oh my God, John!" Her eyes looked four times their normal size. Honestly, it was quite funny, but I chose not to laugh at her, she also looked like she wanted to curse me in every language with all the words.

"What the hell are you thinking? I can't cover half of this bill. I can't believe you have me in this restaurant dining and dashing."

"What? Dining and dashing?" I tried to suppress the smile tugging at the corners of my mouth but failed to do so.

"Yes. Don't sit across from this table looking so smug, as if the amount of this check isn't causing you a small heart attack!"

"Well, I don't know the amount of the check since you snatched it before I had a chance to look at it and when have I ever asked you to cover half of anything when we are out together?"

"Well never, but this is different, John. There is no way you can afford to pay this amount...and even if you can, I can't let you spend this kind of money on me for *food*."

"Vivian. Give me the check. Now." I was tired of playing this game with her and so easily I slipped into my Dom persona and watched as she physically wilted and slid the check over to me.

"Thank you, Vivian. Why don't you go freshen up while I take care of this?" It was not a suggestion. Immediately, she grabbed her new Dooney & Bourke Crossbody purse, and excused herself to the restroom. Meanwhile, I paid the bill with my black American Express card.

"John?" Surprise evident in her voice and on her face to find me standing in front of the restaurant waiting for her.

"Are you ready? I have another surprise for you before we head into Time Square. Do you need anything to keep you warm?"

"Uh...no. I'm good. You just bought this new coat, hat, scarf and gloves for me. Your generosity knows no bounds and for that I am appreciative." She did not look at me, but she didn't need to. I know that those words were as mechanical and forced as that fake bull we ventured on during dinner in western roadhouse themed restaurant. I let it slide, because I knew she was confused by the command in my voice and how easily she submitted to it. We would have plenty of time to talk about everything on the horse drawn carriage ride through Manhattan.

"Vivian. I feel like I owe you an explanation for pretty much everything. I know that I have given you a lot to think about, but more than anything, I want you to trust me. You say that you love me, but you don't really know enough about me to love me."

"The same could be said for you, John. You confessed your love for me and what do you really know about me; other than what I have shared with you?"

"You have a valid point, but I doubt there is anything in your past that would ever cause me to question my love for you. I, on the other hand; have demons. I don't want to share them with you, but I don't want to take this relationship any further without telling you all of it."

"You don't know what's in my past. I have my own demons and from the looks of things, I just keep feeding them and they keep feasting on me." Her eyes were looking down at her leather clad fingers. She refused to meet my gaze and it made me wonder what secrets she was keeping from me.

"So, I guess we both have demons. Are we both willing to share them or should we continue in this relationship like we didn't exist until we met each other?"

"John." She finally looked up at me as the carriage pulled up to the curb and the driver was getting out. "We did exist, and from the sound of things, that's all we did. We didn't live, thrive, love...we just hoped that the days and nights would come and go and leave the broken pieces of ourselves scattered about. Hoping that enough of them would be left behind so that when and if we ever started to live, we could collect them and add them up to make a person."

I helped Vivian into the carriage and we were each given a mug of hot chocolate and about four thick blankets. The ride was cold, even with the blankets. Vivian had never looked more beautiful. A light snow began to fall and the city looked amazing; like something I once saw in a snow globe. I wished that I could trap us in a snow globe. Trap this perfect moment in a glass ball filled with fake snow and fake trees and fake cityscapes. I knew that once I told her what I was determined to tell her that the chances of her staying with me, loving me, marrying me were slim to none, but I wanted this relationship to have a firm foundation and that meant no lies.

"You look so beautiful, Vivian. Are you warm enough?" I was stalling. I didn't want to say the repulsive things that got me to this point in my life.

"Thank you, John. There's something on your mind. Tell me and get it over with. But first, take this." She handed me a piece of paper, neatly folded and pressed like some old note found in one of those big family bibles.

"Do I read this now?"

"No. Later."

"Are you breaking up with me?"

"I'm not going to tell you what's on that paper."

"Why not? I get to read it later anyway. Why not just let me read it now?"

"Because I need you to trust me. I need to be able to trust you. Please don't push this. Just... I'll tell you when to open it. Okay?"

"Okay." I knew whatever was written on that paper would change my life forever, but I would play her game. I completely get it, doesn't make it any easier to not look.

"Alright, Vivian. I paid for the extra-long tour...this ride is going to take about three hours. I have a lot to say to you, I just need you to promise me one thing."

"Anything, John."

"Promise me that after I share my yesterday with you, you won't shut me out of your tomorrow. I need you Viv. More than I have ever needed anyone in my life. I need you to see the darkness inside me and know that because of your light, I can see my way to happy. Promise me, Viv. Promise that you won't leave me or shut me out."

"I promise." Her voice wavered a little. I could hear her breathing becoming shallow. She was anxious and afraid. *I will not lose her. Not when I just found her.*

~21~

Vivian and I cuddled together under the blankets and used our body heat to keep each other warm as well as a little extra something in our hot chocolate. For the first thirty minutes of the ride, we just held each other and enjoyed the city. It was time to talk. Fear gripped my throat and tried to choke the breath I needed to speak right out of me. I was determined to tell Viv everything. *I can do this. I can tell her my most horrible secrets and she will still love me and she will still want me.* I kept repeating the words over and over in my head. Time to put it out there.

"Vivian. What I have to say to you is not easy for me, but I really need you to know who you think you're in love with. I am not...just listen to me and try not to interrupt me and then I guess, we'll see."

"Okay John. I'm listening."

I took a deep breath and exhaled slowly. I watched as my breath crystallized in the cold New York air. I felt like my blood was doing the same...freezing in my veins. I grabbed her hand under the blanket and nervously rubbed my thumb over the back of her gloved knuckles. *Now or never, pussy.* How the fuck did Earl's voice get back into my head. I did not need his shit. Not now.

"Alright. I'll start where it matters. I was thirteen years old when my mother married this piece of shit, white-trash named Earl. He came from nothing, wanted nothing and was determined to leave my mom with nothing. He was a fucking cancer and he slowly spread throughout my home...my life. I never knew who my father was. He didn't stick around long enough to lay eyes on me; much less be in my life. My mother still saw fit to give me his name; although I dropped the junior from my name a long time ago. All I know is whoever my father was, he had to be boot-lick black because my mother could pass for white and well...I am pretty damn sure no one would mistake me for being white." I let a nervous laugh slip through my lips and tightened my hold on Vivian's hand. I looked up to see if she was paying attention and my chocolate gaze met her caramel gaze and I thought in that moment that she already knew everything about me. I felt naked and laid bare before her.

"Anyway. I hated Earl and I started to hate who my mother turned into with him in her life. She, my mother, she used to be so strong and so brave. She worked hard and loved me more than her own breath. I never saw my mother take any shit off anybody and if she felt like someone was threatening me, oh...she would kick ass and ask questions later. I felt strong because of her strength. You know what I mean?" I swept my eyes up slowly and quickly looked away before she could pin me with that sweet, golden gaze.

I could feel Vivian's eyes boring holes into the side of my face, but nothing in me was ready to see what look was on her face. If it was the look that said, *poor John...neither his mother nor his father loved him enough to protect him*, I don't know what I would have done, but it would not have been pretty. I felt her shift on the carriage seat, she moved closer to me. Giving me comfort the only way she could. I loved her in that moment more than I knew was possible to love someone.

"Are you cold, do you need more hot chocolate?" I had to ask, even though I knew damn well why she snuggled even closer to me.

"No, I'm fine. I just wanted to be closer to you. Is that okay?"

"Yes, everything you do is more than alright, Vivian." I squeezed her hand under the blanket to let her know how much she meant to me. I hope she got what I was trying to say with that simple gesture. "Well then." Pulling her a little closer, I continued with my confessions.

"After my mom married that jackass and brought him to live in our house, everything changed. We were by no means rich, but with it being just my mom and me, we always had more than enough of everything. After that asshat, Earl, moved in, we never seemed to have enough of anything anymore. Not enough food, hot water for showers, time for television watching, towels, or soap...shit, we didn't even have enough toilet paper anymore.

Everything changed with two little words. *I do.* Earl was the most disgusting man I had ever met. I mean, Viv, he rarely took baths and always seemed to smell like athlete's foot and shit. He would wear the same clothes for days at a time and never thought to brush his greasy hair or his rotting teeth but complained every time I took a longer shower or brushed my teeth after each meal. More than anything, I hated watching my mother go down.

My mother was beautiful. Not just beautiful because she was my mother. No, she was *beautiful.* By the time she died, she had aged at least fifteen years and was unrecognizable. She gained weight, stopped caring about her hygiene or her appearance. I knew that her lack of personal attention was due to her psycho husband. I fucking hate his guts." I took a few calming breaths to reign in the anger that rose up in my chest, looking for an outlet. I couldn't let her see that shit in me. "You still with me? Do you need a break?"

"No baby. I'm fine."

"Okay then. I was sixteen when I bashed my step father's head in with the same baseball bat he had used to bash my mother's head in several hours earlier. The same baseball bat he used to crack my skull when I came home that afternoon.

After years of watching him beat, rape and sodomize my mother…" I noticed how Vivian tensed up and the hairs on the back of my neck stood up. *What the hell was that?*

"I didn't feel any regret for bludgeoning him. I called the cops and they came over and looked at my mother's beaten and bloodied body and took one look at me, still holding the bat at my side and blood caked on my head and in my hair and said that the bastard got what he deserved. I was free to go about my life." I felt my head hang down and I was waiting for her to scream for the carriage driver to stop and let her off, but she didn't. She only placed her hand on my thigh and squeezed it gently to let me know she was *supporting* me. *Somebody up there fucking loves me, because I don't deserve to have her with me at all. Violet, it must be you. How the fuck do I tell her about what Violet and I had together and how I hastened her death with my careless driving?*

"Vivian." My words were quiet. I wasn't sure how much more I could tell her about me, but I wanted to tell her most of my truth. "If you've heard enough and don't want to hear any more or if you want to go back to the brownstone and pack...I will take care of that for you."

"I'm still listening."

"Alright." I slid my eyes over her face and didn't notice any tension or fear registering, so I felt better about continuing with what I was saying.

"Well. I was a late bloomer when it came to sex. I was still a virgin after the eleventh grade. That summer changed everything for me. I killed my stepfather, buried my mother, lost my virginity in a BDSM relationship with an older woman in my neighborhood and eventually became her Dom." I waited for something, anything...but Vivian was as quiet as a church mouse. *What was she thinking? Did she even know what BDSM meant?*

Does she understand what it means that I am a Dominant? I was shaking next to her, I hope she just assumes I was freezing my ass off. "Vivian?"

"Yea John?" Her voice gave nothing away.

"Did you hear what I just said? I was introduced to sex by an older woman who trained me to be her submissive and then nurtured the Dom in me."

"I heard you. Is there more to the story or are you done?"

"There's more. Are you alright? I mean, are you alright with what you've heard so far? I know how fucked up it all is and I wouldn't tell you any of this shit if I didn't want to give you all of me...for the rest of my life."

"Yes. Just listening. Trying not to process."

"Okay. I—uh. I had never even kissed a girl before. Auntie, that's what everybody in the neighborhood called her, invited me into her house. It was so hot and everyone knew that she kept her house cool with four air conditioning units. Everyone also knew that she chose a young boy every year to take as a lover. At least that's what we though we knew…it really wasn't the case, but I learned that over the course of my summer with her.

When she chose me, I was scared as hell. Nobody ever talked about what happened during their summer with Auntie. Over the course of the summer, she trained me to submit to her in all things. She took all the decision making away from me. When I left my mom's house and went to her house, I didn't have to worry about what I should or shouldn't do to please her. You know what I mean? I didn't have to think about simple shit like; should I fuck Auntie's ass?" I watched Vivian's body tense up again. *Something about anal sex freaked her out. But she said she had never chosen a lover before. Probably not important.*

"I'm still with you. Still listening." Her voice sounded strained and almost sad.

"My training was hard. She gave me my rules, what she expected from me sexually and what she expected from me when I was in her home. She also gave me my consequences if I broke any of her rules or did not meet her expectations. It was so liberating. I knew what she wanted, I knew what would happen if I didn't give it to her. There was no gray area. She knew that I was going to mess up and she loved teaching me how to be what she needed me to be."

"You liked having her control you?"

"I liked not having to be in control. How can I explain this? At home with mom and Earl, every rule and expectation was arbitrary. I never knew when the rules or expectations would change and I never knew what the consequences were going to be. With Auntie, I always knew. You know? I didn't have to guess or try and control myself and hopefully hit the invisible mark that had been set by a lunatic and was subject to change. By giving her permission to control me, I gave myself permission to breath. I was always holding my breath at home, always too scared to take a fucking breath because it may have been my last one. With Auntie...I could breathe."

"What else did she teach you?"

"Auntie taught me so much more than how to fuck and submit. She taught me about music, art, fine dining...she taught me how to be a gentleman. She taught me how to control my emotions and my physical urges. In a word...she taught me how to be a man."

"That's eight words." I heard the smile in her voice.

She was being cute. *God, I loved her.*

"Vivian. Are you listening to me?"

"Every word. So, how did she make you a Dominant if you had been her submissive?" I hadn't really thought about it much until she asked me. Did Auntie *make* me a Dominant and had ever really been a submissive?

"She didn't make me a Dominant. I am a Dominant. A person either is or is not and there is nothing that anyone can do to change that. Being a Dominant isn't a lifestyle choice, no more than being a submissive is. Either you are or you aren't." I watched as her scrunched up eyebrows formed double mountain peaks at the top of her nose. "Let me try to explain it better. If I had never found my way into the lifestyle, I would still be a Dominant…it's who I am, not what I am. Make sense? *I felt like a fucking idiot trying to explain this to her.*

"I get it in theory, but if you are a Dominant as in noun…how could you submit to her and if she was a submissive; how could she dominate you? It's a perplexing dichotomy."

"I get that. Really. I do, but you have to…if I told you that you are a submissive, what would you say?"

"I'd say, not anymore."

"What? What do you mean, not anymore?"

"Exactly what I said. For most of my life, I let certain kinds of people walk all over me, but not anymore."

"Being a *submissive* is not the same as being submissive. A submissive is a noun…like woman, house, and car. Being submissive means acquiescing to the needs and wants of others before yours are considered. Most subs are not submissive in their lives, in fact most are dominating in everything they do. You are not submissive, by any stretch of the imagination;

however, you are a *submissive* by nature."

"Answer my question, John. How did she…how did you become her Dom?

"I don't even know exactly how it happened, really. It was the beginning of July, which meant that our time together was coming to an end. My senior year would be starting in August and at least I would go back to school knowing how to fuck a girl into another state of being." I chuckled and realized I was laughing by myself, so I stopped. *Stick to the sincerity, dickhead.*

"Anyway. It was July 8th and hot as hell outside. I had been seeing Auntie for a little over a month now. My day was so structured, I knew exactly where I'd be; even if I didn't know what I'd be doing. I needed that structure, I needed that routine." For a moment, I was lost in my thoughts and felt myself bird walking down memory lane, exactly where I did not need to be.

"What was I saying? Oh, yea...I walked over to Auntie's house early in the morning. I wanted to see her and I wanted to get the fuck away from Earl and my mom. Auntie had me working in her backyard. I did not feel like being out there, but I also did not want to face the consequences of not following instructions. So, I worked. Weeding her raised flower beds, her container gardens, removing old flower pots and planters from her shed...you know, all the shit that she thought she was too good to do." I couldn't help the smile that curved my mouth up on one side as I remembered hearing Auntie's voice purring to me about how she was too yellow and too beautiful to be in the sun doing field labor. "If I was a slave, I would be in the big house, fucking Massa." I mimicked Auntie's voice and didn't even realized I had done so until Vivian let out a little giggle.

"So, she was funny and made you laugh? I thought

Dominants only gave their submissive pain, pain, and more pain."

"It's not always about pain. There is so much more than pain involved in a Dom/sub relationship. Is their pain? Hell yes, but it's more pleasure than anything." I realized that my voice had turned a little gruff and I had to reel in my frustration. '*Still so protective of that whore.*' Shut the fuck up Earl! I returned my attention back to Vivian with a much lighter tone.

"And to answer your question; God yea, she was so fucking funny. She would say the funniest shit and not even crack a smile. Auntie was fair skinned, just like my mother. She had long, black hair that fell in waves down her back. Her eyes were some funny shade of purple, but sometimes they looked gray or even blue. She was beautiful, but sometimes I felt like she hated looking like that." Vivian's face was a blank slate and that had me worried.

"So, this is the woman who left you the brownstone we're staying in?"

"Yes."

"Oh." Silence

"Yeah, okay." I cleared my throat and continued on. "I had been outside working for about three hours. One of her rules was that I could not ask her for anything. If she wanted me to have something, she would offer it to me. I did not have the right to interrupt her to ask for something she obviously didn't think I needed, because if she did think that I needed it, I would have had it.

Well, like I said, it was hot as hell and I had on some shorts and a tee shirt, but both were sticking to my body and doing little to cool me down. I was just about to deal with the consequences and ask for some iced water when Auntie came out of the back door with a glass of sweet tea. I was so hot and thirsty, I almost ran up the steps to meet her on the porch. 'Where do you think you're going?' Auntie had not come to quench my thirst...she had come to teach me a lesson."

"What did she want you to learn, how to fuck an *animal*?" I could hear the malice in Vivian's voice. I didn't say anything about it, just kept on telling the story.

"Long story short...she wanted me to experience what true powerlessness felt like. Willingly relenting my control to her is one thing, but never having the choice to be in control of one's life was something completely different. She made me take all my clothes off in her backyard, then she turned her water hose on full blast and aimed it at me. I knew I could not move and I could not make a sound.

Those were her rules and those were her expectations; take whatever she gave me and do so quietly and with appreciation. At first the cold water felt amazing against my sunburned skin, but then the cooling water started to feel like liquid bullets on my back and legs and chest and ass. I couldn't even cover up my dick and balls. There was nothing I could do to defend myself against the onslaught of water.

As she sprayed me, she started talking about how all of those passive men and women in the fifties and sixties just stood there and took the water, the dogs, the humiliation and even death. She continued to taunt me verbally, abuse me physically and emasculate me until she didn't anymore." I faced Vivian and tried to gage her reaction to this, I didn't see anything in her golden eyes, just flat discs.

"I hated her so much, but I hated myself more. I let her do this to me. I continued to follow her stupid rules and continued to try and meet her expectations. My mind was numb and all I could see was my mother being beaten, raped, sodomized, forced to do all sorts of vile acts with her husband and me being forced to watch all of it. Then Auntie's voice broke through the haze and she asked me how I would take back my power if she gave me permission to do so. I didn't even have time to think of what I would do, before she said the four words that changed my life…'I give you permission'."

"What happened then?"

~22~

I took the hose from her, wrapped it around her body and pushed the end of the hose into her sex and fucked her; she came so hard she couldn't talk or hold herself up. That's when the transformation started. That was my first foray into acknowledging the Dominant I had always been.

"I spent most of that night at Auntie's house. I took care of her. Bathed her, moisturized her body, fucked her, punished her, fed her... I took care of her as if she were a child. We spent as much time talking as we did fucking. She told me I was her first lover in over 16 years. Of the six boys that she had taken in over the years, I was the only she had sex with, the others just did chores around her house. She needed me. Knowing she needed me felt like a drug being shot into my veins. I was so high...I could not believe someone as beautiful as Auntie needed *me*." I tried to quell my enthusiasm, but I fucking loved how much Auntie had needed me.

"That's the same night my mother died and I killed Earl. I left Auntie's house at about ten o'clock. I was feeling invincible. Feeling like a *man*. Feeling like if Earl fucked with me, he would be sporting a broken nose and a couple of black eyes. When I got home, something didn't feel right. I wasn't sure what it was, but I knew something was off. As soon as I stepped through the door, *Crack!* Earl hit me in the top of my head with a solid wooden baseball bat. I felt the blood running down my face and saw Earl cocking the bat back to hit me again. I grabbed the bat as he brought it down and took it away from him. It was then I noticed the dried blood splatter. I knew then he had killed my mom and she had died a horrible, painful death."

"Oh my God. That's so horrible."

"Yeah, well. I wanted him to suffer for every sadistic thing he ever did to my mom...I started bashing his head with the bat, until I could see brain matter. I killed him and didn't feel like I had done anything wrong." *Someone should thank me.*

"It was because I had finally accepted myself for what I was, a *motherfucking monster*, that I was able to do what I did. It was because Auntie showed me my power that I was able to kill that white-trash fucker and walk away."

"Do you know how to have a *normal* relationship? After all of that, John? Do you know how to be normal with a woman?"

"No and I'm not interested in a *normal* relationship. I want my lady, my fiancé, my wife to willingly submit to me. I need her to trust I will take care of all her needs. I need her to believe I will never take her further than she can go. This is what I want with you, Vivian. I want to be your Dominant. I want to take care of you and love you and make sure whatever is giving you those bad dreams at night, will never come back to hurt you."

"John. I... uh...I don't know. This is not something I wanted or needed. I don't know what to say. I. There are things in my past...things I am not ready to share with you or anyone, really. I don't think I'm able to be this person you want me to be. I'm really scared I will lose the person I'm trying so hard to become." Her breathing was coming in short burst and pants. There was a look of pure terror and confusion sifting through the beautiful sunshine and blue sky that were her eyes.

"Don't panic, Vivian. I will never ask more of you than you are willing or able to give. You set the pace for this, but I really want to try to do this with you. I'm not asking you to be anything other than what you already are; a beautiful, strong-willed, intelligent woman who is used to carrying her world on her shoulders. I don't want to take that world from you, I just want to give you a place where you don't have carry it 24/7. Do you remember the first and only time you let me taste you?"

"Yes."

"I topped you. I asked for your submission and you willingly gave it to me, that's how I knew I could share this part of myself with you."

"I did not *submit* to you. You were the one with your head between my legs, I don't recall sucking your…" Her words trailed off as she no doubt remembered her performance in the bathroom our first night in New York.

"Think back to that evening. You asked me to kiss you, I obliged. I told you what I wanted you to do and how I wanted you to do it and what did you do, Vivian?"

"I did it, but I was really turned on. That doesn't count."

"Why were you so turned on, Vivian?" My voice dropped and my posture changed subtly, but she noticed it and responded as expected.

"Because you were so…I don't know. It was. It felt good to not have to think about what I was going to let you…about what I asked you to do to me. It felt good that I could ask you to do that and you agreed to do it. I listened to you, because I wanted you to…I wanted you to be as happy with me as I was with you."

"And do you know why you wanted that for me, Vivian?"

"Why do you keep saying my name?"

"Answer the question, Vivian." I smirked at her and watched her eyes drop to her lap.

"I wanted it for you because your happiness made me

happy. Knowing that something as simple as listening to you and doing what you told me to do…knowing that it made you happy made me want to do it even more. Oh God! What's wrong with me?" Tears caught on her eyelashes and became diamonds.

"There is nothing wrong with you, Vivian. What you experienced that evening is called a power exchange. You asked me to do something for you and I said I would. That made you feel powerful. I then asked you to submit to me and you did…now, how else did you feel when you realized that doing what I wanted you to do made me want to do what you asked me to do all the more?"

"Powerful."

"Why, Vivian?"

"Because I knew that if I said stop you would. I knew if I didn't do what you asked me to do that I wouldn't get what I wanted from you. I knew I really wanted to please you because pleasing you makes me feel powerful and wanted and needed and important. This is so fucked up." She whispered the last five words, but I heard them.

"No, Vivian it isn't. It's who we are and how we are together. Tell me, how did you feel about the conversation we had before you asked me to kiss you?"

"I felt relieved that you asked me what I wanted and assured me that if nothing happened, you would still love me. I felt comfortable talking to you about sex and I have never been comfortable talking about sex…with anyone. I've never talked about sex with anyone except you."

"Good. How did you feel about what happened after you asked me to kiss your beautiful flower of life, Vivian?"

"I thought I would feel shy and ashamed, but I didn't. I

felt like I deserved to have you kiss me like that and I felt you deserved to be obeyed because you didn't ask me to return the favor…you were only asking me to do as you told me to.

I felt brave for asking and elated that you said yes. When you made me, *orgasm*…I had never experienced anything like that in my entire life and I was so grateful to you for giving me that gift that I wanted to give you me."

"Vivian. As your Dom, that is all I will ever ask you for. Let me give you the gift of power, bravery and more pleasure than you can ever imagine and in return all I want is what you are willing to surrender to me of yourself. I won't take more than you want to give and I won't ask for more than I am willing to give to you."

"I want that. Does that make me submissive?"

"No, Lovely. That makes you my submissive—noun."

"Okay."

"Okay? We won't rush it, we'll take it slow, I promise."

"I trust you, John. It's just. I need time to accept that I love you, that you love me and that you bought a ring for me after running into me at the horseshoe. I need time to accept that you seem to have a handle on your life and I have no idea what the hell I want in my life. I just need time."

"That's just it. As your Dom, I'll deal with all of that. I'll help you decide what you want in life. Be my submissive and you don't have to worry about any of that. I make the choices for you about the tedious shit and then you have the freedom to make the important choices for yourself."

"You want to make choices for me? Like what…what do you consider to be tedious shit? Her voice was high and worried.

“Tedious shit like clothes, food, where we live, how we live...the unimportant shit.”

“That *shit* is the important shit to me! What I wear, what I eat, where I live, and how I live are crucial to me.” She takes a deep breath and I watch her frustrations take shape in the dropping temperature.

“Lovely, I’m not saying that those things aren’t important. I’m saying that they are tedious. Why concern yourself with purchasing clothes, underwear, shoes, outerwear…when it will cause you stress?”

“I’m not a fucking idiot, John. I can shop for myself and not have goddamned breakdown in the store. What the hell?”

“Vivian!” Dom voice and face in full effect.

“Yes, John.” Her voice is soft and contrite and my dick is straining against my zipper. *Not the time, Jughead.*

I know you’re not an idiot, if I thought you were an idiot I would not be wasting my time with you. You are overwhelmed and out of your comfort zone; I get it, but that does not give you the right to jump down my throat because you are confused. Okay?”

“Okay.”

“Baby, this will take so much of your stress away. I can take so much of your stress away.”

“Is there anything else you want to tell me?” She dismisses the topic.

“Yes. I know you are concerned with how much I spend on you, but let me explain my financial situation to you. I am attending Carolina on a full academic scholarship. I don’t have to pay for anything. I don’t need the money at all, but the poorer people think I am, the better off I’ll be.

When my mom died, I received two insurance checks. One for my mom in the amount of two hundred and fifty thousand dollars, the other in the amount of one million dollars. She also left me the house. I made some investments and start letting that money do some of the work." I heard her sharp intake of air and smiled a little.

"A lot of shit happened between the time my mother and Earl died and the beginning of my senior year in high school. I was going to ask Auntie to move to Columbia with me while I finished my senior year and started USC. I still needed her, even though she had turned over the reins of our relationship to me. I was alone and had absolutely nobody who cared for me. After taking care of some business, I planned a romantic dinner for Auntie, whom I called Violet after becoming her Dom, to ask her if she would move to Columbia with me."

"Why did you call her Violet, was that her real name?"

"No. I called her *Violet* because she had the most amazing eyes I had ever seen…until I saw yours. Where your eyes are sunshine and blue sky with a little green grass; Violet's eyes were fields of lavender interspersed with blades of Kelly-green grass. I had never seen anything like them and I doubt I will ever see anything like them again."

Vivian had her head down and wasn't really looking at me or anything really. I took a deep breath and let the words rush out of my mouth before my heart tried to suck them back into the black hole reserved for that one thing.

"I bought Auntie a beautiful dress and shoes, and picked her up in my new Ford Mustang 5.0. I felt like such a big shot. I mean, I was a sixteen-year-old millionaire. After dinner, I planned to drive three hours to Tybee Island and ask her to come with me. My thought was that I would use the drive down to assert my dominance over her...you know, have her suck me off while I drove, slide my fingers into her pussy and get her off on the way there."

Vivian was sitting as far away from me as she possibly could in the carriage and her back was ramrod straight and the temperature dropped about forty degrees around her. *No woman wants to hear how you planned to fuck another woman, whose house you are currently trying to fuck her in. I knew you were a stupid son of a bitch.* Shut the hell up Earl. Shit, but he was right.

"Baby. I'm...uh...I'm sorry. I got caught up in the story. I didn't mean to be so insensitive. Please come back over here, it's cold and I don't want you getting sick. Come back, please?" She slowly slid across the bench seat and made her way over to me. I grabbed her hand and squeezed them in mine until she reciprocated. I could see the hurt and something else that I couldn't name blooming in her eyes. It gutted me like a fish.

"I was trying my best to get Violet in the right frame of mind while I was driving. I didn't pay attention to the road; one thing led to another and after it was all over, she was dead. The only person who gave a shit about me was dead and I had *killed* her." I took a shuddering breath and tried to blink the tears out of my eyes and swallow the tears clogging my throat. Vivian squeezed my hand and put her head on my shoulder.

"Some days later, on my seventeenth birthday, a package came to my house from Violet's attorney. She left everything she had to me. She didn't have any family, either. She loved me, Vivian. She loved me more than she had ever loved anyone else. I was also given a handwritten letter dated May of 1991. That was the first day she called me into her house. She wrote the letter after the first time she met me. In this letter, she told me she was dying of brain cancer and there was nothing that could be done to save her. She said that she wanted to spend the last couple of months of her life giving the gift of power to someone who couldn't recognize it in themselves." I couldn't help the tears that slid down my face and would have frozen on my cheeks, accept Vivian quickly wiped them away.

"She was dying and I... I was left with over seven million dollars in cash, property and other assets. I'm telling you this because I don't want you to worry about what I spend on you, I have turned that seven million into seventeen million."

I placed my right palm against her left cheek and turned her face to mine. I wanted her to be looking into my eyes when I told her the last of it.

"All I have is yours. Trust me, we will not want for anything. I promise."

"I love you, John. You are the strongest man I know and your strength will eventually be what frees me from *my* past. Let's bring in the new year." She placed the sweetest kiss on my frozen cheek and just like that, my past didn't matter. I knew she would be what I needed her to be. *I was damn sure going to be whatever she needed me to be.*

~23~

Time Square on New Year's Eve was absolutely amazing. It was everything I saw on television-only without the commercial breaks and the FCC rules that bleeped out all the drinking, cursing and blatant sexual acts that took place right out in the open. After the conversation that Vivian and I had on the way to the party, I was a little self-conscious about all the sexual stuff happening on the streets. I kept sneaking glances over at Vivian, hoping I would not see disgust on her face and thankfully, I didn't.

"So... what do you think?" I was nervous. Something wasn't sitting right with me. Vivian accepted my past too willingly. *Should I have told her about Bryan or the other shit Earl did...I don't know. No, I'll tell her someday, but not today.*

"It's beautiful, but I am freezing my ass off. Even with this overpriced coat and hat. It's cold." A shiver ran down her body and her mahogany skin had hints of red just under the surface of her cheeks and nose. It was the sexiest blush I had ever seen. I didn't even know skin so dark and creamy could blush, but like so many other unexpected things, Vivian was changing my perception.

"Do you want to get a coffee or tea?" I grabbed her gloved right hand and squeezed it in mine...I was hoping to warm her and keep her out here with me. I had always wanted to bring in the New Year in Time Square and to be here with a woman I was pretty sure I loved, made it even more special.

"No. I'm good. Where do we need to be to see Pearl Jam perform?" Her hazel eyes were shining brighter than the New Year's Eve ball. I smiled down at her and silently thanked whoever was up there for letting me bump into this girl. But, I was still nervous. Something just seemed off. Did she say she would use my strength to tell me about her past one day? *What past did she have? She never chosen a lover, but then she sucked my dick like it was second nature. A thought for another day...not now.*

"I can't wait to get you home...I really want to make love to you, Vivian. Correction. I really *need* to make love to you. Tonight. There is more I need to tell you, but words won't convey it...I have to show you." I looked at her and every part of my body that could get hard decided that moment to do so. Her eyes darkened and her lips parted. She was aroused and I was ready to forgo this whole ball dropping shit, but I knew she wanted to see Pearl Jam and I would be pissed at myself if I let my dick keep me from seeing the ball drop.

"I know we talked about us making love in New York, but I don't know if it is still something you want to do. If you feel like you need more time, than I am more than fine with that." I was anxious; although I would understand her not wanting to make love after all the shit I told her, after hearing I wanted her to be my submissive...yeah, I would totally get it if she wanted to back out of *that* deal, but God, I really wanted to her.

"No... I have been waiting for you to tell me when you were ready. After our first night…" Some guy shoved passed us and bumped into Vivian's shoulder, pushing her into me. He grabbed for her shoulders and mumbled something and just that quickly, a white-hot anger tore through me. I pulled Vivian into my side and glared at the guy. He held up his hands as if to say I don't want any trouble and began to back away.

"Are you alright?"

"Yes. I'm good. It's really crowded out here. I'm surprised that no one else bumped into us before this." *Nervous smile and giggle.*

"Yea, well. Stay closer to me, I don't want some

dickhead putting his hands on you again." Anger dripping from my words like venom.

"John. That guy didn't mean any harm. You need to calm down and just...just relax and enjoy this evening." Her voice was colored with confusion and accusation.

"I don't need you to tell me how to act. Not everyone has good intentions when it comes to a beautiful woman in the middle of a busy city street. I'm looking out for you and your safety...that's my job as your Dom." Authority dripping from my words and burning away the happy like acid.

"I never said that I would be anything other than your girlfriend and I know I didn't agree to be your submissive; whatever that means. I will not be controlled by a *boy* who lacks the self-control needed to not start a fight in the middle of Time Square on New Year's Eve." Defiance and willfulness caress her softly spoken words and race down my spine, challenging my balls to put up or shut up.

"If you want our relationship to continue, then you will agree to be my sub. This is the only kind of relationship I am interested in having." Shaking with rage and regret. I knew I had just signed her walking papers. *Shit. Stupid ego.*

"Then, take me back to your brownstone so I can pack my things and if you don't mind having your driver take me to the airport. I am ready to go home as a woman...not a fucking submissive." She made a right on 7th avenue walking towards the theatre district and away from me. I knew I had messed up and had no idea how to fix it...then her voice floated into my mind. '*Having this kind of relationship requires trust and communication. Remember John, you are asking me to relinquish the freedom of choice and control to you. I have to trust you enough to do that...I have to trust you enough to know you will not use my gift of submission against me. My submission is the most precious gift I can give you...more precious than my body, my heart or even my soul; don't abuse it.'* In that moment, I knew what I had to do…

"Vivian. Please stop. Vivian, I—I'm sorry. I didn't mean to react that way...I'm new at this. Please Vivian." She stopped at the intersection of 7th Avenue and W. 46th Street. She turned on her heel and pinned me to the cement with honey dipped daggers and just held me there. She was shaking. At first, I didn't know if it was from the cold or her fury. From the look on her face, I felt confident in saying it was the fury.

"Is that an order, sir?" Contempt pushing every word towards me.

"Vivian! Stop this and no these are not orders. I fucked up and I'm sorry, but dammit...can you stop acting like a child and talk to me?" Frustration and fear driving my words. No breaks and no way of slowing down.

"Child! There is nothing more childish than a *little boy* trying to play big boy games even when he does not have the right *tools*." Attitude scratching the surface of her beautiful voice, making everything sound harsh and ugly.

"Please stop this Vivian. I will not further engage you in this conversation. I know you feel the need to protect yourself from me and my seemingly crazy request and I get it, but I am a selfish man and I want you. I will not let you walk away from me. From us. If you are ready to return to South Carolina, then I will be returning with you. I still have an apartment in the city and we will stay there until the holidays are over." Power and composure sat on my shoulders like a mantle. I can sense her response and know she would not only talk about our relationship, but she would make love with me tonight.

"Fuck you, John. That bullshit may have worked on that weak ass old lady who let a sixteen-year-old boy fuck and control her, but trust me, I am not her and you will never tell me what to do." She turned and continued down W. 46th Street. I had no idea where she was going or what the hell I was going to do so, I ran after her and yanked her around to face me and planted a kiss on her beautiful mouth. It shut her up long enough for me to come up with a plan.

"Are you quite done? And don't you ever speak of Violet again. You don't know what the hell you're talking about. Your ire is for me, don't bring a dead woman who meant a lot to me into the shit-storm brewing between us. Alright?" Looking into her eyes and adopting my Dom stance. Immediate softening of her face, a deep breath, and then blessed silence.

"I'm sorry, I should not have spoken of Violet like that; if at all. John, I don't know how to be what you need or want. I only know how to survive and I don't want to have to survive you. I love you. I want to have my forever with you, but you scare the hell out of me and then you want this weird Dom/sub relationship.

I can't lose the part of me I have fought to have. I know you don't know my story and I am not ready to share any of it with you, but please understand...I am learning how to be me. Learning how to heal. And what you want. What you need...I can't give it to you without losing me." Crystal tears from golden eyes froze on blackberry cheeks. In that moment, she owned me.

"Baby. I love you so much, it hurts. More than anyone I've ever known, even Violet. I'm scared, too. Loving you like I do makes me vulnerable. I need control to ensure I'm safe and you're safe. I don't want to talk about this now. I can't explain myself. Vivian, please? Just come back with me, we'll bring in the New Year together and then I'll make love to you and everything will be clear." *Begging. Pleading.*

"Okay, John." Acceptance and trust bend her words.

~24~

We stayed in Time Square until the ball made it all the way to the bottom. We counted down with the all of New York and the world. We kissed and cheered and told each other how much love we had between the two of us. After staying up late every New Year's Eve watching all the happy people in New York City kissing and drinking as they ushered in another year, I finally understand how easy it is to get caught up in the euphoria of it all. I was drunk on happy and joy and most of it vicariously experienced from those around me.

"Oh my God! This is so amazing. John, in all my life...I never thought that *I* would be in New York City on New Year's Eve. I never thought I would be sharing this special time with someone I love. Thank you. If I forget to tell you later, this is the best night of my life." She had her left arm looped through my right one as she looked up into my face with the biggest smile I had ever seen. Her eyes were shining and her hair was blowing in the wind. Soft, delicate curls the color of fall leaves that framed her beautiful face and highlighted her golden gaze. She took my breath away.

"Amazing. You are amazingly beautiful. Thank you for being here with me. Thank you for staying." I leaned down to give her a soft kiss and quickly, the kiss became something different. Her lips were soft and cold. She tasted like hot chocolate and sin. I slid my tongue along the seam of her lips and she opened for me. Reminding myself to be patient, I slowly pushed my tongue into her mouth and licked across the inside of her cheek. I wanted to taste and feel every part of her mouth. She darted her tongue out and I felt it slide across mine. Something exploded in me and I lost control. I pulled her around so she was standing in front of me and then I grabbed the sides of her face in my gloved hands and held her how I wanted her and began to drive my tongue into her hot, wet mouth. She met me stroke for stroke and then we were eating at each other. I was sucking on her tongue and nibbling on her lips. She tasted so good. We were just teeth, lips, tongues and swallowed moans.

"Brownstone. Now."

"Yes. Now."

"Are you sure?"

"Yes. Don't give me time to change my mind."

"I won't stop until I'm buried inside you. There is no saying no once we cross the doorway."

"I know."

"No. Listen to me Vivian." I stop and push her slightly away from me as melted chocolate drizzled into caramel pools. "Even if you say no once we have crossed the threshold I won't stop. I will have you."

"I know. I understand. I have until we cross the door to say no."

"Please be sure. I won't be able to stop myself once we cross over. You will be mine to do with as I please. If you say yes, you are saying yes to everything. Do you understand?"

"Y-Yes. I trust you, John. I *trust* who I am when I'm with you. I'm tired of letting fear dictate how I live."

"Let's go." I grabbed her hand and guided her to the front of Rockefeller Center to wait for the car.

We waited on the driver and as soon as he stepped out of the car and opened the door for us to slide in, I extricated myself out of my good boyfriend skin and took a deep breath, reveling in the freedom my Dom skin afforded me. I looked at Vivian.

Tonight, I would start training her to please me... to be my sub.

"Vivian?" I let the question of her name linger in the air between us. I wanted her to be a little on edge. I needed her uncomfortable, a little anxious and confused.

"Are you consenting to being my sub?"

"I—I don't know. I just know that I want you and if that means I have to be your sub to have you, then I guess I am consenting to be your sub." Her eyes remained lowered.

"Good. I am pleased you have consented. Before we start, I need to clear some things up for you. Okay?"

"Yes." Her expression deadpan and uncompromising.

"In order for our relationship to work, you have to trust me and I have to trust you. Your submission is a gift to me, Vivian. I will cherish and protect your gift every day of my life. I don't ever want to do anything to break your trust in me or abuse your gift of submission." I stroke over her knuckles with my thumb to reassure her of my love and commitment for and to her. "To ensure neither of these two things happen, we have to communicate openly. You must be willing to tell me any and everything that is going on with you. I have to trust that you will always be honest with me and you can be sure I will never lie to you and I will respect and take care of you and all your needs. Understand?"

"Yes. I I get it." Her voice was flat and insincere. *It made me a little angry*. I turned immediately to face her in the back of the 1993 black Lincoln MK 8. I narrowed my eyes almost to slits and leaned in close to her. So close, I felt the heat coming off of her body. My lips were a harsh scowl across my face. I glared at her, letting her see the displeasure in my eyes as I spoke to her in a cacophonous whisper. My words were laconic. There was none of the warmth in my voice; only disapproval and disappointment.

"When I address you from this moment forward, you will call me Sir. That is with a capital "S". I expect you to mess up, because you don't know what the hell you have agreed to, but you said yes and that means we have a verbal contract and that means you are mine. In and out of the bedroom. So, when I asked you the question, your correct response should have been what, Viv?"

"Yes. Sir?" Her voice still had a slight edge to it. *She's going to have to work on that.*

"Don't question it. I have told you what I expect and you will meet that expectation. Do you understand? My voice deeper, harsher; this is my Dom voice and I see her relenting.

"Yes, Sir." Her voice stronger and surer. I allow myself one quickly fading smile.

"Good girl," I say with a softer, warmer voice. I let my words caress her and my eyes shine with approval and acceptance. I watch as a small smile graces her lovely face, but it is gone before she realizes that she is pleased with my approval.

"When I ask or tell you to do something, you should respond in the affirmative. Even when you are not sure you want to do it because you have to trust me, Vivian." Authority dripping from my voice.

"Yes, Sir." Her voice is soft and compliant. She wants another approving praise from me. I will make her work and wait for it.

"Now. I will assign you a 'safe word', this word is to be used only when you are reaching a point in our play where you just can't take anymore. The moment you say the word, I will stop doing whatever I am doing with you. But once the word is uttered, I will not resume whatever was happening. Be careful with this word. Your safe word should not be used just because. Your training will be difficult. I will push you to see how far I can take you in certain things and you will learn how to please me. In the end, Vivian, you will set the pace for how this relationship goes. Do you understand?"

"Yes, Sir."

"Good girl. I am so proud you have consented to be my sub. You will not be in gilded cage, you will have your regular life and I will have mine, but when we are together...*wherever* we are together, you are my sub and I am your Dom. Regardless of what I ask of you, you will do it immediately. I will never misuse your trust."

"Thank you, Sir."

"God Vivian. You're making me hard."

"What don't you want me to do with and to you; physically and mentally, sexually?"

"I don't want to have anal sex with you...something about the thought of that...I just know I do not want to have it." Her head shaking back and forth while big fat tears slipped down her rosy cheeks.

"My heart. What are the tears for? Talk to me. Tell me what's making you cry."

"I. Sir, there are things I have...seen. Dark things that wake me up at night in cold sweats, things that cause me to lose my breath when I think about them. I will tell you, someday, but for now...just trust me. Please, Sir."

Wiping a tear from her left cheek; she leans into my touch and takes a deep breath. "I will trust you and you will tell me about these things when you are ready, but for now, no anal play. I am fine with that."

"Thank you, Sir." Her eyes are kept down, looking at her basket weave fingers. One last tear falls into the basket that are her hands and her shoulders relax.

"I'm going to tell you to do something. Remember, don't talk back to me, and do as I say immediately. Understand?"

"Yes, Sir."

"Good girl. You look so beautiful. I can smell how wet you are for me, it's making me hard. You smell like every favorite meal I've ever had." The driver cleared his throat and rolled up the privacy glass. I was so caught up in the moment, I hadn't realized the damn thing was open.

"Thank you, Sir.

"Remove your shoes, tights and panties."

"What?" Horror and fear drench her words. *Chastisement must be immediate and swift.* I reach out and grab her hand, squeezing the spot between her thumb and pointer finger with enough pressure to cause her discomfort. With gritted teeth and a growl in my throat, I reprimand her for her mistake.

"Shit! John. What the hell do you think you're doing? I am not a child, you don't have the right to fuck…" I grabbed her lips between my thumb and pointer finger and looked her in the eyes. She wilted under my gaze and finally lowered her eyes and relaxed her face to something beautifully contrite.

"Yes, dammit. You are like a child when it comes to this and I have every right as your Dom to punish you and correct your behavior. It is part of the training, Vivian. I have to make sure you know how to please me and you know what I expect from *and* of you. I need you to trust that I know what you can take and what you are willing to give. My corrective actions will be as simple as a look or as physical as a spanking. I will never go farther than you are able to go. Never. That's why you have to trust me and tell me the truth at all times."

"Sir. May I speak to you?" Voice low and quiet. *Her submission was making my balls heavy. She had no idea what her submission meant to me.*

"I believe you owe me an apology." No warmth. She had to atone for her mistake.

"Sir. I am sorry for my outburst. I was out of line." *Perfect. She will be a perfect sub and partner.*

"You may address me, now. My lovely girl." She knows that she is forgiven. Small upward pulls tug on the corners of her full lips, but she doesn't allow them to form a smile.

"I am afraid of this agreement. I don't want to give up my freedom. I just got it." *What the fuck does that mean? Just got her freedom from whom? From what?* "I want to be what you want and need me to be, but Sir, I am scared right now. I need my independence. I need to be able to make my own choices and do what I believe is best for me. It does not sound like this *relationship,* will allow me to do that." She was out of breath and winded by the time she was done. The look on her face broke my heart. I knew that look. It was the same look my mother wore. A look that said I have no power. I am a slave. *How do I reassure her that this relationship will not be like that?*

"Don't be afraid of what I'm offering you, sweet girl. As your Dom, I am all things to you. Your protector, provider, shoulder to cry own, joke-teller to make you smile. In this relationship, I will make all of the difficult decisions and free you up to deal with the ones that mean more to you than paying bills and deciding on where and what we eat. Just the opposite of what you think will happen is going to take place.

As my sub, you will experience a freedom you have never known. Freedom to explore who you really are and what you really want in life. You don't have to worry about where you will stay for holidays, how you will get what you need as the seasons change. All you have to do is study, make good grades, graduate and work if you want to. I will take care of all of your needs. I will set you free, Vivian." *Shit. She's on the fence. I don't have anything else to say.*

"I want that. I want that more than you will ever know. Where do I sign?" A small smile kisses her gentle mouth.

"Nowhere to sign, but I do need to address your previous outburst. I will correct you when you are out of line and discipline as I see fit. You will accept your punishment and learn how I want you to behave. Don't hesitate or ever question me when I tell you to do something. Do it quickly and without complaint. Do you understand me?" I slipped back into my freezing voice and allowed my frostbitten words to kiss her cheeks and temples. I saw the moment she felt the lash of cold wind.

"Yes."

I cut my eyes to hers and leaned into her lithe body. "Yes what?"

"Yes, Sir?"

"Don't question it. You have to learn to trust yourself enough to know that who you are is all I need you to be and that I will never find displeasure in you. Trust yourself enough to believe that you deserve all the wonderful experiences and gifts I will give you. Don't question it. Know it."

"Yes, Sir."

“Good girl. Now. It seems you still have on your shoes, tights and panties.”

I watch her bend down to remove her shoes and she placed them neatly on the floor. Next, her shaking hands reach under her wool skirt and begins to tug her tights down over her beautiful ass and thighs and off her feet. She methodically rolls them into a ball and stuffs them in her right shoe. The last piece of clothes to come off are her panties. They are black cotton bikini briefs with a small trim of black lace around the waist and leg holes. They should not have been sexy, but damn if looking at the simple panties didn’t have my dick straining against the zipper of my pants. Once the panties were neatly rolled and placed in her left shoe, she fixed her skirt and sat facing me with her hands in her lap. Twisting them into that lovely basket she tends to weave.

“Place your right foot in my lap.”

At the first touch of my thumbs to the pressure points on the bottom of her foot right below the center of her heel, she moaned and looked wide-eyed at me. I smiled inside. She didn’t know her foot could make her feel so good. She knew so little and yet, something about the way she looked at me, or responded to somethings I said, told me she was not as innocent as I may think her.

~25~

The car pulled up to the brownstone and the driver opened the back-passenger door where I waited to get out. I told him I would get Ms. Bruno. I opened her door and bent down to lift her from the car. She carried her shoes, with her tights and panties tucked into the toe, in her hand. She wrapped her left arm around my neck and her right hand dangled at her side. My chest burned with what I felt for her. Looking at her, knowing what I was going to do to her this night, made my body tense up and refuse to let my breath pass through my lungs. She kept her eyes lowered and her head down. *She was such a natural submissive.*

We got to the door, and I placed her bare feet on the stoop and got my keys out to unlock the door. I'd given the staff the next week off...I had plans and they did not require an audience. I hoped when Vivian and I left New York, we would leave as Dom and sub. With proper training, one week would be more than enough time to introduce her to this lifestyle; however, I would invest the rest of my life in this relationship if that's what it took.

"Are you hungry, Vivian?" *I wanted there to be no room for doubt that she had my full attention at all times.*

"No…" Paused and with a small shake of her head, a correction. "...Um. No, Sir."

"Good girl, Vivian. I like that you corrected yourself. You continue to surprise me." I notice she has not moved from the spot I placed her in front of the door when I carried her in. A small smile danced across my mouth, she makes me happy. "Come...let's have some tea and talk about some things you can expect to happen in the course of the next week. If you still say yes, then we will begin your training tonight." I held out my hand to her and she placed her long, delicate fingers around my larger ones and walked behind me...head and eyes down...silent in her movement. *She needs to tell me her story, it's almost like she has been trained to be a sub by someone else. But who? Who could have had my Vivian?*

"Sit."

She sat down at the table and rested her hands in her lap. She still hadn't looked up or raised her head. *Odd. She is so natural at this.*

"You can look at me as well as speak to me. What are you thinking about, Vivian?"

"I'm just trying to process what has changed in our relationship and why I didn't see this in you before this trip." Her voice devoid of emotion; giving nothing away. She spoke as if she were reading the ingredients from a box of bran flakes.

"Tell me about the perceived changes in our relationship and what is it that you see in me now that surprises you?" I busy myself with making our tea. Absentmindedly, I place a small plate of snickerdoodles in the center of the table and slide a cup and saucer over towards her.

"I really enjoyed the easiness of us. There was no pressure to be or do anything...it was just easy and light. You didn't make demands on my time, my body, my behavior...for the first time in my life, I was free to be myself. I didn't get enough time to explore who that person really was...you know?

I didn't have enough time to see who she could become. I already miss who I saw her becoming, but I'm so far gone with you... I can't walk away from this. From you or from us." One tear, thick as oil, meandered its way down her wind burned cheek. Something caught in my chest and threatened to choke the life from me at the sight of it.

"I don't want to take the easiness away from us. I need it as much as you do. It's still just me and you, Viv." I had resorted back to my normal self and she noticed the difference in my tone and in the way I moved. I saw her shoulders visibly relax as she exhaled for what looked like the first time in a long while.

"I don't know any other way to be with a woman. This is all I know...all I can give. I don't want to crush you, Vivian. I want to free you so that you can be who you really want to be. You know?" I heard the confusion in my voice and something in me felt week for trying to explain myself, but I knew if I was going to have her the way I wanted her...the way I needed her; I would have to make her understand. *Wait...who the hell made demands on her time, body and behavior? What are you keeping from me, Vivian?*

"I know, John." She slid her eyes over to me trying to gauge if she had made some mistake...I let it slide, because she needed me to.

"I know what you want and I even understand why you need the confinement of this kind of relationship, I just wish you didn't. I have fallen in love with you and now I won't be able to show you unless I have your permission." Staring at the steam rising from her cup of tea. Eyes absent of life and light. She looked so different, I didn't like the look.

"Do you think I feel anything less for you? I can't see me without you, but I can't show you how I feel if we aren't in this type of relationship. I need the control. I need to know that I can keep you safe, make you happy and well…take care of you." My mind flashed back to the image of my mother's body lying in the middle of her bed; bloodied, bruised and broken. Her once beautiful eyes, flung open in terror and her mouth twisted in pain. Brains, grey and red, lay beside her gaping head. "I have to know you are protected and no one can get to you.

That no one can hurt you, ever again."

"What?"

"What?"

"What do you mean, no one can hurt me ever again?"

"Oh...nothing. I didn't mean to say ever again. I was just..."

"John, I trust you. I love you desperately, but I am scared to death of becoming a shadow without substance. No purpose. Why would you want me then? I would only be a puppet, a doll for you Living to serve only your needs. I don't want that for myself I want more. I want to breathe. On. My. Own." Each word punctuated with a slap of her flat palm to her chest. She echoed my feelings perfectly. I knew what she needed...a reason to take a breath, a reason to exhale and breathe again. I knew exactly how to help her do that. Auntie taught me well. I would take her gift of submission and in turn, give her the gift of freedom.

"I want those things for you, too. Vivian...let's forget about all of the Dom and sub shit. At least for tonight. For tonight, I just want to take you upstairs, get naked in the shower, and then find myself deep inside you. We can talk about all this other shit later. I need you and I'm going to make you feel so good that *whoever* hurt you...will be erased from your mind." I got up and reached my large hand out to her, she gently placed her shaking hand in mine and flashed me a shy smile. *She's so damned beautiful...it makes me crazy thinking about someone else having her. Did she say that she was still a virgin or that she had never chosen a lover?*

"Vivian. I know someone hurt you...and they hurt you badly. I know that whoever did that to you, took away your power to choose what would happen to you, when and with whom. I don't want to do that with you, ever. I wish I knew who did it. Who took your right to choose away? Will you tell me?"

"I can't. If I ever told you...that would be the end of us. Of my smile...my joy."

"There is nothing you can do or say that will ever make me love you less."

"I have a hard time loving me, John and I know what happened. I hate me. I *hate* all that I am... all the horrible things that created me. I don't even remember who I was before the terrible things...it's like I didn't even exist until the terrible things started happening." Tears trickled, unchecked down her cheeks even as her bare feet stood firmly on the stairs. She was trapped in her own personal hell. I tugged at her hand and continued to lead her upstairs towards the master bed and bath.

"I. We will get through this, I promise." *I have to make her my sub... she will be healed, her fractures, mended. I will break her and then rebuild her. She will become something altogether whole and beautiful.*

"Get undressed and meet me in the shower in five minutes."

"Yes, Sir."

"No. Vivian. It's just you and me. Call me John or asshole as you sometimes feel the need to do." A small smile cracks her beautiful mouth in two half-moons. She was so lovely. So broken.

"I'll see you in five minutes, John." My name was a small whisper on her lips. She broke my heart and I felt humbled.

***

Vivian must have been standing in the door watching me move around in the bathroom for a short eternity, because I jumped when I turned away from the deep breaths of steam exhaled from the shower and caught her eyes staring into my soul, or so it seemed. She was naked and beautiful. I could gaze at her all day. At 5'11", Vivian was a stunning specimen of womanhood. She was thin without being emaciated. Her long legs were toned with skin pulled tightly across lean muscle. Her flat stomach was defined, but not overly so...she had the tone of a six pack, with the softness of woman. There was a simplicity to the curve of Viv's breast. From the side, a perfect upward arch met a perfect slope and came together to form the most beautiful nipples I had ever seen. She had a graceful neck that begged me to sink my teeth into it. The most exquisite feature that Vivian had was her face. High cheekbones, delicately defined jaw line with soft and feminine mouth.

Everything about her was perfect...well almost everything. Where her thighs and hip joined, there was what looked like scars left from deep scratches or *screwdrivers?* The scars were present on both sides, just a shade or so lighter than her beautiful skin. The weird thing about those scars is that they were perfectly symmetrical. Whatever had caused them to appear on her flawless skin, had been apportioned in precise measurements. Round scars vandalized the vertebrate of her spine; starting with the thoracic and stopping at the lumbar. I counted seventeen in all. She never answers me when I ask her about them, but I hope one day, she will trust me enough to share how they got there.

"So. Do you like something you see?" I asked her as I turned around to face her, completely nude. I was so hard for her, I thought I was going to come just from smelling her arousal. I allowed a small smile to play at the corners of my mouth when I noticed her eyes sweep over my body. *Hell yeah!*

She liked what she saw. She couldn't take her eyes off of my dick...she was basically panting and drooling over the damn thing. Good signs...both of them.

"Yea, the shower feels just the right temperature. After standing out in that cold night air, I am still freezing. My nipples are so hard, they could probably cut glass." She flashed a cheeky grin at me as she slowly walked towards me; hips swaying seductively she allowed her nipples to rub across my back as she stepped into the shower. *This little minx is going to be the death of me.*

"Yea. It was pretty cold out there tonight. Does explain a lot." I realized I had nothing clever to say. I opened the shower door and stepped into a soft porn scene that made every part of my body that wasn't hard, tighten up. I felt my balls draw closer to my body, my own nipples beaded into hard little points and my skin suddenly felt too small for me. Vivian stood under the water, covered in soap, her hands moving slowly over her breast and flat stomach towards her perfectly shaved pussy. She had her head thrown back and the water ran in small rivulets down her sensuous neck and caressed her nipples before running over her stomach and onto her thighs. Thighs that made me imagine what it would feel like to have them wrapped around my waist squeezing me as I thrust deeply into the wet heat of her sex over and over as her nails scored my back.

Before I knew what I was doing, I had my right hand wrapped around my dick eyes closed, mouth opened and fist pumping hard and fast in the race to come. I needed relief, badly. Just as I start to spurt all over her stomach; I heard her scream my name in horror and disgust, I was made painfully aware of what I had done. "Shit. Baby, I'm sorry. Wait, let me clean you up. Don't go. Wait, Viv. Shit!"

~26~

Before I could grab her right arm to keep her in the shower with me, she had one foot on the thick bath mat just outside the shower and her left arm resting on the wall closest to the shower head. I was so embarrassed, I didn't want her to stay, but I couldn't let her leave thinking whatever she was thinking about me.

"Vivian. Don't walk away from me."

My voice was a softly spoken command and she had no choice other than to obey. So, she stood stark still in her movements. Her foot hovered in midair, her hand barely resting on the shower wall and her breath stopped in mid exhale. She didn't move...couldn't move. I had not given her permission to do so. Vivian had been someone's submissive before, but whose and why did she not tell me.

"Go sit on the bed, just as you are. I will bring you a towel and we will talk about what just happened. Do you understand, Vivian?"

"Yes, Sir."

I quickly turned the water off and wrapped a small towel around my waist, covering the offending member of my body and grabbed a big, warm, fluffy towel from the warming drawer for Vivian. When I reach her sitting on the bed with her head and eyes looking at her hands folded in her laps, her wet hair hanging in large chunks around her shoulders and down her back, and silent tears streaming down her cheeks; I felt most of my heart break for her. I unwrapped my small towel from my waist and knelt before her. I lifted her head up using my pointer and middle fingers so that I could wipe the tears away. Then I asked her to stand for me, she did so without protest. After prying her hands apart, I wiped the drying semen from her stomach and trailed worshipping kisses along her beautiful skin, apologizing between each soft touch of my lips to the soft skin on her abdomen. The last thing I did was asked her to sit down on the edge of the bed, giving her a choice by telling her she didn't have to if she didn't want to. She chose to sit on the edge...she chose to gift me with her submission.

"Vivian, I want to talk about what happened in the shower and why you reacted the way you did and why you responded the way you did when I told you what to do afterward. Okay?"

"Okay."

"And then, Vivian. I really want to make love to you. I understand if you don't want to...I mean, if what happened in the shower grossed you out or made you not trust me or something...I get it, but...God, I really would love to be inside you tonight, this morning...I really would love to know what you feel like wrapped round my dick."

There was no command in my voice. I was talking to her just as I would talk to anyone else I would ask to get into my bed. This would not be a night for us to share as Dom and sub. No... this would be a night spent as a woman and a man sharing each other's' bodies. I have to have her. I have a lifetime to have her as my sub, tonight I want her as a woman to have and explore. Someone beautiful to fuck, hard and without mercy. Someone to pound my dick into and make scream and cry out for me. I'll make love to her later… for right now, I'll fuck her until she screams for me to stops while her body begs for me to keep fucking her.

After wrapping her in a warm towel and watching her choose a small corner of the bed to perch on, I came to rest beside her on the bed. I let my bare thigh touch hers. She didn't jump or take in a deep breath of air, both good signs, she was not skittish. *Good, I didn't need her afraid of me, I needed her to trust me and know I would never hurt her beyond anything she could take.*

"Now. Vivian, tell me why you reacted the way you did when you saw me pleasuring myself and then when I came all over your lovely belly?" I did not look at her, left my voice impassive and left a wide-open space for her to fill as she wished. The space was safe and inviting.

"I—I wasn't expecting to see you doing that to yourself. I mean. I knew you wanted me but, I didn't think that you would do that in front. I didn't think you would…"

Her stuttering and dancing around words were beginning to grate on my nerves.

"What? You didn't think the sight of you naked and all the ways I had been thinking about fucking you wouldn't drive me to stroking my dick until I came? You are a fucking goddess, Vivian. I have seen and known many beautiful women, but none of them come close to you. Everything about you is uncompromisingly perfect."

I watch as a lovely cherry-plum blush moved up her sexy neck and over her jaw unto the apples of her cheeks. That blush would surely put any white woman ever celebrated for her *beautiful* blush to shame.

"I am not one bit ashamed that you saw me *pleasuring* my body in that way, because it was either take care of myself in that moment or do something stupid I would regret for the rest of my life. Given how precious you are to me, I took the lesser of two evils. My desire for you lies somewhere between insatiable and sadistic. The insatiable I'm sure will be great for both of us; I'm not so sure how we will fair with the sadistic.

I don't think my need will be that great for either of us,

but it is what I know and how I know to experience pleasure and how I know to give and share pleasure. I want to share my world with you, but I don't want to destroy you and something in your reaction tells me that sharing my predilections with you at this moment would do just that. Destroy you." Her eyes were downcast and she refused to look up at me. *What the fuck was she thinking? I couldn't tell if she was afraid and ready to run or if she was a little turned on. Damn it to hell.*

"Say something Vivian, you didn't answer my question." I kept my Dom out of my voice and left everything command free...I really just wanted to talk to her like we used to talk, easy like we always had.

"I don't even know what your question was, John." Her voice was no stronger. In fact, she sounded breathier...more turned on than ever. *What the hell. Was this turning her on? I was tempted to just put this whole talking thing on the back burner and just fuck her, but I needed to know where her head was before I made her lose her mind.*

"The question was, why did you react the way you did when you saw me masturbating in the shower and then when I came on your stomach?" I kneeled in front of her, parting her knees and scooted in the space I had made between her legs, casually draping my arms over her knees where I began rubbing small circles on the outside of her thighs with my thumbs. I looked into her caramel colored eyes and waited for her to answer my question. *Fuck, she was so damn beautiful, it made my heart hurt to look at her There's something unreal about her, it was as if she had no beginning to taint her and would never know an end.*

"John…" Her words trailed off and her little pink tongue darted out and licked her bottom lip. I was immediately hard.

"John there are things about me I just don't want to ever have to think about again. Horrible things done to, in front of and with me by horrible people I don't want to...I don't. I can't talk about. You are the first man to look at me like you want more from me than just what's between my legs. With you, I have a choice." She dropped her lids and shook her head as if trying to clear her thoughts.

"In the shower, I just didn't feel like I would have a choice. You wanted me *too* much. You didn't look like you would be able to stop yourself if you got close to me, and you looked like you would just take whatever you wanted from me. Take my choice away from me, again." Her eyes were rimmed in red and oil-slick tears threatened to topple over the top of the puffy rims. I reached up and ran the index finger of my left hand under her left eye and down the delicate line of her jaw, she let one than two tears fall onto my large fingers.

"Vivian. Look at me. I do want more than what you have between your legs. I want all of you. I love you. I have loved you since the day I knocked you over in the horseshoe. I have not been able to get you out of my mind. Fuck, out of my heart since that day. I have wanted you in my life, my arms, and I won't lie, my bed since that day." I had to stop and take a breath, calm myself the fuck down. I was still hard from earlier. We need to get dressed, before I take both of our choices away from us. I looked up into her summer time eyes and confessed, "I'm so hard right now, and I may have to go take care of this shit again in the bathroom before we continue this conversation."

"I can help you with that. I mean if you want me to, John. I know that you are suffering. Frankly, so am I. Please can we talk later. I wonder what it would feel like to have a man suck on my nipples and squeezed them hard enough to hurt but still feel good, too. John, can you do that to my nipples? I've never had toys or other things I've read about inside me, but

John can you do that to me and not hurt me?"

It was something in her voice that made me want to love her forever. In that one moment, I knew that I would. Knew that I would love her forever.

"Vivian, I will train you to be my sub, because I need you to be obedient in all ways, in all things, but for tonight, for now I just want to make love with you. Is that okay?"

"Yes, that's fine."

"Good. Listen. You are going to have to *guide* me and let me know what feels good and what doesn't feel good. You have to be honest with me. If something I do to you hurts or makes you feel uncomfortable, let me know immediately. We will not use safe words, yet. You only need to say stop or no and I will stop, okay?"

"Okay." She nodded her understanding.

"Now, we've tried some things before. I've made you come with my hands and mouth; although, not aggressively. I would like to take you a little farther tonight. I would also like to pound my dick into your beautiful pussy. We started birth control two months ago and you have been taking them, even with that, if you want me to still use some type of prophylactic, I will. It's up to you." I made sure to keep all traces of my Dom out of my voice, something about that part of me made her so compliant and I didn't want that from her the first time we made love. I wanted to know who she was in bed. I wanted her to be as wild as I thought she would be when given the opportunity to make her own decisions. Something told me those beautiful tiger eyes were not as tamed as they appeared to be and I wanted to let the beautiful pussy out to play; at least for a little while.

"No John. I want to feel you skin to skin. I only have one request. Please don't try anything with my—um. I'm not really into um...oh God…" She took a huge breath and blew it out quickly, her eyes rolling back into her head betraying her frustrations. "I don't do anal play or sex, John. That's one thing I won't back down from, okay?" She tried really hard to sound confident, but on the end, her voice wavered and I could hear the fear and embarrassment in her voice.

"I remember you saying that earlier. I won't lie, I really enjoy anal sex and hope that one day you will come to enjoy it, too; but for now we will leave it alone. Will you one day tell me why you don't want to indulge?" *Somebody messed Vivian up really bad, I intend to take a look when I get back there tonight...this morning. She won't tell me, but I will find out who hurt her.*

"Yea. Some day."

"Are you sure you're ready for this?" I asked as I grabbed her hand and pulled her towards me. My eyes never left hers, I needed her to know that I saw her completely.

"The only thing I'm sure of is that I love you and whatever you want is exactly what I want."

~27~

We were already sitting on the bed, we were already naked and I was already painfully aroused. The light scent of jasmine and feminine arousal perfumed the air in the bedroom and made it pretty obvious that Vivian was more than ready to do more than talk about what was about to happen. She was so beautiful, there was a vulnerability in her eyes that made me want to take care of her and make this first time for us incomparable; to start erasing every bad memory she had that made her so reticent about being with me...about giving herself over to me completely.

"Vivian, I want to see you. Will it bother you if the lights are on?"

"No. I'll be fine with the lights on...just...yes, that's fine." She smiled quickly and looked down at her intricate basket weave hands. *I wonder if her shyness could be explained away by the scarification on her thighs and back.* I thought they were beautiful; however, I know that they did not come from a beautiful place in her life. I looked at her as I had formulated an idea in my head. I hoped this would not make her bolt, but would make her uncross her knees as my knees were uncrossed

"Are you sure? We don't have to leave the overhead lights on. What about the bathroom lights on with the door ajar?" I got up, my nude body on display for her, showing no shame or embarrassment. I was proud for her to see me naked, proud for her to see my erection and how much I wanted her. When I returned to the bed, all of the lights were off, except for the bathroom lights, which were behind an almost closed door and provided only a small sliver of light into the almost completely black room. Just enough light to see shadows and silhouettes

"Is this better? I want you to be comfortable. Give me your hands."

"Where are you? I can't see a foot in front on me."

"Oh, now I'm too dark to see in a dark room?" Humor was evident in my voice. I moved three steps towards her and I felt my penis brush across her lips. She gasped and I smiled as her hands moved to grab my hips. I pulled back just a little. I did not want a blow job just yet, but was glad that she was so willing to give me one.

"Can't see me, but I guess you can find my dick just find in the dark, huh?" I felt the smile that played on her beautiful lips as they curved up and kissed the head of my throbbing cock.

"Keep that up and this will be over before we even get started. Where are your lovely hands, Vivian? Give them to me, I want to hold them, now." She placed her long, delicate fingers inside of my larger, unforgiving ones and I closed my hands tightly around hers. I pulled her from the bed and the towel fell from her body just as I hoped it would. I watched as her beautiful hazel eyes stayed locked on my own and she took the necessary steps to close the distance between us so our bodies meld together. All of her soft, female parts lined up perfectly with my hard, male parts and all I could think about was stretching her out on that king-size bed and fucking her into another week, but I also wanted to savor this meal...feast slowly on her and enjoy her sweetness.

"Vivian. You are indeed made for me. You belong to me. You. Are. Mine. Forever. Nobody. Else. Will. Ever. Have. You." I meant each word I said. I punctuated each word with a soft and gentle bite to her neck...I had to start marking her immediately. I had to start letting people know that Vivian belonged to me, that if anyone so much as looked at her, I had the right to fucking kill them and I would not hesitate to do so.

She is mine, to do with as I please. "I am going to take such good care of you, Vivian. We are going to be so good for each other. Can you see how good we're going be together? Me taking care of you, looking out for you, taking care of every need you may have, ensuring that every desire you have is made available to you.

Vivian, I will worship you with all I have and all I am, will I punish you...yes, but I will teach you to love it and you will look forward to the punishments as much as you do the love making and getting rewarded for pleasing me." At that moment, I heard a small gasp of her breath and her body tensed up a little. I knew she was going to have a problem with the punishment, but I could get her through that, just like Auntie got me through it. Not all punishments had to be painful. I hope my next words would put her to rest.

"Don't worry, I have a feeling you will receive far more rewards than punishments. Vivian, I love you so much, I can't wait to make love to you." I had been licking her neck and leaving small bites along a hot path to her mouth. In between my licks, kisses and bites, I repeatedly rubbed her body in places I knew would flood her pussy with sweet cream she would want me to lap away later on. The rough pads of my thumb found their way to the sensitive nipples of her breast, my fingers found a scorching pathway to her amazing abs and her sexy little belly button that was obviously an androgynous zone for her. When I rubbed my thumb over it, she let out a small yelp and a quick breath.

"Lay in the middle of the bed Vivian. Spread your legs for me. I want to look at you for a minute. Maybe for a lifetime. Who the hell knows? I could gaze upon your beautiful sex forever and never discover all of its mysteries. Fuck, you're so beautiful." She crawled on the bed like some kind of sexy panther. *God, I just wanted to jump on her and dive right inside her wetness.*

"Like this, John?" Her voice was a question and her body was the answer...she looked so damn perfect laying on the bed with her leg wide open and her breast standing at attention...everything about her called to me on some carnal level. I felt more animal than human with her. I saw a timid finger dip between her wet, shining folds and began to rub a hardened nub of pleasure...it appeared that she couldn't wait to get to the big O either. I smiled and shook my head. "Not yet, Vivian. When you come, I will get you there. Remove your finger from your beautiful pussy. I will not allow you to touch yourself tonight, understand?" Slowly her hand moved away from her glistening violet petals and the look on her face spoke of her disappointment. There was a little pout where her full, smiling lips used to be and a furrowed brow where a perfect arch once was. It was so cute, I almost told her to continue as she was, but I made it a mission to never go back on my words. *Just the way I was.*

I crawled onto the bed and settled between her legs, she spread them even wider in anticipation of what, I don't know. *Me, was she waiting for me, hoping that I would fuck her? Yes...My Vivian wanted me as much as I wanted her to want me.* I started at her ankles and worked my way up the inside of her legs and stopped at her knees where I took special care to lift as I kissed my way up her toned thighs toward all that cream her body had been making for me.

"Vivian. Either you're cold, scared, or really ready for me to taste you, because you are shaking like a leaf down here. Which one is it?" Her voice came out just as shaky as her legs were.

"Well, I'm not cold or scared, so I guess that means I'm ready for you to taste me." Her voice was still shaky.

"Are you sure about that. Your voice does not sound like you're ready at all. Are you scared of what I'm going to do to you, Vivian?" I asked her as I let my index finger slide from the top of her clit to the end of her opening and back up again in a slow and lazy sweep. It was nice to hear her voice catch and shutter on my way back up.

"No... I'm not *scared.* John. I'm. Not. Oh...*God.* I'm ready for you."

On the next sweep down, I let the one rigid digit slip into her creamy, warmth. I had entered her this way before, but for some reason, this felt so *different*. It felt like unlocking a treasure I never had the honor of seeing before. I felt like I was coming home. "Christ, Viv. You're so wet!" I couldn't keep the amazement out of my voice. I knew she would be, but to feel her tight, warm walls that wet around my finger made me so hard."

"I can't help it, I want you."

"I don't want you to help it, Vivian. I want you wet for me all the damn time. Just like this." I moved my finger in and out of her wet channel, slowly...back and forth. I added another and then another. After adding the third, I watched as her back arched off the bed and her hips pumped up and down in time with the movements of my fingers as I searched out her G-spot just on the front wall of her pussy behind her clit.

"Look at me Vivian." The command was obvious in my voice even though I barely spoke above a whisper. I know she heard me because her eyes popped opened and she locked her caramel gaze onto my chocolate stare. There were small pearls of sweat dancing across her forehead, her beautiful full lips were opened in silent praise, her hands gripped the duvet...she was so close to coming. I knew from other times when I had made her come with my mouth or hands. I did not want her to come like that this time. I wanted her to start learning to control her climaxes. When Vivian came, it was like watching the most destructive nuclear explosion detonate in the most beautiful work of art. Every time she came was like the first time it ever happened for her. It was life affirming.

"I know you are close, but whatever the fuck you do. Don't you dare come. I know you want it. It's so close you can see it and smell it and taste it. Don't reach for it."

"How. D--D-d-d-do I. Oh...Do I St--Sto…? Her legs were shaking, hell her entire body was shaking. Tears was running down her ravished face and she was wound up so tight, she looked like she was going to explode if she didn't come.

"Breath. In through your nose and out through your mouth. Keep your eyes on me and focus on your breath. I promise, it will be worth it." She worked so hard to focus her eyes on me and then to gain control of her breath. I stilled my fingers inside her, but left all three of them where they were. Rigid, unyielding reminders of who and how I would be in her life. Her breathing slowed down and her back relaxed ever so slightly onto the bed, it was at that moment that I started to remove my fingers from her garden. One at time. They dripped with her essence; I took my time and licked her flavor from my fingers.

"You taste so good, Vivian. I will never tire of having your taste on my tongue or the scent of you all over me. Everything about you is perfect for me. How are you doing up there?" My words were accompanied by two freshly licked fingers sliding in and out of her still sopping, slit. Immediately, her back bowed off the bed. Her breathing hitched and soft moans left her throat. I loved the way she reacted to my touch. But this was about teaching her a lesson and about taking her somewhere she had never been before.

"Vivian. Vivian." I had to call her name twice to bring her back to me. I could feel her walls tightening around me in anticipation for a climax. Her pussy got so hot and tight when she was getting ready to come. *I can't fucking wait to feel her walls squeeze around my dick as I'm pounding the perfect climax out of her.* Vivian's eyes opened with recognition and locked onto mine, immediately, she began breathing slowly through her nose and exhaling from her mouth. She never broke her gaze. *Such a perfect submissive. She's so fucking smart...tell her one time, she's got it.*

"Good girl, Vivian. I'm so proud of you. That's perfect. That's exactly what I need you to do. I'm going to keep fucking you with my fingers, you're going to keep breathing and holding me in your eyes. Don't come. You're going to want to, don't. If it gets to be too much and you are getting close to the point where you can no longer hold it off just sat my name. If it is at the point where you have to come and there is nothing you can do about it, say "Sir" and then come. Do you understand?"

"Yes." Her answer was a breath. My fingers began to dance inside her again and her hips swayed to a rhythm we were making together, just us. "Remember to breath and don't break eye contact with me. I am your anchor, Vivian." I curved my two fingers up inside her and found that small, spongy spot on the front wall of her pussy. It was soft and rough and smooth and hard all at the same time. This fucking spot was Vivian. I rubbed it softly and then with a little more harshness...the texture was so erotic *I* almost came. I could feel Vivian's pussy tightening up. She was so hot. So close. I changed my physical bearing and the plains of my face, slightly. My chocolate eyes were coals burning in fire and brimstone, I saw a frisson of fear wash over her face and then there it was...contrition. Her breathing evened out, her pussy stopped clenching around my fingers and the heat that was scorching my fingers ebbed back and there was only a soft warmth left caressing the gentle thrust of my digits. I was losing myself in the beautiful pools of liquid sunshine that were staring back at me. I watched as a small tear slid down her cheek when I mouthed to her, "Come softly for me, Vivian. Come oh-so softly."

"Thank you." She whispered to me as every muscle in her body slowly tensed. Her orgasm started in her core, I continued to stroke her G-spot and added my thumb to her engorged clit to ensure that this climax would set the tone for the rest of them. I watched as her orgasm moved through her body; a tsunami moving in slow motion. So much power and beauty...the ability to bring both life and death...how awesome to share this moment with her.

I saw the exact moment her body released the tension...her faced opened into one of the most beautiful smiles I had ever seen in my life. I quickly removed my fingers and continued to rub her clit, but there was no way I was going to let the deluge of her fresh cream go to waste. My tongue touched her and she screamed my name as she began to come again. I must have eaten her out for hours. She came so much and for so long... I was full and sated. I fell asleep with my head laying on her soft pussy.

~28~

The morning was happy and bright, but if there was to be a competition for good moods, I knew I had that win in the bag. How could I not wake up in a fantastic mood? I gave Vivian so many orgasms last nights and into the morning...and more importantly, I took none for myself. She wanted me to take her, to let her suck me off, to fuck her...but I didn't. I wanted her to understand, that last night was all about her. We have five more days in New York. My brownstone is stuffed with food and drink; we will not be leaving until it is time to board the plane back to Columbia. I gave her an amazing night with light training, today and the rest of our time here, I will began teaching her how to be my submissive.

Although her training started last night and I'd hoped she noticed that it is was gentle and most of her position as my sub involved me taking care of her needs and making sure she had what she needed and wanted; both emotionally and physically. I was her Dominant, I was there to satisfy every craving she had, regardless of how large or small. Rather it be for sex, conversation or food...as her Dom, I was responsible for providing it. Getting her to trust me and have faith that I could provide for her, more importantly, that I *wanted* to provide for her was an important part of the training.

"Wake up sleepy head. I have breakfast for you." I stood beside the bed next to her head and brushed her abundant curls back from her beautiful face. One brave and reluctant eye opened and peeped at me. Her husky voice floated up to my ears and instantly, I was hard for her.

"Morning. I should be giving you breakfast in bed...you did all of the work last night." A small smile curved the left side of her mouth up into something that looked both sinful and angelic at the same time. *How did she do that?*

"You may have misunderstood me when I said I have breakfast for you. I should have been clearer about what was on the menu." I couldn't help the chuckle that fell from my lips both her eyes snapped open as she threw both her legs over the side of the bed and set up right. Her new sitting position placed her face right in line with my unyielding dick that was currently being stroked by my large right hand. I slowly moved my hand up and down my considerable length; squeezing the large, purple crown enough to draw a bead of pre-cum to the tip. I rubbed my thumb over the slit and brought it to her mouth.

"Open."

"Yes, *sir*." Her lips parted just enough for me to slide the tip of my thumb inside and she sucked my flavor off...hard. Then in a move that surprised me, she bit me...harder.

I grabbed a handful of her thick, silky curls and gently pulled her head back, I know that it didn't hurt her, but she gasped all the same.

"Don't bite me unless I tell you to. Do you understand me, Vivian?"

She nodded her head furiously.

"You have a beautiful speaking voice Vivian, use it." I put a little more pressure on her hair, still not enough to hurt her, just enough to let her know that I could hurt her if I wanted to.

"Yes. John. I understand."

"What exactly do you understand, Vivian?"

"I understand that I am not to bite you unless you tell me to, *sir*."

"Good girl, Vivian." I released her hair and rubbed the area where I had held her hair. Again, I knew I had not hurt her, but I needed to let her know whenever I needed to punish her, that I would always take care of her afterwards. That I would be the one to make it better. While rubbing her scalp, I dropped small reassuring kisses on her forehead, eyes, cheeks, chin and finally her lips.

"Are you still hungry, Vivian?"

"Yes, John. I am."

"Good. Your first course will be my dick, down your throat. Do you know how to deep-throat, Vivian?" Her wide eyes and the small frown that marred her soft lips told me she did not. No one had ever had her throat. I would be the first to fuck her there. *Good. I wasn't too sure about her virginity, but there were certain parts of her, that would belong to me and me alone. And her throat would be one of them.*

"Get out of the bed. Go wash your face and brush your teeth. You can't have breakfast and not have done your morning hygiene."

"Um...Okay. I mean, Yes, *sir.*" Confusion danced across her beautiful features and skidded onto the floor.

She scooted off the bed and ran into the adjoining bathroom. She seemed ashamed of her body. We would have to address that today. There would be no clothes for her for the next two days. *How could someone with a body like that ever be ashamed of it? Someone did a head job on her...I will find out who it was and they will pay.*

I straightened the bed and pulled everything nice and taut to ensure that her "table" was neat for her breakfast in bed. I had just finished smoothing things over when she walked out of the bathroom covering herself with her arms.

"If you would just give me a couple of minutes, John. I could get a shower and put some clothes on...I would feel better if..."

"You won't be wearing any clothes for the next two days. You are a beautiful woman. You cover up that gorgeous body of yours in clothes that old librarians wouldn't wear...why? Why don't you want people to see how fucking beautiful your body is?"

"It's nobody's business what I look like under my clothes. The fact that I have chosen to share my body with you was my decision and I am starting to regret it." One tear, then another. Pretty soon, there was a flood pooling under her chin.

"I am a fucking mess. John...I'm trying to be normal here. I don't need anyone, especially you, figuring out I'm not that special. Can't you see that? I don't know why you even think so." She was no longer standing in the bathroom door. She had lumbered over to the foot of the bed, her hands still covering her breast and her lady parts. Lady parts that I had been so intimately acquainted with last night and this morning. Her entire body was shaking, tears streaming down her cheeks and her eyes were filled with self-loathing. There was nothing I wanted more than to take her in my arms and talk her off whatever ledge she had walked out on, but she didn't need that right now...she needed me to be her Dom, and I needed her to calm the fuck down.

I changed my baring just so, I was taller, more angular in my stance. My face was harsher, colder. My eyes went from a soft chocolate to a rough and dark night. She noticed immediately. There was a change in her breathing and her hands fell away from her body. She stood in front of me, bared and naked. Her breast firm and high; nipples beaded and pebbled. There was nothing out of place on her body. Her eyes cast down, but her shoulders did not drop. In three steps I stood over her, close enough that I could feel the heat rolling from her skin and I know she could feel mine. I did not touch her, just stood over her, breathing her air and allowing her to breathe mine. I did not want to speak to her, just wanted her to know that I was there and that she belonged to me and that her fear and anger and every other emotion she had belonged to me, too...for the rest of her life. After a few moments of silence, I notice her take a deep breath in through her nose and exhale slowly through her mouth, she had calmed down, finally.

"Lay on the bed, Vivian. Make sure your head is hanging from the side. You still need breakfast." My voice was quiet and calm, but there was a command that not even I recognized in there. Where it came from, I do not know. Then something that Auntie said came floating through my mind, "*As you mature and become more comfortable in in your position as a Dom, you will find what you need to control your submissive will become as natural to you as breathing. Don't worry, John, you were born for this role, you are a Dom.*" I guess I am.

I looked down at Vivian and she was laying on the bed, exactly as I had told her. She had not made a sound, just doing as I had told her. Was she afraid of me, had I scared her? I didn't want her afraid of me, I just wanted to be obedient, to listen and know I would take care of her.

"Vivian, are you comfortable?" My voice still soft and commanding.

"Yes, sir." Her voice soft and reverential.

"Good. I'm going to feed you my cock and you're going to take all of it until it reaches the back of your throat." I looked for some kind of reaction in her face. Her eyebrows scrunched up and her lips made a small frown, but then she put her relaxed features back into place.

"This is different then what you gave me in the shower."

"How?"

"I'm going to use your mouth… I don't want you to

suck, lick, or swallow when my cock is in your mouth. I'm going to fuck your face. Hard."

"Yes, sir"

"If it gets to be too much and you feel too full, hold up your index finger on your right hand." I held up my index finger to show her what I would be looking for. If you feel like you are going to vomit or gag, hold your index and your middle finger on your right hand and I will pull out, okay. Again, I held up the two fingers on my right hands to show her what I was looking for. "Are we clear on the hand signals?"

"Yes, sir."

"Do you need any water or anything to drink before we get started?" At this point, I was more nervous than she appeared to be. Something in Vivian needed to be controlled. I was more than ready to meet that need in her.

No, sir."

"Good. I'm so fucking hard for you, Vivian. I've had your mouth once, but this is for me. Your willingness to let me use your mouth to take my pleasure is an amazing gift. I'm almost as excited to be inside your throat as I am to be inside your pussy." I began stroking my dick again as I moved to stand in front of her face, her eyes looking right up at my balls.

"That performance you gave when you came from the bathroom made me want to do two things to you." I grabbed my balls with my left hand and began rolling them around as my right hand increased in rhythm along the shaft of my cock. Small beads of pre-cum began drip onto her face. *Fuck! I had never seen anything so erotic in my life. She made no move to remove it from her face. She was so still. Her golden eyes wide open, watching me pleasuring myself, her face filled with longing. She wanted me in her mouth. Her patience was wearing thin. God, I loved this woman.*

"The first thing I wanted to do was protect you. You looked so scared and alone, like a little girl that needed someone to keep the monsters away." Some shadow sifted through her eyes; a mist of pain and fear. There was a vulnerability that didn't belong to her, but she carried it anyway. It faded quickly, but I'll never forget seeing it there. My heart ached for her.

"The second thing I wanted to do was take you across my knee and spank the living shit out of you for speaking to me that way. You confuse me, Vivian. You make me want to protect and punish you at the same time. I don't think I've ever felt that way before." I moved closer to edge of the bed, removing my hands from cock and balls, resting my fingers on my hips.

"Give me your hands, Vivian."

"Yes, sir." She raised her hands up and waited for me to take them. She had no idea what I was going to do with them, but she trusted me.

"Good. Do you trust me to take care of you and not hurt you, Vivian?"

"Yes, John. I do."

"Good. I'm going to place your hands on my thighs. Don't move them. You're going to want to move them...don't. Okay."

"Okay." I placed her hands on either of my thighs and bent down slightly so that the tip of my dick was touching her full lips. I knew that she wanted to taste me, she had begged me all night long, but she didn't make a move to do anything. *Such a good submissive.*

"Open that beautiful mouth of yours...don't worry about

making it wide enough, just open it for now." Her lips parted just enough for me to slide the tip of my cock past her teeth and rest on her tongue.

"Are you alright?" She looked up and the corners of her lips curled up into a wicked smile around my dick. Gone was the high-strung girl who had been ashamed of her nakedness. She had been replaced by my playful vixen.

"Good. Relax your throat muscles and don't try to swallow me. I just want you to take this gift I'm giving you, okay? Remember your hand signals. Index for when you are uncomfortable and index with middle when you need me to pull out, got it?" A small nod of her head caused her bottom teeth to lightly scrape the sensitive underside of my dick, an uncontrolled growl left my throat. "Fuck, Vivian." Another smile graced her sexy lips, but she kept her eyes lowered in a submissive manner. *Good girl, I can't wait to fuck your throat, again.*

Slowly, I began to ease my cock into her mouth. I felt her mouth opening wider, she wanted so badly to suck me down, her tongue started to dance along the underside of me...tasting me. It felt so good. Her hot, wet mouth around me. I wanted her to suck me off, forget having her throat, I knew she wanted me to come in her mouth and it was everything I wanted to do and none of what we needed at this point in her training. "Viv. Shit...stop that! Don't do anything. Don't move your tongue, just let me get myself in your mouth and down your fucking throat or this will be over before we get started, do you understand? Do not move your goddamned head." My words were harsh, but my tone was a plea. *I was begging her and still trying stay in control of the situation. It was funny as hell, really. Now I had to stop myself from smiling which would lead to laughter, this was not going as planned. Okay, get your shit together John.* I was in the role of Dom, but she knew in that moment, she had all the control and I think she fucking loved it.

She never looked up, but that smirk that danced on her lips...it told me she understood her power. *Maybe I should have been the one having my breakfast in bed this morning. Stupid ass move, dickhead. Stupid motherfucking move. Oh well, too late now.*

"I'm going to give you more of me, Vivian. Remember your hand signals. Use them if you need to." I was so worried. Something about her eyes told me that this was hard for her and that her bravado was more to protect her than anything. I still had so many questions about her past, but they would have to wait for now. I began to feed my cock into her mouth, to my surprise and pleasure, she followed my instructions and relaxed the muscles of her jaw and throat. I felt the head of my dick hit the back of her throat and gasped.

"Fuck. Vivian, don't you have a gag reflex? My dick is touching the back of your throat. Shit, it's so tight. I'm going to lean forward and start moving, if you can, suck me and try to use your throat muscles to swallow me…kind of like…" I noticed the fingers of her left hand were wrapped tightly around her left thumb. *Where the hell did she learn that trick.*

"God, Viv… so good. So fucking good." At that moment, she took a swallow. I damn near came. Her throat was amazing and wonderful and made me think about how great it was going to be when I finally had her pussy and her ass, but right now, she was sucking me, licking me and swallowing me down.

"God Vivian. Your mouth. Shit, it's so...*Fuck*, baby. Yeah, like that. Keep sucking me, just like that." I leaned forward slightly and dipped the index and middle finger of my right hand into her wetness and with my mouth, I started tugging on her nipples, pulling and nipping them as I pumped my dick in and out of her throat. I wanted to give her back some of the pleasure she was giving me. At times, I sucked them really hard, almost to the point of pain, Vivian would moan, making the sound vibrate along my already over-stimulated length. I bit into whichever nipple was in my mouth extremely hard and at the same time I thrust deeply into the back of her throat and back out again. I thought this was the perfect time to press the two fingers that were buried inside of her against her G-spot' pulling away from her beautiful tits, I growled in her ear, "you better not even think about coming. You will take all of this pleasure I'm giving you and, make my dick feel all of it. Every last drop of your pleasure belongs to me." Her face was contorted with the effort to stave off her orgasm, she was going to come, but so was I... And we would both be no good after we were done.

A deep moan tore from her chest and the vibration ricocheted through my balls and shot cum straight up through my dick and into the back of her throat, coating it in bitter, thick cream. Even after coming that one time, I still had so much more to give her. My erection was no more contained than it was when this little game first started. That's when I noticed Vivian's hips pumping up and down and her moans becoming whimpers and muted cries. Small, muffled breaths escaped the sides of her mouth as she fought to find her equilibrium and balance after experiencing her own white-hot orgasm.

"Vivian. Are you alright? One finger for yes, two fingers for no." She held up a hesitant two fingers. I pull out of her mouth immediately. I was a little disappointed, because I was on the verge of coming again, but she looked tired and her mouth looked puffy. She looked like she would protest, but I glared at her as I pulled her from the bed sat her on my lap to cradle her in my arms.

"Well done. You were amazing. Don't ever wait to tell me when something is not quite right. I'm proud of you, baby. How did you enjoy your breakfast in bed?" I pushed her face up so her eyes could meet mine and saw that she had a mask of shame covering her beautiful features.

"What did I say would happen if I saw shame cloud your eyes again?" I slipped into my Dom gaze so easily, I sometimes surprised myself. Her eyes lowered for an entirely different reason. She didn't respond. *Hell, I can't say that I half blame her, I'd be intimidated by me if I had to face my Dominant self.*

"Answer me, Vivian."

"Um. You said that you would punish me."

"Excuse me, Vivian." My voice quiet, but demanding.

"You said that you would punish me, sir." She was quiet with acceptance.

"Good girl. Now what should your punishment be?" I spoke softly to myself

"I don't know, sir." She whispered, knowing I did not request her opinion.

"Oh, you thought I was asking you. You silly girl. Come. Kneel down at my feet for a minute." Again. Not my usual thing, but I had no idea what to do with her. She had me so confounded with the whole face-fucking thing. She claimed she had never done that before, yet someone had to have taught her that and taught her well...too well. She rose clumsily from the bed and settled at my feet, head bowed, eyes lowered, hands clasped together in her lap. She spoke in the softest voice I had ever heard her use.

"What will you have me do, sir?"

"Just sit for now. Tell me, are you really alright and why are you acting so odd?"

"I don't know if I am alright. My throat is a little dry, Sir. Even with the torrent of cum you gushed in my mouth. My face hurts and my muscles burn, but I think I'm alright and as for me acting odd, I'm just trying to be what *you* want me to be." There was a catch in her voice. Almost as if she were getting ready to cry or trying her best not to cry.

"Are you crying, Vivian?" My voice was still as void of emotion and warmth as I could keep it.

"No, sir. It's just. I told you. I've never done anything like this before and I really want to make you...see, your happiness means a lot to...making you..." She took a deep breath before continuing. "Ensuring that you're happy means more to me than I thought it would. I don't want to disappoint you, so I try to do what I can to be what you want me to be, Sir"

I looked down at her and I saw her tears as they filled the tangled basket of fingers. She didn't dare look up from her lap. We were both bared. Naked physically and she was opening her soul to me. I had given her pieces of myself, but she needed more from me than the fragmented shards I had given her. Broken soul to broken soul. I stood from the bed and absently stroked her head in a gentle petting motion. She looked so small, kneeling down on the floor like that. Her proud head bowed, caramel tears streaming down her mocha face and an uncompromising sexuality flowing from her body.

I will never have her kneel at my feet again, I know now, I don't want a pet. I want a lover who will submit to my will sexually and in other ways, as well.

For today; however, her punishment would be to follow me around the house on a leash attached to a collar of my choosing, doing whatever I tell her to do. I left her sitting there, tears dropping from her eyes and falling on her breast like liquid crystals; seeking shelter in the basket her elegant fingers had made. I found the diamond collar I purchased for her five months earlier when we started our weird friends with benefits, but not real benefits relationship. I knew that Vivian would be mine forever, I knew I would never really need this collar to show her this, but she needed this right now and I would always give her what she needed. That was my job as her Dom and my honor as her lover. I dug a little deeper and found the matching diamond leash and attached it to the collar. As I made my way back towards the bed where I left her kneeling, I told myself that she needed this. We needed this if we were going to make it.

I stood over her, my right hand stroking her hair lovingly. She didn't move. She didn't take a breath...she just sat there. So still. So obedient, I wanted her violently in that moment, but she had to be punished and I knew I would never hit her as punishment. She would never learn from that, she would learn this way.

"Stand Vivian." She did. Without hesitation. She was a little wobbly, I steadied her by holding her left arm, my grip a little tighter than necessary because I wanted her to notice it. She did.

"Your punishment will last for the duration of the day; that means until the sun goes down and we are once again surrounded by night. Do you understand how long you will be punished?" My grip tightened around her arm, just a little. I had not look at her and her eyes remained focused on the floor and her hands clasped together at the base of her belly. At least her tears had dried up. "Answer me, Vivian." My voice was a soft growl full of latent power and contained fury, but just under the surface was the constant hum of my love for her.

"Yes, sir. I understand." A whispered sigh floated to my ears, so much contrition in her response, it made my dick hard immediately.

"I've decided what your punishment will be." Her breath hitched and then a small whoosh of air left her body. You will not be allowed to wear any clothes today, you need to get comfortable with your nakedness around me. You are beautiful and your shame will not be tolerated in our relationship. Got it?"

"Yes, sir." Nothing else. Just two small words spoken in an even smaller voice. I would accept it for now.

"The second part of your punishment is not really a punishment in this lifestyle that you have agreed to join me in. In the Dom/sub relationship, when a Dom chooses to collar his sub; it is his way of showing her that he wants her in his life in a more permanent way. It is much akin to an engagement ring in a more traditional relationship. Tonight, I will use it as a part of your training in combination with your punishment, but not as a punishment. I don't want you to ever confuse the two. Do you understand?" There was a tension in my voice that I didn't like, but it was there and it was nothing I could do about it. I needed her to be able to differentiate between her punishment and what an honor it was for me to place this collar and leash around her neck. She could not combine the two in her mind.

"Lift your head and look at me. Your head is not to be bowed anymore today. At all times, you should look me in my eyes and speak directly to me. Whatever happens between us today, you will meet my eyes and do so with a boldness, alright? I need to see you, know what you are thinking and feeling."

I moved closer to her, so close that the curve of her beautiful ass pressed lightly against an already painful erection and drew a low grown from the back of my throat. She noticed and pushed back into me once more. I wanted to stop her, but her ass felt so damn good pressed against my straining cock, I reached out and grabbed her hips. "Vivian, you need to stop whatever the hell you're doing right the fuck now." She chose that moment to roll her hips in a counterclockwise motion and I yanked her ass back tightly onto my stiff dick. I slapped the heavy, diamond collar around her neck faster than I thought possible and felt my control return on a deep inhale and a slow exhale that seem to steal her breath away. Instantly her body went still and the earlier vixen who had been trying to take back her power, willingly gave it over to her Master.

“Vivian.”

“Yes, sir.”

“How does your collar feel?”

“If feels like I belong to you, sir.”

“And do you, Vivian? Belong to me?”

”Yes, sir. I do.”

“Prove it. For the duration of your punishment, you are to call me Master. Can you do that?”

“Yes, Master.” No hesitation.

~29~

I led her into the bathroom and closed the door behind us. I knew she thought that something sexual was going to take place, and something sexual would take place, but the sex was a training tool, not something to get me off. She had a lot to learn about being my submissive, and I wanted this to work...I have to teach her what I need from her. I watched her in the mirror, her eyes looking at the collar and the leash; secretly wondering if the diamonds were real, wondering when I purchased them and were they only for her. A small smile played on my lips, she really wanted to know, but was too afraid to ask.

"Do you have something to ask me Vivian?" No command in my voice, just me, just John.

"Um, are these diamonds real, Master?" She was unsure if she was to call me Master because of the normal tone I had taken with her.

"Of course, they are. The stones in the collar as well as the stones in the attached leash are all real. You have over 60 carats of diamonds around your neck, Lovely." Her eyes were as large as I had ever seen them and the look made me so happy. I could almost jump up and down. The look on her face said if she could have killed me and fucked me, she would have. I smiled at her and went towards the shower.

"I'm going to clean up, I want you to kneel beside the shower closest to the nozzle; I won't be long. Keep your head up and your hands clasped together in your lap while I am in there; however, when I come out, be ready to dry me off and suck my dick, I want to come hard and fast." I stepped around her and looked her in her beautiful eyes. Any warmth that had been in my eyes a minute ago was gone, replaced by the icy stare that belonged to the Dom that lived within the gentler man who loved Vivian more than his own breath.

"Yes, Master." She began to fold her amazing body down onto the floor, as I stepped over her and got into the shower. She was so beautiful and so willing to listen and please me. The travertine floor was cold and unforgiving, and yet she did not complain as she settled down with her hands interlaced on her lap and her head held high and proud. Something about her softened the hardened son-of-a-bitch Dom in me and I gruffly offered her one of the fluffy, warm towels from the warming drawers behind her. She met my eyes, and quietly thanked me and pulled one out to rest her knees on as she waited silently for me to finish up.

***

That was the most perfect shower and blowjob I ever remember having. I felt so satisfied with Vivian and her fantastic mouth, I rewarded her with a jasmine scented bubble bath and the sweetest kisses I could give her. She was so happy that she pleased me, so fucking perfect. Her training was going quite well, except I couldn't shake the feeling that she was only serious about this lifestyle when it came to the sex. I don't think she fully understood that being a Dom is who I am and when she agreed to be my sub, she agreed to be my sub 24/7. I don't want our relationship to be what Auntie and I had, it was severe and I loved every fucking minute of it, I don't think that Vivian could take handle that type of relationship. After her decadent bath, I led her downstairs where we currently stood in the kitchen.

"Are you hungry, Vivian?" This was really an unfair question. A trick. If she answered yes, without regards to my needs first, she would be punished. My heart rate sped up in anticipation of her answer.

"Yes. *Master*, I am hungry. But not for food." The little siren was back and wanted to play. *God, this girl is never going to be the sub I need her to be...not if I don't nip this coquettish behavior in the bud.* The sing-songy way she said master was so disrespectful, Auntie would have had my dick and balls in the gates of hell, and there was no getting out of that bitch. Damn it Viv, two can play at this game, but only one will win and it won't be you.

"Really? Well if it is not food that you desire, what is it that you want? Vivian?" She was kneeling beside the island in the kitchen, completely naked, hands clasped in her lap, head raised and her caramel eyes looking defiantly up into my chocolate ones. Fuck, she was the most beautiful woman I had ever seen in my life. Nothing in me wanted to really break her...not even the Dom in me wanted her broken. She was too much fun, but in order for us to work...she had to offer me her submission. She had to gift me with her submission; willingly relinquish her control. I needed that from her more than I needed to breathe.

"Well, *Master*. After having the pleasure of sucking you off in the bathroom, being left with the taste of your flavor on my tongue, I would really appreciate the opportunity to service you with some other part of my body. Um, *Master*, Sir." A small smile played at the corners of her mouth. She thought this shit was funny and was not taking what I was offering her seriously. She really thought this was a fucking game and would just add some spice to our sex life that hadn't even gotten started, yet. I had yet to fuck her properly and she was nowhere near to getting my dick inside her with the way she was mocking me. Time to stop playing with her and show her the darkness I didn't want her to see in me.

I moved around the island so fast and knelt down in front of her, I'm sure she didn't see me coming. I was a blur of angry motion that bled fear and damnation around her knees. She began to shake. "Don't fucking look at me, or you will not only be naked for the rest of the day, you will be blindfolded, as well. Wipe that smirk off your lips, I'm sure you enjoy sucking my dick, but even cock suckers get tired after two or three hours of nonstop deep throating." My voice, a chilly breeze of dry ice, blowing across her face. I saw the moment she realized something had changed.

"I tried to introduce you to my lifestyle in a less severe way, Vivian, but you have been mocking me for quite some time…" I continued to kneel down in front of her and I grabbed her chin between thumb and index finger, rather roughly and yanked her face towards mine, forcing her to stare into my furious eyes. I said nothing. My face, implacable and my breathing, even. I waited until I saw what I needed to see in her eyes...intimidation and contrition. Not the bullshit contrition she's been feeding me for the last couple of days. No, I needed to see real contrition that a Dom recognizes and holds in his soul as ransom. Ransom for the one thing that means more to a Dom then sex, love, loyalty or even devotion. Control.

Knowing that his sub has willingly given him her submission and ceded control over her body, and in many ways her life...nothing outside of that gift really matters to a Dom. But it must be gifted, the sub has to gift her submission and she has to willingly cede her control. If it is taken by the Dom, then it means nothing and it will cost both the Dom and the sub everything. I didn't see it. I willed it, I needed it to show in the willful stripe of tiger's eye that was staring back at me, but it did not show.

"Vivian. You are free to leave." Six words spoken slowly and evenly. It was an eternity spoken in less than three seconds. I stood and walked away from her. I did not go far, just into the front room, where I stood in front of the window and watched the snowfall over the sidewalk. The snow knew exactly what its purpose was and it executed it without fail, no questions or confusion, just fall from the fucking sky and make everything beautiful. I have never been that sure of why I was here and even when I thought I knew, Vivian made me second guess that.

In this moment, I was ready to walk away from her and this failed attempt at making her my submissive, my lover...fuck, at making her my wife. I had nothing else to say to her. I was done, it was obvious to me she did not want what I was offering her, and although I felt like my heart was being ripped out, I would not be made a fool of. I didn't hear any movement coming from the kitchen, and at that moment I didn't give a shit. Part of me wanted to run back into the kitchen and grab her shoulders and shake her into compliance. To take what I felt was rightfully mine, her submission. She was made for me...made to be my sub. Why the fuck was she denying me what was mine?

"You know what? Just...just fuck it." I was so angry, I pushed away from the window, through my hat, scarf and coat on and walked out of the front door; slamming it behind me. I didn't need this shit and I decided that I didn't need Vivian in my life if she was going to be such a mocking bitch.

SACRIFICE

"If you're going to try, go all the way. Otherwise, don't even start. This could mean losing girlfriends, wives, relatives and maybe even your mind. It could mean not eating for three or four days. It could mean freezing on a park bench. It could mean jail. It could mean derision. It could mean mockery--isolation. Isolation is the gift. All the others are a test of your endurance, of how much you really want to do it. And, you'll do it, despite rejection and the worst odds. And it will be better than anything else you can imagine. If you're going to try, go all the way. There is no other feeling like that. You will be alone with the gods, and the nights will flame with fire. You will ride life straight to perfect laughter. It's the only good fight there is."

— Charles Bukowski, Factotum

~30~

The house was dark when I returned some five or six hours later. I had gone out to about three or four bars, but didn't drink any alcohol. I just had to get out of that house where she was. The house was quiet. Maybe she took me up on my offer, maybe Vivian was gone, maybe she was…

"Good evening, Master." Vivian walked out of the kitchen wearing a pair of Christian Louboutin stilettos and the most scandalous Agent Provocateur lingerie I had ever seen. She stood in the doorway that separated the kitchen and the family room, her five feet, eleven-inch frame silhouetted by the moon shining through the window. My eyes did a slow sweep up her body, I couldn't believe what I was seeing. Legs that went on for days leading up to sinfully sheer pair of full panties that did little to hide her beautiful waxed pussy, attached to the center of the panties is a *necktie?* The necktie, as it was, leaves both of Vivian's ample breast completely exposed save for two black pasties covering her nipples. My dick is so hard, I fear that it is going to break in two if I try to move.

"Turn around for me Vivian."

"Yes, Master."

"Oh. Fucking. My." What I'm staring at when she turns around is utterly breathtaking. Her back is completely exposed, the scarification that adorns her skin is pale in the moonlight and makes her looks like some kind of warrior going off to fight. I feel like she has claimed me as her last fuck before she goes off to battle for her right to live the way she chooses. But the most extraordinary sight is the bottom half of this lingerie. Everything is normal about the back of these shear panties except, Vivian's ass is exposed and instead of just a regular waistband, there is a cute little bow. Her hair is pulled back from her face in a severe bun at the base of her head, showcasing her luminous eyes and high cheekbones. She is beautiful without effort or apology.

"Come to me Vivian."

She falls to her hands and knees and slowly crawls over to me. Her breast are so beautiful, they move in such a natural fashion, I want them in my mouth. I want to fuck them. When she gets closer to me, I see it. The collar and leash, still around her neck. Tears were on the edge of her gorgeous eyes, threatening to overflow. I bend down and pick the leash up from the floor, rubbing it between my thumb and forefinger. She looks so beautiful kneeling at my feet. I can't keep my hand from petting her hair and whispering, good girl over and over. She bows her head and allows her tears to fall freely.

"What are you doing Vivian? What are you trying to prove?"

"Master, don't leave me. I will do better. I want what you want to give me. I'm sorry I've been mocking you and what you are offering me. I want this, Master. I want whatever you want...I don't care what it is, I just want you." Tears are falling freely from her eyes now and dripping onto her breast and she looks so goddamn beautiful, I want to cut all this macho bullshit and make love to her right now, but I can't.

"Vivian, this is me. This is what I am, it's the only way I know how to love you. I have never wanted to love someone before. I am offering you all of everything I am... this is not just some kinky-spice-up-our-sex-life game for me. It's how I live. It's not just in the bedroom. I need your submission in all things...in our bedroom, where we live, how we live, who we associate with, what you wear. I need you to willingly submit to me in all things. I need it so I know you are safe, so I know you are healthy and that nobody will ever be able to hurt you, again." I saw her eyes lift up to mine, her body went tense and she flinched. I knew that someone had hurt her and had done so badly, she had yet to tell me her story, but I knew whatever it was, it was bad.

"How do you know? You always seem to know, Master."

"Damn it Viv, I hear you crying at night in your sleep. I hear you begging *them* to stop, to get off you, to please not touch you anymore. You're not ready, but when you are, tell me who damaged you. I need to protect you, and this is the only way I know I'll be able to do that." I dropped the leash and I took both of her trembling hands into my two much larger ones and pulled her into my arms, glad to feel her body next to mine again. Glad to have her back where she belonged.

"Now Vivian. Tonight, I will make you mine in every sense of the word. After I have you, there will be no questions left, you belong to me and I will have you anytime I want you, anyway I want you. By accepting me into your body tonight, you are accepting me as your Dom."

"Yes, Master."

Grabbing the leash, I pulled her up the stairs and into the master bedroom. I did not bother turning on the lights or music or anything; I just wanted to get her naked and, in the bed, as soon as I could.

"Go stand by the bed and bend your body forward with your chest laying on the bed. You have to be punished for your behavior earlier today and that punishment will be a spanking. Leave your beautiful lingerie on, it's perfect for what I have in mind. Do you know what you did to earn this spanking?" *I said that I would never spank her, but I know that she needs this. She needs my hands on her and God help me, but damn I want to feel her ass warm under my palm.*

"Yes, Master" I watched as she folded her long, elegant body over the bed; her beautiful, round ass sitting high in the air, inviting me to spank her. Hard.

"Good. I'm going to go with twelve licks and you are going to count them while I give them to you. When I am done, Vivian, we're going to make love."

"Yes, Master." There was a tremble in her voice and I knew she was afraid, she should be, but she could stop me anytime she wanted or needed to.

"Do you remember your safe words, Vivian?"

"Yes, Sir. Er--Master."

"What are they?"

"Um...Red and Green. Master."

"Good girl."

Thwack! "Count Vivian"

"One: She cried out as my hand came down hard on her left butt cheek, before moving to the right cheek and repeating to action on that side. Vivian cried out again."

"Three! Master." I never hit her in the same spot on her ass, always in a different place, but always on her cheeks. After each lick, I caress the offended spot and speak soothing approbations in her ear. Once we reached 12, she is winded and crying. I send her to stand in the corner of the bedroom for five minutes to think about what she has done to earn her punishment and what she will do in the future to ensure that she won't ever be punished for the same reason again. I use the time to undress and get the bed ready for our first time. I can't wait to get inside her, to feel her walls around me.

"Walk over to me Vivian." My voice is low, but the command is obvious and there is no mistaken the fact that I am in full control of this situation. I will not allow my penis to become erect, I do not want her to know how turned on I am right now. She needs to understand when I punish her, it has nothing to do with getting me off and everything to do with teaching her how to behave in a manner that is pleasing to me as her Dom.

"Sit in my lap." She does; although gingerly.

"I love you more than I have ever allowed myself to love any other woman romantically. Hell, I may very well love you more than I even loved my mother. I am willing to share everything I have with you, because none of it means anything without you in my life. Having said that…" I pause, taking a deep breath and began to stroke her bare back as she lays her head on my shoulder and hugs my neck.

"I will not have you make a fool of me. Your need to be independent is what makes me want you so much, my need to protect and take care of you is what makes me have to have you. We have to reach a compromise and the only one I see working out, is me being your Dom and you being my sub. I can't have it any other way, Vivian. You may speak."

A deep breath brushes over my neck and sends electricity shooting down my spine. I don't move, she can't know how affected I am by her, not in this moment. I am waiting for her words. I don't know what they will be. This is the first time I have punished her with a spanking, she took it well, but she has had some time to process it and this could go either way.

"John? May I call you John?" Her voice is a small wave in an ocean of uncertainty.

"Yes Vivian. Talk to me, lovely. I need to know what you're thinking, what you're feeling."

Deep breath in and then a small voice spoken into my

neck. "It scares me that you *want* me like this, but it scares me even more that I *need* you to want me like this. There is so much about me that you don't know and even more about myself that I don't really understand. I just know that you as my...my *Dom*, I need that, but it scares me, so I fight against the safe feelings that come over me when I submit to you." She never looks at me, but I feel her tears, although her voice doesn't break, I feel the moistness on my neck.

"Lovely, don't be afraid of those feelings. I was afraid, too. The first time, Auntie introduced me to myself as a submissive; something felt so wrong about wanting what I wanted...but it was right for me. It was exactly what I needed. You deserve to feel safe, let me take care of you.

Let me love you and give you the security of being cared for. I want you Vivian and I have an entire world to give you. Let me. You are a natural submissive. You were created to submit."

I paused to gauge her reaction, I didn't have to wait long. Her head lifted from my shoulder, at first there was a hint of defiance in her eyes and then a softening that stole my breath away from me. She gently laid her head back down on my shoulder and exhaled a breath that I don't think she realized she had been holding. I continued on, feeling more confident in what I was saying.

"I don't think you would be happy if you could not submit to someone; if you didn't know someone was here to take care of you, to give you rules and consequences for breaking those rules. As your Dom, I will do that for you and your life will be easy. I will be completely responsible for you. As your lover, I will make sure your needs are met and that your desires are taken care of. Whatever they may be, there will be no secrets between us, Viv...none. Don't be afraid of us, Vivian. Let me love you. TPE."

"TPE?"

"Yes, total power exchange. You willingly give your control over to me, give me your power and in exchange for all that I'm promising you...I will take care of you for the rest of your life. Every need, every want, every desire, fantasy, hope and dream...I will make sure you have it. That is my promise to you, lovely"

"Make love to me, John. Please. I want to become yours."

"Stand up and turn around with your back facing me. And Vivian...Call me Master. You may look at me and speak freely. I need to know what you like and don't like. Before we get started, is there anything besides anal play that you won't do?"

"I--Er, I don't know. Master."

"Why don't you know? I still wasn't sure if Viv was a virgin or not. *Time to go fishing.* "You have had sex before. What things didn't you like?"

"Master, um, this is the first time I have ever *chosen* to have sex with someone...I have *had* sex, but it was for a different ...it was different...it was under different circumstances." Her voice trails off and a dark shadow drifts through her eyes like mist and then it's gone. "Master, I'm sure I will like whatever you do to me. I have loved everything up to this point." Her voice barely above a whisper. Shy Vivian was sexy as hell and was really speaking to my Dom. I wanted to fuck her seven ways till Sunday. Patience *Jughead,* our time is almost here.

"I wish you could tell me what the hell happened to you, I want to go and rectify that shit right now, but I know you won't." I stood behind her, my hand poised on the bow, ready to undo the beautiful binding as my fingers moved slowly up her exposed back. I loved the feel of the scars on her skin, her muscles bunched under my soft ministrations. It was good to know that my touch could affect her so much. I deftly undid the clasp at her neck at the same time I undid the bow at the base of her spine, the entire ensemble fell to the floor leaving Vivian standing before me completely naked except for her Louboutin stilettos and her collar. I had taken her leash off earlier. She looked like my favorite wet dream come to life.

"How did you feel about your punishment, the spanking and being placed in the corner for five minutes?" My right hand snaking around the front of her neck as I slide my tongue from where her shoulder and neck meet all the way up to her earlobe where I began to gently suck and nibble. She moans and leans her head further over to the right, giving me better access to the spot I know for a fact is making her wet for me. Another moan, but this one comes from the back of my throat.

"Answer me Vivian, or I stop making you feel good." My left-hand sneaking around her body and grabs her right breast. A gasp escapes her perfect lips as my index finger and thumb began to rhythmically pull at her hardened nipple. I kiss on her neck and bite her earlobe, tugging on her sensitive nipple and overall driving her crazy and she is supposed to be able to tell be how she felt when I spanked her. *This should be good. Maybe even good enough that I get to spank her again, but for pleasure...hers and mine.*

"I—I felt humiliated, but...oh. My. God." Panting and deep breaths, but no words. I pinched her right nipple and bit down on her earlobe. "Master, I can't think when you do that to m-me." Another sharp tug on her nipple.

"You need to be able to do what I ask of you, regardless of what I am doing to your body. Now answer the question. Focus on answering the question, because doing so will please me, and that is what my submissive lives for, Vivian. Your soul's purpose is to please me, to make me happy. Doing so, will make you happy. Understand?"

"Yes, Master." Words spoken evenly. I am pulling on both nipples now, pinching and massaging the supple flesh of her breast.

"How did you feel?"

"I felt Humiliated at first, but...then after the first three…" Deep breaths—I count three all together before she is able to continue. I drop my right hand between her legs and began to pet the outside of her pussy... just rubbing her smooth, soft lips.

"After the first three licks, something inside of me sh-shifted. The humiliated feeling left and then I started needing the feel of your hand on my ass…" Four deep breaths. I slip my middle finger between her wet folds and began to rub her along the seam of her opening and sensitive arch of her vulva. She pushes her ass against the thick bulge between my thighs. My hands stop immediately I pinch her vulva between my fingers, hard enough to cause her pain. She cries out and I continue to pinch her sensitive area.

"You don't have my permission to grind that beautiful ass against me, do you?"

"No, Master. I'm sorry." Words squeeze through clenched teeth.

I release her and continue to stroke her and make her feel good again. She whimpers softly, but does not continue to tell me how she felt about the punishment.

"And then what?" My voice is harsh, but it does the job in bringing her back to the conversation at hand.

"And then, I needed to feel the pain of your hand

connecting with my behind, I needed to know that you set a boundary for me, and would punish me for crossing that boundary. The pain, your hands, the idea that you were punishing me...it *quieted* something in me that I didn't know was screaming." Her breathing is labored and she's so wet, I hadn't even entered her with my finger again and she was dripping onto my hands. She was ready. It was time.

"Not all spankings are for punishment, Vivian. That spanking will be as hard as it will ever get with my hands, I hope to never use anything other than my hands on you, unless I think it is something you and I need to introduce into our relationship. I never thought to use that type of punishment with you, but I thought you needed it. I'm glad to know I was right?" I slid two fingers inside her sopping pussy; making wide circles, ensuring that I touched every surface of her slick walls. The air whooshed out of her mouth and she leaned her head back onto my shoulder and bit into the flesh of her full bottom lip and then she came; clenching violently around my fingers. Tears ran from her eyes, down her chest and landed in her navel. *What the fuck was that. Shit, she just came, hard...I barely touched her, and she just came. What in the hell? Is she crying? She keeps throwing me off my game.*

Once she got her breathing back to normal, she held her face up and turned to look at mine, embarrassment shining in her eyes she tried to speak but I silenced her with a lush kiss. My tongue delved deep into her mouth seeking to find all of her secrets. I only let up when neither of us could breathe.

"Come with me, Vivian."

"Yes Master." She did, on wobbly legs.

"You are so fucking beautiful. Everything about you is perfection." I walked around her, looking and appreciating her perfect female form. I allow the tips of my right-hand caress her flat stomach, back and everything in between. Her skin was like silk and I just couldn't stop touching it. There was nothing out of place. I was a lucky son of a bitch and I knew it.

"Lay on the bed, Vivian and spread your legs for me. I want to see you."

"Yes Master." She gracefully laid her body onto the king size bed; she was a flower opening to the morning sunlight, her legs opened wide, revealing the most addictive drug known to man. I knew at that moment that I would never get my fill, I would always need more and more of Vivian, and that my addiction would consume and destroy us both.

"I have tasted you, you have tasted me. You know what I want and need from you. You clearly understand what consummating our relationship means, you understand that choosing to wear my collar means you belong to me and that I *own* you, Vivian. You are mine to do with as I please. That you are mine 24 hours/7 days a week...you don't get a break from being mine. If you mess up, and you will, I will punish you because you need to know how I want you to behave for me; in and out the bedroom. If I do anything you're not comfortable with, let me know. If I am approaching your limit, let me know by saying 'yellow', if I have reached your limit and you want me to stop, let me know by saying 'red'."

"Yes, Master."

"Vivian, I want to hear my name spill from your sensuous mouth. We both know I own you, but you have to know that you fucking own me, too. Like no other human being on the face of this earth has ever owned me; you have me by my heart, my throat and my balls. I can't be me without you. Call me John, unless I say differently."

"Okay, J-John."

I half lay my big body down over hers so that one of my legs is in between both of hers. Propping my head up in my right hand and looking into her amber eyes, my future looked back at me and I saw fear, hope and *love. Shit. I wasn't expecting to see love there, but Vivian loved me. There was no doubt in my mind that this beautiful, fucked up, broken woman loved me...an equally fucked up and broken man.*

"I want to be inside you now Vivian. I know you are ready for me, you are wet and swollen. I will make this last until I feel your walls squeezing my dick and then I'm going to pound myself into your wet pussy until I have flooded every part of you with my cum." She pushed her pelvis up to meet my eager dick and that was all the answer I needed.

Her eyes never left mine as I shifted my body to fit in between her spread legs; she opened them wider to accommodate me, our bodies seemed to be made for each other's.' Like two halves of one soul, we fit perfectly together. My dick lay heavy between the lips of her wet heat, she felt so good, I knew I would have to exercise every bit of control Auntie had drilled into my head and body to make our first time last. I looked down at her beautiful face as I moved my right hand between our bodies to position myself at her entrance. She was so fucking wet, slick with wanting me. I dripped my pre-cum onto her mons and a weird sense of pride welled up in my chest. I knew that it was caveman behavior, this need to mark Vivian with my cum, but I needed to do it, and I knew I would come everywhere I could in and on her body tonight.

"Please. Please John. Make love to me. I need you inside me. Please."

"God. I love hearing you beg me Vivian. You are making me even harder. Fuck...beg some more. Beg me to make love to you again. Tell me how you want it, lovely."

"I want you to feed your long, thick cock into my wet pussy. Give it to me slowly so that I feel every stone inch of you penetrating me. Please, John, don't make me wait any longer. I need you. I need to feel your dick pounding away inside me. Please."

"Yes." That was the last word she heard before I pushed my dick inside her. I met no resistance. She was so wet and warm and soft. There was nothing between us. On the first thrust, I was half way in. "Damn Vivian! You're so tight. You are squeezing my dick like a fucking vice; so damn good." I pulled out a little and prepared to slide in deeper this time, but Vivian's walls were clenched so tightly there was no way *Jughead* was going to get inside.

"Lovely, you have to relax if you want me to be completely inside." She flung her eyes open and tears swam in them along with the pain and sorrow of something horrible. I tried to pull out, I don't know what evil had been put upon her, but I didn't want to be associated with it. I pulled the rest of my hard dick out of her tight heat when I felt her hands on my shoulders. Tears streaming down her beautiful face as she let me see the horror she could never speak of.

"No John. Please. Don't stop. I need your touch to take away their touch. Please. Make love to me. GREEN...Keep doing what you're doing. PLEASE. I *need* it. I *need* you." I slid back in... balls deep. She gasped, involuntarily and tried to breathe through the discomfort of being stretched too wide and filled too deeply. I knew I was too big for most women, but I hoped with Vivian being so tall, that she would be able to take me better than the others I had been with. She was small and tight. *Wait! Hold-the-fuck-up. What did Vivian just say? She needed my touch to erase their touch. Who is their...what happened to her. Why won't she tell me what happened to her and who the fuck are they. How many are they...what did they do.* I kept moving inside of her, working her with my dick—in, out, left swivel...right swivel. A guttural moan left her throat, eyes rolling back in ecstasy, hands clawing the sheet restlessly, and mouth opened and screaming silence into the room. It was the single sexiest thing I had ever seen in my entire world. Sexy enough to pull me out of my own head and focus on her. She hadn't even come yet, and she was lost to me.

"I'm going to take you deeper, lovely."

"Yes." She was mindless with the need to come.

I placed my hands under her fine ass and lifter her up into a deft roll of my hips as I pumped deeply into her soft flesh. I could feel the end of her, I knew that once I came inside her; we would make memories that would start to undo the shit she's been carrying around with her, but refused tell me about, I just needed her to come. I started feeling around inside her with my dick...what I was looking for became more important than finding my own release. I had to make her come again.

"Fuck! Vivian. What are you doing?" I felt her squeeze my dick so hard, I thought she was having an orgasm, but then she did something that no one else had ever done. She squeezed and rotated her hips, putting me in direct contact with the elusive spot deep inside her pussy, exactly what I had been searching for.

"Is this what you want, John?"

"Yes. I would have found it eventually, you know. I didn't need any help with that." The entire time, I'm rubbing the flared head of my dick against the spot Vivian has so kindly put me in contact with. The sexy sounds she makes, makes me want to fuck her into another dimension.

"I wanted y-you to f-f-find it sooner r-rather than la-la-la. Oh-fucking-my…John…John…John!"

I was pounding myself into her like a battle ram. Vivian was coming like crazy. I lost count of how many times she came after the fourth one. Her body was like water, she was completely at my mercy I loved it. “Oh, shit Vivian. I’m going to come so hard for you.” I felt my balls draw close to my body; so close, I was scared my body would suck them into itself and then that familiar tingle shot up my spine and zinged back down, setting my shit on fire. Making my cum hot and ready to shoot out of the tip of my cock. I had been holding off, I wanted to make this last as long as I could for Viv. I wanted my touch to wipe away as much of whatever the hell she had been talking about earlier. I hope this worked a little.

“Oh fuck. Holy fuck, Vivian. Never felt anything like this before. Never felt anything like this before, shit. What are you...d-doing?” Vivian’s long legs wrapped around my waist and squeezed me with all her power at the same time, her wet walls began to pulsate around me as her own cosmic orgasm tore through her with enough force that her entire body began to shake uncontrollably. I was squeezed from the inside, squeezed from the outside. She shook on the outside as her wet, slippery walls shook on the inside...the effect was like nothing I had ever experienced. My mind shut down and my heart stopped beating...I was on instinct only.

We were fucking like two wild animals whose feral veracity caused our bodies to slam into each other’s’ with little concern for the bruises that would be there in the morning. My hands clawed at the soft, tender flesh of her hips and her nails dug into the smooth skin of my back exposing pink flesh...causing blood to run in rivulets down towards my ass. I only felt pleasure. I marked her like the animal I was. Small bites along her neck, breast, shoulders, arms, legs and belly. After all, she belonged to me and could do with her as I pleased. On some unconscious level, she must have felt as territorial about me as I did about her, she marked me with her nails and teeth. Bite marks, scratches and hickeys is what I would find all over my body the next morning when I woke up tangled in the arms and legs of the most beautiful woman I had ever known.

It was done. I claimed her for myself. My lover. My submissive. My life. The next morning, I replaced her diamond training collar with a beautiful *Belle Époque diamond and Conch Pearl Choker.* I knew this simple piece of jewelry would look lovely around Vivian's neck and only she and I would understand the significance of her wearing it. Only I would know I had spent more than $89,000 on such a simple piece, but to me...that amount of money was equivalent to $89.00.

She would never really know the extent of my wealth, I wanted her to want me for me. To love me for me. We will live a normal life, nothing extravagant...just normal and middle class. The next three years will be spent training Vivian to be the best submissive, wife and lover she could be. I can't wait to marry her and give her my world.

~31~

Back in Columbia, South Cackylacky and back to school. I didn't know what to expect once we returned to school and our real lives, but nothing changed. I told Vivian I didn't want her living in her apartment with her roommates any longer and I wanted her to move into my home with me. I expected her to put up a fight, but she didn't. She simply said that she would need some help moving. She has been amiable over the course of the second semester and that she has scares the shit out of me. *What is she going to pull on me for the summer? I don't think I'm going to like whatever it is at all.* Vivian isn't fooling me at all with 'Master this and Yes, Sir that', she is definitely up to something...I just don't know what it is, yet.

***

"I can't believe my first year of college is over. I really can't believe I made it out with a 4.0 and a full scholarship to *France* for a study abroad for two months. I'm so excited!"

"Vivian, I'm so jealous of you, but your *boyfriend*, he doesn't seem to let you out of his sight for too long, does he know about France? What has he said about you going there by yourself?"

"I haven't told him, yet. I wanted to be sure I had it first. I'm sure he will understand what a great opportunity this is for me and he'll be happy for me. I hope he will…"

I watch as Vivian chews on her bottom lip and mumbles to herself. She looks nervous, she should.

"You hope he will what, Vivian?" She jumps at least two feet high and lets out a squeak before she turns around to find me standing in front of her. It wasn't that hot, yet so I chose a lightweight Ralph Lauren chino short in cerulean blue paired with a Ralph Lauren button down; white with pale pink stripes. Sleeves rolled up to reveal my forearms. I saw the moment her body responded to me, the way I trained her body to respond to me. *I own you Vivian. Mind, body and soul. Let's see how this plays out.*

She swallowed hard, her mouth was slack. I watched her nipples become hard, achy points under her thin tee shirt, and she clenched her thighs together because her core was no doubt pulsing and becoming slick with moisture. It was always so fucking sexy to watch Vivian's body come alive and knowing that she couldn't do anything to stop it from happening, regardless of where she was, made me instantly hard. Good thing I left my shirt untucked or Jill would get an eyeful of what keeps Viv so damn happy. *That thought makes me smile a secret smile that usually makes lovely weak with anticipation. She notices and her eyes go dark and hooded. Fuck me! I love having so much power over her.*

"Vivian, I believe I asked you a question. Don't you think I should get an answer? Vivian?" I use her name as a weapon against her fraying nerves. She knows that she only has moments before I bring out a more potent weapon; only moments before I slide deeper into Dom and then she would be lost to me completely. My will becomes her will.

"Yes, John. I do believe you should get an answer. However; I would rather discuss this matter with you at home, if it pleases you." She left the 'Master' unspoken, but it was heard just the same. I gift Vivian with one of my *I'm going to fuck you into submission* smiles and her knees almost buckle under her. I reach out to take hold of her arm and pull her into my body where she feels safest and just like that, my will becomes hers.

"Well, it seems as if you and your lovely friend, Jill were already discussing the topic, may I join the discussion or is it a-*girls*-only discussion that an ogre like myself wouldn't understand?" I have slipped completely into Dom persona and I really like it.

"John, of course it was not a girl only discussion and you are by no means an ogre. We were discussing our plans for the summer." Her voice is repentant and her eyes are lowered in response to her Dom. She continued in the same voice, "Which is why I wanted to continue our conversation at home; as we have not discussed *our* plans for the summer, yet."

It was obvious that Vivian didn't want to make any assumptions about what we are doing and not doing. My face gives nothing away and she knows that I don't for one minute believe any of the bullshit she just prattled on about. I am sure she would rather be alone when she tells me what her plans are for the summer, so that when I go bat-shit-crazy, she will be alone when she cries. *How little faith she has in me...there will be no need for her tears if she would only trust me more. I already know what her summer plans are.*

"Okay lovely, we may continue this discussion at home. I drove. Jill did you need a ride somewhere?" I turn to face her forgotten friend and give her one of my reassuring smiles, because she is looking at me like she will be calling the cops when she gets home. *Fuck off, Jill. You don't understand a thing about the nature of what Viv and I have together.*

"Uh, no. I can walk where I'm going." Jill turns to hug Viv and whispers in her ear as she does, "Don't let that beautiful bastard take this from you. You deserve this, Viv." *This stupid little girl can't whisper to save her soul. Stupid twit...I love Vivian too much to take anything from her. My soul purpose in life is to give her everything she never had and all that she doesn't even know she wants.* I get out of my head long enough to hear Viv tell her, "You, too. Have a great break. See you next fall." I take a deep breath and turn around to face my greatest accomplishment and worst weakness. "You ready?"

She walks slowly towards my outstretched hands and hesitantly places her smaller one into mine. *She knows she has nothing to fear from me. I'm going to need to do some checking into this Jill bitch.*

"Are you ready to go home?"

"Yes." I gently squeeze the hand she has placed in my own and she walks quietly beside me. I know she really wants to go to France this summer, Fuck, she deserves this, she's worked really hard for it...I look over at her and wonder what she's thinking and that's when I see one then two fat tears...and then all she had been fighting to hold back fall unceremoniously from her eyes and land wherever they choose.

We stand at the passenger door, her back to the door and my body facing hers. There is no breathing room between us, just us. I lean down and kiss the tears from her eyes. Silently, I move my unholy mouth...the mouth that knows every part of her body; I move that mouth over to her ear and whisper in a voice that sounds like a choir of angels and my words are meant to end her. Five words meant to undo her completely.

"Summer in Paris is beautiful." I open the passenger door and places her inside, buckling her in and effectively shutting the door and her mouth. She watches me slide behind the wheel of my car and I turn the music on, *Arrested Development,* Everyday People, pours from the speakers in the back of my car. The ride home is quiet and the only sound I hear is the blood rushing through my ears and the music from my CD player. Before I know it, the car has come to a stop and I'm opening her door, pulling her out and walking us to the front door of the home we have shared for the last five months.

"Go get changed into what I have laying out for you on the bed and come back in here, kneel beside me wherever I'm sitting or standing."

"Yes, Sir." She moves quickly into the bedroom we share and finds a beautiful *Agent Provocateur* lingerie set. At this point, I imagine she's realizing her mistakes...all of them concerning the Paris situation. I would pay good money to know what she's thinking, but I won't have to pay one red cent.

I heard her as she walked out into the living area, looking for me. Not finding me there, she made her way to the kitchen where she finds me standing beside the kitchen sink with my arms crossed over my chest, my left arm resting atop my right arm and my left hand rested on my chin. *I've never given Vivian a reason not to trust me. I always endeavored to be honest with her. To think that she thinks I would be so petty a lover, so controlling a Dom as to hinder her success...hurts.* I didn't realize Vivian had walked into the kitchen and kneeled at my feet and was waiting patiently for instructions.

"So, tell me lovely. Do you love your new lingerie?" My left hand now rests on the crown of her head. The pressure, I know, relaxes and calms her for some reason she doesn't seem to understand. *When will Vivian learn that there are no secrets between us? I know everything about her, before she even knows it about herself. Except what the hell happened to her.*

"It's one of the most beautiful ensembles you have ever gifted me, Sir. I don't feel I deserve it. I know you know I have kept a secret from you. How do I apologize for that, Sir?"

"You can't. There is no way you can apologize for this."

"Will you punish me, Sir?"

"Spanking you is not enough. Orgasm denial...not enough. I promised you I would never introduce any other implementation into our relationship...lovely, but you have really disappointed, no that is not the right word. You *hurt* me when you don't trust me enough to know whatever you want for yourself is what I want for you?" I keep my eyes averted from

Viv's. I don't want her to see the full extent of the hurt she's put there. It is not right for her to know how much power she has over me, I don't need her to know how much I love her...how much I want her to be happy. Not yet, she hasn't earned that right.

"Sir, may I speak freely?"

"Yes."

"I know we agreed you would only ever punish me with your hand, but I know I have displeased you and I want to please you. I am stronger than you think, I need for you to punish me properly. I deserve it, after all."

"Lovely. You don't know what you're asking for? Seeing to you in that way would make me happier than you could ever know, but it would also open a door in our relationship I don't think you want to walk through. Once the door is opened, there is no closing it. Do you understand what that means?"

"Yes. Sir." Her voice is shaky and unsure, but she sounds like she wants this. I can't...won't deny her this.

"Go into the playroom. Lie over the spanking bench...take the panties off, leave everything else on. I'll be there shortly. And Vivian, think about why you're in our playroom, why you're getting this punishment and why it's with more than my hand."

I watch as she unfolds herself from her kneeling position and she walks like a fucking goddess towards our playroom and I can't help my body's reaction to her. I don't want to punish her, I just want to bury myself inside her warm, wet walls and fuck her until she's a boneless pile of nothing in our bed and then I want to take care of her. *Why the fuck she wants to be punished for this, I don't know, but as her Dom, I have to do this.*

I have to find some instrument to beat her beautiful ass with to show my displeasure with her lie of omission. I knew she had that scholarship to Paris, hell, I funded the damn thing. I wanted her to go to Paris this summer, I wanted us to have this summer together in the city of love.

I find my long, slim paddle hanging on the wall in our playroom. I glance at Vivian laying prostrate over the azure leather bench, her amazing ass high in the air, her hair spilling down her back and across her shoulders. She is the most beautiful woman I have ever known and I can't believe that she is all mine. *I have not used a paddle in a long time, God I hope I don't mark her permanently. She is so beautiful and she's already so beautifully scarred on her back and thighs...I don't want to add to her markings. Or maybe I do and that's why I'm so reluctant to use anything other than my hand.*

"Vivian, I'm going to spank you with a slim paddy whacker. We'll go for ten licks. You will count, then I will fuck you...you may not come. Understand?"

"Yes, Master." Her voice was thick with some emotion that I could not name, something I had never heard in her before. It tore at my heart and I no longer wanted to punish her or fuck her...I just wanted to hold her and make everything between us easy again. I knew she needed me to do this, so for her I would, I would be a heartless, bastard and beat her.

"Lovely?"

"Master"

"What are your safe words"

"Red to stop and yellow if I'm coming close to breaking, Sir."

"Ready?"

"Ready."

Deep Breath...Thwack

"One."

I gently rub her ass with my right hand, hoping it helps.

"Two"

I find a different spot to hit her this time...never hit in the same place twice.

"Three"

Her voice is softer, thick with unshed tears or hurt or anger. I can't tell.

"Four"

I move the paddle lower, so that it hits between the juncture of her thighs and her ass. I can't take it anymore. I rub her ass, it's warm to the touch and there is a beautiful color blooming where the paddle has made contact with her behind. I spread her thighs a little and move my hands between her legs and find her warm, wet opening...one, no two fingers glide into her pussy. I close my eyes, relishing the feel of her walls around my fingers, remembering how good she feels around my dick. As I push my fingers in and out of her, I hear the moans from the other side of the bench, she is turned on and wants what I want.

"Six more licks, lovely. Can you take six more?"

"Yes, Master." Her voice seemed stronger, perhaps she thought that I would let her come.

"Five" More determined, stoic and resolved.

"Six" Numb and dejected. I'm losing her again.

"Lovely, remember that with pain there is pleasure. Tell me where you are...be honest. Red, yellow or green?"

She takes a deep breath; her arms are slack at the front of the bench and her head is lolling around...she looks so out of it. I have not been easy on her. Her voice is soft, almost a whisper.

"Orange." *What the fuck? Did she just make a new color? Orange falls in between red and yellow. She's close to telling me to stop, close to telling me she has reached her limit.*

"Lovely?"

"Yes, Master."

"Do you want me to stop with the beating and just fuck you?" God please let her say yes...please.

"No Master. I deserve this. I will take my entire punishment. If it pleases Sir."

"Are you sure, lovely?"

"I need to learn to trust you and this will help me, right?"

"Yes lovely, this will remind you that you are mine and you have to trust me in all things, because I know what's best for you"

Thwack

"Seven" Breathless and pained.

"Eight" A whispered breath that I barely hear.

"That's enough Vivian. I'm done. No more. I don't want anymore, Okay?"

"No Master!" Her voice is so soft, but she is vehement about this punishment. "Only two more. I will take it...I *deserve* them, you are within your rights, Master. I was wrong, I lied to you. I kept it from you, please don't stop. Please don't stop. I need to know you still care enough about me to punish me, Master...please still care enough to punish me." *I didn't know what to do or say, I had never seen her like this before. Well except for that time in New York. She had to know I loved her insanely, didn't she?. Maybe she didn't.*

I dropped the paddle and went to the front of the bench, pulled her from the leather and into my arms. She was shaking like a leaf, tears flowing from her eyes...carving the Nile and the Congo down her cheeks. I didn't know what to do to get her to calm down, so I did the only thing I knew how to do well...the only thing I knew would get her to focus on me completely. I walked her back and placed her against the St. Andrew's cross on the adjacent wall, forced her hands into the bondage cuffs and spread her thighs wide, wrapped her legs around my waist and shoved my cock into her wet sex. All of me in one hard thrust. I try to never make her take all of me like that...I know it's too much for her, but she wants me to punish her, so be it.

"Jesus. Fuck. John. Master."

"No sound from you...No words Vivian...and this is for me...you may not come at all."

"But Master, I--can't...I'm too close to stop, please..."

"You better fucking control your body. You know how, I've taught you. Not a word and no sounds...no fucking coming, Vivian. Do. You. Under. Stand. Me?" Each of my words were punctuated with a shallow thrust and swivel of my hips.

"Yes. Master." I felt her tears on my shoulder. I knew she was crying, but I had to see this thing through. She wanted me to punish her.

I fucked her for what felt like hours. I was tireless. I made our coupling last forever. There was no foreplay except for the paddling and that could hardly be considered foreplay. She was tired and soaked with my semen. I had come three times inside her, but I had not let her come at all. She had been denied the right to come every time she had been on the precipice.

She was out of her mind with the need to orgasm. Her legs and pussy trembled every time I moved and her eyes had lost focused hours ago. She was tired and sad and angry and on the verge of being broken...that was the last thing I wanted for her. I didn't want to break her. I took pity on her and leaned down to her sagging body and told her that she could come, but she would have to get herself there. *V*ivian has always shied away from masturbating in front of me...I've been dying to see her using her fingers to get herself off.

"Did you want a toy to help you out, lovely?"

"Please untie me, Master. I don't need a toy or anything at this point."

Walking over towards her, I undo her wrists and lean in to give her a kiss after her wrist are free, but she side-steps me and goes to the settee where she sits on the edge and places her feet in the ankle straps and pulls the lever to open her legs so that they are spread as wide as they can go, putting her naked pussy on display for me. I watch as my cum dribbles out of her slit and rolls into her ass. *God, the things going through my mind right now are criminal.* This might be the sexiest thing I've ever seen her do. And she is still wearing all of that lingerie I brought her. I want to fall between her legs and lick her until she falls apart in my mouth; on my face, but I don't.

"So, Master. You wanted me to make myself come."

"Yes, lovely. I believe that is what I told you to do."

"Will you watch, Master?" Her voice contrite and every bit the perfect submissive.

"Yes, I would pay good money to watch you pleasure yourself, Vivian."

"Lucky for you, Master, you don't have to pay money because I already belong to you."

The little minx wants to play word games. Game on, Viv. Let's see if you are willing to put your money where your sexy mouth is.

"Yes. Lucky for me, you are all mine and I want you to come like a freight train, so let's help you along with that. Shall we?" *Yes, Vivian. Don't ever forget your place. I am the Dom and you are the sub. There will be no topping from the bottom. Not in this relationship.*

I saunter over to my chest of toys and pull out a vibrating dildo with bunny ears. We've played around with vibrators before, but she has never used one on herself before and if she has, I have never watched her do it. I know how wet she is, I can smell her in the air and I've come so many times inside her, this fake dick should meet no resistance.

"Just for you, lovely." I present one of the largest dildoes I have in the chest. It is still in the packaging. I want her to know it's knew and I purchased it just for her...just for us.

"I don't need this. Er...Master. I mean. Thank you, Sir--I mean, Master. Oh my God...I am able to get myself there with just my hands, I assure you."

"Lovely. I want you to use this." I shove the oversized, phallus with bunny ears in her face and give her an all-American boy smile. I should have just finished spanking her with the paddle...it would have been easier, but not as much fun.

"Alright. Can you please take it out of the packaging for me, Master?" I want to go get cleaned up a little bit, if that is okay with you."

"Lovely, *anything* for you." She disappears down the hall and I hear water in our bathroom where I assume she is taking a quick shower, what she doesn't want the fake dick to know that I've fucked her six ways to Sunday?

She comes out looking refreshed and a little readier to take this fake cock on. She walks tentatively back to where she was sitting and demurely crosses her legs, even though she is as naked as the day she was born. I smile and push a lock of her hair away from her face.

"Give me your left foot, lovely." She does without a grumble. "Good girl."

"Now, your right." Again, no argument, just sweetness. "Thank you, lovely." With both feet securely in the ankle straps and her legs spread wide and her amazing pussy on full display...I hand her the now room temperature vibrator with bunny ears. She takes it in her hands and looks at me hoping I will take it from her and just fuck myself with it, but oh well... Tonight, the real punishment is her fucking herself with this big, fake dick and getting off on it.

"Lovely. I don't have all night. Is your pussy not wet any more...do you need some lube?"

"No. Master. I'm ready. Will you be standing right there? Won't you get tired after our earlier activities?" She looks down at her open sex and back up at me, embarrassment clouding her gaze.

"Thank you for your thoughtfulness. I should probably take a seat." I pulled a low sitting stool that put me at eye level with her sex and I sit directly in front of her. "Anytime you're ready."

"Where is the lube, Master?" Something in her look and her voice changed. Vivian still looks like my beautiful submissive, but in that movement, she seemed altogether someone else. I hand her the lube and she smirks at me while she lubed the vibrator and pushed two fingers into her sex to lube herself up, too. *What the fuck is going on. It's like someone just snatched my girlfriend's body. Looks like my lovely, but something's off. Really the fuck off.*

"Do you have a good enough seat, this is probably going to be fast, I mean you wouldn't let me come for like three or thirty fucking hours, so I'm going to come pretty hard and pretty fast." Vivian's voice was different. Not different if you didn't know her, but I knew her like the back of my hand, so I knew it was different. And wait, she didn't call me Master or Sir. I was off the stool before I knew what I was doing. Kneeling between her legs, slapping her spread pussy...hard. She cried out after the fifth slap.

"Do you know why you received that, Viv?" I looked into her eyes and she seem to change in front of me again. Like she softened and became her old self. *What the fuck is going on here? Is she sick? I mean I'm pretty fucked up, but...no, Vivian is fine. Nothing is wrong with her.*

"I don't know what I did to deserve that, but I know that whatever I did, warranted the punishment. Master, I've been experiencing 'black-outs' lately and I don't know...I just don't know what happens when I'm out."

"Come on, let's get you in the bathtub and taken care of. We have a lot to discuss." As I was taking her feet down, I realized she had not come, yet.

"Lovely, I've been rough with you today. I kept your release from you and the paddle...let me make it up to you. I'll be tender with you."

"You only did what you should have done, Master. My behavior has been horrible. Keeping secrets, not trusting you to want what is best for me, and talking to others about plans before talking to you,"

"It takes a long time to build this level of trust for person who is not *you*, and you are *you*...trust comes hard." I am walking her out of the playroom and into our bedroom into our bathroom. I run a warm bath with lavender oils and vanishing bath salts, while I take a look at her ass in the mirror. It's not too bad, but it is bad enough. I pull some *Balm of Gilead* salve from the cabinet.

"Vivian, I want to make love to you now, hold on to the sink...bend down and put that sweet ass in the air."

"Yes. Master." Her voice is hers again. *Thank the Lord.*

I rub her cheeks, they are still warm from the paddling, still beautiful in color. Her breath hissed out through her teeth when I touched her ass, she is sore, the sick bastard in me feels amazing about this. I'm instantly hard. I love that she took the pain from me; took the pain *for* me. She took it and wanted more... *for* me, because she loves me and she wants to please me. I never thought I would love someone so much as I do Viv. I love her so much, it hurts to think about it. There is some other part of me; though, a part I put to rest when I killed Earl that knows I should not be happy Vivian is in pain, but I can never really bury the beast that saved my life.

"When I start making love to you, I want you to touch your clit, okay? This won't be a fast fuck. So don't rush when you're touching. I want you to touch your pussy like you love it, because that's how I'm going to fuck it...because I do, Viv. I fucking love your pussy. Almost as much as I love you. You ready, lovely?"

"Yes Master." Vivian's voice was full of tears, but they were tears full of love and emotion, no sadness this time. *In this moment, she fucking owns me. All of everything I am.*

We made love all night, she learned to touch herself the way I touched her, I learned to see myself through her eyes and I told her all about the scholarship and how I called in some favors from some of the families I knew from the private school I went to. She thanked me with the best deep throat I ever had. We turned a corner and although I thought I would enjoy the paddle, it was too much. I could never do that to her, again.

Tonight, I realized I had carved out just enough space in my heart to love Vivian. And love her I did.

~32~

Our summer in Paris was more than I thought it would ever be. She studied under one of the better-known French curators of the smaller museums in the city, while I made valuable contacts in the financial district. The one thing I grew to love about France was its openness to sexual exploration. Vivian and I didn't feel the need to hide our lifestyle in France; in fact, we were able to find clubs where we could openly practice our lifestyle if we chose.

It was by accident that we stumbled across one of these clubs. We had been out to dinner and wanted to go burn off some of the rich foods we had eaten, so we went in search of a *discotheque*, when we were walking down rue François Miron looking for someplace to blow off some steam. After making sever turns, we happened upon this little club about twelve miles from our starting point on rue Thérèse. From the outside, it looked like any other after-hours club, so we were not expecting what we found once we paid a rather hefty cover charge.

Our visit was just an exercise in viewing. We were not allowed in some of the areas of the club because we were not members; however, we were allowed access to a few of the more tamed spaces in the club. I wasn't impressed with what I saw, and I could tell that Vivian was weary. I always knew she had a little bit of voyeurism tucked away deep inside her, but this place was a little dark for her taste. We were allowed in the store area to purchase appropriate fet-wear, then into the socializing and open play area. That's as far as we were given access to on the this visit. Vivian's voice was whisper soft as she told me her selection for costume.

"I think the black, sleeveless halter top and the black leather pants will do. What do you think, Sir? I would also like the knee-high boots, I like the heels on them." My cock jumped in my linen pants as a small, nervous giggle bubbled up from her throat. I nodded my head and walked her over to the dressing room. I had selected some black leathers for myself; therefore, she would either be wearing the skirt or the skimpy shorts I had tucked away under my selections.

Choosing to wear the shortest shorts I'd ever seen in my life, Vivian stepped from the dressing room looking like my naughtiest fantasy.

"Turn around, lovely." Although we had not discussed how we would addressed each other if ever in this situation, we had talked about what her collar meant and how others in this lifestyle would treat her because of that neck jewelry. Somehow, Vivian just knew what to do and how to behave in this situation. She really was perfect and amazing in all ways. *I had done nothing to deserve her, and yet she loved me unconditionally. Somebody, somewhere wanted me to be happy. Thank you, Violet.*

"Yes, Sir."

My greedy eyes devoured her. There were so many beautiful things to feast on; her pebbled nipples pressing against the barely-there leather of her halter top, her amazingly sexy navel tucked away in even sexier abs. She was just too fucking much. I wanted to tie her up to a bed and fuck her until we both passed out from pleasure, but she was mine and I would never let another see her like that. Even when we fucked like animals; we made love. There was no way in hell I would ever share that with anyone.

"Vivian." Her name, an epic poem no less important than the works of *Homer,* was whispered in her left ear as my fingers caressed her shoulders.

"Yes, Master" Hearing her call me Master did something to my soul. *I didn't even fucking know I had one left.*

"I'm going to need to put this leash on you. It is not to humiliate you, but I know I would fucking kill anyone who looked at you like they wanted to say bonjour to you. This leash along with the collar will ensure they won't even breathe in your direction." The look on her face told me this was not the first time someone had put a leash around her neck to make her feel small and humiliated. I felt like a piece of shit for asking this of her and more questions needled around in my head about Vivian's past which she only talked about in bits and pieces.

"Do you have to use a leash, Master?" Her voice whisper soft as a lone tear slid down her cheek. She fucking broke my heart, in the end there was no leash for her. I could *not* do that to her.

"No lovely, I don't have to. Stay close to me and keep your left hand on my right shoulder at all times. If I don't feel your hand there, the leash will be on...*you understand?"* My chocolate eyes melting her golden irises into caramel pools.

"Yes, Master. I understand." A small, gracious smile playing at the corners of her luscious lips. Another Dom walked in with his sub crawling in with him. She was naked on her hands and knees. A leash on her crude, leather collar and fresh, angry scars all over her back and buttocks. Her stringy hair plastered to her face and neck, she looked and smelled as if she had not bathed in much too long. Her anus was a gaping hole and her pussy looked no better. Both Vivian and I looked at her, but only I look at the Dom, Vivian did exactly as she should have...she kept her eyes low and did not make eye contact with the new Dom or myself. *I was so proud of her, I couldn't wait to get back to our apartment and reward her tonight. I* had *to think of something amazing.* Vivian placed her left hand on my right shoulder and kept her head and eyes down and averted. I didn't have to remind her or tell her, she just did it. I wanted to get us both out of there as fast as I could, something about the shape of the sub told me that this Dom was bad news.

"Zyu due not 'ave zyour pet on zee leash? Ah, *zyu* must be zee pet." His laugh is tinker bell deep and fake. He is trying to get my hackles up, it is not working, but good effort. I look at him and his sub with pity in my eyes. Vivian and I are leaving the fet-wear shop and the asshole goes a little too far. I hear a small gasp escape Vivian's mouth and then she says as only she would, "Get your fucking paws off of me, you piece of shit. I belong to--" Her words are cut short and before I have time to turn around, a large, meaty white hand drew back and open-fist slapped Vivian across her cheek. Her head turned savagely to the right and spittle flew from her mouth as tears burned a path down her face into the hollow of her neck.

The room went black and when I came to myself again, Vivian was sitting beside me in the hospital and she looked so worried, so concerned. She had been crying, but I couldn't worry about that right now, because I noticed the giant cop standing in the corner. *What the fuck had I done at that club?*

***

"John?" The question in her voice was one of pure concern for my wellbeing. Not one of accusation or disappointment that I kept hearing over and over in my mind. The voice was my mother's. She had come to hate me as much as Earl did by the time he killed her. She thought I was as much a fuck up as he did, if not more so, because I was blue-chip black where she was high-yellow. But Vivian wasn't my mother. She wasn't like any other woman I had ever known. She loved me. Without condition, without reason. Vivian loved me past all understanding.

"Yes." One word scratched out over pumice stones, barely reaching the ears of my lovely. She somehow heard me and leaned over to press her small ear closer to my mouth. I couldn't resist it. A small kiss on the outer shell to let her know I was acutely aware of her presence. Her delicate breath gusting over my face, "I missed you, John. I thought, I—I Love you." Tears either hers or mine wet my cheeks and that's when I realized that I couldn't lift my arms from the bed. At first, I thought that I had broken my arms, but then I heard the telltale clink of handcuffs.

"What the fuck is this?" My voice deceptively soft. Almost a whisper. Only Vivian knew how dangerous I could be when my voice was that quiet, that soft. She pushed her chair back, slightly and spoke in placating tones.

"Master…" Her voice soft and cajoling in an effort to calm me down.

"Standing in the corner is the *Police Nationale, he* is the officer assigned to the case, but he is here to simply take your statement and ensure that the crazy uh...uh Dom doesn't show up. His name is officer Beaulac."

"Can officer Beaulac get these fucking chains off my wrist? I'm not some fucking *sub*... I don't take it in the ass...get these fucking irons off me right fucking now!" I roared like some out of control animal; so embarrassed by my current situation and lowered status...being chained up like I belonged to someone...like someone had the right to collar me...I didn't even notice that my collared-someone had left the room. "Shit!"

Officer Beaulac was beside my bed before I even realized that Vivian had taken the short walk from my bed to the door and out into the hall. I knew she had issues with all things anal and that she was not all that comfortable with me talking down her station as my sub and I had just done both...I just kept right on shitting where I ate, literally.

"Bonjour, comment vous sentez-vous ?" (*Hello, how are*

you ?)

"Je suis allé` mieux, merci. Pouvons-nous faire quelque chose a` propos de ces menottes ?" (*I am better, can we do something about these handcuffs ?)*

"Je ne vois pas pourquoi pas." (*I don't see why not.)*

"Merci beaucoup. Parlez-vous anglais ?" (*Thank you very much. Do you speak English ?)*

"Oui, I do speak English; with a heavy accent, but well enough to communicate. Your French is impressive, why not continue in the language of *love*?"

"Love is not what I am feeling at the moment. Why am I handcuffed to this bed and what happened at the club to land me in the hospital?" My voice still did not belong to me and my eyes watched as the police officer methodically took the cuffs from my wrist. I rubbed them noticing the dull soreness as the blood pounded through my veins, trying to restore life back into my hands. The sensation took me back to an afternoon in Auntie's house when she had me handcuffed to the bar inside her closet. She had worked me over with her favored flogger; it was a pink and black leather one she had ordered from Wian Studios. It could cause a lot of pain in the right hands and Auntie had the right hands. I loved every minute of it, every lash, and every moment she broke me down only to build me up. Every time she made me fuck her to within an inch of my life. I loved all of it and now I was the one in charge of doling it out and my little lovely had fled the room because of my insensitivity and lack of attention to her needs. *Fuck me two times on Sunday and once on Monday.*

I was drawn back to the conversation at hand with this pansy cop. He was asking me some stupid question about why I was at the club. *Why the fuck do you think I was at the club?—* Where is Vivian? I really need her back in here with me, I need to tell her I'm sorry for what I said. It serves me right, if she has gone back to our small apartment, what was I thinking? *Oh, I wasn't thinking. I was just feeling sorry for myself.*

"Monsieur?"

"Yes."

"Uh, you were in a sex club last night. Correct?"

"Yes."

"Thank you. Uh, why were you in this club? What were you looking to get *into?* No pun intended." He chuckled at his lame joke. I just glared at him, wanting to punch him in his fat, red face. Nothing he said was funny

"I wasn't looking to get *into* anything. I... that is, my girlfriend and I were looking for a night club so we could dance off some of the extra rich food we had eaten, we saw this club and went inside."

"You guys looked pretty comfortable in this kind of environment. You looked like you engage in a lot of *activities*. Are you familiar with the BDSM lifestyle, sir?" This cop wasn't wasting a word? "Will you continue to frequent sex clubs while in our country?"

"Thank you for your kind words, and yes, my girlfriend and I do plan to visit more upscale clubs once we get settled in." There was no shame in my voice or no need to explain myself. I knew both Vivian and I wanted to go back to a classier club that caters to people with discriminating tastes. If this pussy cop thought we were scared because of an even bigger pussy *Dom* and I got into it at some low rate club, he had another think coming. "Are you arresting me or can I discharge myself and go home? I am not a fan of hospitals and I don't feel any worse for wear, so I'm ready to go."

"No. You are not under arrest. The man you had the altercation with, fled the scene, although I don't quite know how. From eye witnesses, he should not have been able to walk, much less run away from the scene. Apparently, you are skilled in the martial arts?" His balding head inclining slightly to the right, his pale blue eyes staring at me as if waiting for me to confess some big secret.

"Yes. I am a second-degree black belt in Jiu-Jitsu." Dark chocolate meeting ice blue...nothing happening, just some kind of weird power stare down, he looked away first. *The ten-year-old in me is yelling in victory about winning the staring contest. I'm such a fucking child.* I shake my head slightly and continue to look at the officer, hoping he gets the picture.

Before I can ask him does he need anything else, in walks my reason for living. God, she is so beautiful...she is not wearing her submissive leathers; she in her floral sundress and sandals, looking like she stepped out of a Leon Giran Max painting. Everything was glowing on her except her eyes. Vivian's eyes always told me exactly how she felt. Her wide smile said she was happy I was up and unshackled to the hospital bed, but her eyes told me I had hurt her, cut her deeply and left her open to bleed all over the bare floor and she would not be getting over this particular hurt any time soon. *Yes, I was royally screwed and it had been of my own doing. No need in saying I'm sorry, I knew it wouldn't help.*

"Ah, Bonjour mademoisel." Officer Beaulac spoke with even more of a French accent if that was possible. He dropped his voice an entire octave, his back straightening and within seconds, he was standing beside Vivian. *Standing entirely too close to Vivian.*

"Um...Hi officer Beaulac." Vivian stepped away from the Frenchman and walked to the left side of the bed. Even though I had hurt her, and had done so badly, she still sought me out to protect her and something about the cop scared her. She reached down and grabbed my left hand and noticed the dark bruised starting to form around my wrist. A small 'V' formed between her eyebrows, she didn't like the idea of me being bruised, yet I marked her all the time. *I did not deserve this woman.*

I looked at her, a small smile playing with my lips, "I'm good, sit. How are you, have you eaten anything this morning?" Her face dropped. All the answer I needed, but I couldn't find the fire to be angry with her.

With a clearing of his throat, Beaulac reinserted himself into our small bubble. "Je suis content que vous nous avez rejoints, mademoisel. Je voudrais vous poser quelques questions si cela vous convient." (I'm glad you joined us miss. *I would like to ask you some questions, if it's fine with you.)* His words over sweet, his feet moving ever closer towards my Vivian. Why in the hell is he asking her if she has time for questions… what the hell has he been talking with her about before I woke up?

"Beaulac, Pourquoi tu vas parler à Vivian en français, quand tu sais que tu parles anglais ?" (*Beaulac, why are you speaking to Vivian in French when you know you speak English ?)* My scratchy voice blew volcanic ash and smoke across the small room and landed against the pale cheek of the French cop turning it a bright red. I was only a little satisfied, because Vivian chose that moment to answer him in perfectly accented French.

"Bien sur." (*Of course.)* A demure smile gracing her full lips and she had the nerve to turn her head away from me and look the officer right in his eyes and turn her charm up to megawatt power. *Of, course*, she purrs and she knows she has the tiger by the tail, she also knows she has the advantage because I used her hurt to rub my insecurities on and there was nothing I was going to do to add to that hurt...*Fuck, she had me by the short and curlies and she was getting ready to go in for the old grab, twist and pull. This was going to hurt and I mean bad.*

"Sprichst du deutsch?" (*Do you speak German*?)
GRAB.

"Ja, ja ich tue. Meine Mutter ist Deutsch." (Yes, yes my mother is German.) Shit eating grin on his overly, happy face. I want to punch him. *What the fuck are they saying?*

"Stört es dich, wenn wir Deutsch sprechen, wird es meinen Freund pissen. Lachen, als ob ich etwas Lustiges gesagt hätte." (*Does it bother you when we speak German, it will piss my friend. Laughing as if I had said something funny.*) *Why are they laughing? Did she just ask him to speak in German? I heard something about piss and laugh. What the hell?* TWIST

Du bist ein sehr lustiges und schönes Mädchen. Ich sehe, warum er dich liebt. Sollen wir jetzt sein Elend beenden?" (You are a very funny and beautiful girl. I see why he loves you. Shall we end his misery now?) Vivian looked into his glacier blue eyes like he had said the sweetest thing she had ever heard. Her beautiful caramel pools melting for him...for that cock sucker. *What the actual fuck*?

"That's enough. It was enough when you two started speaking fucking *German*, laughing and making soft fucking eyes at each other. Vivian, you know your place and this shit ends NOW. Stand down." I am not yelling, I don't need to. I keep my voice controlled and even, but I'm vibrating with anger.

"I let you have your fun, because...well you know why, but this has gone too far." I felt the vain on the left side of my head throbbing as hard as my dick was. I wanted to take Vivian's sweet ass and throw her across the bed and fuck her until she remembered who she belonged to. She'd obviously forgotten who her Dom was. She would know after we got home this afternoon. I would show her and she would remember. *Note to self: stop by the market and get some ginger root.*

"Yes, Sir. I'm sorry, Sir. May I address Officer Beaulac, Sir?" Her voice perfect. She is back where she belongs. My perfect little submissive...she will still be punished.

"Yes. Briefly."

She stood and walked over to Mr. *Beautiful Lake* and looked into his eyes, my jaws were clenched so tightly, I knew I would need to see the dentist after whatever the hell she had planned took place.
"Vivian...Get on with it please."

"Danke ihnen so sehr für das Spielen mit mir. du bist ein Schatz. Jetzt Kommen und Kussen Sie Mich auf die Wange." (Thank you so much for playing with me. you're a sweetheart. Come now and kiss me on the cheek.)

I don't speak German, but I know I heard kiss and come… "Vivian, if he comes to you and Ki—" My words are snatched from my mouth as officer Beaulac leaned in and kissed my Vivian on her mouth...no tongue, but enough heat in his eyes to let me and her know that he would love to kiss her other set of lips, too. PULL

I was out of the bed before I knew it. My naked ass swinging in the breeze, I saw the surprised look on Vivian's face, she wasn't expecting that. She had probably told him to kiss her on the cheek or something innocent to make me mad...I told her never throw rocks in a placid lake. Well she threw them.

Ripples for days. "Don't you ever put your fucking lips or hands on my lovely again, okay? Glad we could come to an understanding." He shouldn't need too many stitches, if any.

We left the hospital to return to our apartment without

words or feelings shared. Vivian sat so far away from me in the taxi I couldn't touch her if my arms were made of rubber. Even if she were sitting in my lap, I wouldn't be able to touch her, she was closed off from me because she had gone somewhere deep inside herself. I had seen her do that before... seek refuge in the pink and grey matter of her mind.

It was the strangest and scariest thing I had witnessed; and I've seen some pretty scary shit in my short life. Her eyes were open, but the vibrant, golden microcosms with kisses of blue sky that made the sun emulous; those beautiful eyes were now sun-scorched tumbleweed rolling on deserted roads that went nowhere. H*ad I caused the perfect day to leave her eyes? She always left me questioning myself, my role and place in her life...shit...in my life.*

"Vivian." I called softly to her. No response. Her head bowed down and her eyes glued to the rainy city passing by as the taxi zoomed at a bit too fast a speed for my liking, but I don't say anything. I reach across the proverbial line that seems to have been drawn in the seat between us and she flinches away like a scared animal. Like I'm going to hurt her...I mean really hurt her beyond what we have agreed upon as hard and soft limits.

"I'm coming over to you, Vivian. I won't touch you until you tell me I can, okay?" *What the fuck is going on here? She's never behaved like this before. I have to be gentle, when all I want to do is snatch her over here and ruck that skirt around her waist, rip her panties off and shove my dick into her tight pussy...claiming what rightfully belongs to me. She must be bat-shit crazy if she thinks that this shit is ever going to fly again.*

"Vivian, I know you hear me. What's wrong baby. Talk to me. Whatever it is, we will deal with it, I promise. I love you. I got that you were playing a little game in the hospital. It doesn't mean that I'm not going to punish you, but it will be so much more than any dark pleasure I've ever given you, trust me." Her breathing changes a little, but she is still trapped inside that beautiful mind of hers.

"Your game...you speaking German when you know I only speak French and Spanish...You fucking turned me on…" Finally. Her eyes blink and sweep up to look into chocolate craters that leak concern and fight for hope. Gone were the dry tumbleweeds with scorched skies. They had been replaced with those beautiful amber pools that I fell into searching for green grass and purple haze. "So fucking beautiful...your eyes are enough to get and keep me high. Where did you go, lovely?"

~33~

A smoky finger of Remy Martin pointing accusations that don't belong to me, but lay blame all the same in my direction; expecting me to somehow take ownership for some painful, undiluted hurt spilling from those dark, amber oceans…trying to pull me under. I know I can't take the hurt from them, but I also know I didn't put that hurt in them. Those aren't my Vivian's eyes and I'm too chicken shit to ask whose they are again. So, I turn away and look out onto the rainy city and hope like hell Vivian comes back to me by the time we get back to the apartment, I can't be alone with this stranger much longer.

***

We enter the apartment and immediately, Vivian walks into the bathroom and stays in there for an eternity or at least it seems. I use the time to finish up some business that needs my attention. We have only a few more weeks in the city and I want to make this time count for future investments.

"Je dois voir la propriété encore. Si j'aime ce que je vois, alors nous parlerons des contrats." My voice was low and curt. Not my Dom voice or any voice that Vivian has ever heard. She has no idea my liquid assets are worth over five million and my other assets are moving into the billion-dollar-man club. I will never tell her this...she never needs to know.

"What properties are you looking at...is it a small apartment for us?" She asks with Vivian's voice. No more hard brandy accusing me of hurting her, just my soft and contrite Vivian. I smile because I'm happy to see her, even more happy because I have such plans for her tonight.

"Yes, Vivian. Were you eavesdropping? I was hoping to surprise you with a small get-a-way we would sublet, but here you are ruining the surprise." I spoke and as the words fell from my lips, I allowed my Dom to slide around each one, to caress and make love to them; the effect was exactly what I knew it would be...Vivian's face fell as an aspect of fear passed across her amazing cheekbones, her eyelids fell as she dropped to the floor on her knees, hands spread on her thighs, legs slightly parted and mouth full and waiting. There she was, my lovely.

"I missed you. Where have you been, Viv? You lost your damn mind in the hospital with that panty-waste of a French cop." It was damn near impossible to keep the anger out of my voice as I think about that cunt putting his lips on what belongs to me. "And then in the cab ride over, what the hell was that all about?" I had not given her permission to speak, so she simply sat there with her hands spread on her thighs and her eyes down cast. It was so fucking perfect seeing her like that, my dick was instantly and painfully hard, but *Jughead* would have to wait for a while longer*...or maybe he wouldn't.*

I placed the phone on the small side table and turned to face Vivian again. I caught her looking at me with a small smile playing across her lips. It was during times like this when the vixen in my lovely made herself known and Christ, it made me want to fuck her until she passed out. "Vivian." Her face became a blank slate; eyes down, her mouth in that sexy ass natural pout of hers. She didn't answer me. She didn't even look up...not one little peek from behind her long lashes. *My mind went crazy with thoughts of all of the filthy ways I was going to bring Vivian to heal tonight. I knew that it was going to be a hard night for her, but she had to know her place as my submissive. She had to understand she would never be allowed to assert herself like she did in the hospital again...not and continue on as my submissive.*

I walked casually over to the radio and found a station that still played music from the early twenties and the wobbly voice of Josephine Baker came spilling from the speakers in her imperfect-perfect French. I smiled to myself before turning back towards Vivian. Walking in measured steps back to where Vivian knelt on the floor...waiting for whatever I was going to do to her. My mind was going a mile a minute. *Fuck me, it was going to take every lesson Auntie had ever taught me as her submissive and as her Dom to get me through this night...Vivian might leave my ass and I may well deserve it after what I do to her.*

On my best day, I could not have planned a more fitting sound bite on the radio. There are so many things I want to say to Vivian, but words would be useless in this moment to adequately convey what needs to be conveyed to her. There is obviously my love for her, my need to protect her and know she is alright and cared for. I need to know whatever she needs and more importantly, whatever she wants, she has it even before she knows she needs or wants it. I can't explain my unending desire to satisfy her curiosity about life.

Her questions fascinate me. She wants to know about the everyday things and nothings that most eighteen-year olds just know about. Sometimes, it like she's lived a sheltered and secured life away from so many normal things, but her knowledge of all things depraved is depressing *and* sexy as hell. It makes me want to give her sunlight and rainbows to balance out some of the dark clouds and beautiful, chaotic lightning storms we create together.

"On your knees, lovely. I noticed you found something amusing earlier. I don't really care what it was, but I don't recall making a joke so there was no reason for you to smile." I poured two even piles of course grounded salt on the hardwood floors in front of her and watched as she placed her knees on either pile. My breath caught in my throat as she took a deep breath to center herself. I began to walk a circle around her body. The fresh smell of soap and honey-almond oil floated up to my nose letting me know that Vivian had showered and washed her hair. *She smelled so fucking good. Most of her smell was just Vivian alone. She smelled like summer time and fresh cut grass after it rains.* "You may speak to me when I ask you a question. How are you feeling, lovely?"

She takes a big swallow of courage from the air. I know she is afraid of what will happen to her tonight...she should be, because she knows what she did in that damn hospital room was completely unacceptable. "I'm scared, Sir."

"You know I don't want you to ever fear me, lovely. It is not my intention to have you afraid of me. It is only my intention to punish you to reinforce a set of behavioral standards we agreed upon to ensure you are safe and both yours and my needs are met in this relationship. Today in the hospital, one of us forgot that agreement and it sure as fuck was not me. Now was it, Vivian?" I tried and failed miserably to keep the savage roar and wrath out of my voice, but there was no help for that. With every increase in tone, my steps got heavier and closer to the front of my submissive, whose entire body was visibly shaking by the time I stood in front of her with my hands on my belt buckle...fumbling to undo it and undo my pant front.

"No fucking tears. Pick your head up and look at me. Now. I'm going to ask you again, Viv. How are you feeling? Give me the kind of answer a sub who has caused her Dom all sorts of heartache and suffering should give when she finds herself in this situation. Ready?" I placed the index and middle finger of my right hand under her wet chin and forced her watery eyes up to meet my angry, dry ones. My dick was hanging out, hard and leaking my arousal down the front of Vivian's chin. What I saw in her eyes scared the shit out of me, but I was not willing to back down. "Answer my fucking question, how are you feeling?"

"I'm feeling sorry for causing you so much worry and trouble, Sir. I never should have asserted myself in such a way as to cause you concern." Tears, thick like oil slid down her face and I didn't know if they were coming from her words or from kneeling on the salt. My heart was breaking, but I had to see this thing through. I wiped her tears away and leaned over her to kiss her forehead...I thought I felt her flinch just a little. I kissed a path to her ear and whispered how much her words made me happy and how much I loved her and her gift of submission. I kissed my way back to her soft mouth, which is always softer when she cries.

"I love you so fucking much, lovely. But you...you have to know how far you can go before you go too far. Today in the hospital, you went too damn far. I could stop right now and just fuck you. Not let you come at all, not for the rest of the night...and that might be enough, but I know you. You need something that will remind you for the rest of your life that we have a contract and you don't have the right to fucking break that shit, ever!

I am not willing to let you go. You wear my collar...that means you belong to me; forever! I am going to marry you; do you understand what I'm saying to you? You are never going to belong to anyone else, so don't do shit that will make me have to punish you like I'm doing tonight again. I fucking love you, lovely. I. Don't. Ever. Want. To. Have. To. Do. This. Again. Do. You. Fucking. Understand. Me?" I slammed my dick into her mouth and down the back of her throat with such force, she almost fell on her ass. I caught the back of her neck and began thrusting in and out of her mouth as if I was fucking her tight pussy. I realize somewhere outside of my lizard brain I had not reminded her how to let me know if she needed to stop, but my lizard brain was in control… she knows she can tap me twice on my thighs. *Fuck, I hope she knows.*

Somewhere between grabbing her neck and deep-throating her, I lost my mind and starting coming...I didn't hear her gagging and coughing. I didn't feel her trying to push me back and out of her mouth either; until she bit down on my cock and I reach back and slapped her face. I slapped her so hard she fell to the floor coughing and choking on my cum and then she just stopped. She stopped coughing. She stopped choking. She stopped moving.

You know when people say the world slowed down and every sound was magnified, every color was sharper? That's what happened as I watched Vivian laying on the floor, not moving.

There was a thick, red something pooling beside her head, my mind would not let me call it blood. I knew I should go to her, do something, check on her and make sure she was still alive, still with me. I was so afraid. Afraid I had killed another woman I was supposed to protect. *What the fuck is wrong with me? All I do is hurt the women I love...I hurt and love them to death. I am the one that's fucked up...Earl was so right. I'm the one that's fucked up. I'm the shit-for-brains— My* self-loathing was interrupted by a low moan and then a soft cry of my name. I fell to my knees beside Vivian, afraid to touch her and afraid not to. She looks so fragile, so scared.

"Sir?" She licked her swollen lips and turned her tearful, caramel gaze to me. Fear oozed down her cheek and in that moment, I knew that she was not afraid of me, but afraid for me. My heart broke for her, because I did not deserve her love or her submission and I never would.

"Lovely. I. Am. So sorry. Please forgive me. A Dom never has the right to treat his sub the way—"

"No Master, I should not have gagged on your cum, I should not have bitten down on your cock, Sir...Please don't turn me away. I love you." The tears ran freely down her cheeks and I scooped her up in my arms, knowing that it was I who should be begging her forgiveness, but also knowing she would never allow me to do so. I held her close to me and rocked her in my arms, whispering my love into her hair as I checked her for the cause of the bleeding. It appeared she had hit her head and sustained a small cut. A small bandage would fix her right up.

~34~

As her Dom, it is my job to see to her aftercare. To make sure she is both mentally and physically intact after a scene or punishment. Right now, I wish I had someone to see to me. I am a mess, but I can't let Vivian see that in me. I will deal with my weakness later, after I have put her to bed. She needs me to love her, to be her boyfriend now. First her aftercare, then her boyfriend. *Fuck. I'm tired of all these roles. I just want to be with Vivian. I just want it to be John and Vivian. Wait, if that's what I want, then why can't I have it? Why the fuck not? Why, because I need it. I need parts of our lifestyle to keep me sane, but there has to be a middle space, right?*

Getting Vivian out of her head took some time, but a warm bath, hot tea and hand-fed dinner seemed to do the trick. I made love to her for hours; denying myself the pleasure of coming while making sure she got hers in spades. It was my way of submitting to her without conceding my power to her. When her body was boneless and limp in my arms from coming and fucking, I told her I had given her permission to use my body, now I would like the same concession.

"Yes, John." Her voice light and airy as she lay on her back and spread her legs wide for me. The rain pelted the tin roof and her pulse beat in time with the irregular beat of the cleansing water.

"I'm not going to fuck you anymore tonight; you'll be sore in the morning...rub your clit with your right hand and don't come again until you feel my cum on your stomach."

"Yes, John." Her hand slid between her thighs and with her middle finger she began to stroke around her wet opening as heel of her hand massaged the center of all her pleasure. *God her face was a picture. Something that should be framed and placed on every man's wall to show him the look he should put on his woman's face when he's fucking her.* Her eyes were soft, her full mouth was slightly parted, her skin was covered in a fine sheen of sweat and most importantly her usually cool hands were warm and wet with the sticky nectar of her flower. She was lost under her ministrations and it was a thing of beauty.

It was not a conscience decision, it just happened. I ran my entire hand down the length of Vivian's wet pussy and immediately wrapped said hand around my pernicious dick. All I could see, hear, smell, and feel was Vivian. Poor *Jughead*! I squeezed and jerked him so hard, he may not be talking to me after this. Vivian's essence coated my dick and watching her fingers fucking into her beautiful flower made cum boil and bubble in my balls like my mom's grits use to when she left them on the stove too long.

"Oh my God...John! I'm...I can't stop---I'm going to come."

"No, the fuck you're not." It was more a growl than spoken words.

"John, can't stop it." Her hips pumping into her hands and three fingers work themselves into her wet channel, the heel of her hand rubbed her hardened clit...driving her insane.

"Stop fucking yourself. Wait for me, dammit. Wait for me, I'm almost—shit, Viv...I'm almost...oooooooh." I fell onto Vivian like water being released from a dam. Slapping her hand out of the way, I slid into her warmth and began coming immediately. Her muscles gripping me...clamping down on my dick so tightly I cried out from the tightness of it. The painful euphoria of our joined climax was too much. Our breathing slowed down and our heartbeats crept to just enough to move blood.

Vivian was facing me, laying on her right side with her

head on the pillow. She was so beautiful. I leaned in, nuzzling her neck. Because I'm a fucking caveman, I bit down on the smooth skin just below her ear. Always needing to mark her. Needing to let any and everyone who saw her know she was taken. "I need you as more than my sub" I whispered into her neck as my tongue soothed the fresh bite mark. "You have to put me out of misery, be my wife." Some long breaths later, after I had rolled to my back and pulled her to my side, her head resting on my chest and was making lazy circles on Vivian's back, I realized she had not responded. I knew she wasn't asleep and I also knew she was scared shitless.

I kissed her shoulder to let her know it was time to talk about my proposal of sorts. Shit, I don't even know where to start. *I had not meant to bring the subject up just yet, but oh well... fuck it.* "I don't plan for us to marry before we graduate from Carolina." The words hang in the air for a few moments, she doesn't say one word, she doesn't even move. *I hope to fuck she's breathing.* I pressed my hand between her breasts to feel her chest rise and fall. *Okay, she's still with me*. "As I said, we're not getting married until after we graduate, but please know immediately after graduation… you will become Mrs. Johnathan Raynard Ellis. There is no need to wait. There is nobody else for me or you. You're already wearing my collar...we have the next three years to perfect our relationship and make sense of our monogamous Dom/sub lifestyle. You may not always be my sub in the traditional sense, but I will always be your Dom and we will work that out. Do you understand what that means, lovely?"

"I love you, John. I know that I love you and nothing else really matters."

"I love you, too."

We didn't wake up until 2 pm the next day.

***

Summer in Paris proved to be amazing and wonderful and all the things people said it would be for a pair of young lovers. We will never forget our first time in the city of love. I was happy to purchase the small apartment, it was a great investment and over the years it also became a great getaway for times when *I* needed to get away.

As much as Vivian and I enjoyed Paris, we were ready to get back to the states and finish up our college experience. Carolina had many lessons to teach us and most of those lessons were learned outside the classrooms of the hallowed halls of the university. Three years left to earn our degrees. Three years left to earn each other's' trust and love. Three years left to work the kinks out of our kinky relationship. Three years left until Vivian became my wife. I could wait that long. I would have to.

~35~

I had forgotten how hot South Carolina was in August. Returning home was a necessary evil and one I both looked forward to and dreaded. The sooner we were back, the sooner we could finish with our degrees and the sooner we could be married. I needed those papers, my ring on her finger and prefix of Mrs. in front of her new last name...Ellis. Mrs. Vivian Ellis

"John, I can't find the box marked, kitchen. Have you…" I wrapped my arms around her waist and pulled her to my chest and urged her to wrap her long legs around my waist. She did, among a fit of giggles and pretend complaints. "We can unpack later. Right now, I want you and you don't have the option of saying no." I walked slowly down the hall towards our bedroom. I loved the house she thought we were renting. It was an older home in the prestigious Shandon area. I got it for a steal, as it was in foreclosure. I knew this area would only appreciate; therefore, my investment would yield a big return when I went to sell it down the road. It had three bedrooms and one bath. At a little over 1500 square feet, the house was small enough that we would have to be close to each other, but big enough to give each of us the space we would need in the coming three years.

Kicking the door open, I dumped her on the California king size, four post bed. Our bedroom and closet had been the first room to be unpacked and decorated. The walls were a deep shade of tyrian purple and the bedding was all grays and black. "Don't move." My voice dropped, and my stance changed just enough to let her know that she was in the room with her Dom, not her doting boyfriend. Her response was instantaneous. Her eyes turned down, shoulders relaxed, and her head bowed. *Fuck, I love us like this. I love her like this...so fucking perfect for everything I need her to be. What will I do with lovely today?*

"Take your tank top off and your bra. Hand them to me when you are done."

"Yes, Sir." *Fucking perfect.*

Vivian sat up in the bed and removed her white tank top. Crossing her arms in front of her and reaching towards the hem of her top, she slowly pulled the flimsy material away from her scarred skin. Revealing small expanses at a time, making my dick hard enough to pound nails into the wall. Once the shirt was under her breast, she licks her full bottom lip and pulls it between her teeth...slowly releasing it. *Little vixen. She knows that I'm going to make her pay for teasing me and I think she wants to pay. I hope I haven't turned her into a pain-slut. The thought disturbs me...pleasure punishment.*

Finally, the goddamned shirt is over her head of bouncing curls and she is sitting on my bed in her champagne colored lace bra. A growl bubbles up from my throat. It's a warning and she seems to get the hint, because her bra comes off much quicker than her top had. A small smile flirts with her lips. She is in a good mood today.

"Now come undress me. Don't take all day, Vivian. I have things to do and so do you." She crawls towards the edge of the bed and then slowly swings her long legs off the side of the bed before standing and walking over to me as I folded her top and bra before I place them on the dresser behind me. Turning to face her, I am transfixed by the gentle sway of her breast. *So. Perfect.* Her hands reach out for the bottom of my shirt and she begins to pull it up towards my head. I bend forward to help her take it off.

Her eyes have not left the floor. She folds my shirt and places it on the bed. Nimble fingers undo and remove my belt from my Levi's, she coils it and places it beside my shirt. Her hands are on the waistband of my jeans, eight fingers resting on the inside against my pubic hair and two thumbs making circles on the outside against my dick. *Viv, you're killing me, babe. I want to take her by the shoulders and throw her on the bed, rip that little skirt into shreds and slam into her wet pussy. No underwear allowed in the Ellis household. Fuck, I like the sound of that. Focus, John!*

"Lovely. You are playing with an intense fire. Think carefully about your next move." My voice is quiet and soft. This is when I'm at my most dangerous. She knows it. I know it and neither of us wants me there right now. "Get these motherfucking jeans off me, get down on your knees and wait for me to fuck your mouth." I sound menacing to my own ears and then flashbacks from the horrible ordeal in Paris flood my brain. Trembling hands undo my button-fly and she slowly pulls my pants down. *Because I'm a sick bastard, her fear makes me harder. A part of me hates myself for it, but most of me is fine with it.* My dick springs out and hits her in the face...on the chin. I have to stifle a laugh. Once I step out of my jeans and they are neatly folded, she places them on top of my shirt, my socks on top of my jeans and my coiled belt on top of all of it and walks silently over to the dresser to place them on my side.

"Sir?" Her voice is wavering, and she sounds like a little girl. Gone is the playful vixen who teased me earlier and in her place, is the most submissive version of Vivian. I didn't want her this way...she's afraid of me. She's remembering Paris, too. *Fuck! Should I turn off my Dom and just make love to her? I don't know what the fuck to do. God, I hate feeling like a scared, little boy and in my own house, too.*

"Yes, lovely." I decided to stay as her Dom. We have not had oral like this sense Paris. She's going to have to get back in saddle.

"Would you like for me to finish undressing?" Her voice is high. She's aroused, but scared. I know exactly what to do for her. I'm going to fuck her mouth... No, I'm going to make love to her mouth. Slow shallow thrust and then deep, slow thrust. *Yea, my cock likes the idea, too. Jughead weeps at the thought of taking Vivian's mouth like that.*

"Yes. Go ahead and undress. I want to see your beautiful body. Your lovely scars and that amazing, beautifully tight pussy of yours." I keep my voice low and sexual. Her reaction to my earlier outburst help to put me back in my place. Moments later, she returns to stand in front of me, head down and eyes on the floor. There is a visible shiver running over her body and I know she's not cold...no this is fear. I place left hand on her right cheek, she leans into my touch and closes her eyes completely at my gentleness. *She is so sweet. Deserve her, John. Prove you deserve her.*

"Lovely. Look at me, please" I move my hand, so my thumb is rubbing her bottom lip, it's so soft. I can't wait to suck it into my mouth and nibble on it. *Focus John, you selfish son-of-bitch. Focus on making her feel safe.* Vivian's eyes sweep up to meet mine and every-fucking-time she looks at me, it's like an electrical wire to the brain. I have never seen eyes the color of Vivian's. Liquid gold running through green grass while flirting with blue skies. "I am not going to hurt you. I know we have not tried this position sense my stupid blow-up in Paris, but Vivian I really need to know that you and I can do this. Don't be afraid of me. I will *never* treat you like that again. I love you too much.

Me treating you as royalty is self-preservation, baby. Your smile, your joy... that's what keeps me moving forward. That's what keeps me breathing, my heart beating. I. Will. Not. Hurt. You." Each word punctuated with a soft kiss to both eyes, the tip of her nose and two to her amazing mouth. She took a deep breath and graciously dropped to her knees in front of me. I had gotten a little soft, but the sight of her willingly submitting to me in this way; when I know that she is scared out of her fucking mind, makes me immediately and painfully hard. With her hands behind her back, her eyes on me, I wrap my right hand around the back of her head...burying it in her thick curls. With my left hand, I press head of my dick to her lips, she opens for me and I release the breath I'd been holding. *Fuck yea! She's going to let me in her mouth. God, I don't deserve her trust or her love, but thank fuck I have them both.*

"Vivian? Are you okay?" I had the head of my cock in her mouth, she couldn't speak so she gave me thumbs up. That was our nonverbal signal to keep going. "Good girl. You look so beautiful kneeling before me. I'm so fucking happy right now. I want all of your mouth. My control...do you trust me, Vivian?" Thumbs up. "Open a little wider for me, that's it. I wrap my left hand around the back of her head, grabbing a handful of curls and start to move deeper into her mouth. I keep my tempo slow and my thrust shallow. I feel her tongue swirling around the tip on the underside of my dick and I almost lose it. I push deeper, moving her head on and off my cock. Her mouth is so wet and the sexy sounds she makes while sucking me off make me crazy. *The animal in me wants to ram my dick down her throat and fuck it until I'm coming. I want to use her mouth as my personal fuck hole...but that's not going to happen. Not today.*

"God baby. Your mouth is my own private heaven. So warm. So wet." I'm all the way in and I feel her throat working on a swallow and she swallows what feels like half of my dick. *I can't come, yet.* Closing my eyes, I pull out and start with shallow, fast plunges into her greedy mouth. "Fuck, lovely. Do that again." I grit out as she scrapes her teeth across the bottom and top of my dick. She is moaning so loudly, I feel like I need to make sure she is not touching herself. I did not give her permission to. Her hands had better be behind her back or I *will* fuck her mouth... *hard*!

"Just like that, lovely. I want your throat. Please thumbs up if it's okay." I hope like hell I see a thumb's up. Thumbs up. *Thank fuck.* I grab her head in earnest and plunge into the back of her throat. She swallows repeatedly, knowing how much I love that shit, then I start to move. Deeply, slowly. In and out of her throat. Every time I go back in, she swallows; pulling me deeper into her tight, wet throat. I want nothing more than to come and I can't stop myself this time.

"Lovely. Shit, baby. Ohhhhhh yea! God-You...Oh Fuuuuck." Then I'm coming—hard. I shoot my seed down her throat and it just doesn't stop. My groin is plastered against her face and I'm pumping my hips like a race horse and she just doesn't stop swallowing me. I feel my dick jerk in her mouth and I start pulling out of her throat and mouth and she whimpers. *If I didn't already love her like a crazy man...I do now. God, I would kill for her.*

I'm barely holding myself up, but I bend down and pick Vivian up by her shoulders to bring her on the bed with me. She is breathing as hard as I am, she's as turned on as I am. The evidence of her arousal is running down her thighs. I lay her against my left side and tuck her in close...I need to hold her for a minute. That was the most intense blowjob I've ever experienced in my life.

"Vivian, are you awake?" She so quiet.

"Yes, Sir." She doesn't say anything else.

"Are you alright? That was pretty intense for your first time back in the saddle." I say with a smile in my voice. Something feels off, so I try to lighten the mood.

"Yes, Sir. I'm fine, Sir." Nothing else.

"Viv..." No more Dom in my voice, just concerned

boyfriend who's scared to death that he's broken something in his fragile girlfriend.

"Yes, John." Good she noticed the difference.

"Talk to me. Where did you go just now?" My voice is low and husky. Her smell is fucking with me, I'm getting hard again, but we need to deal with this before I make love to her.

"I came, John. I don't know what happened... I-I have never come from sucking you off and no, I didn't touch myself. My hands were behind my back the entire time." She holds up her right hand and presses her fingers under my nose to prove her point. *Well, fuck me running a marathon; that's the sexiest thing ever*. I'm stuck on her fingers, when I realize she's still talking. "I came when you came, and it was—*cathartic*." She sounds amazed and embarrassed and a little bit scared, which my wayward dick notices and starts to rise to the occasion.

"I thought that you had come, but honestly I was so far gone, I wasn't sure if I was still conscious. You sound...frightened." I lift her chin and force her to look at me. This time I'm prepared for the punch in the gut I get from those eyes. "Talk to me, Vivian."

"It's just that it has never happened to me and I didn't have permission to come, but it was so fast. The moment I felt you get bigger in mouth...I knew you were going to come and it triggered something. I don't know what, but something opened up the biggest orgasm ever and I was...*am* just scared. I didn't mean to do it and I don't know how to stop if it happens again." A tear slid down her cheek as her voice cracked on the end of her words. I licked the tear from her cheek and kissed her lips, softly. They're so soft when she cries.

"Don't worry, lovely. You will always get a pass when this happens. It makes me crazy that it turns you on so much to give me pleasure. It is the most selfless thing I have ever experienced. Without any physical stimulation, you orgasm from my pleasure alone. Wow! As your Dom, nothing makes me happier. As your lover, nothing makes me happier. I love you." I kiss her, softly at first, but then she reaches up and pulls my head down to hers. She takes over the kiss and I let her.

Her tongue is sliding against mine, licking and eating at my mouth. She sucks on my bottom lip and then with just enough pressure to cause the right amount of pain, she bites down. *Oh my God. I feel like I'm in the bed with someone completely different. I have never seen this aggressive side of Vivian, well not in the bedroom. Holy fuck, it's sexy as hell. Wait she was like this the last time we went to our favorite sex club in Paris. Something had changed...*

"John." Her voice was husky and lower. It snaked its way around my neck and slithered down my chest and stomach to hug my balls. I wanted her, and I would have to analyze the change in her later.

"Yes Vivian." I could hardly get the words out. She was working me with her hand, running her fingernails over my balls and my dick—driving me out of my fucking mind. She pulled on my shaft so hard, I saw stars. This was different and hot.

~36~

"John, turn over. Please. I want to ride you." Something feels off, but I can't put my finger on it. She is so fucking sexy like this and normally there is never any topping from the bottom allowed in our bedroom, but she's just so hot when she wants me this badly. I want to give her this, because she has given me much more than I ever thought I would have.

"You want to ride *all* this?" I'm trying to lighten my mood...as turned on as I am, something just doesn't feel right.

"Yes, John. I want *all* of you inside me. I want to feel you pounding into me, jerking my hips down to meet your thrust, rubbing your thumbs over my clit and I want to feel *all* of you fucking *all* of me." Her words, her voice and the sexy come-here-and-fuck-me-now look she's giving me makes me forget my name and my concerns fly out the open window facing the backyard. I flip over onto my back and open my arms wide in invitation. Vivian is crawling on the bed looking like some kind of sex kitten and she drags her nails down my chest before straddling me,

"Please John. Help me. You know it's hard for me to take you this way." *My pride wells up in my chest and Jughead gets bigger and harder. She shouldn't be able to do this to me with a few little words, but I fucking love that she can.*

"Come here, Viv." I hold out my right hand and she grabs onto it with her left, squeezing it tightly. I'm a tight fit for her in other positions, but with her on top...it's almost impossible to get all the way in, but I never fail to fit. *And Vivian never fails to take all of me and her greedy pussy just keeps sucking me deeper. So good.*

"Lift up on your knees and scoot that delicious ass up

towards my dick. You want me to fuck *all* of you...that's what you said, right? Does this mean that you're finally going to let me—" The words are snatched out of my mouth by Vivian's hasty retreat to the other side of the bed. *What the fuck?* By the time my addled brain processes what happened, I realize that she is balled up, her long arms wrapped around knees that are pushed up to her chest and hiding her face. Soft whimpers coming from some broken part of her that she has yet to tell me about.

"Viv, baby." My voice not above a whisper as I scoot over to her and place my left hand on her back and began to rub small, firm circles between her shoulder blades.

"Baby. What is this thing that makes you so afraid? Who hurt you, tell me and I'll find them, and they will bleed." The soft tone of my voice was for Vivian, the razor sharp, cold as ice edge that slid under and over my words was for whoever hurt and destroyed parts her.

Dark caramel eyes with stormy clouds of gray, looked at me with such pain and fear and... *loathing*? I had to look away. "They always hurt me. Too many to name, too many scars to heal. I put them in jars and set them up on shelves in my soul." Her voice was flat and completely devoid of emotions. I thought she was done...I really didn't understand what she was talking about, but before I could ask for clarification, she started talking again. "John. I am a filthy whore and you are, too good for me. You deserve a good and decent girl…that's not me. I—I have done...things have been done. I saw so much—you should have better. You should punish me every day for all my transgressions. I am a dirty, filthy whore." Sobs and shudders rack her body. I am stunned into silence. My heart has stopped beating and I can't breathe. *What the fuck happened to my lovely? She's as broken as me.*

***

I've given Vivian a bath and fed her, her favorite meal, pan seared tuna, sweet peas and roasted herbed potatoes; and now she is sitting quietly in a chair looking out the window at our backyard. She hasn't said one word sense her outburst and I don't know what to say to her. I'm watching her from the living room like a scared little boy, because I feel helpless and confused and impotent. *I hate this fucking feeling. I haven't been this fucker in years and just like that...I'm a sniveling pussy.*

"John?" Her soft voice pulls me from my dark thoughts and the question in her tone makes me pay attention. "Yes, lovely. How are you feeling?" I keep my voice even and low. I've averted my eyes from her, but I feel her standing to my right, waiting for me to tell her to come over, but I can't… not, yet. "I—I... want to s-say that I'm s-sorry for…" A sob rips from her throat and I'm on my feet, pulling her into my arms and kissing her hair. Her body is shaking and her 5'11" frame feels small and vulnerable in my arms. "Lovely. Shush, don't apologize. I pushed you and I know you have scars that don't show. I shouldn't have pulled scabs from them. I'm the one who is sorry." Her sobs have subsided and her body melts into my own.

"Do you want to talk to me?"

"No."

"Do you want to go for a walk?"

"No."

"Do you want to make love? No D/s... just a love-sick guy who wants to be with his beautiful girl."

"Yes."

I take her hand and lead her to our bedroom and for the rest of the night, I show her how much I love and worship her.

“Tomorrow will be better, lovely. We'll put the house together, go buy books and find our classes. Our second year of college awaits us.”

“Thank you, John. One day, I'll open these jars and share them with you.”

“I know, lovely. When you're ready, I'll be here. I love you... now,” In my Dom voice, “...go to sleep. This is not a request.” I feel her smile against my shoulder and I don't feel like a pussy anymore.

~37~

Sophomore year of college is more of the same bullshit, just more work. Navigating my college career takes little effort; join the right clubs and organization, attend the right meetings and social gatherings and kiss the right professor's asses. This is all a game and thankfully, I never lose. Navigating my relationship with Vivian is a whole different story. Every day feels like a lesson in diplomacy. I am learning so much about her and still, there is a gaping hole in her life I just don't have access to and she does not seem to be willing to share it with me. Granted, she does not know any more about me than I have told her and that isn't nearly the entirety of my depravity, but she doesn't seem to need to know more. She is content with what I give her. Why can't I be more like her...happy to have whatever she gives me? But it is not enough, it will never be enough. I have to possess her, own her...I can't do that if I don't have access to all of her.

"Baby, it's a month or so before Christmas break." Vivian walked into the kitchen in a pair of Levi's 501 dark denim jeans that set low on her hips and fit tight all over. She paired it with a beautiful white cable knit crew-neck sweater with a green turtleneck...she looked like the reason holiday colors were invented.

"Yea?" I could barely get a word out of my mouth. Most of my blood flow was heading south and that left a miniscule amount for my brain to function on.

"Well, last year you took me to New York... so?" She stuck the thumb of her right hand in her belt loop and cocked her hip out to the side, she looked like every dirty fantasy I ever had.

"Are you trying to figure out if I will be taking you somewhere this year?" I gaze at her as I pass her a cup of coffee and give her my sexiest smirk...the one I know makes her panties wet. *God would I love to see if it's working. Those eyes...staring at me after what she did for me last night in our basement playroom...God, I fucking love her as my submissive and I worship her as my girl.*

"Well."

"Well, what?"

"Stop being cute, John,"

"Will you let me handle our Christmas plans, please?"

"I just want to know…" I cut her off with a sweet, slow kiss and she forgot all about Christmas plans and melted on my tongue. The sounds that came from her were so sweet and perfect. I didn't want anything more from her than the soft moans and sweet sighs...they made me feel content and needed.

"Come, we have another week of class and then your holiday awaits you. I can't wait to spend my second Christmas with you, lovely. Last year was so amazing, so fucking perfect. Every time I see my collar around your neck, my heart burst with pride and love. And now...I have already said too much."

"You are such a tease, but I'll let you have your fun. I know how much you love to surprise me and I love you for it. Let me get my stuff and we can go. Can you drop me off at the Cooper, I have to meet Byron there to go over our notes for English." She came back into the kitchen wearing a thick hat that barely contained her thick, cinnamon-hued curls and her favorite short ski jacket.

"Why are you working with Bryon? I thought we agreed that you would not work with that sleezeball again after the last time. Do you not remember what that horny bastard did the last time...or did you like it?" My voice was low and soft. I'm sure she knew I was pissed. *How dare her work with that priapic fucker after he pulled out his pathetic excuse of a dick and told her that she could suck it for him and he would give her twenty dollars. What the fuck is she thinking?*

"I didn't have a choice. My professor made me work with him. I even went to her after class and begged her to let me change partners or work alone, but she said no and that I would have to learn to work with different personalities if I was going to be successful in this world. What was I supposed to do?" Her voice was agitated and she was trying to hold it together, but I saw her facade cracking. She was trying to be strong and brave for my benefit.

"Lovely, I will be at the library with you for this meeting and I will have a few words for our young Mr. Byron. Let's go."

I didn't have class for another hour and that's how much time Vivian had to meet with Byron. "You have about forty-five minutes with this son of bitch, you got me?" I didn't wait for her to respond as I got out of the car and walked around to open the door for her. She took my hand and stepped from the car.

"Thank you, John. I'm glad you're staying. I won't have to meet with him again...he makes me feel, *dirty.*" Her voice was barely above a whisper and words from the day we moved into our house floated into my mind. "*John. I am a filthy whore and you are, too good for me.*" I grabbed her hand and rubbed my thumb across her soft knuckles. *She fucking slayed me. One word. I'm going to fuck Byron's shit up and he won't even know it until it's over.*

The study session was tense, to say the least. I sat beside Byron with my dick out under the table and ran a twenty-dollar bill up and down his thigh. *Childish? Very. Effective? Hell yea*

***

The final week before Christmas break was a blur of

cramming, fucking, testing, making love, eating and *playing*. My kind of week and not a bad way to usher in the holiday season.

"Babe, I'm home. No thanks to you. I'm glad you got us these new cell phones." Her voice was terse, but humor danced around her words as they left her sinfully, decadent mouth. I heard her knee-high, heeled boots clicking on the hardwoods as she searched for me in the house.

"It smells like pine...Oh. My. God!" Her mouth was opened wide and those beautiful golden eyes were glowing. *Perfect. Just perfect.*

"Click.". The *Nikon* shutter immortalized my lovely's reaction to our first live Christmas tree in our first home together.

"It's so big!"

"Yes, that's what she said."

"John! I've never had a tree for Christmas. Not one inside a house where I lived. Thank you, baby. It's beautiful." Tears oozed out of her eyes and ran like thick baby oil down her cheeks.

"Me either. I've never had one and never thought I would want one until I saw your eyes light up when we looked at that big ass tree at Rockefeller Center last year. I wanted to see you look like that in our own home. I wanted to give you the Christmas you deserve to have. Start some traditions."

She walked over to me and placed her arms around my waist and laid her head on my shoulder "Thank you. You are so good to me. Too good to me. Do we have decorations?"

***

Christmas morning was an experience in *bliss*. There

was no other word to describe the look on Vivian's face when she walked into the living room and saw the gifts that had *magically* appeared under the tree over the course of the night. *Now I see why parents plan and stay up all night to play Santa Claus. Wait, where the fuck did that thought come from?*

Vivian handed me the only gift she had for me in a beautifully wrapped box. I shook it and nothing happened. I squashed the small stab of disappointment at not hearing something in the box. "Open it." Her voice was so soft, I had a hard time hearing her. What I found nestled in between soft silk handkerchiefs in more shades of blue than I've ever seen, was an envelope with my name on it

"What is it?"

"My gift to you."

"I know it's your gift to me, but what is it?"

"Open it, John. Please."

I took the envelope out of the silk handkerchiefs and sat down in the chair beside the window. She walked over to me and knelt down at my feet with her head bowed and her eyes down. She didn't say a word. As still as a statue and just as silent. I opened the envelope with deliberate movements. *What in God's name will I find inside. My heart is beating like a drum and... shit, are my hands trembling. Get your shit together, Ellis.* I pull out a tri-fold paper that smells of jasmine and will my hands to stop shaking. I look over at Vivian and she has clipped a leash onto her collar. *Where did she get that from? It's the diamond one from New York.* I return my eyes to the letter...no wait, it's an IOU.

I Owe You...

I owe you a debt I can never pay. I don't have the correct currency.

I am sorry to default on this debt, but I can't afford the cost of loving you. (Don't stop reading to ask me what this is about ☺)

I would gladly pay any price, but I don't think I have what it takes to do so.

Please accept this I. O. U. in lieu of payment.

I owe you my life. I gladly exchange my dying breath to make you happy. In the moment when everything looks like it won't get better and you are sure your joy will not return, I will give my last breath to give you back your happiness. You may cash this I. O. U. in when you need that glorious smile back. Your happiness is the one thing that lifts me from the darkness that is my yesterday. The reality of what I was before I met you. Your joy is the talisman that keeps the boogeyman away from me, thank you. <u>My life for your happiness</u>.

I owe you my joy. I gladly exchange my joy for your pain. In the time in your life when you are consumed with pain, a pain so terrible you can't see a way out of it. A pain so visceral, there is no recovering from the scars it will leave on your soul...I will gladly give you my joy. My lightness. My ease. I freely give it and I will take your pain as my own. I will shoulder it and add it to the many scars that already adorn my body. The scars left by your pain will be counted beautiful by my soul, because your pain is a gift for me to bare. <u>My joy for your pain.</u>

I owe you my soul. I gladly exchange my soul for your sins. In a time when all you have ever been and all you will ever be come together and reveal any flaw...any blemish that may mar you...I will gladly give you the best part of my soul. The good part. The clean part that your love has made whole. I will give you my soul and take your sins as my own. I will wear them as a badge of honor and one day…I hope to be worthy of wearing your sins. My soul for your sins.

Who I was does not matter because I was nobody until I met you. I owe you my contentment. My body as an offering…a sacrifice. I sacrifice the darkly erotic place for your peace of mind. At a time when nothing else can bring you peace your mind seeks, I will gladly exchange my peace of mind for yours. Use this I. O. U. carefully, for it is only redeemable once. I only have the one time to give this to you, after that time…I will have restored your peace of mind and will take your fear, pain, anger, and confusion as my own. My body, anyway you want to use it, for your peace of mind.

I love you,

Vivian (soon to be) Ellis

I looked up from the letter and watched as tears ran down her cheeks. *Holy mother of God, she has just gifted me all of her in a way that a collar, a wedding band, not even a D/s contract could do. I don't deserve this, but the bastard in me will take it.*

"Vivian. I—I don't know…"

"Sir. May I speak freely?"

"Get up, lovely."

"Sir. I need to stay here. Like this, for now. Please."

"Why?"

"Because I can't do this any other way."

In my Dom voice because she needs me to be that for her, "You many speak freely, Vivian." I see her relax and I know in this moment I was right...Viv needs my domination.

"I was not sure what to get for you, Sir. I thought I had found things in Europe, but none of them felt right. I saw so many sides of you in Paris and I saw a darkness in you I had not let myself see before. I know that darkness. I understand it, *intimately*." She is still not looking at me, and this time I'm glad. She has seen the monster in me and still she gives me this gift. I don't say anything. I can't.

"This semester has been amazing and scary and fun and passionate and hopeful and disappointing. I wanted to make this Christmas as special for you as you made last year for me, but I didn't know how." I hear the smile in her voice and I slant my eyes to her beautiful face and catch the smile playing with the corners of her mouth. It makes me smile.

"Anyway. I wanted to give you the one thing that no one else will be willing to give you."

"What is that, Vivian?" *I'm dying inside, hoping that it is not some fatalistic suicide pack she is hoping to make. I don't understand what is going on here and I don't like not knowing.*

"Unconditional access to every part of me with no hope of receiving anything in return except for your smile, your joy, your absolution and your peace of mind. Whatever it cost me to give this to you is still not enough to repay the debt I incur for having you love me like you do."

"I love you."

"I know."

"I don't deserve this gift and I don't deserve you."

"I know."

“Then why?”

“Because without you; my life has no meaning. I need to know that through me, you are redeemed. I need to be that for you, because that’s what you are to and for me. You are my *Messiah* and I want to be your *Shekinah.* Let me. Please, Sir.”

This time, it was me who had tears leaking from my eyes. *I never cry. I have never felt this feeling in my chest and I hope I never lose it.* “I don’t know what to say. Please get up, sit on my lap...I need to hold you.” She gets off the floor and climbs into my lap, placing her leash in my hand and laying her head on my shoulder soothing me with sweet kisses to my neck and words of adoration and love in my ear. I cried for every horrible thing I had ever done to anyone, because I wanted so badly to deserve her and I knew that I never would.

***

In a million years nothing could have prepared me for her gift. I have a safe in the house and in the safe is my gun, five thousand dollars, our passports, Vivian’s engagement ring and the gift she gave me for our first Christmas in our first home. I had it mounted and framed. Of all the contents in my safe, her gift is the most valuable item in there.

She was pretty stoked when she opened her multitude of gifts under the tree. She made out like a bandit. An all-Black Barbie collection with its own display case, diamond earrings with matching tennis bracelet, and the gift that had her in tears...keys to a brand new 1995 Volkswagen Cabriole; candy-apple red with a convertible roof. She could not believe it and said it was too much, but in the end, she graciously accepted her gift from her lover, but only at the insistence of her Dom. It’s good to be the Dom in this D/s relationship.

~38~

Everything I do for Vivian is a gift to her, at least in her mind. Christmas break was amazing. If I never receive another gift from her, the one that sits in my safe will always be too much. We went to our share of parties and drank too much champagne on New Year's Eve and day. Now it's time to finish up our final semester of our second year in college. Two down, two more to go. We both decided to go to summer school in hopes of shaving a semester off of our four years. may-mester, summer I and then summer II. It's going to be horrible to spend the summer in all this heat, but I am planning a two-week trip to Ireland for the end of the July.

Vivian loves the architecture and there are several museums I know she wants to see. As for me, there is a really good opportunity to get in on the ground floor of a micro-brewery in the land of the little green people. Should be fun and hopefully cooler than South Carolina in the days of hell that are June-September.

***

"Vivian? What's this note about...the one sitting on the table?" I was reading a note from some dude named Parker Daniels and he was confirming plans to meet later on this week at his apartment in the Five Points area. *What the fuck is she going to his apartment for? This will not do.*

"John. I told you I had to meet Parker later this week, we're working on the end of the semester project—" She stopped talking and seems to be looking for something.

"No. You didn't tell me anything about it. He needs to bring his—" Her voice interrupts me from the bedroom.

"—for our Italian Renaissance art class. We have to

reproduce a famous work from that time with emphasis on a modern social issue facing our generation. We just got the—" Another pause and then I hear her bare feet padding towards me.

"—ass over here. There is no way in hell I'm letting you go to his apartment." I look up from the note and she is standing in front of me with her newly forming locs hanging around her face like ropes of soft vines and her hands on either side of her perfect hips. But that's not what makes my dick hard enough to pound nails into the concrete, no she is wearing some flesh colored bodysuit that makes her look like she's naked. There is nothing left to the imagination in this body-hugging outfit.

"Vivian, what the fuck are you wearing? I can see the outline of your pussy and your nipples are damn near poking my eyes out." *She better have a damn good reason for wearing this shit and it better begin with John and end with Ellis.*

"John." She smooths her hands down her sides and then blows out an exasperated breath as she looks at me with those caramel eyes being kissed by the blue sky.

"John, this is the suit I'm wearing while Parker—"

"Wrong fucking name, Vivian." My voice deadly quiet. My body braced to pounce. My heart beating out of my chest.

"John, it's for class. Listen to me please. He has to wrap me in plaster and this suit will make sure that I don't get too hot and that my body cast is as real as it can get without me being naked." She had the good sense to look down and step back a couple steps.

"NO FUCKING WAY!"

"YES, FUCKING WAY! You will not jack my grade up in this class because of your misplaced jealousy. I am doing this assignment and there is nothing you can do about it." She flounced back into the bedroom and slammed the door. Shortly after, I heard the shower running. I've got to get out of here before I do something I will regret. *She has lost her damned mind if she thinks for one minute that this shit is going to fly.*

I quickly write a note on our communication board that simply reads, "Going for a drive, I have your car keys. Stay in the house until I get back. Be in the Playroom in two hours." I left and locked the house up just as the shower turned off.

She won't be able to put anything on her body for a while once I'm done with her.

I return to a silent house, too quiet and I immediately know that Vivian is not at home. My stomach is in my throat as I walk to the kitchen. *God, don't let her things be gone. I can't lose her, I love her too damn much.* I turn towards the communication board and see her neat handwriting telling me she went for a walk and will be back when she gets back.

"Guess I'm not the only one who needed to cool the fuck down." I grumble as I make my way to our bedroom. I turn the side table lamp on and stop cold in my tracks at what I see on the bed. Her voice startles me and I look up and see her standing in the doorway looking like the fucking goddess that she is.

"You hurt my feelings and undermined my autonomy. I don't know what happened after that, I just know that I fucked up the bed, but I don't—" I'm moving towards her and I see that she's shaking like a leaf and tears are swimming in her sad, scared eyes. There are gray clouds where there should be blue sky's dancing in sun-kissed wheat fields. She's in my arms and all of anger leaves my body in one whoosh of my breath.

"I have you, lovely. Give this to me, let me take it." She wrapped her arms tighter around my waist and tried to talk.

"I'm s-sorry. I don't...I think I'm losing my mind, John."

She's shouting and I'm scared shitless. The silk threads holding her formidable mind together are unraveling right before my eyes. *Maybe I need to take Viv to the hospital...have her evaluated by a psychologist.* I look at her walking in circles, her hands gesticulating her anguish and confusion as she mumbles a mixture of English, French and German. *Fucking Beaulac!* And I know in *this* moment the only thing my lovely needs is her Dom. I'm what she needs.

"Vivian." I give her a few seconds to register the change in my voice and the subtle change in my body before I continue. "I told you to be in the *Playroom*...you're four minutes late. This does not bode well for you or your delicious ass." I feel her body surrender to the submissive in her and she takes a breath and moves back a step, but I thwart her retreat. "Look at me." Her eyes sweep up and she meets my gaze. Chocolate meet caramel and a galaxy forms between us. Her breath catches as I reach out to torment her bottom lip with a firm caress of my right thumb. "Are you okay...to *play* I mean? We can't do this if your head is not where it needs to be." Our playtime is special and we can't bring any outside shit into that time. No anger, no fear and no intimidation beyond the normal D/s dynamic. "Now. Are you okay to play?" I looked into her face and implored her with my eyes to say she couldn't go...she wasn't ready, but she didn't. She lowered her eyes and nodded her head and began to make her way to the Playroom.

Fuck! I *needed* her to say no. She will safe word on me and that will undo so much of the trust we've built with each other. I'm her Dom and she is not where she needs to be, but she thinks she needs to be punished for the shit she did and if I don't meet that need in her then she will not feel safe and cared for in this relationship. *I'm fucked if I do and fucked if I don't.*

"Vivian. You may address me as Sir."

"Yes, Sir."

"Get up and walk over to the Chesterfield, don't sit down." She moves like liquid sex and I am as hard as I've ever been. I look at the $4500 Chesterfield; bespoke in vintage teal blue, English leather with its tufted, deep cushions and high back and sides. When I saw this sofa in a magazine, I knew I wanted in my playroom. A few modifications; adding restraints and a drawer in the exposed wooden frame to store supplies, made it perfect for all sorts of amazing days and nights of fucking Vivian right out of her mind.

"Bend over the arm of the chair and stretch your arms as far as they will go."

"Yes, Sir."

"Now, spread your legs as wide as you can. Wider. Good." I hear her breathing and see her arousal trickle down her leg. *That is the sexiest thing I have ever seen. In. My. Life.* My mouth is dry and I try to regain composure, but she is so ready for whatever I have to give her. I start to doubt my plans for her, but I find my resolve and my voice at the same time. I go to stand behind her and she knows better than to move a muscle, but she can't help herself and presses her perfect ass against my hardness. *God, what I'd love to do to that ass, but she won't relent.*

"I'm going to measure your legs from hip to ankle and then your arms from shoulder to wrist. I will add those two numbers together and divide the sum by two; the quotient will be how many punishments you receive for your offensive behavior today. Do you understand, lovely?"

"Y-Yes, Sir." Her voice is breathy and soft. There is trepidation and fear, but mostly there is arousal. This spurs me on and the monster in means roars to life and can't wait to get started. *Pipe the fuck down, patience is important. Slow and steady, remember?*

"Legs are thirty-five inches. Now for your arms." I move around the side of the Chesterfield and kneel down beside her. My lips are close to her right ear and I see she is still shaking a bit and it's not cold in here, it never is. "Lovely, we don't have to do this now. Part of my role as your Dom is to make sure what we do is done in a safe, *sane* and consensual space." I emphasize the word sane, because frankly, I am questioning her sanity. Something just doesn't feel right and I know that this will not work if her head is not in the right place.

"Sir?" I barely hear her. I continue to measure her extended right arm.

"Twenty-four inches long." I allow my fingers to take a leisurely stroll up her arm, over her shoulder and down her spine.

"Sir." Louder this time.

"Yes, lovely."

"I'm scared of myself right now and I think there is something wrong with me. In my *head.* The blackouts are getting worse and what I did today. Destroyed clothes and lube and the—the… I peed all over our bed...I don't know what to do. Please help me. I'm so scared of—" She breaks down into uncontrollable sobs. My heart is breaking for her. I scoop her up off of the sofa and place her in my lap. "I love you too fucking much, Vivian. If your world is cracking, then my world is cracking. Tell me what you need, and I *will* give it to you. Anything, Viv. Just let me take whatever this away."

"Punish me. I deserve it and I need to know you still care enough to correct my behavior. Please, John. Punish me and then...do whatever you want to me. No anal, but whatever else...*use* me." I sit her on the sofa and rub circles on her back as she calms down.

"Twenty-nine and a half minutes of orgasm denial.

Twenty-nine and a half minutes with both nipple and genital clamps in place. Twenty-nine and a half minutes with a large rabbit in your pussy and on your clit. Twenty-nine and a half minutes of watching me jack off and come until I'm dizzy. Walk over to the cross and stand at the ready...hands raised and legs spread." She obediently walks over and raises her arms and spreads her legs. She is still visibly shaking, but there is a calmness in her as she waits for me to shackle her.

I have clamped her nipples and her clit with the connecting clamp attached to a thin 25k gold chain. She flinched three times and a single tear ran down her cheek, but that was all. I kiss her tear away and remind her of her safe word before I blindfold her.

"You may not come until I tell you that you can. Do you understand?"

"Yes, S-S-Sir." I had been pulling the chain connecting all three clamps away from her body causing her nipples and her clit to sing with pleasured pain. *At least I hope there some pleasure in it for her. My monster is happy as a motherfucker at what he sees. He is salivating and dammit, so am I.*

I insert the rabbit in her soaked pussy and there is a sucking noise that tells me just how wet she is. "So beautiful. Vivian, you look like a goddamned goddess on this cross. Sacrificing yourself for me, for us... I love you, lovely." I position the rabbit ears right up against her over sensitized, clamped clit and turn the vibrator on to level three. I don't want to blow her sensitivity out, but I want her to come—hard and fast so that we can get the fuck out of this room and I can make love to her.

I can't see her eyes, but her mouth is wide-open, and she is screaming her head off. Tears are rolling down her face and it looks like she's having a seizure. Nothing coherent is coming from her and the monster in me is jumping up and down, beating his chest like a damn caveman and before I know what's going on, my dick is in my hand and I'm coming all over her soft, flat belly.

A life time passes and I finally stop coming and I notices that the screaming has stopped and her mouth is closed. She did not come, and she is breathing deeply like she is meditating. She looks so calm and I realize she has slipped into subspace and I guess right now that's where she needs to be.

It's so damn hot that she has this much control; my dick is hard again and I'm stroking *Jughead* from root to tip with so much force I know I am going to be sore in the morning. I'm coming again, this time I angle my dick up to spurt on her tities. *Go ahead, send me to hell. I love her like this. I love me like this. I love when we're like this together.*

***

We are laying in our freshly made bed and Vivian is too quiet. She hasn't said a word sense she fell into subspace. I'm afraid that I broke something in her. Something in us.

"Hey, babe? Are you okay? You've been so quiet and you haven't moved a muscle in as much as I've been moving you about." I felt my frustration rising with her and I didn't want to be in that place.

"You made it go away."

"Made what go away?"

"The noise and the darkness. It's gone and all I can hear is your voice and my own voice."

"Vivian, what are you trying to tell me? Have you been hearing *voices*?"

"Not voices, John. I'm not crazy!"

"Babe, I know you're not crazy and you need to calm your ass down. I'm trying to understand what the hell is going on with you." *I hate feeling like I don't have control over a situation and I am truly out of my depths here.*

"John. I can't explain what this absence feels like. I just know that something was causing me to *black out,* and that something isn't here anymore...you took it away, just like I knew you could." She smiles up at me and I accept her explanation because I want the crazy shit that's been happening to be over. *I need the crazy shit to be over.*

***

The end of our sophomore year ends wonderfully. Vivian and her punk-ass partner got an A+ on their assignment and he made quite a nice female form with a little help from a couple of drag queens I know. Two down, two more to go. *I love my life and my girl. Life is one giant gift and I am going to keep partying until the gift stops giving.*

BROKEN

"Trust is like a mirror, you can fix it if it's broken, but you can still see the crack in that mother fucker's reflection."

— Lady Gaga

~39~

<u>Three Years Later</u>

"Babe!"

"Yes?"

"Cuff links."

"Box."

Vivian walked into the bedroom wearing just her white cotton panties and matching bra. I never thought cotton was a sexy lingerie ensemble, but on Vivian it looked like Victoria's biggest secret. She was standing there looking at me with a smile on her lovely lips and a lustful glint in her beautiful eyes.

"What?" My voice, a little gruffer than I intended, but most of my blood was collecting in my groin and my only thought was getting Vivian naked.

"I love that we can have one-word conversations and know what we are talking about. This is so *normal*, so what a young married couple would do." I looked up at her as I pulled my gold cuff links out of an unassuming dark walnut, wooden jewelry box given to me on June 15, 1997 by my new bride. She went on and on about the designer, Arthur Umanoff and how excellent the quality and attention to detail was. All I ever see when I look at it is a wooden box that she spent almost two thousand dollars on, but what the hell do I know?

"We're already *normal*? I'm wounded, lovely. We've only been married a year and we have already become *normal*. I must not be doing something right." I tried to keep my voice light, but the tension in her shoulders tells me that she hears the undercurrent of something unnamable in my voice. *I don't know what she means by normal, but that is not what I signed up for.*

You are still my sub, sweet Vivian and I am still your Dom. Perhaps, I have been on the honeymoon a little too long.

"I don't mean...*normal.* I mean, we—you know...we fit together. We know each other and we work. You know? I'm not getting the words out right. We're not boring or anything...God! Just forget it. Forget I said anything." She walked towards the closet and I grabbed her left arm, a little more roughly than I should've, but I didn't let it go.

"Don't walk away from me, lovely. We are in the middle of a discussion and you know I don't appreciate rude behavior." My voice, a subtle growl and my stance more angular and harder. She immediately acknowledges the presence of her Dom and her contrition is absolute.

I hold her there for an eternal heartbeat and then release her arm. She does not move. Her hands clasp in front of her at the base of her belly, eyes on the floor and her head bowed down. *So fucking perfect.* "Tell me again about how *normal* we are. Is this *normal*, Vivian? You standing in your underwear, unable to do anything unless I give you permission to. Is this *normal* for young married couples?" I have no idea why that word has pissed me off on our one-year wedding anniversary, but it stings the back of my eyes to think my wife believes we live like every fucking body else. *I don't know anyone who lives and loves and fucks like we do. No-goddammed-body!*

"You may answer me Vivian."

"No, Sir." Her voice is small and afraid. Not what I wanted on our anniversary. *What the hell is wrong with you, Ellis? She's your wife!*

"No, lovely. Not normal at all. I don't want to give you a normal life. I want to give you an *extraordinary* life. One filled with every dream, fantasy and whimsy you can think of." I move to stand behind her making sure not to touch any part of her. I feel the heat coming off of her body and see the slight tremor racing up and down her spine. I lean forward, still not touching her, but placing my mouth close to her ear as I continue.

"Normal is for those married couples who go to work and come home and pay bills and eat the same food every day and make love when they're not too tired and hope that once a year for maybe a week they can go down to Myrtle Beach for vacation." I step closer to her and wrap my left arm around her waist, pulling her back flush with my front and instantly I'm hard. My fingers dig into her side and I whisper a shout into the crook of her neck, we are not fucking normal!" She flinches with every word I speak.

When I come to myself, I turned my wife around in my arms and look at her and see the tears sliding down her face and I feel about one inch tall. She hadn't meant anything by it, just excited to be in a healthy and safe relationship and to just be...happy. Happy to be comfortable with each other. She was just *happy*, but now she isn't and that is entirely my fault. *Way to fuck up the special day you had planned for you and your wife, Ellis.* Shut the fuck up Earl*!*

Vivian looked so crushed and hurt; there was no way to salvage this day. I have so much shit to tell her. So much to talk to her about, but now that I went all caveman on her...she won't hear anything I have to say. Fuck! Something changed when I signed our marriage license. Something changed in me...not her. I haven't taken her to our playroom in months. I haven't put her in her submissive role in months. I don't know how to reconcile being both her husband and her Dom. It was easy when we were just boyfriend and girlfriend, being both was seamless.

Now, I'm the one struggling to make this shit work. I know she needs this, I know she needs me to be her Dom and still, I can't see treating my wife the way I treat my sub. I can't see me *fucking* my wife the way I fuck my sub. She needs this shit as much as I do, but for some reason, my head and my soul are not working together. *Yea, shit for brains! Both your heads and especially your soul is broken.* Shut the fuck up, Earl!

"Viv. I don't know how to do this." My voice was flat and I didn't even recognize it. She looked up at me with a sadness I had only seen in her when she didn't know that I was watching her. I didn't dare look around the room. I held her gaze and let her see my shame and hopefully, she saw my love.

"John. I need to finish dressing. I don't want to be late for whatever you've planned for our day because I don't want the plans I've made for tonight to be put off." She turned and walked into the closet to finish getting ready. She was so quiet, I didn't think she was actually doing anything. Minutes later, she breezes out the closet in a beautiful white sundress that falls just above her knees. The halter top is covered in a delicate lace that makes the simple white cotton material it lay against, whiter, fancier even. The waistband sits right under her breast and was covered in what looked like tiny seashells and sea glass. The skirt flounced out from her waist and accentuated her shapely hips and thighs. There was no embellishment on the bottom of the dress, just a plain, white cotton skirt.

"I'm ready, John."

"Jesus, Vivian!"

"What John? You said that I should wear something that would look great on the water...I hope this will suffice."

"Yes. It's just that you—you look so beautiful. I wasn't expecting to see you in all white. You are as stunning in white cotton as you were in white silk." I couldn't keep the wonder out of my voice. Never in my life had I seen a woman wear the shade of white more beautifully than my Vivian. Her mahogany skin glowed when she wore white.

"Thank you, John. I'm glad you like what you see. I spend my life trying to make you happy. Your happiness is everything to me." Her eyes gazed at me and for a brief moment, she wasn't my Vivian. Her eyes were vacant and belonged to someone who seemed to hate me. This *person* peeped through the caramel oceans being kissed by wisps of blue skies that hit me like a punch in the gut every time I looked at them. Then it was gone. Like that look never existed, she was my Vivian again. *What the fuck is going on with lovely? She has been all over the place lately and sometimes, I really feel like I'm living with a total stranger.*

"I do appreciate what I see. lovely, come here. I need to apologize for earlier... I need to know that my stupid outburst hasn't ruined our anniversary." She floated over to me and stood between my spread legs while I sat on the edge of the bed. My hands shot to her hips and I held onto them like they were my lifeline. *She is my fucking lifeline. Everything. I am is nothing without Vivian.* Looking up into her beautiful eyes as she peered down into my undoubtedly unsure ones, I took a deep breath and prepared to beg for forgiveness, but she snatched the words from my mouth by kneeling in front of me and placed her hands behind her back and bowing her head in the submissive pose that I've seen her in so many times, but not once have I seen her like this as my *wife*. My dick got so hard it hurt. I didn't realize how much I missed seeing her like this.

"Vivian. What are you doing?"

"Sir. May I speak?"

"Yes, lovely." I slid into my Dom effortlessly and watched her shoulders relax at the sound of my voice.

"I know I'm disappointing you, Sir. I don't know how to be just your *wife*. I need to be all of everything you have taught me to be for you and..." Her voice wavered and I watched a tear slide down her cheek. She needed me, her Dom and I had failed her.

"Stand up, Vivian."

"Yes, Sir."

"We don't have much time, so I'll make this quick. Lift your dress and hold it to your waist. Don't let it drop for any reason. Do you understand?"

"Yes, Sir." She pulled her dress up and stood there looking remorseful and beautiful. I reached out to touch her demure cotton underwear and I smelled her arousal. I saw how damp her panties were. *God, I can't believe I've been such a selfish bastard.* Pulling her panties down, I helped her step out of them and I couldn't help it, I held her soaked panties up to my nose and inhaled her scent. I watched as a shudder passed through her body and a trickle of arousal dripped from her pussy, slicking her inner thighs. *Fuck! We are going to be so late.* I tucked her panties into my pant pocket and lifted her left leg up to rest her knee over my right shoulder. Keeping my left hand on her right hip to steady her, I ran my nose up the length of her pussy and breathed in the most intoxicating scent in the world. All woman and flowers and the best smell in the world, Vivian.

"I'm going to eat your pussy out and you are going to stand here and take all the pleasure I give you, but you will not come. Do you understand?

"Y-Yes, Sir."

"Good girl."

I bent my head to lick at her supple flesh. She was so smooth and soft and warm. She may not come, but I probably would. I licked her from the base of her pussy all the way up to top of her pubic bone and back down again. Long laps of my tongue, spreading her open like the flower she was. I wanted to plunge my fingers into her wet heat, but it wasn't about me...this is for her. I speared her with my tongue and her sweet arousal flowed down my throat, fucking her delicious sex with shallow thrust and then returning to lick her honey into my mouth. She was making the sweetest sounds, trying so hard not to come. I blew on her to bring her back down, she whimpered. A fine sheen of sweat covered her thighs and she held onto her dress like she would float away if she let it go. I returned my lips to her swollen, hard clit where I begin to suck in slow pulls. *Giving Vivian head always made me want to do extra nasty shit to her...shit that wasn't even legal in most states and certainly not in good old South Carolina.*

Smiling at my wayward thoughts, I sucked extra hard on her clit and bit down with just enough pressure to cause her to cry out. I felt her body starting to tighten up and I knew she was close. Pulling back from her, I blew on her over sensitized sex and let her calm down a bit. Seeing her breathing evening out, I dove back in to continue feasting on her sweetness. Licking, fucking, sucking and blowing. That's how it went for the next twenty minutes. She never came and I never saw her look more lovely than I did in those moments when she was fighting her body and denying herself the release she so desperately needed.

"How was that, lovely?" My face was covered in her juices and I smelled like her. I stood and kissed her perfect mouth. She opened for me and I plunged my tongue deeply into her mouth, letting her taste herself on my tongue and lips. She sucked on my tongue the way she would normally suck on my dick and I swear my balls drew up so much they were inside my body. Her moaning and kissing were driving me over the edge.

"Fuck! Vivian. You're going to make me come in pants like some teenage boy." As soon as I said that, she licked her tongue across my chin and back up to suck my bottom lip into her mouth and I shot my load in my pants like some punk-ass who had never seen a naked woman. *What the fuck was that? You're just like your stupid bitch of a mother...a quick fuck.* Shut the fuck up, *Earl!*"

"I've got to change my pants. You made me come, so you won't be wearing any underwear today on our outing. Come. Let me clean you up and I'll get changed so we can go."

"Yes, Sir."

"Viv, is this what you need from me; me as your Dom? You need more of what we were before we got married?"

"I need and want you, Sir; the same as always. I just want all of you and that includes you as my Dom, my lover, my best friend, my punisher, my protector, my provider and most of all...my husband."

"Understood. Let's get cleaned up. How do you feel?"

"Sir. I feel like I'm ready for my evening plans." A shy smile reserved just for me, her Dom played on her full lips and now I'm wondering what the hell her evening plans are for us.

"Okay. I'm intrigued and my dick is getting hard again...let's go. I don't want to miss the day's activity that I have planned for us, we're kind of late, but it's alright. You are so beautiful and sexy. Thank you for being you and still being able to love someone like me."

"I'll always love you, Sir. I'll always love you, John. I'll always love us." She walked into the bathroom and waited for me to wipe her down and dry her off. Once she was good to go, I gave her permission to let her pretty white dress fall from her hands. She perched on the bathroom counter and watched as I peeled myself out of my sticky boxer briefs and pants. She smiled when she saw how hard I still was, licking her lips and taking a hard swallow. I cleaned myself in silence and gave her the show I know she wanted. After I was clean and dry, I took myself in hand and stroked my dick from root to tip, pulling a bead of pre-cum from the head and smearing it over the shaft as I begin to jack myself off. My hips moved involuntarily and my breathing came faster. I knew that I would come soon, but I wanted to come in something warm and wet.

"Viv, Your mouth. Now!" She jumped from the counter and scrambled to the floor on her knees. She had me in her mouth and down her throat so fast I didn't have time to register that I was fucking her throat until she swallowed me the way I loved for her to. *Holy motherfuck...* "Like that, Viv. Keep doing that shit." My voice sounded like I was channeling the devil himself. "Your mouth. So damn good. Yea baby, I'm going to--Oh yea! Shiiiiiiiit! Vivian! That's it, baby. That's it!" I screamed my orgasm and poured my seed down her open and willing throat. I was dizzy and brain damaged, but holy mother of God...that was the best blow job I've ever had in my life.

"Thank you, baby. We really have to go." Fifteen minutes later, we were in the Mustang heading out to West Columbia for the first surprise of the day. *Alright this helicopter service, better make this flight as special as you promised you would...I'm certainly paying enough for it.*

~40~

"Oh my God! John, I can't believe you did this. I didn't even know this place existed and you did this for me." The smile on her face was worth every penny I had spent to make this helicopter tour happen. We were strapped into our seats, each with a glass of Champagne Krug Brut—1988. At just under a thousand dollars for the bottle, I was pleased that it tasted as good as it did. I wanted everything about this day to be perfect for Vivian, just like she had made the first year of our marriage perfect for me.

"There is nothing I wouldn't do to put that smile on your face, lovely. How's the champagne?" I hope she didn't hear the anxiousness in my voice. I slid a seductive look her way to mask my anxiety, I know it worked because I watched her press her thighs together and listened as her breath caught in her throat.

"John, everything about this day is perfect. You won't tell me where we're going." She didn't ask a question, but I felt I needed to answer her all the same.

"If I told you where we were going, it would ruin the surprise that awaits us when we get there. Trust me?" She smiled and I knew she would go anywhere, do anything I wanted her to. It was such an honor to have this much power over another human being and not having to use my fist or pain to be gifted with it. This gift was something I would never take for granted, nor would I ever abuse it. I know all too well what that looks like and how that scenario plays out. *This shit is too dark to be thinking about right now. Only happy, sexy thoughts Ellis. That's all you get to be today...Happy and sexy.*

We settled into our flight and were told through the oversized headphones that we should arrive at our destination in roughly an hour and ten minutes. I look over at Vivian, who is relaxed and looking extremely fuckable as a smile creases my lips just thinking about the next part of our outing. We flew east towards our destination and when we reached the halfway point, the pilot's disenchanted voice came through cans. "If you'll look outcha winduhs on either side, y'all see what's called the Santee Cooper Lakes. Made upof two lakes, Moultrie and Marion. It's—it's quite a sight from up'ere. We 'bout halfway through y'alls' flight. Sit back and enjoy the ride and the views." The way he pronounced his words reminded me of the old white men back home who would try to scare us when we were kids walking through old cemeteries. My skinned felt too tight. Once he was done with his spiel, I heard his mic go off and I knew that whatever I said to Vivian would only be heard between us.

"So... where do you think we're going?"

"Charleston? I hope to God it's Charleston!"

"Of course, it's Charleston. Bet you can't figure out what we're doing when we get there."

"Eating I hope. I love low country cuisine. Shopping in the Market? Pralines and salt water taffy."

"Well, naturally all that. But there is more to do in Charleston than eat and shop."

"But...you won't tell me and now my mind is going a hundred miles a minute trying to figure it out."

"Nope. Not going to tell you. I love keeping you tied up in knots—" I laugh quietly at my choice of words and the irony was not lost on Vivian, either.

"Anytime, Ellis. Anywhere. I love being tied up in *your* knots." Just that fast, my dick became painfully hard.

"Careful Vivian. I may have to take you up on that offer sooner rather than later." My voice had dropped lower and I knew she was wet for me. I could smell her. *Fuck! When is this thing going to touch down? I need to be deep inside her and that's now!*

***

We landed at the Charleston airport and made our way through the terminal to step out into the liquid air that instantly made my clothes stick to my skin. "God! It is hot as fish grease out here." I was immediately uncomfortable and sweaty. I glanced over at Vivian and saw the beads of sweat collecting on her forehead. "Lovely, let's find our car and get out of this heat." Grabbing her right hand, I walked down a ways until I saw a tall, white guy in a black chauffeur suit and hat holding a placard that read *Ellis: Party of Two.* Moving towards him, I registered the surprised look on his face when I extended my hand and introduced myself.

"You might be an Ellis, but this car is for someone of *means*." His heavy, magnolia laced drawl grated on my eardrums and turned my hands into fist.

"Well, of course this car is reserved for a man of *means.*" My southern genteel voice oozed contempt for the man's station as a driver. I slid into a dominant stance that I reserved for white people who wanted to start shit with me and waited quietly for this pompous son-of-a-sharecropper to recognize who the fuck I was. *There it is. The light of recognition that seemed to dull his watery gray eyes to a shade of the sky just before it rains. I love moments like this. When they have to see me as more than just another Black man...when they have to acknowledge me as a motherfucking man. Because that's what I am. A man.*

"Sir. I'm so sorry...I was expecting someone who looked...well—I thought that you would be…um, *older*?" His eyes studied the sidewalk so hard, I thought he had spotted some money.

"Well, of course you did." I chuckled and put every bit of the disdain I felt into the hollow sound of my voice. "I understand completely. I am quite young to be a man of...what did you call it? Oh yes. *Means.*" Vivian's hand slid into mine and squeezed it slightly, reminding me that this was not the time to provide a lesson on the new southern Negro to this driver. "We are ready when you are." I smiled, but it didn't reach my eyes and my voice brought the temperature down to a chilly thirty-two degrees Fahrenheit.

"Yes, sir. Mr. and Mrs. Ellis, please allow me to open the door and get you safely to your destination." He opened the rear door of the black Lincoln Town Car and stood to the side. I waited while Vivian slid in. I placed my hand on the door to signal the driver that I needed to speak with him. He looked at me the way Earl used to look at me and I lifted the corner of my mouth into something that resembled a smile but felt more like a sneer and looked him in his eyes. "If you have any doubt about who I am and what I can afford, please know that even though I only need your services for a total of one hour, I have paid your salary for the entire day. Rest assured, you are driving for a man of *means.*" His face fell and darkened as he nodded his head in understanding. I slid in beside Vivian and appreciated the feeling of having just set that backwater driver to straights about who the hell I was. "Ready for the fun to start?"

"I'm ready to soak up some of this air conditioning." She giggled softly as her long-fingered hand fanned her face and neck. I couldn't take my eyes off of the slow, winding path of sweat that trickled down her neck from the back of her hairline.

"John! The driver...he...Mmmmm, that's good." I continued to lick and nibble her salty skin from just behind her ear to the juncture where her neck and her shoulder came together forming the perfect cradle for my teeth to bite into her flesh.

"I could give a damn about *Farmer Brown*. Do you want me to stop?"

"No. Never."

"I didn't think you did. Shit, Viv. You smell so good. Can't wait to get to where we're going."

"I know you didn't just fly me to Charleston in a helicopter only to check into some hotel and have your wicked way with me." Indignation colored her words, but her body was colored by a whole different emotion...lust. She squeezed her thighs together, her breathing increased fractionally, her lips plumped and those beautiful honey colored eyes glowed like a bottle of Greenore Irish Whiskey.

"You wouldn't really be that upset if I had, would you?" My voice low and seductive, for her ears only. I keep my face impassive, like I don't really care about her answer, when really, I'm not sure I'm even breathing as I wait.

"No." One word and she gives me back my right to breath.

"I didn't think you would, but no. I didn't rent a helicopter, fly you to Charleston just to take you to a hotel and fuck you fifty ways till Sunday. But…"

"But nothing. Where are we going?"

"To hell if we don't get right with God." She snorts out a laugh and pouts. Her bottom lip, poking out a little further than her top lip, eyes slightly angry and narrows and her cheeks have some heated color to them. "You're just too fucking beautiful, lovely." I realize I have not hidden the wonder and amazement in my voice. Sometimes I can't and right now, I don't want to. I want her to hear the wonder in my voice. I want her to hear how desperate I am for her. Something in me resonates with something in her. She's looking at me and I can see my feelings reflecting back in her eyes.

“I love you, John. So much. It scares me and makes me feel safe. I know that sounds all kinds of crazy, but... it’s true”

“You are so sweet. Come here, Vivian.”

~41~

The salty air kissed our cheeks as we walked down The Charleston Harbor Marina towards The Fish House restaurant where we would be eating lunch before our sailing expedition.

"Wow! This is so beautiful, John. We should work really hard over the next couple of years and get a home on the coast for vacation." Vivian had no idea of my wealth and I loved that she used the pronoun, *we* when she spoke of working hard to achieve a goal. *I should probably tell her we already have a house on the coast...well, on the west coast.* "Babe? Did you hear me? We should look—"

"I heard you. We can check it out while we're here, if we have time. If not, then we will look into it later, okay?" I dropped her right hand and snaked my arm around her waist, pulling her close to me. *Too many men taking too long a look at my wife. Back off fuckers, she's taken.* I leaned over and whispered to her about how good she tasted on my tongue this morning and licked the outer shell of her ear. She trembled and moaned low in her throat as I pulled away. "I love how you respond to me. Let's eat some lunch and then on to the real treat. The look on her face told me she thought the helicopter and town car ride was the real treat. *So grateful for every small thing. Vivian, can't you see you deserve so much more?*

"Come. Food and then we take to the water and test your sea legs." Her smile was enough to calm the savage beast that wanted to feed on her soul and ravage her body. Darker and darker thoughts crept into mind where Vivian was concerned. I wanted to do horrible, sadistic shit to her and make her love it. Make her *crave* it. *That's why I haven't indulged in the D/s aspect of our relationship...I'm so damned scared of breaking her. Breaking her like Earl...Fuck! I will not think of that bastard today.*

***

We boarded the chartered sailboat and made our way to the deck. I was nervous to see how she would respond to sailing and being on the water. Vivian looked around the boat and out into the water and her beautiful mouth fell open and then snapped closed again.

"This is... *amazing*!" She burbled. Her voice was filled with wonder and joy. I loved seeing her like this. Her eyes and face so open and expressive. I didn't have to ask her if she loved it; it was written clearly in the beautiful, sunset of her eyes.

"So....? Happy anniversary, lovely. I thought this would be a great way to celebrate our first year of marriage. You, me and the open waters off the coast of South Carolina. What do you say to that?"

"I love you, Sir. I love every inch of you. From your brilliant head to your sexy bare feet... I love all that's in between. Sir, what do you have planned for us on this beautiful boat?" She didn't look at me and her voice was soft. It's like she was speaking directly to my dick. *She needs this, Ellis. Don't be a chicken shit and wimp out on her.*

"Lovely. A crew member will escort you below deck to the bedroom. Undress, completely and wait for me. There are ten items on the bed, choose four that you would like to play with today and place them on the floor next to you. I will be in shortly."

"Yes, Sir."

Vivian followed the young woman below deck to the master suite. She looked so calm and relaxed, like she was taking her first real breath in the year since we were married. I stepped towards the guardrails and placed my hands shoulder width apart and held on so tightly, my knuckles cracked. I knew Vivian needed me to be this *monster* for her...to her, but I am so fucking scared I'll hurt her. *The shit I want to do to her. Nasty, vile shit that no man who claims to love a woman should even be able to think about.*

"Fuck it." I said to the ocean and to whoever else was out there laughing at my silly ass. The items I left for her to choose from are going to scare the living shit out of her, but that's what I want to happen. I need her to *not* want this bullshit to be a part of our married life. I can't have Vivian as both my sub and my wife.

She's been pushing me for a while now and I hope she takes a look at my choices and is able to see the full extent of my depravity. I was not easy on her in those early years; Paris had been fan-fucking-tastic. She was such a great sub, but she's an even better wife and right now that's what I want from her. I just want her to be my wife.

She seems to be changing all the time. Her passion for art comes and goes and sometimes, when I look into those sunrise eyes with blue skies lurking just below the surface, I swear someone completely different is looking back at me. I'm scared out of my fucking mind when that shit happens. Why is she be changing so much? My conversation with the wind is over and now it's time to fish or cut bait. *The sad part is that there is a part of me that wants so badly for her to be waiting with her four objects, my body burns to do it. I shouldn't want to hurt my wife, but God help me, I fucking love her tears. Game on Ellis.*

"Vivian." I push the door open and walk inside. I hope she can't hear the trepidation in my voice as I try to coax my Dom out of hiding. I immediately look to the floor for her, she isn't there. My eyes sweep the room and I find her sitting on the bed, staring at all of the shit I left there for her to choose from. Her pretty white dress is still on and her hands were absently caressing the blade of the beautiful African ceremonial knife made of copper alloy with a wooden handle. The blade had a beautiful patina and the shape looked like an elongated maple leaf. This is the sort of knife that would have been used in a scarification ceremony. I chose it for that reason. I wanted to add my own scars to the chaotic loveliness that already marred her perfect body. From the first time I saw those scars, I knew I wanted to add my own right along her ribs. *Such a sick fuck…that's me.*

"Lovely, why aren't you undressed and kneeling on the floor; are you still choosing the *toys* you want to play with?" No response, her hands move over to the brown, braided leather handle that led to a gruesome cat o nine tails that was tipped with metal beads in various sizes. This beauty was designed to leave beautiful raised welts on the body. The welts would heal, but the scars would stay forever. There would be some blood from the skin puckering and opening up some; however, that simply meant more tears, more blood and more of her soul. *Fuck Vivian! I crave your blood, your tears, and your oenomel soul.*

"Sir." A watery drip of her usually sensual voice slid over my overheated skin and felt like acid dripping in open wounds. "Why have you chosen these…ur…*toys?* If I may ask, Sir?" Her eyes did not leave the bed. She skipped over the electric shock nipple clamps and landed on the large, black rubber butt plug and then on to the anal beads that boasted a bead the size of a tennis ball. Her hands were shaking, and I couldn't see her face all that clearly from this angle, but God her body was ramrod straight and rigid would have been too loose to describe her. *Maybe you went too far, asshole.* I think that maybe I did, Earl. Now fuck off!

"I wanted to try something different for our first foray back into playing. I wanted to really push your limits today, you know...see how far I could take you. Take *us*. Are you questioning your Dom, submissive?" Her hands immediately went to her laps and folded in on themselves, her head bowed and eyes lowered. She slid from the bed and onto the floor at my feet and waited for me to meet out her punishment. I wanted to grab her hair and haul her head up and shove my dick down her throat, but I didn't. I couldn't. "Get up, Vivian." My voice soft and endearing. No heat, or Dom, just John. I held my hand out to her; she placed her ice-cold fingers in my palm and rose with the grace of ballerina. "Look at me, Viv." I led her to the other side of the bed and we sat down , her left thigh pressed against my ight. I continued, "I need to see your eyes when we have this conversation." *I need to make sure it's you I have staring at me and not the stranger I sometimes see peeking out from your beautiful face.*

"I'm scared, Sir...ur, John. These things will really hurt me, maim me, scar… *abuse* me. This has never been a part of our play. Why now?"

"Because you asked for this. You want me as your Dom, your husband, your provider. You want it all and if I'm going to be everything to and for you, then you have to be everything to and for me, too. Vivian, I am a dark son-of-a-bitch and if you want to bring this into our marriage then it won't be like it was before. Before, you were my girlfriend/sub. I had a non-legally binding contract with you, but no legal right to call you truly mine. However; according to our marriage license, you are mine to truly do with as I please. The control and power over you is absolute and irrevocable. As my wife/sub the possibilities are endless and if this is what you want from me, then this is what you have to be willing to give me. So?" I let the words hang in the air like fog too thick to see through as I watched her face shut down. There was nothing left of her after only ten seconds. No summer sun. No blue skies. No amber whisky...nothing, just flat and lifeless and empty. *The ball is in your court, Vivian. If you want this shit…you will have to deal with it all. What will it be?*

"John. I—I don't know what to say. This isn't who you are, really, is it?" Her eyes landed on the black leather ball gag that would cover her entire head and neck. Heavy leather held together with bronze chains suspending the large, rubber gag in the bronze opening where her full lips would fit. The headpiece had cut-outs for her eyes, nostrils, and mouth. This was the most severe ball gag she had ever seen and the longer she examined the medieval looking bondage contraption, the more deviant thoughts flooded my mind. *There is no way in hell I won't do serious fucking damage to her if she lets me get my hands on her with any of this shit. Shut her down, Ellis or regret your one-year anniversary for the rest of your life.*

"So, Vivian, what will it be? You are either all in or we will not have any part of the lifestyle as a part of our marriage. Your call, but you should know that either way, I will be happy. I love you as my wife. I love you happy and sassy. But as my sub…" I allowed my voice to trail off as memories slammed into my brain from those heady days of training her to be what I needed her to be. I didn't want my reaction to those thoughts to make her think that I wanted this shit in our marriage. "As my sub and my wife, there are no hard limits. Your body is mine and the first thing I intend to claim is the one thing you have never given me access to. Your gorgeous ass will open for me today and every time after this." Her face fell and her eyes flashed; thunder and lightning causing stormy gray clouds to block out the sun and blue skies.

"No! No! No! No!" Vivian's voice was a needle tattooing her pain and fear onto my eardrums. Before I realized what I was doing, my arms were around her waist lifting her from the bed and burying her head in my chest while cooing softly into her hair. Her body shook violently and I rocked her to calm her. I felt her breaking and I knew I had to be her binder, hold her together.

"Vivian. I just want you and me. I just want us…no D/s. I don't want playrooms, just bedrooms and us loving each other. I know myself, and I am a dark, sadistic man. I don't want to be that man with my wife. But, I'm weak, lovely. I'm weak when it comes to you and owning you. I'll hurt you and ruin you and break you; and I don't want to do that. I love…no, I worship you, Vivian. Don't make me debase the only God I've ever known and trusted and loved." Tears from my eyes mixed with her and we were lost to each other in a way that only love, pain, truth and passion could hide two people.

I put my Dom to rest on my one-year anniversary and I have never felt so whole and complete. Making love on that chartered sail boat for the rest of the afternoon to my wife was the most transcendent act I'd experienced to date. Fuck you, Earl! I will never be like you and Vivian will never be my mother.

The afternoon belonged to Vivian and she did not disappoint. We had dinner at our home, which had been turned into a French chateau with all the trimmings. She turned our backyard into a replica of a Jardin du Luxembourg in Paris, France. We were treated to the first meal we shared in Paris in that resplendent summer so long ago. We sit down to a feast of poulet vallee d'auge. The chicken was perfect and the dry, crisp, white wine was delectable. The night ended with Vivian playing her acoustic guitar while she sang a song she wrote just for me and her.

I watched Vivian bury her sub as she disrobed in our backyard and led me to the most interesting piece of outdoor furniture I had ever seen. Making love under the stars to my wife on our first anniversary while Tone, Tony, Toni sang 'It's Our Anniversary' made for a sublime ending to an era and the most auspicious beginning to forever.

~42~

Time seemed to be moving at the speed of light when it came to my marriage, my company and my ever-growing wealth. Vivian and I sold our first home in Shandon and had a custom French Country home built on three acres of land on Lake Murray. I didn't want to live in the city any longer and Viv loved being by the water. In the years that we've been together, she never inquired about my money or how I was able to afford everything I gave her. She knew about the real estate that Auntie had gifted me, but she didn't know about the money and the investments and the other endeavors I had been busy with. What's more important is she didn't care. She loved our new home and all of the beautiful Art Deco furniture and Country French accessories to complement the softer French Provincial style and design inherent to the 8500 square-foot space.

We had just returned from celebrating our four-year wedding anniversary, which we spent in The Caves Resort in Jamaica. Beautiful amenities built into the sides of caves…the most intimate moments were shared between my wife and I while there. As I sit sprawled on the grey, silk-linen blend Chesterbrook in our living room, absently playing with Vivian's locs that hang down her back in a riot of red, brown and strawberry-blonde waves, I can't help but wonder what she is dreaming about. Her face is a puzzle that's not quite put together, but it's only missing a few key pieces before it can be complete. A small "m" of concentration sits between two perfectly arched brows and the corners of her full, lush mouth are turned slightly downward—giving her the appearance of a sullen child. Otherwise, her face is impassive and nothing seems out of place.

There are times when I feel like this woman is turning into someone I don't know. Someone who is strange and yet familiar. There seems to be an emptiness growing inside her and I can't help but wonder if she is starting to seek fulfillment in another…maybe a Dom. Shit! I hate questioning myself and hate that she is making me do it. I want to punish her for making me feel this way, but I took that off the table when I gave her the ultimatum…wife/husband or slave/Master.

"Hey, baby." Her sleepy voice is husky and makes my dick twitch against my zipper. I know she can feel me swelling beneath her head and I want her to.

"Hi. How was your nap?"

"Great. I didn't realize I was so tired. Um, John?"

"Yes." I knew she was getting ready to ask me about my ever-present erection. *That's right Viv; I am always ready to fuck you right back to sleep.* "Go ahead, ask me about it and see what happens."

Her voice was a small challenge when she whispered and her warm breath blew against my zipper. "I can't help but notice that *Jughead* is feeling a little firm…were you dreaming about me during your nap?"

"I didn't go to sleep, Vivian. I stayed awake to watch you sleep. When you woke up and spoke to me with that sexy, sleep-husky voice you wake up with…well, I want to fuck you now."

"Really, just my voice? Do you think that you could come from just listening to me?"

She wanted to play, but she also knew that the D/s shit was not an option, but kink was always on the table with us and it seems that Vivian was feeling a little bent out of shape. "Do I think I could come from just listening to you talk? Do you want to find out, Vivian?" My voice sounded like fallen angels making love with demons, low and smooth with a hint of brimstone and a touch of heaven.

"Yes." One word and I was almost ready to explode in my shorts. She knew what she could do to me and she loved the power she had. She loved knowing that she could bring me to my knees with a look or a touch. Vivian was so damn sexy when she felt this powerful; I'd give her anything she wanted in moments like this. In moments like this, there was no question about my wife being the woman I was madly in love with and the woman I wanted insatiably all the damn time.

"Get up, lovely. Meet me in our *playroom."* Although we no longer had a D/s aspect to our marriage, we still enjoyed kink and to that extent, we really enjoyed our playroom. Gone were the implements of torture and punishment, but we still loved bondage, domination and submission as roll-play. There was no discipline or sadism and certainly no masochism to speak of, but sometimes Vivian needed to be dominated sexually to feel safe and secure. I didn't mind giving that to her, when she needed it. Something was riding her hard, and I knew she needed this release in order to reset her equilibrium. To be honest, I needed to dominate her to appease this need to punish her for making me question myself. *Perfect fucking timing for her to want to go into the playroom. I have to make sure I stay in control, but I won't leave feeling as if there are any questions unanswered when I'm done with her.*

Vivian was walking towards the playroom with her head held hi and her back straight. Her lace shorts hit a little below the point where her beautiful ass and toned thighs connected. She was so painfully beautiful it hurt to look at her sometimes. Graceful and powerful, she moved like a panther; sleek and dangerous, but beautiful and sensuous as well.

"You ready, Vivian?" No reply and I didn't expect one.

"God." My breath left my lungs and left me searching

for air. She had taken off every stitch of clothing she had on and stood in the middle of the room with her feet shoulder width a part, hands on her hip and her breast pushed high in the air. My panther had morphed into an African warrior-princess with the tribal scarification to boot.

"You like?" She purred and something was a little off, but I was too turned on to pay attention. She looked like a fucking goddess and I was going to let her have her way with me. I would worship at her feet, her legs, her knees, her thighs, her pussy, her belly, her breast, and drink from her mouth. God she was magnificent. And she was all mine!

"You know I do. Now, make me come with your voice. If you can't do it in five minutes, I'm going to fuck you until you scream and you will not be able to come, deal?"

"Deal, get naked John. You know I love looking at your body as much as you love looking at mine." I start to take off my clothes and she starts talking and holy mother-mind-fuck…the things she says."

"The first time I saw you without your shirt on, my pussy got so wet I thought you could see it dripping down my thighs. I was so embarrassed and too turned on to do anything but squeeze my thighs together in hopes of alleviating the pressure that was building between them." Stops and licks her lips and swallows audibly. *So fucking sexy.*

"Anyway, when you started doing those push-ups and the muscles in your back and arms flexed, my clit started pulsing to the rhythm you set in your work out. Every time you went down, my clit pulsed out…reaching for you. Every time you came back up, my clit pushed in—hard…wanting to suck you in deeper. I was gushing. Panties so wet, I could smell myself and prayed you didn't have a wet spot on your bed when I stood to leave."

"Vivian." My voice was barely audible. It was so low and rough with arousal, I was having a hard time talking. She just stood there on display for me, talking filthy shit with a shiny, wet pussy staring me in the face. My shirt was off and folded on the cabinet and I was pulling my shorts and boxer briefs down as she continued talking.

"When you rolled onto your back, I wanted to climb down off of the bed and crawl over your body and lick the sweat from your belly. Your nipples were flat and dark against your defined chest and I wanted to bite them. You put your arms behind your head to start your sit-ups and your biceps flexed…oh my God! My entire pussy clenched. I couldn't get the image of your arms holding me down while you fucked me hard and deep… right out of my head. You were counting and I was squeezing my thighs together trying to stop my hips from fucking the air. I was so empty, but I couldn't fuck you…it wasn't *right.*"

"I need you, Vivian." My hand was fisted around my dick and pre-cum was pouring from me in ribbons of milky white liquid. Standing in front of her as naked as she was, as hard as I've ever been and she would not budge. She just kept talking.

"When you reached 100, I came so hard, John. It hurt. My entire body tightened and my pussy was so empty, but it didn't stop her from sucking in and pushing out. The emptiness didn't keep me from taking pleasure from the sheer beauty of your body. There was no way you wouldn't notice the wet spot I was leaving on your bed. I didn't make a sound because I didn't want you to know what the hell I was doing. When you stood up; your feet planted shoulder width a part, your hands on your hips and your chest and abs working to regulate your breathing…I wanted you to slam you dick down my throat and fuck my face, but you just looked at me like you knew something about me that I didn't and that made me want to be yours."

That was it. I hadn't even stroked my cock. Just had my hand fisting it, tightly and it happened! I came in a torrent and in a blur of movement, she was on her knees with her luscious mouth open to drink me down. "Holy fucking hell. Shit, Vivian! On your hands and knees, now!" I bit out between clenched teeth. Never in my life had I thought it possible to come like that, but it wasn't enough. I needed to be inside her as hard and fast as she had made me come.

I yanked her hips towards me and put my left forearm in the middle of her back and forced her chest to the floor. She pushed her ass higher in the air; her pussy was so wet, so swollen for me I almost came again. "Vivian, this will not be an easy ride for you." That was my only warning before I slammed into her all the way to the root. Her tight, wet pussy sucked me in and clamped down on me so hard I saw stars and lost my breath.

"John!" She screamed my name like I had broken her. I was too far gone to stop myself from fucking her to within an inch of her life and I just didn't want to stop, even if I could. "John…I. Can't. Do. This!" Her body was shaking so badly…but I had to move. I had to fuck her…get as deep as I could inside her. I needed to not leave any room for anyone to move in and dominate her. She was mine to dominate and only I had the right to see her like this. To take her like this. To *fuck* her like this. She would never want another man to dominate her, she was mine! And with that final thought flying out of my head, I started fucking her like I was punishing her and in a way…I was. I wanted her to never make me question myself again.

She was trying to get up and away from me, but I would not let her rise. I pushed harder on her back, putting most of my weight onto her as I wrapped my right arm around her waist and used my knees to spread hers wider so that I could get deeper inside of her. I wanted to crawl into her and take possession of her soul. *God, I need to stop. Help me gain control, I don't want to hurt her. I want her ass…What if she lets some other man claim her ass. It's mine…I have a right to it. She won't dislike it…I won't give her an option.*

My mind made up, I yanked my dick from her tight pussy with a loud, sucking pop and slammed it into her even tighter rosette. I begin fucking her hard and fast and deep immediately. "Baby. You fucking feel like heaven. I knew that you would love this. Yes, Vivian. This was worth the wait. Your. Ass. Is. So. Very. Fuckable." Every word accentuated with a deep, hard plunging of my dick. "Every hole in your body belongs to me. I will come everywhere in and on you. Feel how hard you make me. Feel how much I want you." I was growling at her, holding her down to the floor and fucking her ass off, literally.

"I own your ass and you love that I do, don't you? You want me to pound this sweet ass of yours. Holy shit, Vivian. I—I think I'm gonna to come. Yes! Yes! Lord, your ass is fucking AMAZING!!!!" I pound into her once, twice and the third deep penetration, I come in her and find myself floating above our bodies and I have never felt better.

I didn't realize that her body had gone lax as I came with an animal-like roar that made my throat burn. I didn't notice the blood running down her thighs and coating my softening dick until I pulled completely out of her gaping asshole. I didn't notice the bruises forming on her back and shoulders from where I held her down until I moved my arm away from her. I didn't notice how much she looked like that *esclave* we saw in the Parisian sex club until I looked at her broken, bleeding and bruised body.

I backed away from her and she fell over on her right

side, bringing her knees up to her chest and wrapping her long, toned arms around herself in the fetal position. I thought she was crying, but there was no sound coming from her. No movement after she got herself all bound up. I glared down at my dick and thighs, covered in her juices, blood and my semen and felt my stomach roil…I ran to the bathroom and just made it to the toilet in time to throw up. I wretched until I was left with only dry heaves racking my body. I ran a bath and poured scented Epson salt and bath oils in to make my apologies to Vivian. I will give her aftercare and we will go to our bedroom and we'll talk about what just happened and I'll hold her and everything will be fine. *Nothing is ever going to be fine again. I just raped and sodomized my wife. I can't fucking fix this…I can't fucking fix this. Shit. Shit. Shit. I am Earl.*

~43~

I take a quick shower and wash the evidence of my depravity from my body. I watch as Vivian's blood runs pink down the drain and the noises that I couldn't hear when I was deep inside her ricochet off the tiled walls of the oversized shower as I stand under the scalding rain water that's pelting my back. A scream like a wounded banshee tore from her throat when I breached the tight ring of her sphincter muscle and pushed past her limits and shoved her out of her mind. I didn't hear it then, but it is pounding inside my fucking head now. *What in the hell was I thinking. I knew she wasn't ready for that...would never be ready for that. I raped and sodomized my fucking wife. I turned her into esclave when she chose to be my wife.*

I step from the shower and dry my sated body with an Egyptian cotton bath sheet and walk into the playroom where I expect to find Vivian laying in the bed that sits in the corner facing the lake, but I don't. She hasn't moved from the floor where I left her about 15 minutes ago. She hasn't moved one muscle...she is still laying on her right side wrapped up in the fetal position. She was not crying and I wasn't even sure is she was fucking breathing and most of me was too afraid to find out, but I had to go to her. I have to provide aftercare for her, it's the least I would do if she were my sub. Tentatively I approach where she is lying on the floor and I squat down beside her. Her eyes are open, but she does not seem to be there. I've seen her like this before, but this is worse than any of the other times I've witnessed this particular state of being.

"Vivian." It's not a question, but it sounds like one. I don't know what else to say to her. "I'm going to lift you and take you to the bath. After we get cleaned up, we will go upstairs to our bedroom and talk about what just happened in here and then I just want to hold you until you won't remember how badly I fucked up tonight."

"Yes, John." She unfolds herself from the floor. Blood and semen run down the backs of her thighs and down her legs. She is barely able to stand but won't accept my help when I offer her my arm. I watch as she limps towards the bathroom and her long, elegant fingers wrap around the door knob and she turns it slowly before stepping inside. *I think that she is going to be alright. She's talking and walking and she hasn't yelled at me and she's not crying. Ha! I'm still good...we're still good.*

"Viv, I put your favorite Epson salt in the bath, that's going to help you feel much better. I...We are not going to talk about this until we are both cleaned up and I know you're physically alright with what took place just now."

"Yes, John." She is stepping over the lip of the bathtub and as she lowers herself down into the hot water, she winces as her sore bottom and bruised pussy touches down. Something flinched across her face, but it's gone before I can put an emotion to it. Now she is sitting in the tub like a marble statue—her face is impassive; her limbs don't move at all and her back is so straight it looks like she is sitting with a steel rod up her ass. *She did have a steel rod up her ass and that's why she's sitting like that, stupid.*

"I'm going to get into the tub with you so that I can get you all cleaned up." I don't want to hear her say 'yes, John' again.

"Yes, John."

"Vivian!" She jumps and I realize I have just yelled at her and I'm standing over her as she begins to shake uncontrollably in the hot water surrounding her in the tub. My hands are fisted at my sides I know I look terrifying to her right now, but she's pissing me off with this act. So, I fucked her ass, get over it already.

"John. I would like to bathe by myself, please." She looks up at me and the sunshine eyes with beautiful, blue skies have gone a whisky river brown with stormy, grey clouds lingering in the corners. I've never seen her look so lost before and I know I did that to her.

"No. It is my job to look after you when something like this happens. I have never left you without giving you aftercare and I will not do it now. Let me look after you, lovely. It is my honor and privilege."

"I'm not your fucking sub, John. I'm not your slave, either. I'm your motherfucking wife and I want to bathe by my damn self. Now leave me the fuck alone."

I can't breathe or move or process that my wife just spoke to me the way she did. I don't know whose looking at me or who just spoke to me, but that was not my *wife* and I know that for a fucking fact. I bend down next to the tub and fold my forearms on the edge and get right up in Vivian's space to stare into a face I know and love, but eyes I have never seen before. They don't even look like the strange eyes I sometimes see starting back at me. *What in the hell is this. Vivian has lost her damn mind or she must think I've lost mine if she thinks she can talk to me like this. Okay Ellis, let's nip this shit in the bud. Now.*

"I'm sorry, Vivian. I don't think I heard you clearly. You mind saying what you just said again…face to face." I'm all Dom and ice and fury and calm. I have spoken softly and slowly, making sure to enunciate and allow my smooth baritone to caress every word that falls from my lips. I want her to become aware of her mistake before I have to point it out to her implicitly. I wait for her response…it better damn well be what I expect it to be or she is going to have more to deal with than having her ass fucked by her husband.

"I said, John…" She pauses and turns her hardened face towards my own hardened face and looks me in my eyes as she continues her response. "…that I am not your *fucking* sub. Nor am I your slave; remember, I chose to be your *wife.*" The way she says wife makes me flinch. I felt like she had reared back and punched me in my throat. Like wife was a four-letter word that tasted like shit on her tongue.

"Excuse me?"

"You fucking heard me, you coward. I am your wife and you just raped and sodomized me like I was some kind of *slave*. I'm not that person or that thing and I don't need aftercare, I need time to decide if I'm going to press charges on you or if I'm going to walk away from this bullshit marriage or if I'm going to slit your goddamned throat."

This is not my wife and I know in that moment that I have broken her. I just broke my wife and I don't know how to put her back together again. I have to find a way to put her back together again, I love her more than my next breath and I will fix her. I will fix this.

"All right Vivian, I'll leave you to it then. Let me know when you are ready to come upstairs and I will come and get you. I love you and if I hurt you… I'm sorry. I love you so much, lovely." I'm hoping that my words will somehow bring my Viv back to me, but I don't see her. In a soothing voice I continue to cajole my wife back from whatever hell she is in. "I've been rough with you tonight and there is no excuse for how I have treated you, but I want you to know how much I love and need you to be safe and whole and mine." I stand and back out of the bathroom, my eyes not leaving the stranger sitting in the tub posing as my wife and then I see her. Tears streak down her face and the beautiful summer sunshine and blue-sky eyes look up at me with rain showers obscuring them, but she is here and I have never been happier to see her.

"John, don't leave me. I'm scared and I need you. My jars are breaking, John and I'm so scared."

"I'm never going to leave you, Vivian. I love you and I will help you put your jars back together again." I had no idea what the fuck she was talking about with these *jars*, but she was here and that's all that matters. I broke her and now I have to fight to put her back together again.

AUTHORS NOTE

Thank you all for reading my first novel, Âmes Brisées. I am humbled to be able to tell stories. I have been with John and Vivian for almost five years. In fact, this is not the first novel I have written; however, it is the first one I have published. The first novel, Ménage a Trois: Three Souls was written from Vivian's perspective and left me with so many questions about John, I had to write his story to find out what was going on with him. It turns out, John's story needed to come first. I thought of making this book a prequel to the first book, but realized it needed to be read first in the series because everything else that happens between John and Vivian has its foundation in Âmes Brisées.

I wanted to take a little time to talk about how I wrote this novel… well all of them, really. I have never been a planner. Some writers can sit down and map out their entire novel, including character profiles, settings, conflict and the whole shebang. I'm not that girl. I like to consider myself as a more organic writer. They, whoever they are, tell us to live as organically as possible to be as healthy as we can be, so at least I know my writing meets the health standards established by them. But really, I don't map anything out. I spend a lot of times with my characters in my head. Sometimes, I feel as if maybe they're more real than the people I see every day. I hear their voices, the image of their faces and bodies; how they move and express themselves physically—all of it burrows in my brain until I have to write it down to make room for more.

My characters are pushy and demanding! If I'm not writing what they want me to, when they want me to… they will keep shouting and pushing until I sit at my desktop and get it down. I guess one could say that my novels are character-driven as opposed to plot or trope driven, I am more interested in the characters of books than what is happening to them. How many different scenarios can romance writers come up with about forbidden love or the bad-boy billionaire? I want to know how the characters respond and grow or regress when placed in different situations. That is usually what I connect with and what I hope my readers will connect with in my writing.

I call myself a reluctant romance writer because I don't know if I care about my characters finding the HEA, but I do care about how they grow and change. What they discover and reveal about human nature and the overall human condition. I love using eroticism in my writing and with this book, there is no way I couldn't reach out to my old friend. I use erotic situations as a mirror or sorts. Characters engage in erotic acts that show not their sexual depravity, but their human vulnerability. Shows their need to be accepted for who they are and how they are. The entire Broken Souls Series is written in the Southern Gothic style. If you are not familiar with this genre or style of writing, allow me to share a little bit of what to look for.

As a Southern Gothic writer, I focus on several elements in my novels. My novels are set in the south; although, my characters may travel all over the world, their lives begin and end in the good-ole-south. I also focus on the macabre and grotesque underbelly of society. Incest, death, sexual deviancy; you know the things polite people don't talk about with outsiders. That's another focus in my writing, the outsider. Southerners don't like dealing with folk whose family lineage is unaccounted for. If the history of a person is not known, then we southerners will create one for them… usually a horrible one based in fear and jealousy, lol. This genre also focuses on violence and social issues. My novel deals with mental illness, moral integrity, race relations, and classism. I hope my readers are able to pick out the Southern Gothic elements as they delve into John and Vivian's story. Yes, the sex is hot and steamy but it is not what I want you guys to get caught up on. Well not too caught up on.

It took me four years to complete this first novel. Much longer than I hoped it would and much longer than it will take me to complete the rest of the series, hopefully. I would be remised if I didn't share with my readers the reason for the elongated writing period. I was diagnosed with systemic lupus five years ago and have been learning how to live and thrive with this disease ever sense. Lupus is a debilitating autoimmune disease which causes chronic inflammation, pain, and fatigue among other symptoms. Lupus cause the immune system to make antibodies designed to attack healthy organs, tissues and systems in the body. Although this disease is not listed as terminal and many people live relatively normal lives while fighting it, those of us who have this illness acknowledge and understand that the cause of death for us will be lupus complications unless we die in some unnatural way.

I was also subsequently diagnosed with the sleeping disorder narcolepsy with cataplexy. I used to make jokes about narcolepsy when my students would fall asleep in my class. We found a YouTube video of a cute, little narcoleptic dog who would pass out if he got too excited. I would play it on Fridays for my TGIF video of the week. My students and I would laugh until we cried. Well, I'm the cute, little narcoleptic writer who passes out when I get over excited, angry, or scared. It's not so funny when it happening to me.

Because I've been learning to live with both of my chronic diseases, it has taken me forever to write this first book but thankfully, I have some systems in place and follow an extremely strict treatment plan that helps manage both of my new companions I hope you enjoyed Âmes Brisées because I enjoyed writing it for you. The second book will be available in November 2018.

Thank you for reading the first book in The Broken Souls Series. John and Vivian's story can't end there. There is so much more to learn about these two Ill-fated lovers. I invite you to read an excerpt from Book two, Ames en Miroir: Mirrored Souls. Available November 2018.

~1~

It's been six months sense John and I got back from The Caves Resort is Jamaica. Six months sense the last time John and I were in the room downstairs in the basement. The room he will no longer allow me to enter. He must think I don't remember what happened in there, but how could I not remember? How could I ever forget what happened in that God-forsaken basement? I will never forget and I know he won't either; if his behavior as of late, is any indication. He remembers ever God-awful act that occurred in the bowels of our beautiful French chateaux on the lake.

Six months, three weeks, and fourteen days sense we created life from the broken soul which now levitates just above my heart and out of reach of my rational mind. I picked my head up from the pillow, searching the recesses of my mind for a reason to get up and be productive. I was so big with the baby growing inside me, I wasn't sure if I had enough room for this baby to continue to grow; parts of me hoped I didn't. I knew for certain, there wasn't enough room for me and whoever the hell else was lurking behind my eyes; waiting for me to slip away and open the window allowing them to peak out and scare the hell out of John.

I found myself pushing a large hand from my exposed belly as the sheet slid from my shoulders and continued its silken glide below my waist, where it pooled around my hips like some kind of virginal shroud. My heavy breasts were barely contained in the gray and black leopard-print pregnancy bra trimmed in black lace with cups big enough to carry cantaloupes, but not big enough to carry these giant ass baby boobs. *What the actual fuck?* My sleep shorts hug my toned thighs and remind me what's happening above my waist is not a permanent situation and will not be my new normal. I have to remember this in order to deal with the fact I'm pregnant as a result of my husband's less than genteel response to some dirty talk he asked for. I remember how this baby was made. For that reason and that reason alone; I know I'll never be able to love it. *I wonder if that's why my mother never stuck around for me? Who the hell knows and who the hell cares.?*

Every morning for the last six months starts the same way—even the weekend mornings. I wake up wondering where the fuck I am and who is in bed with me. Then my reality slams into me in the form of a gruff voice or a long, muscled leg slung over my long smooth ones. I am jolted back into the farce which has become my marriage, my life, and my hell. I used to wake up to this man and I was positive I was the lucky one in the relationship; however, now I know how sour and poisonous his love for me is.

I shove his arm from around my waist where he is protectively holding onto my stomach like he knows if he wasn't making me go through with this fucking pregnancy, I would have aborted this bastard of a baby the moment I found out about it. As I push myself up to fully sitting and prepare to leave the four-thousand-dollar French provincial slay bed that feels more like a prison cot. The beautiful burnished wood with its intricate inlay of darker, more exotic wood and the amazing scroll work which adorned the tops and sides of the California king only serve to further imprison me in this make-believe life I live.

I loved this custom-built home when John and I designed it two years ago, but now the four walls don't feel like home. It's only the house I share with my husband. The house I keep clean and immaculate for my husband. The house in which my husband destroyed every part of me he could, but I knew he would and it's time for me to stop being angry with him. It's time for me to stop punishing him, myself, and this unborn child. And I will, as soon as he turns in the one I.O.U. I hoped he would never cash in.

"John, you need to wake up! You are going to be late, again." I rest my hands

on John's right shoulder and gently nudge him into this world and way from the world where all men want to be him and all women want to be with him. *Fuck if his dream world isn't the same as his real world.* "Wake up, John!" My voice a little stronger and my nudge a little less gentle. John rolls over with a huge grin on his face and pulled me closer to him.

"Good morning, babe. I remember when you used to wake me up with your lips wrapped around my dick. What happen to those mornings, huh? I miss them." His words come out in short staccato burst with soft notes of both laughter and longing playing accompaniment. The minty smell of his morning breath makes me wonder how the hell he always seemed to have freshly brushed teeth. I wrinkle my nose and instinctively turn away from him as I shoot molten daggers of caramel from my eyes and walk unceremoniously from our bedroom. I toss a mumbled thought across my shoulder, hoping the words would fall on fertile soil and flower soon. "Get your fine ass up and start your day."

"I love you, too, lovely." I felt him watching me as I went from my dresser to my closet to the bathroom to get my day underway. God, I hated the distance and anger separating us, but until he redeems the I.O.U. he cashed in, I know I won't be able move pass what happened six months ago. He has been so perfect and has doted on me and the pregnancy, *I want this to be better between us and I need him to take responsibility for his actions… not act as if nothing horrible happened.*

"I love you, too, John. I miss us more than I can tell you." I walked into the bathroom and locked the door behind me. My back pressed against the door and my head pounding with the pressure of the blood rushing through my body. I hoped against all hope he hadn't heard my parting words, while simultaneously praying to every god out there that maybe he did. *I'm tired of being so fucking angry. I want my husband back and I want to love this baby inside me.* He's always dropping hints about how much he misses us and what we were, but he doesn't mention what caused us to move away from each other.

This is my favorite part of the morning. Standing under the spray of the rain shower head while the more than warm water sluices over my body. Outside of my giant belly and more than ample breast, I don't look like I'm pregnant at all. *I guess all of my walking and pregnancy aerobics is paying off.* I'm pretty much done bathing, but the water feels so good and if I'm being honest; I need to come. I love the detachable shower head with its fourteen setting. I know I can't stand the touch of my husband, yet but I need relief from my constant state of horniness. *Pregnancy hormones are crazy. All I think about is fucking. I'm so swollen, I come from simple activities like walking.* Using the shower head, I position it exactly where I need it the most and close my eyes, place my right foot on the shower bench and let my head fall back as the water pulses over my engorged clit. I know it won't take long for me to come but I want to draw it out. Make myself wait for it like John used to do. My mind's eye takes me down a dark tunnel and at the end of it, I find my sadistically sexy husband and I turn myself over to his sublime touch as the water continues to stimulate my sex.

After an amazing orgasm, I put my panties and bra on, grabbed my whipped cocoa and shea butter and walked out into our bedroom. My maternity jeans lay across the freshly made bed along with a white long-sleeve tee shirt and my favorite gray cowlneck sweater. John had even placed my thick woolen socks and comfy shoes out for me. *God, he really is sweet. Fuck, Vivian! You knew the darkness that ran through his veins and you chose to be with him. You recognized it because you'd seen it before. Remember? Give him a break.* What I didn't recognize was the voice in my head trying that's been trying to coax me into forgiving John for the last six months. *Who the hell is this.*

I walked to the door and stuck my head out into the hall to look for John. I didn't see him and I needed him to help me rub this butter on my skin and help me get dressed. "John! Can you please come up here…I need help with my—" My words were cut short when something caught my attention on the bed. I looked closely at the piece of paper that had been placed unassumingly on my pillow. Laying in wait for me to happen upon it. *If it had been a snake, I would be dead already.* I knew exactly what it was. With tears stinging the backs of my eyes and parts of my broken soul fusing back together; I picked up the paper and noticed how it trembled in my hands. How afraid was this piece of paper that it trembled when I picked it up?

John stepped into the room just as I turned toward the door. "Babe, you o—" He stopped in the door, obviously out of breath from his mini-sprint up the stairs to check on me. His eyes scanned my face and moved quickly down the rest of me and back up to my face. He focused on my shaking hands and then back up to the drops of liquid topaz dribbling down my cheeks and held his breath. He knew his entire life hang in the balance between my tears and my acceptance of what that piece of paper meant for them. "Vivian are you alright?"

I swept my eyes up from where I was holding on to the six-year-old piece of paper that had been stamped with a bold red PAID

IN FUL. Questions and hope scorching the sunshine and blue skies of her eyes. "John? What is this?"

"You know what it is. I went to my safe six months ago, Viv. I cut the I.O.U. out and was preparing to give it to you the next morning, but so much happened the very next day and then you went away from me and we've been dealing with the pregnancy and learning how to live with our *new reality* and… I just—I didn't know how to give it to you. He didn't get a chance to finish the words because I was on him with my arms around his neck and my lips sealing over his. My tongue pushing into his mouth and my tears drenching his face. He did it…he redeemed the I.O.U. and now I can love him and our baby. I can love him again. I can love us again.

I clutched the paper in my hand as I ravished his mouth. I had him back and he knew what he had done and he gave me back my trust in him. I am ready to make this work. "I love you, John. I needed to have you give me this. I needed to know that you knew what you did when you took me like that. God! I love you so much." He took the paper from me and read it as tears ran down his beautiful face. We were older and knew so much more about each other than we did when I gave him the poem six years ago, but in so many ways we were still learning who each other was. His voice was hard whiskey over smooth gravel and it made me love him even more for it. I know it killed him to redeem this, but knowing he knew what he had done made me appreciate the sacrifice I made in giving him the I.O.U. in the first place.

ABOUT THE AUTHOR

Ella Shawn is a writer of all things darkly erotic. Not the dark things that go bump in the night, but the dark musings that role around in the hearts, brains and souls of mankind. She spends most of her day creating worlds, beings, and languages... she readily admits she has a God complex, but even a Goddess must cook, clean, and pick up doggy and guinea pig poop.

Born in Columbia, South Carolina, she moved to Charlotte, North Carolina to attend the University of North Carolina at Charlotte pursuing a bachelors in English... she was back in SC after two years. Money didn't grow on trees and even if it did... she wouldn't climb it to pick any off. Being a southern lady and all...

Upon her return home, she promptly enrolled in a technical college to save money. During this time, she began writing poetry, short stories and essays about any and everything. She noticed how her work always seem to dabble in the macabre and leaned more towards an erotic esthetic. At the time, she was not comfortable embracing that writing style and became more political in an effort to move away from the dark and sexy writing that came from her.

After entering The University of South Carolina, she found her courage and her pen. Thanks to a writer-in-residence who challenged her short story about lesbians who fell in love with a twelve-year-old child, she knew she was on to something. After reworking it, the professor told her, "This is your space… don't ever be afraid to play and create here." That was the beginning of her true love affair with erotica in all forms.

Still too shy to share her work, she went into a respectable career as a high school English teacher and shared her passion for reading, writing, and learning with students for thirteen years. After being diagnosed with lupus and subsequently narcolepsy with cataplexy; she left her teaching career to focus on her health. With time on her hands, she picked up her old friend, writing and fell into her space. She shed her fear and began writing her first novel. It's taken five years, but it was well worth the time and effort.

She has let a few people read her work and the response is

usually something like... "Who the hell knew you had such a wickedly dirty mind?!"

Made in the USA
Columbia, SC
04 August 2020

15382646R00202